Paris, where lo[...]
is art and life.
— Maureen Johnson

Left of the
Left Bank

A NOVEL

VICTORIA MASTERSON

Betsy,
thanks for your warm
welcome to K.H. I appreciate it.
wishing you happy & true in
this earthly sojourn. You
deserve it! Best,
Victoria

Left of the Left Bank
by Victoria Masterson

Cover art by Teresa Laurenzo

Cover photography by Teresa Laurenzo

Published by Romeo Jones Enterprises L.L.C.

ISBN-10: 1515228053

ISBN-13: 978-1515228059

Printed in the United States of America

There is naught but a veil between the present and the past . . .
between the shadow of the world and the realm of light.

To my parents, Geraldean and Victor, who though crossed
over, are ever with me now. Their love and inspiration have
made all the difference in my life.

ACKNOWLEDGMENTS

A heartfelt thank you to my sister, Teresa, for her ongoing moral support, for the many hours spent reading the manuscript, for her thought-provoking comments, and for the beautiful cover design. Thanks, Sis. I couldn't have completed this without you.

Another huge thank you to Mary Boardman, who motivated me to pick up and complete my unfinished manuscript while taking her writing class.

And many thanks to James Seloover for the much appreciated help in getting my manuscript ready for publication.

PART I

Denver

VICTORIA MASTERSON

1

Stupid weatherman. That TV jerk said no snow. Right. At least it's not sticking yet. No tracks to worry about. Damn! Where the hell is she? The bitch is never on time.

The lookout had chosen well. The black-clad figure crouched in a vantage point that commanded views of both the rear of the house and the garage just off the alley. A wrought iron fence ended at the garage where a massive gate labored on hinges complaining with each gust of swirling snow. The single streetlight illuminated the near end of the alleyway, tracing shadowy scrolls and flourishes of intricate ironwork onto the wet pavement.

Should've killed that blasted streetlight. Neighbors might get suspicious though. Or little missy. She might not drive in if the alley's dark. This way, she won't know anything's up till she gets in the house. And then it'll be too late.

The whine of gears shifting down broke through the quiet of the early March darkness.

The lookout aimed the flashlight toward the house, switching it on and off twice in quick succession. The signal received, the patio door slid closed and a dim interior light extinguished in response. Night settled under a mantle of determined snowflakes.

The luminosity of powerful headlights at high beam arced into view followed by a vintage 190SL white roadster that

3

swung into the alleyway and purred smoothly into the parking area in front of the garage. The lookout drew a sharp breath, thrilling to the driver's vain attempt to open the garage door with the remote control.

Come on bitch. Forget the overhead door. It's not working. I made sure of that. You're going to have to use the gate. The gate, bitch.

Claire Martelli switched off the lights and engine of the restored Mercedes and stepped out, slamming the car door to satisfy her irritation with her estranged husband. She pulled the hood of her jacket up to cover her head against the falling snow and looked through the open gate into the darkness of the back courtyard. She would have turned on the back lights from inside the garage if she'd been able to get the overhead door to open. Slipping her hand into her pocket she sought the reassurance of her phone. Decision made, she straightened her shoulders and entered on the flagstone path, swinging the gate closed behind her. The creaking of the hinges attested to the fact they hadn't been oiled in a long while. In the seven years she'd lived here, that had always been her job.

The dog run wasn't far, just a short distance to her right, a path she knew all too well. She would get Duffy and be back to the car in a jiffy—a matter of minutes. Her spirits picked up as she headed in the direction of the chain-link enclosure, whistling for the Springer spaniel that always ran to greet her, tail wagging and woofing in his excitement.

"Duffy, I'm here boy. Duffy? Where are you fella?"

There was no answer to her summons.

That's odd. Maybe Chad left him inside today, but why didn't he say so when he called?

She picked her way along the path toward the house, carefully avoiding the dried skeletons of the flower beds she'd planted last summer. But that was then, before her decision to separate and initiate divorce proceedings from her husband and business partner, the architect E. Forde Chadwick. Claire

4

thought back to this morning's call from the man she knew as Chad and already thought of as her ex. He'd asked her to turn on the alarm system when she picked up the dog for the weekend, posing a sheepish admittance that once again he'd forgotten to set it in his usual mad-dash.

"Nothing new. Leave it to Chad," she muttered under her breath. *He knew it would be late when I got here. Yet, the house is pitch black. Duffy isn't in his run. The garage door opener isn't working. The alley gate's unlocked—and open. So what did I expect? For him to change?*

She sighed. *Yeah, right.*

She took the stretch band that held the keys to the house off her wrist, the same one the company's Gal Friday kept in her desk drawer. Claire's own keys resided at the bottom of one of the boxes lining the attic walls of her carriage house, a cardboard testimonial to her failed marriage.

A low grinding noise resonated from the direction she'd just taken. Claire froze in mid stride.

What was that? The gate?

Certain she'd swung it closed behind her, she strained to hear over a gust of wind that scuttled spent leaves and snow around her feet. The hinges moaned with the grating of iron against iron.

No question now. A heavy iron gate doesn't open by itself.

She sprinted the last few yards to the patio door, jamming the key into the lock by memory rather than sight. Heaving the heavy glass door open, Claire rushed inside, hurling it closed and locking it in a single motion. She switched on the back lights. No one there.

Feeling somewhat easier, she flipped the switch for the hall light.

No response.

You're a real shit, Chad. Can't even change a damn light bulb.

Claire felt her way along the wall and around the corner of the laundry room, then stopped short on hearing a soft, but

5

audible, padding on the wood floor. The sound seemed to be coming toward her.

"Duffy? It's okay. Just me, Duff. Here, boy."

She groped for the light switch inside the laundry room doorway and flicked it on, sighing in relief as the blessed light nearly blinded her.

Then her gaze landed on a black and white pile of fur.

"Duffy? Oh no . . . Duffy!" Claire struggled to pull it together. The sight of her much-loved pet sprawled in the corner—tongue lolling, eyes rolled back—stabbed through her like an icy blade. She dropped to her knees beside the heaving animal.

A chill shot up her spine breaking through her immediate absorption over Duffy's condition. Recalling the muted shuffling noises she'd heard before finding the dog, she turned her head toward the dark corridor behind her. She listened, her fingers catching hold of the phone in her pocket. All was quiet. Though the silence caused her more disquiet than the butterflies taking wing in her belly.

Duffy's muscles began to spasm. Hands shaking, Claire grabbed a towel from a laundry basket and wrapped the dog in it so she could carry him.

She leaned down and whispered to her pet, willing him to understand. "Please . . . you've got to hold on, pup . . ."

Claire froze in place, listening to what could only be soft footfalls. The shuffling started up again, seeming to stop in the darkness just outside the laundry room. Her heart lurched in the direction of her throat. Swallowing hard, she jerked her head around, gasping at the black-clad figure framed in the light of the open doorway.

Claire sprang up, her gaze focused on stony blue eyes staring through the slits of a black ski mask. In horror she watched his pupils dilate, merging with the face mask into total darkness.

Mesmerized, Claire barely saw the raised arm coming at her before she felt the ferocity of the punch that caught the left side of her face. Lights exploded behind her eye. She fell limply against the wall. The cold snap of a steel blade pierced her ears, screaming its savage intent. He reached down to release the fly of his jeans. She forced her shaking body upright.

This is it . . . I'm dead . . .

He lunged, grabbing for her hair.

She braced herself to concentrate through the pain.

Nothing to lose . . .

The clarity of the thought sent her adrenaline pumping, overtaking the pain from the blow. She instinctively rolled away, flinging her body to one side. Her attacker crashed into the wall. Spinning around in a fury, he slashed out at her face with the knife. Her muscles flowed in reflex from her years of martial arts training. She automatically sidestepped and parried the thrust, using his momentum to allow the knife to whip by harmlessly.

She knew he would come at her again. She only had a few precious seconds before he regained his balance. Claire weighed her choices—flee or fight. And it was too late to run. She couldn't leave Duffy behind.

Accepting the inevitable, she determined to take the initiative, coupling the proficiency of a high-degree brown belt with the element of surprise. Even as the blood-curdling *ki-ai* tore from the center of her being, she targeted, then kicked-out to his knee, focusing the force of her kick through the knee.

His leg collapsed under him. He dropped the knife, howling in pain. In that instant, Claire maneuvered behind him in a *jujitsu* move that leveraged her assailant's muscular neck into a choke hold. She wrapped her legs around his torso and hung on relentlessly.

Inhuman sounds gurgled from his throat. Enraged and gasping for air, he attempted to buck her off, brutally tearing at the barred arms closing off his windpipe, bouncing her into the door jamb and walls as he staggered on his injured leg towards the patio door.

Fueled by desperation, Claire forced herself to keep pressure on the choke hold, her arms in agony.

Hold on! Hold on! The neon thought flashed a thousand times in the eternity of a few seconds.

Try as she might, she felt her strength ebbing, her grip dangerously close to loosening. She was near panic when his legs suddenly buckled, toppling both of them against the glass patio door, carrying her with him to the floor.

"No!" The sound of her own hoarse cry surprised her.

In the instant she hit up against the glass, her brain relayed an image of a face peering in. Watching.

A face? She blinked and looked again. A reflection. It was only a reflection, she reasoned.

He may come to any second . . . or did I just kill him? Have to get help.

Claire groped in her pocket for her phone only to discover it was missing. She began to crawl on all fours toward the wall housing the alarm panel. She tried to stand. Her legs shook so badly she tripped over the inert black form of her assailant, and landed on the floor beneath the alarm. Her vision blurred, the room began to spin.

No . . . can't black out now . . . Duffy . . .

In a last conscious effort, Claire forced her quivering hand upward to reach the emergency keys that would send a silent signal to the alarm control center.

Lieutenant Grady Owens of Denver's Criminal Investigations Division clicked his phone off and headed in the direction of the stairs leading to the living room. He proceeded along the library-lined gallery that, by day, would be lit with natural light from the long peaked skylight overhead. Just now, the ambient lighting framing the skylight illuminated the snow now falling sporadically onto the darkened glass. Track-mounted spotlights on the ceiling framed niches designed to showcase artwork. Some were empty. He picked his way along the interior railing, around the rubble of broken and littered items the intruder had left behind.

After a lifetime of being a cop and just a few years away from retirement, Owens' senses were honed to the point of acute perception, utilizing this ability in solving cases. He mentally noted the expensive and intact art objects yet occupying a few of the niches, reasoning as to why these items had been either neglected or rejected would become an integral part in unraveling this investigation.

Finished with his cursory inspection, Owens paused to look over the stainless steel stair rail into the open living room below. He noted from what he'd seen so far, the whole place reeked of costly materials and furnishings. He descended the short flight of concrete stair treads to the main level.

The victim, a woman, rested on one of the leather sofas, hands clenched, her face battered and bruised. Owens fully understood and respected the effort it took for her to hold it together. He'd glanced through the initial police report given him by the team of blues who'd answered the security center's emergency call. For the record, he could honestly say that he didn't know of many victims, male or female, who could've handled themselves the way she had. Or do what she had done. But where the hell was the scumbag responsible for all this—the guy she'd choked out?

A uniformed policewoman was in attendance. She rose as Owens entered the room, passing him with a nod when asked to find some ice for the woman's face.

"Mrs. Chadwick," he began, looking down at the name set forth on the report. "I'm Lieutenant Owens from Criminal Investigations. I'll be working the case. The EMTs and the forensics team are on their way," he explained, coming to stand across from her.

"It's Martelli, Lieutenant. Claire Martelli. I use my maiden name," she corrected him, her voice barely audible. "And I don't need the attention of the EMTs. I've already told the officers that I don't intend to go to the hospital. I'll be all right. I plan on staying the night with Abbie as soon as I leave here." At his questioning look she continued, "Abbie is a nurse . . . as well as my mother. So you see, I won't need the EMTs."

9

Looking at the battered face, Owens raised an eyebrow. There was a nasty bump rising on her forehead and a deep split to the side of her left eye where a punch must have landed. The eye was already swollen shut and blackening quickly. Bruises and dried blood covered her hands and arms, as well as several angry cuts that were just beginning to coagulate. She cradled one wrist against her chest in a protective manner, causing Owens to think it might be broken, sprained, or in the least, greatly painful.

"Really? Have you called her yet?"

"Ah, no . . . not yet. I'll call her before I leave." She dropped her gaze.

"Okay, right. Just take it easy, Ms. Martelli," he said aloud, while thinking it wouldn't hurt to let the EMTs take a look at her. Before her mother saw her like this. But it was her call. He toyed with the idea of insisting she go in the ambulance to the emergency room, but figured that would be about as easy as coaxing a cat into a tub of water.

He adjusted his reading glasses, glancing through the half-lenses at the information on the report.

"Your husband, this E. Forde Chadwick, he's out of town. In Vail, right?"

"He prefers to go by Chad, Lieutenant. And, yes, my soon-to-be-ex-husband is in Vail." She awkwardly hugged her arms to her body in an effort to stop the trembling in her limbs.

Owens understood the tremor—shock was setting in. He disliked prodding her but he needed answers. After learning how she'd handled herself during the attack, he knew that she was strong enough to give them, shock or no shock. Talk about strength of character.

He'd also learned that she wouldn't talk to the officers at all until the veterinarian had been called for the dog. Thank God the guy just lived down the block, a neighbor and a friend, she'd explained. The vet and the other officer were working on the dog now in the laundry room—pumping his stomach. Owens reflected on the vet's diagnosis that the dog had been given poisoned meat, probably through the fence of the dog run, then dragged inside. One way to take him out of play, Owens thought.

"Ms. Martelli. Do you know where Mr. Chadwick is staying in Vail?"

"Staying? Oh, he should be at our cabin, just outside of Vail. Technically, it's the company's cabin," she explained, "but since Chad and I are sole partners in the business, we've been using it in turns since we separated."

That's handy, he thought. A cabin. Probably no one around to back up his whereabouts tonight.

"What's the number, Ms. Martelli? I'll have to notify him of the situation." And see if Mr. E. Forde Chadwick indeed has an alibi. He made a quick note to check for a pre-nup agreement.

Claire recited the phone number, adding, "We don't have a land line up there, Lieutenant. That's Chad's mobile."

Owens jotted it down then headed for the hallway to make the call out of earshot.

"I'll just be a minute, Ms. Martelli."

"Lieutenant, wait," Claire called after him, exhaustion evident in her voice. "You should probably know the police have already tried to reach Chad. That was a little before you arrived. He didn't answer." She watched him turn back in acknowledgement of the information she'd just given him. "And, another thing, Lieutenant, why don't you call me Claire, Ms. Martelli is rather formal given the circumstances."

The detective absently nodded at her suggestion to use her first name, preoccupied with the information that her estranged husband couldn't be reached a short time ago. He looked at his watch. Ten thirty-five. A very continental dinner hour, even for Vail. If he didn't answer around ten and it's just under a two-hour drive from here, Owens thought a closer examination of the times merited his attention.

"Interesting," he muttered. But it didn't necessarily mean the husband was in on it. He might be seeing another woman and didn't want to be disturbed. His alibi?

11

"What time did you get here this evening . . . er, Ma'am?" He asked, opting for the middle road in addressing her. Owens was old-school. In his book, it just wouldn't be appropriate to call her by her given name in this situation.

"Please, Lieutenant, I've already given the police the details. It's all in the report."

"I'm only trying to determine the exact time of the attack, Ma'am. Just tell it one more time for my benefit," he requested. "It really helps to get the details straight while everything's still fresh. Tomorrow, you're liable to forget some little thing that may be what cracks the case. The fact your assailant wasn't here when the police arrived is peculiar after what you did to him. Choking him out like that."

He wanted to add there were other circumstances warranting his concern. For instance, there was no sign of forced entry. And the big one. If the guy came to and left under his own power while she was still out, why didn't he finish the job—why didn't he kill her before he left? And why didn't he take the knife with him instead of leaving it on the floor? But he didn't say anything. He knew these questions couldn't be answered until he discerned the motive for what happened here tonight.

He turned to take the improvised ice pack from the returning officer.

"Thanks. And I think Ms. Martelli could use something to drink. Preferably water, but whatever you can find that's wet and cold. And, one more thing. Please check progress on the dog for her while you're in the vicinity."

Claire shot him a lopsided smile. Only the right side of her face moved.

"Ma'am, you just collect your thoughts while I try to reach Mr. Chadwick. Then we'll go through it one last time." He handed her the plastic bag filled with ice. "This should help that eye."

Alone for the moment, Claire gingerly held the ice bag to her eye, easing her aching head back against the soft Italian leather. She'd never forgive herself for agreeing to share custody of Duffy with Chad. All because he'd put on his *poor-me-face*, saying how lonely the house would be after she moved out. The image of the suffering animal still tore at her heart strings.

It was hard to believe what had just happened was real. It felt more like it was all a bad dream. How appropriate, she thought. Just like my marriage. The emotions she'd been holding back for months were so close to the surface, she couldn't keep her eyes from welling up. Teary droplets traced down her face. She wiped at her eyes with the back of her sleeve. The salt from her tears burned like fire into the deep split next to her eye.

The truth was she couldn't ignore her stubborn inner voice that insisted she own up to the cold reality of tonight's ordeal—as well as her failed marriage, it prompted. She sighed, giving herself the luxury of a final sniff. In truth, when she forced herself to look at the whole picture, she had to face the fact that both were about as real as real can get—the attack, and her seven-year marriage to Chad.

She waited, thinking she should feel better now that she'd gotten it through her head she couldn't hide from the reality of either situation. But she still felt like crying, which brought her to wonder why lately her life seemed to be drifting through a highly charged electrical field totally devoid of negative ions.

No, she thought, just let it go. There would be no positive result if she were to harangue herself on that score at the moment. Was she being too hard on herself? After all she'd just gone through with the intruder, she decided to go easy on herself and simply chalk her present mood up to shock and exhaustion.

At least for tonight, she'd been successful. She'd been able to fight off her assailant.

He's gone. The police are here. I'm safe now.

She didn't want to imagine what could have been a far different outcome if she'd not chosen to learn the art of self-defense after one of the gals at the office was stalked, and later mugged in the parking lot of her townhome. Claire knew her martial arts training had paid off in a big way.

Yet, something nagged at her, something hazy in the back of her mind. She couldn't quite bring it into focus. She found herself staring at the dark reflections in the two-story glass wall along the opposite side of the living room. The glass was bare. Chad hadn't wanted anything to obstruct the view. Goose bumps spread down her bruised arms.

The glass patio door . . . had there really been a face outside staring in? Was someone out there watching her even now? She jerked upright at the sound of footsteps on the hardwood floor.

"Sorry, didn't mean to startle you," Owens said, coming into the room and sitting down on the sofa across from her. "He still doesn't answer, Ma'am. You doing okay? I promise this will only take fifteen minutes, maybe less. Then I'll have the officers drive you to your mom's place."

Claire nodded, appreciative of the fact that he declined giving any sympathy or comment on her teary face.

"Take your time. Just tell me everything that happened. A little background helps, and anything and everything leading up to and specific to the incident tonight. And the times. As best you can remember. I'll only stop you if I have questions," he said, opening his notebook.

Claire gathered herself together. Her lips quivered with the effort it took to sip the water the officer had quietly placed beside her. "I'll hold you to your word, Lieutenant. That's about all the staying power I have left, about fifteen-minutes-worth.

"I'm not sure where to start. Guess you should know that Chad and I are partners in the Chadwick+Martelli Design Group. It's an architectural and interior design firm. I handle the interiors. He's the architect. Plus we have a small staff, as well. When Chad planned this Vail trip, he asked me to take

14

care of Duffy while he was gone. I usually pick up the dog four or five days of the week anyway. Kind of a joint custody.

"My original plan was to stop by to get Duffy right after work, around five-thirty. But Chad called in earlier today to say our New Orleans' client was in town and wanted to drop by at six to go over progress on the interior plans for the theme restaurant of their resort project." Claire's voice broke into a hoarse whisper. She paused, sipping more water.

Owens nodded and continued making notes in his book while waiting for her to continue.

"The client finally showed about seven. I had just about given up on him. In fact, I was shutting out the lights when he finally arrived, a little the worse for an extended Happy Hour, I would guess. I suggested we reschedule the meeting to tomorrow, but he was insistent we go over the plans tonight as he was planning to leave in the morning. The meeting lasted till around eight-thirty or so. Then I stayed to make notes regarding his review. Think it was somewhere around nine when I left the office."

Claire stopped for breath, all the while watching the detective's face for any reaction. But as far as she could tell, there was none. "Is this what you want, Lieutenant?

Owens looked up from his notes. "You're doing just fine. I promised not to interrupt but I have a couple of questions regarding what you've just related. What time did Mr. Chadwick call in today?"

"It was right before lunch. I think it was around eleven . . . eleven-thirty maybe."

"Was he calling from Vail or Denver?"

"I'm not sure. Chad didn't say one way or the other, but Susan, his Gal Friday and the office receptionist, thought he was calling from Vail."

"This Susan. What's her last name? Ms. or Mrs.?" He asked, eyebrow lifted expectantly. "And Ma'am, I'll need to talk to her. Okay if I drop by the office tomorrow?"

"Of course," she agreed, her limbs quivering as if a deep chill had entered the room. "And Susan's last name is Farrell .

15

.. Ms. Susan Farrell," she answered, trying to keep her teeth from chattering while wrapping herself in the woolen throw on the sofa, the one she'd forgotten to take with her when she moved out. The one she'd knit in simple color blocks based on an early Amish quilt. The one Chad had hated, saying it wasn't sophisticated and didn't belong in his house.

"Ten more minutes, Lieutenant," she reminded him.

"A couple more quick questions, Ma'am. Was that all Mr. Chadwick called to tell you? About the client coming in right after work?"

"Well, no. He also asked me to set the alarm when I picked up Duffy. Said he forgot. Again. Guess that's why I assumed he was calling from Vail. If he was still in town, I thought he'd go back and set it himself."

"And another question, Ma'am. Why wouldn't Mr. Chadwick tell you about the appointment with the client before this morning? Like before he left the office yesterday?"

"You would have to know him to understand, Lieutenant, but Chad's famous for that kind of thing. It's always last-minute with him. Unfortunately for the rest of us, he thrives on it."

Owens looked as if he was about to say something, but didn't, simply raising an eyebrow at her answer. He noted her remark in his book, then continued his line of inquiry.

"Was his trip to Vail for business or pleasure, Ma'am?"

"Well, he told me about a week ago he'd lined up an appointment with a group who are planning to build a new resort in the Vail area. Our firm specializes in the hospitality field, Lieutenant . . . hotels, resorts, restaurants, clubs, that sort of thing." Claire stopped her account to try drinking water through the straw the policewoman had discovered in the depths of the kitchen's ultra-contemporary cabinets.

"Although, he did say he was also going to do some spring skiing if there was enough snow left on top. Why are you asking me all these questions about Chad? Surely you don't think he had anything to do with what happened tonight? Look at this place." She swept a trembling arm up to include the

16

balcony area. "You can't think Chad would have someone burglarize his own home. Do you? Or poison Duffy, for that matter. Or try to kill, let alone rape, *me*. That's just not plausible. I know we're divorcing, but Chad would never do anything to harm me. I was evidently in the wrong place at the wrong time. I surprised the burglar. He attacked me. It's really quite simple, right?"

"Maybe not so simple, Ma'am. Does this belong to you or Mr. Chadwick?" The detective pulled an evidence bag from his pocket. A circular object glimmered through the plastic. It looked like a small gold medallion, or charm of some kind. He held it up for her to see.

Claire shook her head, grimacing from the pain. "No Lieutenant. I've never seen it before. Does it have some connection with what happened here tonight?"

"It's certainly a possibility. One of the officers found it out back, along with your phone, when he was searching the area earlier. If it doesn't belong to you or Mr. Chadwick, I'll bet my sainted mother's beads that your attacker lost it. The chain probably broke when you struggled, got caught in his mask or clothes, and this little bauble fell off when he escaped. Take another look, Ma'am," he said, handing it to her. He watched her bring the bag close to her good eye to focus more closely on the object.

"The design looks vaguely familiar," she said, passing it back to him. "It reminds me of something I've seen somewhere before. Just not as a piece of jewelry. I'm sure of that. If it comes to me, I'll let you know, Lieutenant."

Owens nodded, stuffing the little bag back in his pocket. He turned toward the sound of approaching footsteps in the hallway.

The policewoman escorted a man in a soiled veterinarian's coat, shoulders slumped in fatigue, his dark hair matted with dried perspiration. She apologized for the interruption, explaining, "He wanted to tell her himself."

"Claire! Oh, honey, your poor face," said the vet, hurrying toward her, oblivious to Owens standing to the side of the door

17

opening. "Looks like I should've worked on you instead of Duffy. Is it as painful as it looks?"

"Tell me what David?" Claire asked, ignoring his remarks concerning her face. She moved over to give him room to sit beside her, putting out her hands to her neighbor, imploring him. "Please, I must know. Is Duffy . . . dead?"

"Well, what I wanted to tell you, honey, is that he's going to be fine. Truly." The veterinarian clasped both her hands in his, smiling his assurance. "I'm going to take him with me for the night. Just want to keep an eye on him. He's sleeping off the sedative I gave him. Out cold. Right now, he wouldn't know you from his worst enemy. Besides, he really needs to rest. He's been through quite an ordeal. You can pick him up tomorrow, or one of my people can drop him off at your place. Smart animal, he only got a mouthful of the meat before he somehow figured it was bad. Just ate enough to make him one sick puppy." He rubbed a hand over the heavy stubble covering his jaw. "Could be that Duffy may have known whoever fed him the meat . . ."

But Owens didn't let him finish, moving into view in the room. "Uh, thanks, Doc. I'll have the officers help you get the dog in the car," he said, ushering the vet from his seat next to Claire.

Claire stood up, her legs unsteady. "Thank you. David." The swelling on the left side of her face caused her attempted smile to contort. "You don't know how much I appreciate this. I'll call you tomorrow to make arrangements to get Duffy."

"Are you sure you're all right, Claire? Your poor face. You really shouldn't be alone tonight." He put out an arm to steady her. "You're more than welcome to stay with us. Margo and I have hardly seen you since the split."

"Thanks for the offer, David," Claire said, her voice now hoarse with fatigue. "You see, I'm planning on staying at Abbie's. I'll be fine. Give Margo my love."

Kessler put his arms around her in a comforting hug, but drew back when Claire tensed.

18

"Okay, whatever you think is best. Don't worry about Duffy. You just get some rest."

The waiting officer touched his arm, indicating it was time for him to leave.

Kessler gave her a quick glare, but nodded his agreement. "Talk to you tomorrow, honey," he called back over his shoulder with a wave as the policewoman escorted him from the living room.

Claire sat back down. "Duffy is going to be okay. Thank God. But why does David think Duffy knew the person who poisoned him, Lieutenant?"

Owens took the seat across from her. "Probably just an over-active imagination, Ma'am." He lifted his head at the sound of a nearing emergency vehicle. "Hear that? The siren's getting closer. Why not let the EMTs give you a quick once-over? Your mom doesn't deserve to see you this way even if she is a nurse."

Claire bristled. "Lieutenant Owens . . ."

He stood up, snapping shut his notebook. "Okay, we'll do it your way. But you'll have to sign a release refusing treatment. Then you need to get some rest. I'll stop by your office tomorrow. Like I said, I've got the basic report you gave the officers to go on. If you'll call your mom and prepare her so she doesn't fall over in a dead faint when she sees you, I'll have the officers drive you there."

Claire allowed him to help her up. It took an effort, but she determinedly straightened her back.

"Lieutenant, the call won't be necessary. I've decided that I'd just as soon my mother doesn't know about this until I get there, so she won't imagine the worst. And one more thing, I'll drive myself. If I can fight off an assailant, I can drive."

This time Owens didn't try to dissuade her. He observed the dogged set of her mouth, simply nodding. "Okay, Ma'am." Short of hog-tying her and taking her to the ER or to her mother's himself, he knew he had no legal means of stopping her. And Lord save him from another go-around with Internal Affairs, who weren't likely to look the other way if he were to do just that. So he went with the only recourse he had left. He escorted Claire to her little vintage roadster, fastening her seat belt for her, and telling her to "Drive safe."

Owens returned to the house where he sat in the living room for a long while, his mind engaged in considering the various possibilities of the case. His thoughts necessarily included the facts and what he had learned from questioning Claire, but that wasn't all. Something inside him said it wasn't a burglary gone bad—just made to look that way. That in actuality, Claire was the intended victim of the attack. Now to prove it.

And yes, she'd had the balls to fight off her assailant. A brave woman. He would hand her that, to be sure. But there were limits. He also figured she had the strength of will to make it to her mother's in one piece. But that didn't stop him from having the squad car follow her with instructions to make it a discreet shadow. If they ascertained she needed help driving, they were to stop her and drive her to her mother's in the squad car. One of them would follow in her car. And in that case, he hoped Internal Affairs would never find out about it.

But enough for tonight, Owens thought as he left the house, making sure the door locked behind him. He mentally checked off the list of people he intended to talk with tomorrow. Claire's estranged husband, Chad, was at the top of the list. Chad's Gal Friday, Susan, next. And he definitely wanted to have a chat with David Kessler. Owens had noticed lacerations on the vet's hands and the cuts looked pretty fresh. He could've gotten them while treating the dog, noting the vet seemed fairly unconcerned someone would see them. Or, did he get the cuts some other way tonight?

David Kessler heard the Mercedes' engine spring to life then drop to a murmur as it hummed down the alleyway

20

behind his house. He would recognize that car anywhere. He'd heard it enough times in the years she lived in the house Chad designed and built on the once-vacant lot down the block.

Kessler finished latching the holding kennel where Duffy lay in a drugged stupor. Flicking off the overhead light, he walked to the back window and lifted a slat of the mini blinds. He couldn't help himself. He watched the tail lights of the sleek little car redden to a brake and then turn out onto the side street. The metal slat bent in his grip.

Muttering about the unfairness of it all, he crossed the room to his desk and opened the top drawer with a key, taking out his private directory. He dropped into his chair and tipped back. He had to think. The whole thing was getting too much. The night's events required some serious reflection.

He ran his hands through his matted hair, staring at the light glowing softly through the green cased-glass shade of the task light Claire had selected for his office when he'd hired her to update his study several years before.

In his mind he envisioned she'd taken him up on his offer to stay the night, even though he knew she would never agree to anything other than being friends. The real beauty of it though, his wife need never have known—Margo was away visiting family in Iowa.

In the kennel behind him, Duffy stirred and whimpered in his sleep, rousing Kessler out of his indecision. He shrugged impassively. His gray eyes stony, he picked up his phone and punched in a private mobile number.

VICTORIA MASTERSON

2

"No, you didn't wake me, Mom," Claire lied, lying prone in bed. It was dark. She adjusted the phone to her other ear and attempted to sound alert after awakening from a deep sleep. The LED clock on the night stand read twelve forty-five.

"Really, I'm fine. The bruises are completely gone now. Thanks to your wonderful care, Paris will see me much like my old self," she lied again, adjusting the pillows and leaning back against the upholstered headboard.

"Of course, I know you'd rather be back in Denver with me right now, but auntie needs you more. I sent a card, but please give her my love and let her know she's in my thoughts. Anyway, it's been a while since you've visited the rest of the family. Please don't worry about me, Mom, I'm fine. Oh, I almost forgot to ask, have you heard when the proverbial wandering gypsy will be back in town?"

She smiled as her mother described her last conversation with Miranda, aka Mandy, Claire's sibling, who was more often than not traipsing around the country on some photography assignment though she made Denver her home base, as did Claire and their mother, Abbie—the three Martelli women.

No matter that her younger sister was nearly thirty-years-old, their mother often threatened to have a GPS microchip injected in her errant daughter's arm so they could locate her

23

blip on a map of the country for those occasions when Mandy forgot to call or share her whereabouts. At those times, Claire would smile at her sister's pained expression and point out how lucky they were to have a mother possessing such an admirable commingling of traits. Abbie was first and foremost a traditionalist, both by nature and through the deeply-planted Midwestern roots of her European-immigrant lineage. Co-existing along with this ideology, she held a modernist's belief in the extraordinary accomplishments of the twentieth and twenty-first-centuries—and in the same manner, the ever-evolving world of information technology, pursuant to the medical field and her chosen nursing profession.

Claire rolled onto her side, continuing her original train of thought. "Yah, I hear you, Mom. Knowing Mandy, I wouldn't be surprised if she gets back just in time to make a run for the plane. But I'm glad we're going to Paris as a threesome. It's been a while since we've taken a trip together. And, personally, I can't wait to get away this time. The headaches and nightmares are getting out of hand."

Sorry she'd revealed this last bit of information, Claire listened patiently as her mother suggested yet another remedy for the incessant headaches she suffered, one of the resulting effects of the attack in March. "Thanks for the info. Yes, I know, Mom, I know. And I promise I'll give it a try. Bye now. Love you, too."

Switching the phone off, Claire changed the ring tone to pulse and set it on the bedside table. She'd gone to bed early, tired from one of many extra-early-to-late days at the office these past several weeks. Her aim was to finish designing the overall interior theme and layout for the New Orleans' resort project. She could then turn her conceptualizations over to her veteran staff who would continue with the required delineations and specifications while she was in Paris. The excursion was slated as a buying trip, as she planned to search for the rustic French antiques she envisioned as the featured décor for the resort's restaurant and lobby.

Claire waited for sleep to take her once more, but worrisome thoughts filled her head now that she was wide awake. She couldn't believe she'd automatically picked up the phone and answered, even if she had been awakened from a deep sleep. Luckily, it had been Abbie on the other end. Although that, in itself, didn't make her less concerned. It was something she generally wouldn't have done, especially in these past few weeks, without first checking the identity of the caller. She hid it well but following the attack her fears escalated with the feeling that someone was watching her. That, accompanied by disturbing phone calls in which the only audible sounds were tracts of frightening screams and dirge-like music from horror movies, had brought her to the point of considering the upcoming Paris trip a much-welcome escape. She hoped the business portion would be productive. And just maybe, the sights, arts, and other wonders offered by the City of Light could help to quiet the relentless nightmares as well as her frayed nerves.

Not that she really wanted to leave her new digs. She'd only moved into the refurbished carriage house in February, a month prior to the assault.

Determinedly, she swept that whole episode from her mind, choosing instead to continue her original train of thought. She knew she was lucky to have acquired the carriage house as structures of this type were getting to be a rarity in Denver. And this one came with privacy in the form of three acres of land on a private eighteen-acre wooded site, thanks to the couple who owned the 'big house', who were both friends and clients of Claire's. They'd purchased the mansion and the multi-acre site with the plan of moving the carriage house and building tennis courts in its original location. And Claire had jumped at the chance they offered.

Now that the renovation stages were pretty much complete, there were only minor things left on Claire's to-do list After tearing down the non-bearing walls in the former small kitchen, she'd added a separate room as pantry and a small morning room that served as her at-home office, increasing the kitchen's work area and revealing the airy great room effect she desired.

Her plan for the enlarged kitchen included an extended custom-built island with work area and eating bar, along with state-of-the-art appliances. The installation of painted cabinetry, stone countertops, and a new natural rock-face on the fireplace, finished the renovations on the first floor.

She looked around the warm and inviting space that was her bedroom, happy she'd gone ahead with the remodeling on the upper floor that she'd originally planned to do at the end of the summer. She'd created her new master suite by adding walk-in closets, a laundry area, and a large master bath with walk-in shower, in the space the original second bedroom once occupied. As a final design element, she'd also added-on a deck off the bedroom.

Claire turned off the lamp beside her bed and snuggled down under the down-filled duvet. As she did quite often these days, she sent a prayer of thanksgiving upward. As related to her new home, she'd been in the right place, and more importantly, at the right time, to purchase the carriage house and then renovate it.

And since the attack, she'd added a second prayer hoping to find a way to alleviate the lingering effects of the ongoing headaches and nightmares.

Claire closed her eyes, attempting to switch off the nagging worries. Unbidden, her thoughts went to the e-mail sent from her attorney that morning, advising her that he was reasonably certain the divorce papers would become final while she was in Paris. She knew what the '*reasonably certain*' meant—without further complications from Chad's lawyers regarding changes in the property settlement portion of the divorce agreement. She could only hope the obstacles surrounding the long-awaited divorce would finally give way. And perhaps they would as she'd given her assurance to Chad that she would remain his business partner, one of his major objections to the divorce.

Just maybe, she thought, Paris will do the trick. All around.

It seemed like she'd just closed her eyes when Duffy roused her by pawing the side of the bed. Claire, a sound sleeper by nature, knew from experience this was his way of indicating a noise he deemed important enough to wake her. Perhaps innocent, like a squirrel hightailing it across the peaked roof overhead. Or possibly, the deer, who visited her wooded property in their never-ending desire to eat as many of her plants and bushes as possible before daylight dawned. Sometimes she couldn't figure out what he actually heard, but this time she was instantly aware of the reason for his wake-up call.

A hushed but audible creaking came from beyond the door to the master suite, the result of weight placed on the wooden stair treads that had loosened over the years. Claire had planned to make the necessary repairs, but the major renovations had taken priority.

She couldn't remember if she'd locked the deadbolt on the bedroom door before going to bed. This had become part of a nightly routine and a clear example of a trepidation that began 'after attack', or '*a.a.*'

In the dim glow of the three-quarter-moon's light coming through the French doors leading to the deck, she could just make out Duffy's shape facing the entry door, silent but vigilant. She couldn't quite see but knew from experience the fur on his neck would be standing on end. She reached to turn on the lamp, but made a quick decision to leave the room in darkness, groping instead for her phone on the bedside table. Her hand bumped the little device and it clattered to the floor. Claire stilled to listen to the sudden quiet beyond the door, her tension notching upward. Duffy's low growl alerted her as she fought for control, her already taut nerves stretched to fragile threads.

Come *on Martelli, get hold of yourself. Think.*

Her thoughts raced to the escape-ladder system that she'd designed and had custom-built on the top-floor deck in case of fire. It was powered by an electric motor that triggered the ladders to engage and move down the shaft on the back of the house. Maybe, she thought, but knew if she had to operate the override mechanism to crank the ladders down by hand if the system was disengaged or the electricity was out, it would take longer than the amount of time she had if someone was at her bedroom door right now. She needed a more paramount solution.

The burglar alarm.

Claire glanced over at the system's control panel that she'd put in as a precaution, a duplicate to the panel that resided next to the door downstairs. The light glowed red, indicating it was on but it could've switched over to the back-up battery power. The alarm system was installed with sensors to pick up movement anywhere on the first floor.

It should have gone off.

Her mind reeled at the thought that somehow someone had gotten in without triggering the alarm. Claire stood up and quickly moved toward the control panel, intent on sending out a silent alarm for help if the system hadn't failed.

Duffy's sharp barks alerted her once again. She stopped short. A crack of light appeared around the door frame. In the full moon's light she could see the knob turning. Had she indeed forgotten to lock it tonight? Just more bad karma, Claire thought, mentally preparing to defend herself without knowing what was coming at her.

A burglar? Please . . . not again.

The door creaked opened to reveal not a person, but an overpowering smoke-filled red luminescence that suffused her bedroom.

Fire!

Horrified, Claire watched as her sleeping chamber radiated into a crimson inferno. The on-coming flames goaded her across the room until she could go no further. She backed up against the French doors, dragging Duffy with her. In a paroxysm of fear for her life and that of her pet, she let go of the dog's collar and scrambled to release the dead bolt, opening the doors and retreating out onto the deck until she hit another obstruction, the railing. She called to Duffy to come to her, giving a quick glance down to see if there was shrubbery that could break their fall if it came to that. There was none; the spring landscaping project only partially finished.

Her mind riveted once again on the escape-ladder system in the storage closet to the side of the doorway. Damn, she thought, it was inaccessible, hidden behind a locked door. And the key was in the top drawer of her desk. Inside. There was no way she could get to it through the flames without being burned alive. And nothing on the deck to pry the lock open. She felt the heat radiating toward her as the murky smoke cascaded onto the deck, seeking to envelop her in smoldering effusion.

With a sinking heart, she realized the full extent of her predicament. There was no sanctuary. Nowhere to escape the growing chaos of the fire without the probability of sacrificing her beloved pet. Spasms of terror shot down her spine. Claire turned toward the open French doors, as if she could force the flames to subside by sheer force of will.

Worse than the flames, an unnatural disturbance gyrated the very center of the maelstrom. Her ears were assailed by a discordant and high-pitched whirring, like the swarming of hundreds of winged insects. Transfixed, she could only stare as a frightening apparition emerged from the fiery center, wearing a dark, hooded long cloak and appearing untouched by the crimson flames. In a repugnant yet almost seductive manner, the specter stalked toward her, seemingly relentless in its quest. The hood was pulled low, completely concealing the face in the shadowy play of flaming crimson. A foul stench of decay emanated from its person as it drew near, permeating the immediate area, and with it, Claire, who stood with Duffy at her side, both rooted to the deck, stunned by the apparition.

Knowing nothing human could've survived the fiery chaos that enveloped her bedroom, Claire's mind refused to process what was happening. One thought reached out for awareness.

If it touches me . . . I'm dead. The silent words screeched inside her head.

She opened her mouth again and again, but no sound emerged. Strangling on her screams, she was only able to breathe in gasps as a dense fog overtook her, beclouding her senses. Without hesitation, Claire knew she would rather go over the rail than succumb to the nefarious visitor.

Beastly talons reached out. Pawing at her. Scorching her.

She fell back, clutching her bloody arm, eyes squeezed shut. Hope vanished.

Claire's eyes flew open, instantly aware that something had pawed at her arm. She'd felt it. But strangely, there was no blood. Her heart continued a rapid tattoo against her ribs. The logical part of her brain comprehended that it had been another of those terrifying nightmares. She frantically searched the darkness for the demon figure, the unbidden monster that roamed at will in the vestiges of her imagination.

Forcing herself to a sitting position, she threw aside the comforter and pulled off her perspiration-soaked nightgown. She groped for her bathrobe, but abruptly pulled back her hand on encountering something wet and cold. Wide-awake now, she became aware of her surroundings from where she sat on the side of the rumpled bed. A wriggling white shape with inky splotches was discernable in the predawn moonlight. Her breathing slowed as she recognized her pet. It was Duffy who had awakened her out of the devilish dream by pawing at her arm. She switched on the lamp beside her bed, and reached down to pat the wagging spaniel.

"Oh, Duffy pup . . . I know I must have scared you, pal. That was a real head trip this time," she confessed to her canine companion whose countenance lit up at his mistress' evident return from where he could not follow.

Claire threw on her robe and shoved her feet into her slippers. The thought of going back to sleep right now, to possibly suffer another such nightmare, was something she would avoid as long as possible. She walked the few steps to her reading alcove set in the dormers of the two-and-a-half story carriage house and raised one of the windows slightly to let in the mild April breeze before settling into the comfort of her chaise lounge.

Appreciative that Duffy seemed to have an uncanny knack of knowing when she was deep into one of the ongoing nightmares, she patted the end of the chaise—a signal for her pet to join her. This wasn't the first time she'd felt the scream rippling up through the watery layers of her semi-consciousness. And once again, Duffy had managed to awaken her.

Claire thought back, hoping to both analyze and demystify the horror of the dreams that invariably began in a darkened room. The one thing she could count on, the plot always took a macabre twist. The only theme that remained constant was the appearance of the demon specter, its shape and face hidden by a dark hooded cloak, its bony hands ever reaching for her out of a relentless chaos of red, like magnets of pure evil, as if to pull her into the raging flames. The whole scene is what she envisioned hell to be like.

The phone vibrated from the bedside table, startling Claire out of her preoccupation. Checking the caller ID, Claire stared at the little screen until the pulsing stopped. Caller unknown. The vibrating sensation moved from her phone into every nerve of her body.

She didn't need to check her voice mail for the message. She knew the only communication would be a discordant dirge of notes and noises, a requiem intended to evoke a hysteric response. She'd almost given the lunatic the game—Whacko 1, Claire 0—when she originally heard the disquieting lament the first few times. It elicited a profound distress, intense in its effect. Especially with everything else going on in her life. She couldn't help wondering what kind of certifiable maniac was doing this. And why. Did she actually know the person? Was it someone she saw and talked to every day? And who was watching her?

Those questions, and the fact that the number of the caller changed every time a message was left, unnerved her because she didn't have the answers.

Claire sighed and returned to the chaise lounge in the alcove. The stresses in her life were taking a toll. Originally, it was the upcoming divorce, added to by the attack and its subsequent nightmares and headaches. And now the phone calls. Paris couldn't come soon enough. She wrapped the knitted afghan around her, picked up one of her favorite Jane Austen novels, and sank back into the cozy recess of the down-filled cushions with Duffy beside her. She knew sleep was no longer an option.

PART II

Paris

Denver

VICTORIA MASTERSON

3

Paris—Claire's Journal, 13 May

Lord deliver me from airlines, airplanes, and airports. In particularly, mechanical problems, delayed flights, or even worse, cancelled flights. Up until now, Murphy's Law has prevailed.

Mechanical problems on our original flight from New York to Paris. Flight cancelled. Talked to every carrier with a route to Paris. All direct flights booked. Finally found a carrier with three seats to London, with an Air France connection to Paris. Made that connecting flight by the grace of God. One piece of luggage still in space somewhere—my business case.

The taxi ride to our lodgings took us through several districts on the right bank of the Seine and into the Saint-Germain quartier on the left bank. The Residence Saint-Germain is a tall, imposing eighteenth-century mansion. Slate-tiled roof, stone façade, four floors—no elevator. Our accommodations, one of the 'quiet and intimate suites tucked away in the rooftops', as advertised. French doors open onto a small balcony overlooking one of Paris' best-kept secrets—a hidden garden, protected by high stone walls. The most incredible lavender-blooming trees line one side of the perimeter wall.

Raining lightly now. The balcony doors are open. The scent of rain-washed blossoms fills the room. Ahh, sweet Paris.

Day One

Paris—Residence Saint-Germain

Claire woke with a pounding headache that matched the incessant whine of what sounded like an old motor, running in high staccato and coming from somewhere very near, but beyond the walls surrounding her. Still entangled in the cobwebs of her dream, the thought finally surfaced that Duffy hadn't used his super-spaniel sensitivity to help bring her back to the world of the living from out of yet another nightmare.

She forced her eyes open. "Duffy, pup?" Not seeing him next to her bed, she peered around with confusion at the jumbled articles of clothing heaped over every piece of furniture and possible protuberance of the room. The chamber held another bed which was rumpled and empty. Then she remembered. Duffy was staying with Loupe in Denver.

I'm in Paris!

Through the partially open door she could hear one side of a conversation that increased in volume and insistence as the clatter grew nearer.

"*Bonjour, Mademoiselle.* This is . . . *pardon,* I mean . . . *Je vous Mademoiselle Martelli. Cintres, s'il vous plait.*" A pause, then . . . "Hangers. You know, for clothes. When we checked-in last night, there were only six clothes hangers in the wardrobes. Six hangers for three people. *Cintres* . . . Hangers. *C'est urgent.*"

Another pause. "Wait, I don't understand, er . . . *Je ne comprends pas.* Do you speak . . . hold on a minute. What is that racket? *Parlez-vous anglais?* No? Then kindly find someone who does, *s'il vous plait. Comprenez-vous?*" The conversation ended on the jangled-nerve level.

Claire stretched, steeling up to full consciousness. Well, so much for Mandy's crash course in French.

"Rise and shine, Claire. Paris is waiting. I'm out of the bathroom. Your turn." The tenacious voice of her sister cut through the last vestige of sleep. "No hangers yet, but I'm working on it. Are you awake? Can't sleep your life away."

Claire pushed back the coverlet and cautiously sat up on the edge of the bed, trying not to disturb her aching head.

I know my robe and slippers are buried in this mess. But where?

Barefoot, she threaded the floral carpet through the forest of clothes and made her way into the cramped bathroom termed *"old-world"* in the descriptive packet sent from the Residence Saint-Germain on the Left Bank.

One look in the quaintly-clouded mirror told the tale of the previous day's extended itinerary from Denver to London to Paris. Her eyelids were puffy this morning she noticed, making the fine network of laugh lines at the corners more pronounced.

But not as bad as I expected, considering the chaotic trip, the jet lag . . . and, of course, that dream again.

The persistent din of the motor droned even louder. It sounded more and more like an old vacuum—a very old vacuum. She sighed, wondering whether the dream brought on the headache or the headache the dream.

At age thirty-nine, Claire generally considered herself one of the lucky ones in terms of her gene pool. Her body, still firm and lithe, was leanly muscled like that of a swimmer. She easily passed for somewhere in the low thirties, a fact that never ceased to irritate her sister, ten years her junior. Her best feature, the tawny eyes that flashed glints of pure gold, was a bequest from her father's Northern Italian ancestry.

From her mother's side, Claire received the complementary gleaming tresses that fell in tousled, honeyed tendrils, no matter how much hairspray and mousse she used to tame them. She picked up her hair brush, attempting to bring some order to the tumbled mane, then gave up and crammed it all into a shower cap, reflecting on the source of that legacy, her maternal parent.

Abigail Campbell Martelli, feet firmly rooted in French and Scottish pedigrees, could out-maneuver, out-talk, and outlast most people half her years. Better known as Abbie, she was at once both practical and charming with an indomitable spirit cleverly packaged in a petite five-foot frame. The clear blue eyes were her most effectual feature, combining innocence with sincerity.

Claire had a sudden thought. She hadn't heard her mother up and around this morning. Absurd as it sounded, she'd told them she wanted to stick to her usual exercise routine and go jogging—on the streets of Paris.

She wouldn't really? But, yes, she would.

Claire was fairly certain she'd be okay, knowing Abbie. She had a knack of taking care of herself, friendly with strangers who invariably were taken in by her artless manner. The sisters had tried their best, begging her to go easy until she'd rested from the jet lag. However, knowing Abbie suffered from insomnia, hardly sleeping more than three or four hours a night, Claire hoped their mother had at least waited until daylight, a reasonable time to go for a jog.

Claire ran the shower and stepped into the dribble that surprisingly turned into a comfortable stream as she adjusted the flow valve. The product of a recent renovation, she concluded, marveling as her headache began to fade in the steamy warmth. As she stood there, letting the soothing cascade do its work, her thoughts automatically returned to the cause of her mother's current sleeplessness. Her dad's last heart attack had changed all their lives.

"In the wild March morning, I heard the angels sing," . . . the beautiful sentiment Mandy had written to mark their father's passing came to mind. Claire purposely willed those thoughts away for now, opting for a happier topic.

Paris. For ten whole days. A working holiday to be sure, she reminded herself. Still, it would be fun. The three women always traveled well together. And not just because they were

38

family. More like good friends. Even with the occasional little difference of opinion that caused Abbie to make her infamous "we're-not-stubborn-just-strong-willed" pronouncement. Or, throw in one of her many Colo-Iowa-provincialisms, like when she used one of Claire's favorites—"Sorry doesn't feed the bulldog"—on Chad when he sarcastically apologized for calling them the three 'mouseketeers'.

Claire's thoughts refocused to the man who had been her husband for the last seven years. Even now, she wasn't sure if she knew the real Chad. Or if there was a real man behind the persona. Chad, the brilliant manipulator? The multi-million-dollar architect? Or rather, as she knew he preferred—the Master Builder.

She thought back to when they first worked together, when he'd engaged her services to design and furnish the interior of the new house he built. This was after his divorce from his first wife, and on the heels of her own break-up with Adam, her longtime significant other.

A sudden wave of goose bumps ran down her arms causing an involuntary shudder in spite of the hot water. She turned off the water and quickly dried herself. Her vivid yellow and pink striped silk pajamas being the only apparel available, she slipped them back on and headed to the bedroom to find something more suitable for her first day in Paris.

The sudden quiet shattered her contemplation. After listening so long to the percussion of the motor coming from the corridor outside their door, the sound of noiselessness was close to deafening. For a scant few seconds, Claire enjoyed the precious tranquility only to perceive new reverberations crashing the walls. It started as an agitated babble of French and English, but quickly descended into a garbled mish-mash. The combative tone was unmistakable in any language.

She grabbed for the nearest article of clothing. Her favorite old sweatshirt was slung over a door knob.

"Mandy," she yelled, "what's going on out there?"

Pulling the oversized 'Rock the Rockies' purple sweatshirt over her pajamas, she raced through the bedroom and into the sitting room. Mandy was already at the open door to the hallway. Over her sister's shoulder, Claire caught a glimpse of their mother in the middle of a small knot of people.

Dressed in a plum and blue jogging suit, silver head shaking indignantly in the matching sweatband, an arm-waving Abbie gestured simultaneously to an elderly Frenchman, a vacuum sweeper, and the door to their suite.

"You were peeping at the keyhole, Monsieur," she charged. "Don't try to deny it. I caught you red-handed. Are you perverted, or just mad? Oh, girls . . . thank God. This old codger was looking through the keyhole into our room when I came up the stairs. He mustn't have heard me because that noisy old relic of a vacuum was in the middle of the hallway, running at full blast."

"But, Mom, look," began Mandy, "the key is still in the door. On the inside. He really couldn't see anything, even if he tried, which I'm certain he had no intention of doing." Her voice rose in an attempt to be heard over the hubbub.

Interrupting her sister's effort, Claire slid past her to get to Abbie's side. The sound of doors opening on the floor below floated up the open staircase as the commotion lured guests up into their corridor. The handful of spectators grew to an even dozen, adding their respective languages to the ensuing cacophony. Sounds like a United Nations debate, Claire thought, fervently wishing for the gift of tongues. She spent an unsuccessful moment trying to disengage Abbie from her tirade on the errant vacuum pusher and those vocally siding with him.

Claire thought it really wasn't likely the little Frenchman, now wildly gesturing and presumably pleading his innocence, could actually be a *peeping tom*. He reminded her of her own granddad, even to his choice of comfortable clothing—a baggy brown sweater worn over a faded checked shirt. The Frenchman's neatly-trimmed beard and mustache softened his lined face under the navy beret.

Claire put an arm around her agitated mother, trying to calm her. "Wait, Mom, I don't think he meant any harm. Look, he has something in his hand. See, he's pointing to the floor in front of the door. Can't quite see what it is though."

Catching sight of her sibling over her mother's bobbing head, she tried to get her attention. "Mandy, can you see what he's holding? Better yet, what's he saying? Miranda?"

Claire watched as her sister's suppressed giggles turned into hiccups, and recognized the beginning stage of the perplexing quirk leftover from her sibling's childhood.

"No help from that quarter," she muttered aloud. "So, where are the Marines when you really need them?"

It seemed to Claire the big black dog came out of nowhere. With one gleeful bound, an enormous wolfhound descended into the fracas. In seconds, the furiously wagging long tail scattered spectators and participants alike, leaving Claire alone in the middle of the hallway, dumbfounded and off-guard. She valiantly attempted to brace herself as the overly-friendly canine reared up on its hind legs and flung its front paws onto her shoulders. Eye to eye, a rough pink tongue slavering at her face, they went down together in a flurry of paws and fur.

A distinctly masculine voice, carrying a hint of a Scottish brogue within an English inflection, came from the top of the stairs. "What's happening here? Oh, I am sorry. Penelope, down girl! Penny, let the lady up."

Fluidly muscled arms lifted Claire from under her captor and set her on her feet. "Are you all right, Miss? Terribly sorry about this," he apologized.

"I . . . I . . . ." gasped Claire, struggling to wipe her face with her sleeve and regain her breath at the same time. Still wobbly, she stumbled against her rescuer's hard torso. Strong hands caught her. He swung her up into his arms. Claire's feeble protest died on a quick intake of breath and, though totally out of character, she instinctively wrapped her arms around his neck. She looked up into the brilliance of sapphire blue eyes and a smile so knock-out gorgeous it sent an unexpected rush of warmth racing through her veins. And all he'd done was smile at her.

Abbie, who'd been standing open-mouthed during the 'dog attack', as she later described it, stepped toward the stranger still standing in the middle of the corridor holding her daughter in his arms.

"Oh, my dear. Claire? Are you all right?" When Claire didn't answer, Abbie took control. "Sir, please, bring her into our suite," she directed, while abruptly dismissing the gaping audience and her former opponent with a wave of her hand. "Everyone, please. Let us through. It's all over."

Upon declaring she would take the *peeping* matter up with the hotel's proprietress, Abbie cleared the way into their suite without taking her eyes off the man carrying her white-faced daughter.

"Please put her there. On the settee. Claire? Claire, listen to me, honey, where are you hurt? Miranda, call the front desk. Tell them we need a doctor. Pronto."

"If you will allow me, Madam, I am a doctor," the dark-haired Englishman said, gently lowering Claire to the small sofa. "And, I am responsible for this old hound here," indicating a chastened Penelope who promptly settled on the floor at Claire's feet.

"For some reason she's rather taken to this pretty lady. Your daughter, Madam?" His question unanswered, he quickly assessed the pupils of his squirming patient. "I don't believe there's a concussion," he said, feeling Claire's head for bumps. "As I'm totally responsible for freeing Penny's lead on the way to my quarters just now, please let me do what I can. My specialty is psychiatry, but I . . ."

"No, *I* believe you've done quite enough as it is," interrupted Abbie.

"Oh for heaven's sake," Claire said, recovering to a more normal breathing pattern and struggling to a sitting position as she pushed the stranger's hands away from her head.

"I'm fine. Really. Just had the wind knocked out for a minute."

At the sound of Claire's voice, the big dog at her feet bounced up, penitently licking the bare foot extending from

42

the sofa before she was unceremoniously dragged off by the collar.

"No, Penelope. Down, girl," her master sternly said. "Please forgive us again, ladies. It looks as if she's trying to say she's sorry. Penny is generally very well-behaved. I think she must have somewhat of a crush on you, er . . . Mademoiselle?" He inquired tactfully.

Once again, his query went unanswered as this time Penelope took center stage. The big wolfhound fixed Claire with liquid brown eyes, the woeful expression rewarded with an impromptu chuckle. The tentative thump, thump—thump, thump of the long tail gained her forgiveness. Claire and Mandy broke into spontaneous laughter, the stress of yesterday's travel delays along with the morning's incidents already receding in the process.

"Oh, Claire," sputtered Mandy in between giggles, "now that I know you're not hurt, I wish I had a video of that whole hallway scene. First, Abbie and the *peeper*, then you and *monster dog*. Sorry, Penelope. It was priceless," she laughed, looking as if she might be trying to seek a measure of composure for the sake of her sister's rescuer. But she gave up the effort; instead, plopping down onto the arm of the loveseat next to her sister, hiccupping loudly.

Abbie gave a relieved sigh upon seeing both daughters' merriment. "Thank the Lord you're all right, Claire. You do look fatigued though. Or is it another of those headaches?" She turned to the man whom she held responsible for her daughter's present state. "Sir, we do thank you for your efforts to help, but as you see, we're in no state to entertain callers." She nodded unmistakably towards the door.

The tall gentleman agreeably nodded back, glancing down at Claire's bizarre attire. Fumbling in the inner jacket pocket of his tweed sport coat, he found a business card and offered it to Claire. He looked pointedly at her ringless left hand as she took the card. It read, *Malcolm Sutherland, M.D., Psychiatrist*, and included a London address.

His smile deepened as he continued. "Please call me Malcolm," he said with a smile for Claire. "And I think your outfit is smashing. I dare say you could even entertain the queen for tea in that attire. And I can heartily agree with the 'Rock the Rockies' sentiment as I have skied the Rockies. In Aspen last winter. And, even been lucky enough to make it to the top of one of Colorado's Fourteeners, climbing with some friends the summer before that."

She looked up from the card she held and, for the first time, studied the ruggedly handsome face above her. The cleft in his chin set off a strong and generous mouth, smiling broadly now to reveal white teeth that contrasted sharply with the early tan of an alfresco addict. The dark hair and expressive brows lent contrast to a pair of impressive deep blue eyes that once again immersed her in a warmth that jumbled her senses. She broke her gaze as a fleeting emotion she'd thought was long dead—or in the least, unresolved—was proving quite the opposite. Color spread across her cheeks.

Noting her daughter's discomfort, Abbie reached out to take the card from her hand while commanding the doctor's attention.

"*Doctor* Sutherland," she said stiffly, "these are my daughters, Claire and Miranda," indicating each. "And I am Abigail Martelli. Now that the formalities are over, I really must insist you take this . . . this animal out of here. She really is a public nuisance, Sir."

"Understandable, Mrs. Martelli," agreed Malcolm in an affable manner, but his body language showed a reluctance to leave as he started toward the open door with the wolfhound in tow.

"I hope you ladies will allow me to look in on you again," he said, turning back at the threshold. "I feel perfectly awful about this. Better yet, could I take the three of you to dinner this evening, as an apology? And, Claire, I have something in my quarters for that headache. I'll be happy to get it for you."

"My dear Doctor," Abbie said, drawing up her full five feet. "I am a registered nurse, and completely capable of administering aspirin. She will be fine. Now, please . . ."

"Yes, thank you for both your help and your dinner offer, uh, Malcolm," said Claire, smiling to soften Abbie's more militant posture. She gladly took the arm he offered as she struggled to her feet, her pulse erratic once again from the brief contact. "I'm afraid we must decline your kind invitation though. You see, this will be our first full day in Paris, and Mandy has her heart set on photographing the city from the Eiffel Tower at sunset. We have reservations to dine at the restaurant there. Your apologies are accepted. Dinner really isn't necessary."

"Ladies, another time then." Malcolm yielded gracefully with a smile and a nod for all, though his eyes lingered on Claire. He left then, whistling an enthusiastic rendition of *The Battle Hymn of the Republic* on his way down the corridor, a dejected-looking wolfhound trailing behind.

Denver—Offices of the Chadwick+Martelli Design Group

In rapid succession, the black shiny lines outlined the perspective of the hotel entrance for the New Orleans Crown Resort project. The title block along the right margin of the blueprint-sized vellum sheet taped to the drawing board read: *Chadwick+Martelli Design Group, E. Forde Chadwick - Architect, Denver, Colorado.*

The architect sat at the drafting table studying the effect of his creation on the paper. Not satisfied, he added a line here and there. He still preferred working up his designs on vellum with a drafting pencil, not the more impersonal computer-aided drafting program, saying he couldn't get the feel of his creation using the computer. Beads of sweat dotted the jowly broad face of the self-proclaimed Coloradan. Impatiently, he pushed his gray-tinted glasses higher on his nose in the habitual gesture that laid furrows up that fleshy feature.

Mopping his forehead with the cuff of a limply-rolled sleeve, he unbuttoned his collar and tugged to loosen the knot of his tie.

Enough!

He surrendered his drafting pencil to gravity as he missed yet another aimed shot at his wastebasket, frowning into the afternoon sunlight that streamed out of the cloudless blue sky and through the glass wall across from his work area. An enormous spectacle, the Rocky Mountains, confronted him. The silhouetted grandeur of the Front Range spread open to his view from Pikes Peak on the south to Long's Peak, his northernmost vantage.

He smugly congratulated himself for the umpteenth time in having planned his office facing this majestic view. Despite the objections of his minority partner-tenants, he'd added a second floor to the original plans for a single-story building. The new space accommodated only the Chadwick+Martelli office suite—and a clear view to the West. He then situated his partners on the first floor of the office complex. And he'd quieted them by threatening to bring in other investors.

"Waiting in the wings," he'd said, "to snap up the golden opportunity generated by this office complex and its exclusive Cherry Creek location." After all, it would be an E. Forde Chadwick creation. Now, for the most part, he ignored their continuing complaints.

"Susan," he bellowed toward the outer office, "didn't you call that twit who has the service contract for the building's mechanical systems? It's hotter than the hammers of hell in here. Oh, Susan . . . your master calls. Susan?"

Interrupted by a light knock on the closed door, he looked around expectantly for the tall, cool redhead who handled the firm's daily Girl Friday affairs. And just as efficiently, certain parts of his private life. Instead, a short and softly-rounded form riveted his attention. The dark-haired woman standing in the doorway was Guadeloupe Smith, better known as Loupe, Claire's second-in-command in the interiors department.

"Mr. Martelli, excuse me, but Claire is calling from Paris. She's holding on line one."

"Loupe. Where's Susan?" he demanded impatiently. "And, it would be very advantageous on your part to remember to use *my* name when you're addressing me . . . which is *not* Martelli."

"Oh, I'm so sorry Mr. *Chadwick*. I don't know why I said that. But I do know Susan is still out running errands for you."

Glancing down at his gold Rolex, he pushed his glasses back in place. "She isn't back? It's four o'clock. I sent her on errands at one. In my new Mercedes," he added.

"Susan phoned in a little while ago. She said she had a flat tire and she's having it taken care of and will be in as soon as she can. Also, the service man called back regarding the problems with the air conditioning unit. The message he left was something about prioritizing service for those who don't undersize the AC unit for the building size. And, um, pay their bills on time. He said you would know what he meant."

"Get him on the line," Chad snapped, his pale blue eyes narrowing through the gray lenses.

"I really don't think it will do any good, Mr. Chadwick."

"You don't *think*? Thinking entails brains," he shouted. "Claire only lets you *think* you're running that infernal department while she's gone."

Loupe stiffened, backing towards the door, then stopped and looked him in the eye. "Claire is still holding on the call from Paris, Mr. Chadwick."

Before he could stop her, she leaned over his desk, punched the blinking line on the phone and handed him the receiver. Cringing in response to the scowl on his face, she escaped through the open door, with a loud exhale that resonated relief.

Chad glared at Loupe's retreating back, then down at the phone in his hand. His palms were sweaty. He hesitated for a split-second. He hadn't counted on her calling so soon. He never knew what to expect any more with Claire.

Pushing the speaker phone on and his glasses further up on his nose, he quickly decided on what tact would ensure him the alpha position.

"Claire, darlin'," he boomed into the mouthpiece, further amplifying the overworked Texas drawl he'd picked up while living in that state in his early years. "Are you there? How are you sweet lips? How's Paris treatin' you? Up kind of late aren't you? Isn't it the bewitching hour over there?"

The veiled agitation in the overly-loud tone was not lost on Claire, on the other end of the line. "Hi, Chad," she answered. "So far, Paris is great. In fact, it's absolutely magic at midnight. The City of Light, you know. We just got back from dinner in the restaurant at the Eiffel Tower. Mandy took *the* quintessential photos of the sunset from the tower, and later, overlooking the lights of the city. It's a stunning sight from the viewing platform. She's doing a freelance assignment, a photo journal of our trip to Paris for one of her publishing clients.

"But, how is everything in Denver? I understand you're having an early heat wave there. How's the New Orleans' job going? Loupe said the interior plans and specs are running on schedule."

Chad's brow knit in frustration in response to the composed voice coming over the speaker. It was one of the things about her that originally attracted him—Claire's seemingly endless reserve of composure. He grudgingly admired her talent. But, at the heart of the matter, the simple fact was that both her character and talent scared him, although he would never admit it. She was a free spirit, and he'd tried his best to break her. He was only aware of a few times in their marriage that he'd succeeded in shaking her natural enthusiasm and upsetting her equilibrium.

"Chad, are you still there?" Claire's voice cut into his thoughts.

He blinked, bringing himself back to the present. It wouldn't do to let her see how much she disturbed him. There was that lilt in her voice that so annoyed him. She sounded so alive. And he couldn't grasp that mental state. Mostly, he just felt empty.

"Everything's fine, Claire. Under control, darlin'. Now you just have a good time. Don't worry that pretty head about it. Uh, Claire, honey, I'm a little busy right now. What can I do you for?"

"Sorry. I wouldn't have bothered you, but Loupe said you were free right now. Here's the problem. The airline made me check my attaché case, but somewhere along the way of last-minute flight connections, they seem to have lost it. There was a message at the desk when we got back tonight that they've located it, but it won't arrive here for another couple days. They found it in Bangkok of all places. Until I get it back, I'm more or less without my head. Everything is in that case: contracts, plans, appointments, and all my contact's names.

"Actually, though, I called to have Susan fax me the complete itinerary I left with her. But since she's out, Loupe can fax a copy of the one I left on your desk. I'll get it in the morning as the Saint-Germain's office is closed for the night. And could you please look right now at your copy to see what date the auction is being held at Simon Boule's, the antique house, and when I have an appointment with him?"

Chad rummaged in the mess on his desktop, despite the fact he already knew the paper with the itinerary and contact information wasn't there. He also knew what he'd done with it.

"I don't see your itinerary right in front of me, Claire honey. Looks like you'll just have to get some shut-eye tonight and wait for the fax in the morning. You need your beauty sleep anyway, darlin'. Is that all you wanted?"

No, one more thing Chad. I'm planning on checking out the antique houses in the St-Germain-des-Pres district that will be showing in the annual exhibition at the end of the week. But you see, the letters of credit are also in my briefcase. So, even though the case was locked, I think it would be wise to have Susan notify the bank, today, if possible. I will let her know if

49

my case arrives intact. If not, the bank will have to cancel the originals and issue new letters of credit.

"And if I do find some antiques for the project, I want to put holds on those pieces. I know they won't do that unless they have a deposit. So I need you to authorize Susan to send me some blank business checks first thing in the morning by one of the overnight express services. A half-dozen will do. I will use them as good faith deposits until my case arrives."

"Consider it done, my pet," his voice lowered to its normal pitch. "I'm ringing off now. Send us a postcard. You know, one of those *wish-you-were-here* types. And don't worry about anything. Okay?"

Claire was silent for a couple seconds, knowing instinctively what went unsaid.

"Okay, Chad. Tell everyone hi for me. Take care of yourself. Bye."

Paris—Residence Saint-Germain

Damn it, Chad, it could have been so different, Claire thought, uncurling herself from the settee in the sitting room. She clicked off her phone and set it on the desktop, then turned out the lamp that lit the Directoire-styled field desk. In the darkness she made her way to the French doors, attracted by the glow coming through the lace curtains. She pulled back a corner of the curtain and looked out. No stars. A partial moon showed itself at times through the drifting cloud cover that reflected the lights of the city. Careful not to wake Mandy or her mother, Claire opened the doors and slipped out. She leaned against the iron railing and closed her eyes to savor the faint bouquet of the herb garden below. Only distant sounds of the city penetrated the rustling night songs of the garden. She turned her face into the soft breeze that ruffled the escaping curls tied at the nape of her neck.

Feels like rain. Still, it's a heavenly night.

No, not exactly heavenly, she amended. More like . . . *cosmic.* Yes, that was it, cosmic.

And something else. She tried to put her finger on it. There was a sense of heaviness also. Like the air was weighted around her, closing her in. Strange that it would happen now, in Paris. She tried to think back to when she'd originally noticed that same feeling. She was fairly certain it had started about the same time she'd filed for the divorce. But till now, she'd only felt that way when she was at work in the Denver office. And now, here it was again.

A muted but distinct sound reached her from the garden below. Her eyes flew open. She looked down to see a brief flare coming from the deep shadows by the old manse's garden wall. Then it was gone. The acrid smell of a lit cigar carried up to her on the night breeze. Claire stared hard but could see nothing.

Her eyes adjusted to the night, yet she couldn't penetrate the inky shadows below. She tensed, waiting. Nothing moved except the clouds skittering across the crescent moon. There was no sound but the rustling of the newly-blossomed trees and faint street noises from the nearby boulevards. Yet Claire felt goose bumps rising on her arms. She pulled her hands up into the sleeves of her old sweatshirt and turned toward the French doors. Quietly, she made her way back into the darkened sitting room and pulled down on the latching mechanism to lock the doors.

The clamoring ring of her cell phone reverberated through the room, causing her heart to skip a beat. Remembering she'd left it on the desk, she fumbled to retrieve it from the smooth wood top.

Must be Chad, or one of the gals in the office calling back with my itinerary.

"Hello," she whispered, hoping not to wake her mother and sister.

"No . . . Oh, no." It couldn't be. "Not here . . . No! Not in Paris."

Her legs turned to rubber, her breath came in great gasps. The only thing keeping her upright was the campaign-style chair at the desk. Claire seized onto the back as if it was a life preserver and she was drowning. Her phone fell from her hand to the floor. But she could still hear the pernicious racket blaring in her head. Like a sound track from a class B horror movie, her senses were assailed by the wild clash of an organ pounding out an off-key lament against a background of tortured screams.

Denver—Offices of the Chadwick+Martelli Design Group

It was five o'clock in Denver, quitting time, and the temperature had dropped thirty degrees in the last hour. Gray thunderheads rolled in from the west, mounting the white-capped peaks to take command of the sun. It was a typical mile-high summer storm, complete with thunder and lightning, and just as quickly as it came in, it passed on, leaving Denver dampened, but refreshed.

Chad had given up his plan to stay and finish the architectural drawings that would represent the theme and facade for the resort. The clients were due in town tomorrow for an initial presentation. In his mind, he had plenty of time. He knew he could complete the drawings before the meeting. And, as he so often bragged, his drawings would be "a thing of beauty and a joy to behold." And, invariably, he was right. Just as, invariably, he left things to the last minute. Working well under pressure, up to and including the very last moment, was another of his perceived strong points. It was nothing new.

He reached over and clicked off the overhead lights from the switch mounted on the side of his desk. Tilting back in his leather chair, Chad contemplated the resplendence of the white peak in his line of vision. In the distance, beyond the foothills, loomed Mount Evans, still clad in the winter mantle that covered its craggy bowl-shaped elevation rising far above timberline. It would be another month before much of the snow retreated from the crowned heads of the high country. At this time of day, the late afternoon light played with the jeweled spectrum of the pine forests, turning the scene before him into an oriental painting ombred in purple-blue mists. Layer upon layer, beginning with the foothills, each set retreated further into gauzy eminence.

Chad admired the mountains. In their shadow he felt grounded. They represented substance and strength, two qualities he lacked, which is why he worshiped his patron saint, Frank Lloyd Wright. In Chad's view, Wright epitomized talent, strength and substance The Master Builder, the authoritative architect whose masterworks still influenced architects the world over.

Chad patterned himself after this often cantankerous genius, even to the manner of genius. If Wright could conceive the design of a structure by way of concentrated thought, not on paper but by visualizing it totally in his imagination, letting it live there, down to the last brick and intimate detail—he should be able to do the same.

If Wright could draw his conception in one sitting, sketching the first drafts of plans and elevations in their entirety, then so should Chad, who did possess some degree of intelligence and talent. But by the cruelest whim of fate, these simply translated by the nature of his character to native skill and cunning. Try as he might, he could never equal the pure genius and true authority of the Master.

Chad mused on the unfairness of life, staring out at the darkening silhouette of jagged peaks backlit by the profound coloration of a Colorado sunset. Not one to remain in low spirits for long, he shrewdly began to contemplate a grandstand play for tomorrow's meeting. Why not chuck the drawings now on the drafting board and draw the whole structure from scratch—while they watched?

He would have to use his colored marker technique, not the thoughtful colored pencil mastery of his demigod. But still, if he could pull it off, what a coupe. He would truly become the

Master Builder of the Crown Resorts. He would have his immortality.

The scent of something sweet-smelling and diaphanous penetrated his senses. He closed his eyes and breathed it in. A cool hand fell softly on his shoulder from behind. One, then two hands began to massage the back of his neck with light, deft strokes, working slowly upward, through his hair. Now, the silken hands played at his temples.

Claire could wait. The Crown Resort could wait.

He leaned back. "Ahh . . . Susan, my love. Don't stop now, *darlin*."

4

Day Two

Paris—Residence Saint-Germain

The heady scent of old-world roses scaled the aged stone walls, filtering through the lacy curtains on the open balcony of the Martelli's sitting room, while morning sunbeams danced across the rose-patterned carpet.

Claire brushed away the last crumbs of a croissant and poured herself a second cup of chocolate. Her headache thankfully gone, she felt more relaxed than she had in days. She didn't remember dreaming last night either, though if she had dreamed, it wasn't filtered through the red haze of her usual nightmare.

She let her mind wander as Mandy provided an animated rundown on the merits of the artists they would see in the *Musee d'Orsay*, the gallery showcasing the work of the French Impressionist movement. While Abbie, the intended receiver of the briefing and a self-proclaimed *visual illiterate*, relished a morning bun slathered with butter, content to nod at the appropriate intervals.

The welcoming cushions of the eighteenth-century reproduction *bergere* armchair enticed Claire to settle back, offering a wide-angle view of the sitting room decor. By profession, she was a stickler for good design. And in the present case, she happily approved of the room's charming mixture of quality reproduction and enduring wicker furnishings done in a rather atypical color scheme of the sort the French seemed to delight in. The palette's neutral hues were accented with deep dusky-rose shades and muted lavender pastels, combined with a pale mossy color on all the wood moldings. The highlight of the room was the burnished gold ornate eighteenth-century fireplace.

Must compliment Mandy. The Saint-Germain was a real find on her part.

Claire knew she couldn't have done any better. The old mansion offered great ambience and style, and was perfectly located for buying antiques for the hotel project.

She drowsed as the warmth of the sun's rays filtered over her, content to relax for a few minutes more before heading to the shower. She didn't even feel guilty about lounging around the suite over a late breakfast.

Claire mentally reviewed her request and Chad's promise to have Susan fax her schedule and contact information this morning. And, hopefully, Susan would get the overnight package out today so she could begin to shop for antiques tomorrow.

Right, but why haven't I gotten the fax at least? It should have arrived by now.

She'd notified the proprietress and her daughter regarding the expected fax. They were to let her know the minute it came into the Saint-Germain office. She also made a mental note to ask Madame Fontaine if she knew which auction houses were likely to provide the best finds in the Saint-Germain area.

Claire resolutely settled herself further in the armchair and relaxed to Mandy's voice droning a soothing background white noise. A pair of deep blue eyes came to mind, belonging to the man she'd just met yesterday while in her pajamas in an undignified heap on the floor. Dr. Malcolm Sutherland. She admitted to herself, although sheepishly, on finding an attraction there. This in itself was unusual. During the past eight-month separation from Chad, her life solely revolved around her design work and the firm's business. There wasn't even anyone she wanted to have a casual dinner with. Until now, she thought, tacking a *maybe* onto those thoughts for good measure.

She wondered whether that meant she was finally getting through the grieving period, and through the could-have-beens and should-have-beens. Odd to think of the resultant divorce like that, but it was really about loss—the passing of a marriage.

Though, like Scarlet, I'll think about it tomorrow. Or, in this case, when I get back to Denver.

She mused on why Malcolm was in Paris, on business or holiday. Strange though he'd bring that gigantic dog with him for either of those reasons.

Dog, huh. More like Gargantua.

Maybe an evolutionary breed, she mused. A genetic link to the Hound of the Baskervilles? But, no, the dog wasn't at all scary, and it did have a rather sweet face. It was probably just an oversized something. A wolfhound, most likely, but which version—Irish, Russian or French?

And her owner? English or Scottish?

There had been a London address on his business card. But she'd detected a slight Scottish brogue. She'd ask her mother if Sutherland was a clan name. Of course, she really didn't know much about him. He could be Jack the Ripper. Or, worse, married—with a dozen kids to boot.

Nah, no self-respecting London psychiatrist, in Paris and accompanied by a monstrous dog with the unlikely name of Penelope, would have a dozen kids. Would he?

A pleasant tingle ran down her spine just thinking about the way he'd looked at her.

"Earth to Claire. Snap out of it my much, much older sister," Mandy said, playfully. "Where were you just now? I'm trying to get a fix on our sightseeing plans. I know I planned Notre Dame for today, but would you rather go to the Louvre with a late lunch somewhere along the Champs Elysees? Or, we could take in the Latin Quarter and check out the artists' colony. Also, I've read about some wonderful cafes, the very ones that Hemingway and that group patronized. It would be great to lunch where they hung out, even though Paris was quite different back then."

Claire brushed non-existent crumbs from the pajama-sweatshirt duo that was fast becoming her favorite outfit in lieu of finding the yet missing bathrobe somewhere in the piled clothing in the bedroom. She kept her head down to conceal the blush that spread across her cheeks resulting from her wayward thoughts on Malcolm.

"Mandy, you've just covered four or five days in one minute. It's now a little after nine o'clock," she said, hiding behind a business-like demeanor to avoid more scrutiny from her sister and their sharp-eyed mother. "It will take us approximately thirty to forty-five minutes to finish getting dressed. Then, transport time. The Metro, taxi, or bus? We could possibly be at any one of those places by ten-thirty-ish. Makes no difference to me, but the Louvre alone will probably take two or three days even at a fast trot.

"We've got ten days, you know," Claire reminded her sister. "Anyway, I think we should let Abbie decide today. Tomorrow we'll plan on getting a much earlier start, Mandy, and then it's your call."

"Mom, please make up our minds," Mandy said, turning from Claire to Abbie. "Then, I for one, am going to zip in and finish getting myself put together."

"You always do this to me, girls," Abbie said. "From experience, there is no way we'll be ready to leave here before eleven at the earliest. If it's my decision, I suggest a stroll along the Left Bank, and a light lunch at a sidewalk café of your choice, Claire. Then, Miranda, if we have time, we can do your *Musee d'Orsay* tour in the afternoon. I'd hate for your art lesson on the French Impressionists to go to waste," she said, smiling at her youngest daughter. "Besides, I've heard so much about the riverside quaint book stalls along the Left Bank. You know, they actually expect you to haggle over the price."

"That's if you can haggle in French. Americans probably pay full price, or more," Claire teased. The thought of Abbie wheeling and dealing with a Parisian bookseller brought a smile to her face.

"You just want to see all the young lovers making-out along the Seine, Mom," said Mandy, already halfway to the bathroom. "I like it. Sounds like a great photo opportunity. Last one dressed pays for the taxi," she called over her shoulder.

"Not fair, Mandy. You'd better be out of there in five minutes," Claire called back, just as the phone interrupted with two closely-spaced jingles, then two more.

Abbie nimbly sprang up from the loveseat and headed for her bedroom before Claire could mobilize. "It's probably for you, dear, and you handle the intricacies of the French language so much better than I do. Besides, Parisian taxi fares are way too rich for my blood," she said with a disarmingly innocent smile.

Claire shook her head, resigned to the obvious as her mother's last words came through the closing door in a muffled fashion. She could make a fairly good guess who'd be paying the taxi fare to the Seine's renowned Left Bank. She picked up the receiver and found consolation in a nasal-accented mix of French and English, telling her a fax had arrived "from the U.S. of A".

Malcolm headed up the venerable stairway from the Saint-Germain's office toward his rooms on the top floor, his lecture engagement at *universite* concluded for the day. He smiled to himself remembering how today's focus on the intricacies of graphology in the mental health realm had taken the thirty-some students in his class by surprise. He'd definitely piqued their curiosity, giving them a reading assignment from books available in the library and a paper to write discussing certain mental problems that could be ascertained using graphology as a tool.

Intent on his thoughts, he opened the door to his rooms, pausing to pick up a folded paper from the floor, remembering that the proprietress had said a fax had come for him earlier, and not knowing his schedule for the day, she had her daughter slide it under his door. Penny rose to greet him from her position as sentry in the entryway. The massive wolfhound stretched and gave a wag before ambling out through the open French doors to nap in a sunny spot on the balcony.

Doesn't make a lick of sense, Malcolm thought, reading the fax from London once again. Why is Grandmother coming to visit me in Paris? I'll be going home after this *universite* session. "Doesn't bode well," he muttered, closing the door and throwing the message onto the hall table. It's almost a command, he thought. Whatever this is about must be serious. He could call her, but knew from experience that she hated talking on the phone, so she didn't answer. Probably wiser to let it go for now, he thought. He would get to the bottom of things when she arrived.

It was part of his daily routine, unless he had private business matters scheduled, to check in at the Saint-Germain office for messages on the way back from lecturing at *universite*. He usually made it a point to chat a few minutes with the proprietress, Emilie Fontaine, or her daughter, Marie-Claude, whichever happened to be manning the front desk. The women all too gladly reported the news and happenings of the day. He had won their confidence with his easy manner and fluent French. It was now six weeks into his stay, as well as the daily conversations, and he had long ago determined the proprietress to be a goodhearted, albeit serious sort, and her daughter, the mademoiselle, an out-and-out flirt. Today he had stopped for his messages and to find out what the ladies knew about yesterday's incident with Dominic, generally known as Dom, the old man Abigail Martelli accused of peeping at their door.

Malcolm walked out onto the balcony and dropped down onto the wrought iron bench, absently petting Penny, while staring out onto the tree-lined garden below. In the past six weeks he hadn't once seen Dom operating the vacuum. Until yesterday that is. He knew the old man to be the Saint-Germain's gardener, and uncle to the proprietress herself. Malcolm had run into him a few times while walking Penny in the park. Dom had been exercising the miniature poodles belonging to the two spinster sisters who leased rooms at the Saint-Germain.

Malcolm thought Dom to be a regular enough chap from the conversations they'd had in the park, at least from what he could comprehend. According to the proprietress, her uncle was born in the Provence region in the south of France, the reason his particular dialect was difficult to understand.

Could be that one of the regular cleaning people didn't show up, Malcolm reasoned, and Madame Fontaine asked old Dom to help out. According to Madame, by way of Marie-Claude, Dom had knelt down to pick up an object from the floor in front of the Martelli's suite. He left the vacuum running for the few seconds it would take to retrieve the article. Again, with respect to Marie-Claude's account, it's easier for the old man to kneel down on one knee rather than bend over because of a bad back. Supposedly, that's why Abigail Martelli found him kneeling at the door when she came up the stairs. Of course Dom had tried to explain his actions in the hallway. But, as Marie-Claude put it, "Dom's English? Not so good."

Turned out the object he picked up was a rather unusual medallion, gold, with a spiraling design and notched edge. That was about all the girl knew, except that her mama had locked it in one of the safety deposit boxes they utilized for their guest's valuables. He decided to talk to Emilie Fontaine herself, and see if she would open the box so he could take a look at the medallion. If old Dom was telling the truth, and Malcolm was inclined to think he was, then someone else was in the hallway outside the Martelli's door. Someone who lost the charm sometime between the night of the three women's arrival and early the next morning. That would definitely clear the old man of Abigail Martelli's charges. But that only meant that someone lost a gold charm in the corridor outside their suite. Perhaps it had been worn on a neck chain that broke. Nothing sinister about that, or was there? His gut still told him something wasn't quite right.

"The devil, you say!" Malcolm slapped his knee, startling Penny out of her dreaming. "It's okay, old girl. But, Penny, I've been so dense. Remember the guy we ran into on the stairway early yesterday morning?"

The big dog watched him intently, as if eager to recognize something familiar in her master's tone. But all Malcolm got in answer was the thump of a tail.

"Well I remember all right. He almost bowled us over. Twice. Once on the way out for our walk and again on the way back. What if this character inadvertently lost that medallion piece, and then came back to look for it when he realized it was gone?"

Malcolm vividly remembered the rather bizarre incident on the staircase as the stranger had taken the steps at a fast clip, deliberately turning his head away as he passed. Malcolm had held Penny at a *stay* command as the stranger went by, when he noticed the hair bristling on the back of her neck and the restrained growl coming from low in her throat.

"Should have listened to you, old girl," Malcolm said, giving the wolfhound a couple of conciliatory pats for not taking the warning seriously. "Okay, Pen, let's see if I can pull up a description of the guy. I remember one thing for sure. He wore one of those tweedy gangster hats, the kind with a brim you always see in the old mobster movies from the States. Like the cap Cagney usually wore. I remember it because it was unusual, it had a green shamrock woven into the top." His mind flashed on the fact that the goon had pulled the brim down so low that it shadowed his features.

"On purpose, I bet, now that I think about it." Malcolm didn't remember anything else of significance. Half the male under-fifty crowd in Paris wore a leather jacket and jeans.

Penny only looked at him, her head on her paws. Malcolm scratched behind her ears. He was used to voicing his thoughts to the big wolfhound when they were alone. It helped him put things in order. He was interrupted by the phone jangling from the console table in the entry hall. The voice on the other end of the line spoke in perfect, though heavily-accented, English.

"Sutherland? Simon Boulle here. That shipment of antiques I'm expecting is due in on Friday, the balance of the lot from the provinces. I'm afraid it will require a quick turn-around on this one. You see the catalogues have already been sent out to our patrons and these pieces are included. The auction is scheduled for next Monday. When can I expect you?"

"There is written provenance on these pieces?"

"*Oui*, all the papers will be on my desk Friday morning."

"Good, I will come by Friday after my lecture at *universite*. About one o'clock."

"Till Friday then. *Au voir*."

Paris—A sidewalk café

"Forget it, Mandy."

"Please, Claire? Come on, humor me. Put on the hat. It set me back a pretty penny at that fancy millinery shop. Just pretend you're waiting for your lover at this little sidewalk café. Romantic, huh? No, not that corny face again. Look starry-eyed, not cross-eyed," pleaded Mandy, viewing her sister through the lens of her Nikon.

"I feel silly in any kind of headgear. Just not my style. And I don't wear this color of red. All right, it's actually more of a vermillion shade." Claire conceded. "Anything to get this over with. Just take the picture, Mandy." She settled the fancy millinery piece with its frothy rows of ruffles on her head. She was not, however, willing to give up her litany of complaints.

"You've got everyone staring as it is. You can be a real serious pain, Miranda Martelli. Anyway, you coerced me into being your model," she reminded her sister.

VICTORIA MASTERSON

"You look charming, Claire. The hat gives you a mysterious look," chimed in Abbie. "And it really does look wonderful with the olive tee-shirt and linen vest you're wearing, dear."

Mandy took a step back and adjusted the focus, "Claire, your hair. The hat is hiding too much of your hair. Could you please let it loose? And pull a few wispies around your face."

Sighing, Claire took off the designer *chapeau* and released her curly mane from the ribbon at the nape of her neck. With a will of its own, the sun-drenched mass escaped in a rippling halo. She jammed the hat back on her head.

"There, that's it. You *are* a good model, you know, Claire. It's your bone structure, or perhaps your coloring. Definitely those topaz eyes," said Mandy. "The perfect *Lady in the Vermillion Hat* composition."

"Don't you really mean as a model I work cheap? You're buying lunch. Right, Mandy?"

Ignoring her sister's sarcasm and Abbie's chuckles, Mandy only smiled from behind the cover of her camera. "Now, think of someone you would like to spend a romantic evening with. Never mind, I know what that frown means. Well, something that makes you happy then. Like all the gorgeous hunks of marble waiting for us at the Louvre. The Venus de Milo? The Winged Victory? The Michelangelo sculptures? Yes. That's it. Oh, it's great, Claire," exclaimed Mandy, excited now at the composition of her sister sitting at a table covered in a black-and-white checked cloth, actually smiling from under the froth of deeply-hued ruffles. "Wait until you see, Claire. You're going to love it. I promise. Hmm, could use just a touch more of something that definitely says you're at a sidewalk café in Paris."

As if on cue, their waiter appeared, skillfully juggling a tray which held three empty glasses and a carafe of red wine, the café's own *vin de table*. The waiter was young, dark-haired and handsome in his Parisian waiter's uniform of white shirt worn under a black vest with a formal bow tie. A long white apron wrapped around his lean waist. Mandy knew he would make the perfect Gallic contrast with his eloquent brown eyes to Claire's golden coloring.

Before he could deposit the contents of the tray on their table, Mandy quickly snapped the shutter in rapid advance mode. After a second's pause, the waiter smiled affably as he placed the three glasses on the table. Mandy stepped back and adjusted her lens to a wider angle. This time she caught the young Frenchman in the act of pouring Claire's glass of wine. Colorful umbrellas and the *maitre d'* greeting other café patrons created the perfect background. After several more rapid shots while the waiter finished his rounds of the table, Mandy noticed her current photo memory card was full. She unslung the camera from around her neck and took her seat at the table, pleased with her photo session.

"Well, I'm glad that's over," said Abbie, pushing her chair back and standing up. "I've been waiting to use the café's facilities. I didn't want to bother you while you were shooting, Miranda, but how do you ask directions to the restroom?"

Mandy laughed. "That's an easy one. It's probably the first phrase I learned. You know me," she said. "The *maitre d'* probably speaks English, Mom. If not, try *ou sont les toilettes*? And add *s'il vous plait* for good measure. Got it? Would you like me to come with you?"

"No thank you, dear. I'm sure I can manage quite nicely." Abbie headed for the open doors leading into the café, repeating the French phrase under her breath.

Claire watched their mother disappear into the interior of the building. "Think I'd better tag along to keep her out of trouble, Mandy. Who knows where she may end up." Rising, she removed the ruffled hat and plunked it atop Mandy's sleekly-bobbed head. "Looks better on you anyway, squirt," she said in passing, using one of the pet names that generally annoyed her sister.

"Okay, Claire. I'll wager you a movie with buttered popcorn you'll be begging to wear the hat again when you see yourself in the edited version of the photo when the guidebook is published," she shot back, rearranging the beleaguered *chapeau* to a more flattering angle.

As her sister walked toward the interior of the restaurant, Mandy took advantage of the quiet to replace the spent memory card in her camera, taking a fresh one from the special slotted card wallet that held both used and new. Like her professional colleagues, she generally transferred the day's photo-takes from the memory card onto her laptop on a nightly basis so she could see the full-size results soon afterward.

As she finished inserting the new card in her camera, a shadow fell across the table. Mandy looked up to see her Parisian model, the handsome waiter with the soulful eyes, standing across from her, empty tray in hand. He stared at her with a shy smile. Mandy smiled back. On impulse, she decided to attempt a conversation to improve her French. She slipped the finished memory card into her pocket to deal with later.

"Thank you again, Monsieur. *Merci beaucoup. Parlez-vous anglais?*"

"I speak a little of the English, Mademoiselle." The voice was soft-toned, the accent nasal, but not the Parisian accent she was becoming accustomed to.

"Well then, we're even. I only speak a little of the French. *Jen e parle pas bien francais.* Just the key tourist phrases, I'm afraid. What is your name . . . er, *comment vous appelez-vous?*"

"I am called Etienne, Mademoiselle, Etienne Geraud. *Et vous?*" he asked, bowing to her.

"Miranda . . . Mandy for short. You know, nickname?" Thinking he wouldn't understand the word, she added, "Never mind. *Je m' appele*, Miranda."

To her surprise, he gravely repeated the shortened version of her name. "*Enchante*, Mademoiselle Man-dee," he said, breaking her name into two syllables and placing the accent on the ending.

Out of curiosity, Mandy asked, "Etienne, where do you come from? *D'ou etes-vous?* Not from Paris, I would wager."

66

He broke into a boyish grin, revealing white teeth that contrasted and set off his olive complexion. "Please, Mademoiselle Man-dee, I will speak English. Mine is not so good, yet I am learning. If you do not mind that we speak slow. It is better than to attempt to speak in two different languages. *Oui?*"

"You speak my language very well, Etienne," said Mandy, slowing her speech down for his benefit. "Much better than I speak yours, I'm afraid."

He colored and gave a slight nod in acknowledgement. "To answer your inquiry, Mademoiselle, I come from the region of Provence in the south of France. My home is near the center of the local perfume industry. Now, I am back in Paris to study more of the English."

"Back in Paris? Did you live here before?"

"*Oui,* Mademoiselle. I was at *universite* for some years and completed the course in the science of horticulture. It was expected I learn this to go into, how you say, the family business."

Mandy would have liked to hear more about his family, but Abbie and Claire returned to the table just then.

"Sorry, Miranda. We had to wait in line. Ahh, here's our waiter now," said Abbie, sliding into her chair. "I was just saying how famished I am. Dear, can you ask him if our lunch is ready?"

"Almost, I think, Madame. I will go to check for you at once," Etienne said, returning to the impersonal demeanor of the Parisian waiter.

"Why, you speak English, young man," said Abbie. "Why didn't you tell us before, when we were trying to decipher the French menu? I'm not sure *what* I ordered."

Flustered by the American's indignant candor, Etienne took himself off to the kitchen after throwing Mandy one last expressive look.

"Well, what was that all about?" asked Claire, noting the creeping shade of pink unusually evident on her sister's ivory complexion.

"It's nothing, Claire," said Mandy, unfolding her napkin. "Etienne was just telling me . . ."

"Etienne?" Abbie interrupted. " You are on a first name basis with the waiter?"

"I know what you're going to say, Mom. About talking to strangers. However, he seems like a very nice young man."

"A very handsome young man," added Claire. "You sure can pick them, Mandy."

"He's probably all of twenty-two or twenty-three," her sister pointed out. "Don't make it sound like a big deal. We chatted a little. That's all. He's trying to improve his English."

Abbie sat back, listening to the familiar banter going on between her daughters. She wiggled her feet out of her expensive new walking shoes, knowing she should have worn her old favorites. She glanced up, feeling someone at her elbow. Etienne had returned, artfully balancing their luncheon selections on his tray.

"Madame," he said to her, bowing gravely, *"your cassoulet toulousain."*

"You know what I've always told you girls, if there are stoves in heaven, I'm not going," Abbie said, scooping up the last bite of *cassoulet* with a crust of *baguette* bread. "Not that I could ever prepare a dish as scrumptious as this, mind you. Reminds me of your father's cooking, only French rather than Italian. Your dad was such a gourmand, I simply had to get out of his way and let him have at it in the kitchen. I was always better on prep and clean-up anyway."

"Well, Mom," said Mandy, "not to say that your soups aren't to-die-for, and those wonderful French pancakes, of course. But you gave up the cooking chores early-on from the stories we heard from dad."

"Well, I planned to continue on with my career in the nursing profession," Abbie said in defense. "Why did I need to know how to cook? Your father did say he liked the first meal

68

I prepared for him. So, I figured, why argue with success? I fixed it again the next night."

"But," Claire chuckled, "over-cooked steak, lumpy mashed potatoes and gravy, and banana pudding? Both nights? If I didn't know you better, one would think you were playing it dumb . . . like a fox. You can knock off the innocent act, we don't call you 'Columbo' for nothing."

"Oh my, look at the time," began Abbie, in her best Colombo-like manner. She didn't finish however, as for the third time since they sat down, café patrons jostled into them as they passed their table on the narrow access aisle. "How rude. Not as much as an *excuse me* from any of them, this time, or before," she said, readjusting her chair.

Claire mopped up spilled water from the table cloth with her napkin. "You know, this establishment seems to have ignored the age-old design principle of flow and function. It's way too crowded in here. Looks like this table was placed in the traffic pattern as an afterthought so they could squeeze in a few more diners. Next time we'll ask for a table on the terrace side."

"Well, I'm ready to leave anyway, girls," Abbie said, slipping her feet back in her shoes. "I'd like to get back to the hotel soon so I can take a quick run this afternoon before I get ready for tonight's opening reception of the INA conference. Somehow the time just slipped by today. Sorry, girls, since I'm the Director at Large from Colorado, I must attend. You two can take in the sights and the galleries without me."

"Oh, that's right. I almost forgot about the International Nurse's reception this evening," said Mandy. "Didn't you say you know the keynote speaker? I'm okay with putting off the sightseeing, Mom. Your conference is much more important. Claire, since the afternoon is open, are you going to look for antiques at the auction houses?"

"I will either need my brief case, which won't be delivered till tomorrow sometime, or the business checks Chad promised to express before I can buy anything, Mandy. So, no, to answer your question," Claire said. "Does anyone care to make a wager on whether Chad actually did have Susan get the package out on overnight delivery?"

"You've got to be kidding," declared Mandy, gesturing to Etienne across the terrace for the check. "I know my soon-to-be, but-not-soon-enough, ex-brother-in-law all too well. The crown prince of procrastinators. No wager.

"You can come with me this afternoon, Sis. Since we'll have some free time, I'm going to the photo shop my friend Jesse recommended. I need more memory cards for my Nikon. You remember Jess? My photographer friend who lived in Paris for a year?"

"Do we remember him?" Claire laughed. "Abbie had the whole wedding planned last summer, Mandy. Or didn't she tell you?"

"Don't tell tales, Claire. He was such a nice thoughtful person, Miranda. So handsome and personable. And you said he was quite talented," Abbie said, shaking her head at her youngest daughter. "Whatever happened to him?"

"The same thing that happened to my favorite candidate," Claire said, "the one who piloted his own vintage barnstorming plane. They both probably became hermits, maybe even monks, after our Heartbreak Kid dumped them. Then there was that musician, the one that unfortunately was no one's favorite. He could play a mean saxophone though," recalled Claire, watching her sister squirm. "Yep, like I've always said, when they get serious, Mandy cuts them loose."

Mandy rolled her eyes heavenward. "Are you through dissecting my love life, Claire? Let's just say I'm not ready to settle down yet, ladies. End of conversation. *Finito*. Amen. Anyway, here's Etienne. Finally. *L'addition, s'il vous plait*."

"I have brought it, Mademoiselle. But, before you leave, I would ask something."

"Yes, Etienne?" Mandy inquired, absorbed with figuring the exchange rate in her head.

The waiter stammered, and reddened. "Would . . . would it be possible," he finally blurted out, "to see you again, Mademoiselle Man-dee?"

70

"Good Lord, another conquest," Abbie whispered under her breath.

Startled by the question, Mandy nudged Claire under the table in a wordless plea for help.

Claire smiled at the young waiter. "We'll be back, Etienne. The food is wonderful and you are an excellent waiter. So, you will see *all* of us again."

Mandy recovered quickly, cueing in on Claire's lead. "That's right, Etienne. Besides, I'm planning on bringing copies of the photos I took of you the next time we come in."

The disappointment was apparent on Etienne's face. "You intend to have copies of the photos of your family holiday before you leave Paris, Mademoiselle?" He asked, politely.

Mandy suddenly realized he didn't understand the purpose of the earlier photo session.

"Etienne, I'm a photographer. I took those shots of you and my sister for my work. She acted as my model, as you so kindly did. Right now, I'm on assignment to take photos for a new guidebook to Paris. May I use your photos for that purpose? *Permissione?*"

Seeing his perplexed look, she tried again. "Etienne, these are memory cards," she said, reaching down beside her chair for the card wallet she'd laid at the top of her open canvas bag when he'd served their lunch. "They're full of the camera shots I've taken during our first couple days here."

Her hand searched where she had placed the wallet a little earlier. Panicked, Mandy looked down at the open valise. She grabbed the bag onto her lap and wildly searched the contents. "They're not here," she said, dumfounded. The alarm on Mandy's face was readily apparent to both Claire and Abbie.

"Look on the floor, Mandy, maybe the wallet fell out and was pushed under your chair when that last group shoved by us," Abbie suggested.

Claire's head came out from under the tablecloth. "There's nothing under the table or the chairs. Look in that monster bag of yours again, Mandy. Maybe it fell to the bottom."

Etienne didn't know what was missing, but could tell by Mandy's actions it was something important. "Mademoiselle, can I help to find what you have lost?"

"My leather wallet . . . with the memory cards inside, it's just not here. Please, Etienne, can you ask the *maitre d'* if someone found it and turned it in?"

"*Oui,* Mademoiselle, I will be but a moment," he said, wheeling off toward the interior of the café.

"I just know someone took it." Mandy determinedly dumped the contents of the canvas bag onto the table. "Probably one of those rude people who knocked into us on their way past our table."

"Mandy, get hold of yourself. Why would anyone want to take your memory cards?" Claire questioned. "Your Nikon is still here. That I could understand someone stealing. Are all of your lenses here? Yes? Okay, but the memory cards?" she continued. "No one would have any idea what was even on those cards, right? And you said yourself new cards are available at all the professional photo shops."

"Well, see for yourself," Mandy said, holding up the empty bag and shaking it for her mother and sister's benefit. "The wallet is definitely not here. All my time, wasted. All my beautiful shots at the Eiffel Tower . . . the Saint-Germain's walled garden . . . just everything" she wailed, her voice trailing off.

"Okay, Miranda, let's approach this from a different angle," Abbie suggested. "We can check under the tables around us. They're empty now. Maybe the wallet got kicked under another one, by accident."

"Good idea," seconded Claire. "You take that row and I'll check over here. Mandy, get off your duff and look under those tables behind you."

"Mademoiselle Man-dee?" Etienne called, coming upon them a few minutes later with the *maitre d'* in tow, who appeared not a little amused at the scenario of the three women, backsides in various poses, hunting for something under his checkered tablecloths.

"Oops. Ouch. It's not here," said Mandy, rubbing her head and backing her way out from under a table to view the lower halves of two pairs of black-trousered legs. When she straightened to a standing position, she was eye-level with the well-demeanored goatee of the café's *maitre d'*. Etienne stood beside him.

"Oh, Monsieur, *merci*," Mandy said, automatically smoothing her pale blonde hair and adjusting the deeply-hued rose hat that had fallen over one eye. "I'm missing a leather wallet with a zippered closure. It held a good many memory cards that I use in my work. I'm a photographer," she explained. "By chance did someone find it and turn it in?"

"Non, Mademoiselle," said the *maitre d'* in English, though his accent was so thick it made his words difficult to understand. "But you must know there is the possibility it may have been thrown in the garbage collection by one of my waiters. Accidentally, you understand, Mademoiselle. But of course, it would have been by accident," he hastened to add. One thing was clear, however, he was obviously enjoying his role in the scene with the good-looking American.

"You are more than welcome to, shall we say, peruse our garbage bins for your missing case. You seem to have much practice on your hands and knees," the *maitre d'* finished with a leer that turned his words into a thinly-veiled sexual implication.

Storm clouds built in Mandy's gray eyes boring into those of the *maitre d'*.

"Monsieur," she said, carefully controlling her emotions. "I will not root through your trash. I expect you to check with your waiters to see if one of them did indeed throw the wallet away, by accident as you say, during this last hour. And, Monsieur *Maitre d'*," she continued, holding his gaze with steely calmness, "I expect an answer by the time it takes to walk from here to your front door."

Silence greeted Mandy's ultimatum. The *maitre d'*'s dark eyes raked her from head to toe.

Etienne quickly broke in, volunteering, "Monsieur, Mademoiselle, I will be happy to ask the other waiters. Please to sit down and wait, ladies. I will be back in, how you say . . . a jif-fee."

The *maitre d*'s face blotched purple in anger. "Monsieur Giraud, you defy me. As of this moment, you are no longer in my service. I will send your wages to your Paris address." Turning on his heel, he tossed back a sarcastic, "*bonjour*," leaving Etienne to gape after him.

The three women stared at each other in disbelief. Mandy was the first to speak. "Etienne, I'm so sorry. I only know the word for this man in Spanish . . . *machismo*. Mom, Claire, come on. Let's get out of here. Anyway, I'm fairly certain the wallet was deliberately taken."

Mandy watched Etienne's face as he stood staring after the *maitre d'*. "Come with us, Etienne," she said, sympathizing. "You lost your job trying to help me. I feel responsible."

Etienne sighed. "It is not your fault, Mademoiselle. Please, not to worry. I will find other employment. I must apologize for Monsieur *Maitre d's* rudeness. And the loss of your card case."

"Well, if it had to be, I'm glad the memory cards disappeared early on in our stay," Mandy said, purposely ignoring Etienne's apology for the *maitre d'*. "I still have time to go back and re-take the shots. I just need to buy more memory cards. It's certainly not tragic, just disappointing. But, they didn't get this one," she said, triumphantly waggling the card she'd dropped in her pocket earlier. "I just remembered I didn't get a chance to put this one in the wallet when Etienne came over to talk while you both were in the ladies room. It's holding the shots of Claire and Etienne, *and* the café, *and* the river walk. Everything I took today."

"Bravo, Mandy," Claire complimented her sister. "I don't think I could've posed at yet another sidewalk café. One hat trick per trip is enough. And, by the way, you did a helluva job handling that slime. I was about ready to drop him with a kick where it would hurt the most. He was so demeaning and it was so unnecessary. I really don't think your cards got thrown in the garbage, 'slime ball' just wanted to see our backsides as we rooted through it. Talk about a sicko."

"Miranda, you were marvelous," said Abbie, adding her praises. "Personally, I was seething inside. The worm. But you had the situation under control."

Claire returned to their table to help Mandy repack her bag. "On a more serious note, Sis, I'm afraid I have to agree with you. Since we didn't find the wallet within a dozen feet of the table, someone had to have taken it from the top of your bag, for whatever reason. The puzzle is, why?"

Etienne took off his apron and laid it over a chair along with his order pad and pen. Responding to the young waiter's obvious dejection, Claire tried to console him. "Etienne, I'm afraid you were the token sacrifice so Monsieur *Maitre d'* could save face. I'm sorry you were let go, though I'm not so sure you won't be better off out of his influence." She glanced at Mandy, who nodded in agreement to the unspoken message that passed between them. "Come," she continued, "we will take you with us to see Madame Fontaine. She might know of another position."

"Wait," cried Etienne, in surprise. "Did you say, Madame Fontaine? Then you are staying at the Residence Saint-Germain?"

Claire and Mandy nodded at the same time, both surprised and intrigued by the response their offer created.

"You see, Madame Fontaine is *tante* to me. I think the word translates as *aunt* in your language. But I am also staying at the Saint-Germain. Though just while I complete my course in English," he added. "*Tante* Emilia and *Cousine* Marie-Claude are my family. From my mother's lineage. But this is wonderful."

"More like unbelievable," Mandy said, shaking her head.

"I say it's fate . . . *kismet*," said Claire, trying to hide a grin.

"It is true, Mademoiselles, I assure you," Etienne beamed.

75

"Then you must also be related to the old man, Dominic," Abbie queried, recovering from her initial surprise at this announcement.

"Oui, Madame. You have met *Grande-pere?* He is my mother's papa," Etienne replied proudly. "When I am in Paris, I assist him with the gardening at the Saint-Germain."

"Mom, you can talk to Etienne about his . . . ahem, charming granddad," Claire said pointedly, "on our way back to the hotel." She fastened the closure on Mandy's satchel while her sister did one last search for the missing wallet and her memory cards. "Ready, Mandy? Mom? This café is history. Please excuse the pun. Hemingway and F. Scott Fitzgerald can have it," she tacitly pronounced, gathering up their things.

"Please allow me, Mademoiselle." Etienne reached over to take Mandy's bag and slung it over his shoulder. "Come, we can go out this way," he said, "it is shorter and perhaps less conspicuous." Offering Abbie his arm, he started toward the break in the hedge that separated the terrace from the sidewalk.

"No, young man, not that way," said Abbie, with a firm pull on his arm. She squared her shoulders and reversed their direction toward the interior of the café. "We always leave by the front door."

The streets of Paris

The train vibrated to a sudden stop, the doors slid open to the platform of the Vavin station on the number four line of the metro system running through the bowels of Paris. Malcolm maneuvered his way out of the congested car and allowed the swell of the crowd to sweep him toward the stairway leading up to the street and into the blessed daylight. He emerged at the conflux of the tree-lined Raspail and the traffic-lined Montparnasse boulevards. In full stride, he headed to his right, toward the smaller thoroughfare that led diagonally in the direction of the Luxembourg Gardens and the area of his lodgings some dozen blocks away. Malcolm tried rationalizing his decision to take the quickest subterranean route—underground for a mere twelve minutes. The above-ground time entailed by the longer walk didn't matter as long as he could see the sky and inhale the open air. He enjoyed the walk. The day was superb.

A gray drizzle had saturated the earlier hours, puddling the morning commute. Now, the city fairly sparkled in an elemental display of sunlight and shadows.

Malcolm looked at his watch, quickening his pace. Notwithstanding his rationalization for taking the long way, he wanted to get back to the Saint-Germain in time to catch Madame Fontaine. She generally turned the front desk over to her daughter around this hour. He still had the same gut feelings about the mystery man on the stairway and the same curiosity about the gold medallion. And there was the hope that Claire would be around later.

Maybe I can talk Madame Fontaine into brewing up a pot of the tea I brought with me from London, he thought. High Tea in the garden. The lavender trees are in bloom. And the lilacs. Why not?

He thought maybe Claire would at least accept an invitation to have a spot of tea on the Saint-Germain's terrace. He abruptly did an about-face in front of the small patisserie shop he was passing by, suddenly homesick for a true English teatime. Turning into the shop, he opted for the house specialty, the small fruit tarts piled high with luscious, ripe berries.

Paris—Residence Saint-Germain

Malcolm turned off the Rue Vavin and onto the quiet side street in good stride. At the farther end of the block stood the Residence Saint-Germain, the stately mansion that stood as sentinel of the street for nearly two hundred years. Nearing the handsome entranceway, a replication of the original according to Madame Fontaine, he sought to juggle his parcels in an attempt to free one hand to open the heavy door. The pastry box was easy, though the two large bouquets proved awkward. The riotous mix of spring flowers, judiciously blended with the more subtle Queen Anne's Lace, was for Madame Fontaine, a thank-you in advance for helping him with his garden party. And if nothing else, he decided they would nicely do service in the antique silver vase she generally kept filled with fresh flowers on the reception desk.

The exquisite fragrance of the other bouquet, Penelope's peace offering to Claire, caused him to inhale deeply. For just a moment, he was back in the English countryside, in his grandmother's garden, and those golden summers that seemed to go on forever when he was young, thinking about how to catch fireflies rather than girls. Yes, he decided, coming back to the present, he'd made the right choice. He looked down at the two dozen delicately yellowed roses edged in a deeper pink hue, as a few of the huge buds were in full bloom. And aptly named. He recalled the flower vendor's discourse on how this French masterpiece, the Rose of the Twentieth Century, came to be known simply as *Peace*.

Malcolm balanced the flowers against his chest and fumbled for the long, hand-wrought handle of the entry door. He hoped Claire was either in her rooms or away from the residence, as he needed a little time to arrange things with Emilie Fontaine—and take a look at the medallion she had locked away—before he saw any of the Martelli's again.

"*Puis-je vous aider*, Monsieur?" the voice came from behind him.

"*Oui, merci beaucoup*, Monsieur." Engulfed in the flowers, Malcolm gratefully stepped back and accepted the offer of help as a white-gloved hand reached around him and pulled open the door. The hand connected to an arm clad in the light blue sleeve of a uniformed shirt. Black trousers, black tie, and a brimmed hat completed the outfit. The braid-trimmed epaulets on the shoulders designated his rank, while the gun in its holster at his side made it official.

"You are very kind, Monsieur," said Malcolm to the French *gendarme*, though he couldn't help thinking of what could possibly have happened that brought the police to the Saint-Germain.

They crossed the small lobby to the reception desk in silence, only the sound of their heels clicking a staccato duet on the marble floor.

A young French woman, chicly dressed in black, looked up from behind the beautifully-preserved Louis XVI desk. Like a cat intent on its prey, her shadowed brown eyes monitored their approach. The deep red-shaded lips curved into a coy smile and her throaty greeting was for the Englishman carrying the beautiful flowers.

"*Bonjour, Docteur, un instant, s'il vous plait*," she purred. She then turned to the gendarme who stood at attention at Malcolm's side, awaiting her acknowledgement. She crisply inquired, "*Puis-je vous aider,* Monsieur?"

"Marie-Claude. I have asked you time and time again to speak in English to our American and British guests when you are on duty." Madame Fontaine's voice scolded through the open door of the small business office directly to the left of the reception. "*Comprenez-vous?*"

"*Oui, La Mere*," returned Marie-Claude, her full red lips pouted. "But it is only Malcolm, Mama. And of course, the police. Oh, *pardon,* Messieurs," she said quickly. "I did not intend bad manners. It is this *anglais la mere* makes me to speak." She smiled beguilingly, punctuating her words with a helpless little shrug.

The *gendarme* smiled back at her. But Malcolm only shook his head. He didn't buy the act. Marie-Claude was probably half his age, young enough to be his daughter, yet she continued to play the coquette around him. He deliberately looked over, not at, the young woman preening at the desk, to her mother who was coming out to greet the policeman, apologizing for her daughter's tardiness in announcing the official. She showed him into her office, and turned in the doorway toward Malcolm.

"*Pardon, Docteur,* lack of manners seems to be the rule today. I did not mean to ignore you. In fact, I have something to tell you. You see, there was a break-in last night." At his shocked look, she continued. "*Oui,* I am afraid I was negligent in securing the gold medallion Dominic found in the hallway. Fortunately, it was the only thing taken. I am telling you, in confidence," she said nervously, looking around as if the Saint-Germain lobby was a hot-bed of spies left over from the Nazi occupation, "because you have shown such interest in the trinket. Please come in, also. It is only fitting that you hear the whole story."

"But how did they get in? How did they get into the safety deposit box? And how did they even know what to look for? I guess the real biggie is . . . why?" Malcolm's head whirled with speculations even as Madame Fontaine shook hers in answer to his last question.

She pointed to the middle set of French doors down the hallway from the reception, leading to the garden. "They came in just there, breaking a pane of glass. Then it was a simple matter to turn the bolt and enter. No one heard them. The police came in early this morning after I discovered the damage and called. When the investigators left, I had the glass from the door cleaned up and replaced before any of the guests noticed. But please," she said, again looking around, "come in so that we may not be overheard. I pray the authorities are wrong, but they have said the situation may not be the simple matter of a break-in after all."

Intrigued by the proprietress' announcement, Malcolm unceremoniously plopped his parcels in one of the chairs next to the desk. He followed her into the office, ignoring Marie-Claude who was occupied with an incoming call, though gesturing for his attention.

"*Oui,* Monsieur, I am sure. *Oui,* I will ring again," Marie-Claude impatiently told the insistent caller on the other end of the line, all the while frowning at Malcolm's disappearing back.

"*Non*, no one is answering in that suite. *Oui*, I have written down that you called once before. It is right here. At ten o'clock today: "*Urgent I meet with you regarding guidebook assignment. Unless I hear from you otherwise, I will be at the Saint-Germain at nine tomorrow. Let's make it a breakfast meeting.*" *Oui*, Monsieur, of course I have your name and number. *Au revoir*, Monsieur."

Marie-Claude sighed as she put the receiver down. She watched the door to the office quietly close, shutting her out, rejecting her. Just like before. She would try not think about it—that other door. The one that always shut on her when she was small.

Briskly she gathered up the morning's phone messages and resolutely started for the pigeon-holes built into the wall behind the desk, the message center for the Saint-Germain's guests.

That's when she heard it—starting up again from somewhere in the back of her head—the thin childish voice chanting that silly little nursery song. Her movements turned to slow motion, the papers floating out of her grasp. She clamped her hands over her ears and squeezed her eyes tight, trying to block out the all-too-familiar sound that brought on the unbidden images. The singing grew louder.

And, there. There she is, hiding in the shadows of the hallway. The little girl. Her dark hair spilling over the eyelet collar of the long white nightgown. And, there. There *they* are—papa and *la mere*—coming up the stairway, arm and arm, smiling into each other's eyes as they enter their bedroom.

They didn't see her. They never did. She held her breath, hoping. But the door closed on her and she heard the bolt being thrown from the inside. She knew she should not be out here in the hallway, in front of their door. She should be in her own room, in her own bed, where papa had tucked her in earlier.

The dark-haired little girl sat in the gloom for hours, singing softly to herself, rocking, holding tightly to the porcelain doll papa had given her when he returned from one of his trips. A very special doll. Usually he brought her sweets, the strawberry tarts were her favorites. She knew the door would stay shut for a long, long time. So long, they would find her in the morning, curled up in the little nook of the window seat in the hallway. She knew it was her fault. Papa was punishing her. He told her she was five now, and a big girl. Too big to sleep with mama and him in their bed. She knew it was her fault—why he never came back to her from that last trip.

The sing-song of the nursery rhyme faded into the background. And now, those other voices would come. They wouldn't leave her alone. They told her that *la mere* was monopolizing Malcolm, just like she monopolized papa before he left them. The door would be closed for a long time, the voices said, all because of that trifling piece of jewelry. And the Martelli's.

And here she was, stuck out here, taking care of the tiresome guests' problems, like answering those uppity Martelli's phone calls. And now there were faxes also. And the stupid clothes hangers the younger one pestered about for several days now. The older one, the mama, she caused that fracas in the hallway. She was a real pain. And then Malcolm met the one they call Claire that same day. Those Martelli women certainly made her life miserable. And to make matters worse, ever since they arrived, Marie-Claude's own mama actually reprimanded her. She said Marie-Claude was rude and lacked in what she called 'social graces,' toward the guests of the manse.

Marie-Claude smoothed a strand of hair into the roll at the back of her head. She had dressed in her most flattering business outfit this afternoon. Just for Malcolm. The voices told her she looked pretty, that the suit made her look like a cinema star. Like her idol, Catherine Deneuve. No matter that the famous French actress was a classic blonde beauty and fairly-complected, the voices said Marie-Claude's darker looks and coloring were more exotic.

She balled her shaking hands into the pockets of her jacket, woodenly circling a path from the office door to the desk, then back the other way.

"*Oh,*" the voices screamed, "*you need to get out of here. Time is running out. Malcolm will go back to London in a few short weeks. He is leaving, just like papa. It isn't fair,*" they said. And she had worked so hard to get his attention.

She stopped pacing in front of the chair piled with the colorful bouquets jacketed in the paper cones. The flowers. They must be for her, the voices told her. Marie-Claude brightened, then puzzled. Why were there two bunches? The roses for me . . . maybe the other one is for *la mere*? That was it. Malcolm wanted his *cherie's* mama to have flowers also. How dear of him. She picked up the larger paper-wrapped sheaf and buried her nose in the pink-ruffled froth of yellowed petals spilling out the top of the wrapping. That's when she saw it, the white confectionary box on the chair. "*Go on,*" the voices urged. "*It's for you. Open it.*"

Some moments later, the little party from the cafe entered the lobby. Spirits high, the three Martelli women, with Etienne happily ensconced in their midst, were taking turns rehashing their impressions of what they laughingly called, *the café caper*.

The merriment died as they approached the reception desk to find Marie-Claude on the floor in front of the closed office door, face and hands smeared with crushed red berries. On the carpet around her, bits and pieces of brightly colored spring flowers, ripped apart. Their mangled heads strewn among the confetti of torn paper. She clutched a bouquet of roses tightly to her breast, rocking to and fro, crooning softly in a child-like sing-song voice.

Paris—The Saint-Germain garden

VICTORIA MASTERSON

Claire lazed in the plump comfort of a chaise lounge, enjoying the cool recesses of the brick terrace in the shade of the most resplendently flowering tree she had ever seen. A book lay open in her lap. Yet, she gazed up, to the blazoning display overhead. Lavender-tinged blossoms massed the gnarly limbs of the ancient tree, emitting an essence that rivaled the finest perfumes Paris had to offer. She gingerly stretched the tense muscles in her neck and shoulders and settled back into the cushions, abridging her view down to the eye-level range of the Saint-Germain garden. She didn't want to think right now, preferring to engross herself in the detail of each planted bed, budding bush, and shady nook.

In the background, a vague drone of honey bees swarmed over the waterfall of white wisteria flowing from the trellis-work at the rear of the manse. Softly, the heady mix of sounds and fragrances stole around her, penetrating her senses. The verdant habitat of this urban oasis captivated her, as she knew it would. Here, in the late afternoon, her favorite time of day, the long shadows played and the color of the light turned golden. She would readily surrender her headache to the peaceful assault of the garden around her.

"Botheration!" The expletive slipped out, though she reluctantly acknowledged it to be appropriate in the literal sense. The disturbing images of the Marie-Claude episode flickered in her mind like the changing patterns of a kaleidoscope. She shivered, chilled by the reality her anxiety prompted, while discerning how best to quiet her present stream of consciousness.

No gym, no lap pool to exercise in. Besides, if I wanted to get all hot and sweaty, I could have gone jogging with Abbie, Claire rationalized.

She decided to try another relaxation approach, meditation, which she often employed with good effect to dispel the goblins of her frequent fright-night dreams. She closed her eyes, normalizing the pattern of her breathing to an easy rhythm as she filled her diaphragm deeply, slowly pushing the air out again. After doing this several times, Claire silently intoned her *mantra*, an Eastern technique she used to de-focus conscious thoughts. But instead of the meaningless syllables, her mind chattered with the nonsensical verse of Marie-Claude's nursery rhyme.

Claire sighed. Just have to let it be, then I'll meditate, she promised herself. She began rotating her neck and then her shoulders, in slow-moving circles, to loosen the knots clumped there. The sudden chill running down her spine was not caused by her self-therapy treatment. She froze in mid-arc, in eerie anticipation that she was no longer alone. She turned in the direction she perceived to be the source of her unease, the rear of the manse, only to be reminded of the similar sensation that interrupted her balcony soliloquy the other night.

Get a grip, woman, she scolded herself. Pretty soon you'll be seeing the bogeyman skulking behind every tree. Just like in Denver. Or in those damnable dreams. Good Lord, is this how paranoia starts? But, I am right, there is someone there. Ahh, it's only old Dom, she discovered in relief.

He saw her at the same time, doffing his perennial head gear, the navy beret, and acknowledging her with a courtly little bow. Claire relaxed. She smiled and waved at the Saint-Germain's peppery little gardener, dressed in a leather work apron tied over a shapeless sweater and baggy pants. He appeared to be heading for the kitchen plot, a trowel and kneeling pad gripped in one hand, a shallow gathering basket over the opposite arm. Claire shielded her eyes and squinted into the whiteness reflected by the trellis-work of wisteria, following his progress down a short path bordered with riotous plantings of balled and clumped salad greens.

He stopped several times, positioning his knee pad to pick a sampling here and there. A little further on, he chose a spot among the radish colony where he began aerating the soil around the plump red spheres intermingled with the white tops of a French *Icicle* variety. Claire observed that the little Frenchman worked in obvious contentment, and seriously contemplated the idea of asking the old man if she could get down on her knees and dig in the dirt with him.

Surely, Dom must know about Marie-Claude's episode earlier today. She is his granddaughter, after all. Not to say he isn't feeling it inside, but outwardly he seems at peace. Claire wished she could say the same, finding the sobering reality of the afternoon's crisis still tugging at her emotions.

But at least I had the good sense to turn down Mandy's offer, she thought. At least in the garden there is the reasonability of a natural order. She recalled her mother and sister's attempts to occupy her in their company after the ambulance pulled away with an anxious Madame Fontaine clutching her daughter's hand. Claire could have accompanied her sister in a mad dash to the professional photo studio in the old Montmartre quarter. Mandy's close friend, Jess, had given this particular shop high praise for carrying the largest inventory of photo equipment and accessories in Paris. But they closed at five on the dot, he had warned.

Claire checked her watch. *I'll lay odds Mandy made it. It's just five o'clock now.*

After seeing Mandy off, Claire had headed for their suite. She wanted to talk before her mother lay down "to rest my eyes," as Abbie had put it, prior to the conference kick-off dinner this evening.

Heaven knows her mother deserved a couple of winks after dealing with the hysterical Emilie Fontaine. Abbie did get her calmed down though, Claire thought. Thank goodness for that, or Emilie would never have given her permission for Malcolm to sedate Marie-Claude. Or, she asked herself, would he actually be sedating the little girl who had taken control?

Claire remembered opening the door to their suite expecting to find Abbie in a robe or similar attire. The periwinkle jogging suit flashed another message. Claire wanted to talk. Abbie did not.

"My dear and wonderful child," Abbie said while brushing back the unruly tendrils of her daughter's golden halo of curls, "we will talk. Later, okay? If I don't jog now, I'll be unfit for human companionship tonight. You are welcome to join me."

"No, but thanks for asking," Claire replied. "And, *please*, mother, stick to the more populated areas? And for heaven sakes, don't stop to talk to anyone."

"As if I could," Abbie quipped, a streak of blue periwinkle shooting across the room. "*Bonjour, comprehend-de*-English?"

Claire laughed. She knew when she was bested. "You're hopeless, Abigail Martelli. Be careful," she called after her.

Out on the streets of Paris, the early evening rush hour toiled on, sounding a vacuous belligerence of tinny horns, to lay siege to the ramparts surrounding the manse's grounds. But Claire heard only the white noise of the garden. Punctuated by unintelligible voices floating out to her from the reception area, dominated by Etienne's provincial tones. He hadn't needed to look very far to find a new job after all. Claire knew Mandy would be relieved when she heard the news. Madame Fontaine had asked him to take over Marie-Claude's duties, as well as some of her own. "For an indefinite period of time," she'd said, charging her nephew with the responsibility of the Saint-Germain as she boarded the ambulance that Malcolm had ordered.

That poor woman. Finding Marie-Claude like that. What a shock for her. For all of us, Claire silently amended her thought. *And, thank God, Abbie and Malcolm were there. Because I don't think dialing nine-one-one would work too well in Paris.*

It had been Abbie who went into the office to break the news to Emilie Fontaine. Though it was the calm and collected Dr. Malcolm Sutherland who first came through the doorway of the office to take control.

"Okay, okay. Admit it. Besides being the man of the hour, he does have a certain appeal . . . in a rugged sort of way," Claire grumbled to herself. Not wanting to complicate her life further, Claire had made up her mind to relegate the good doctor to *Category A: Attractive Men I've Met While Traveling*. This designation was usually good for dinner and maybe a night on the town while traveling on business during the months since she filed for divorce from Chad. Maybe even a couple of postcards when she got back to Denver. But that was all. She didn't have any sub-classifications. Now, she reluctantly admitted he was more impressive than she wanted him to be.

After a thorough assessment of Marie-Claude's condition, Malcolm had taken Madame Fontaine aside to advise her of his diagnosis and recommendations for immediate treatment. Then he'd explained the situation to the rest of them, sensitive to the traumatic effect of the young woman's symptoms. The bizarre posturing along with the deeply regressed and altered state of mind were indications of what Malcolm termed, *catatonia*, further explaining the psychiatric terminology as a condition of catatonic schizophrenia.

Guess I shouldn't be so surprised. Claire reflected, mulling over her perception of Marie-Claude in the two days since their arrival. *But schizophrenia?* She'd never suspected that the young woman's taciturn manner and moody demeanor were indicative of this mental disease. She just figured it was more of what some travelers to Paris called "the Parisian attitude" thing. Only Marie-Claude seemed to take it to such extremes. Claire recalled how the younger woman's moods generally swung from cold detachment one minute to an almost arrogant rudeness the next, both in the context of an inability to deal in reality.

Okay, so forget it already. Claire sternly told herself. *Just because she isn't Miss Congeniality material. So she has problems. Don't we all? But I'm afraid hers are big time.*

Must be hell living with a thing like that, she thought, hoping the clinic Malcolm had recommended could help.

Claire waved away a curious bee that opted for an unscheduled stop en route to the hive. It appeared to be undismayed by the brush-off, circling over the berry smudges on her slacks and buzzing her once in general, before continuing its normal flight plan.

She looked down at the stains on her clothes, remembering how difficult it had been to remove the smeared berries from the carpet when she and Mandy pitched in to help Etienne clean up the mess at the reception desk. They had to literally scrub up the tart remains, from the carpet, the chair, the desk. And it hadn't taken long to figure out why all the guest message boxes were empty after sweeping up the mangled shreds of paper and derelict flower parts.

When the clean-up chore was finished, Claire had gone to see if she could be of any help to her mother or Malcolm. They might have their hands full with both Marie-Claude and Madame Fontaine, she reasoned. And at least she could run errands or perform some other non-medical function. She'd tiptoed through the open foyer of the Fontaine's quarters and on to the only door standing ajar, stopping there, the intended offer of assistance dying somewhere between her throat and her gaping lips.

The Fellini-like quality of the scene that greeted her was never to be forgotten. In her deeply sedated state, Marie-Claude reclined in motionless tension, her black clad shape contrasting the white coverlet draping the bed. She lay in a pool of torn rose petals. From the stranglehold of her cradled arms, a porcelain doll vacantly stared.

Keeping vigil in the charged silence of the bedchamber, her attending cortege waited for the ambulance, amid a flurry of ivory petals that swirled like snow in a water globe, rising with each fresh breeze from the open window. The fragments cascaded over and around her still form and onto the muted roses patterning the carpet.

Denver—Residence of E. Forde Chadwick

Denver's early morning traffic sped down the parkway as Detective Grady Owens swung into the curb parking in front of Chad's house. He checked his watch, smiled to himself, then walked through the wrought iron gate of the newly installed courtyard leading to the front door. It was seven a.m., perhaps just a little early to be making an official call. But then where was the fun in being orthodox? He got things done, though not one of his fellow officers would ever call his methods conventional. He rang the bell.

Through the door he could hear low voices. Then from somewhere within came the sound of a door closing faintly in the background. A few seconds later, the front door opened a few inches and a tousled Chad peered out, looking surprised to see Owens standing on his doorstep.

The detective greeted him, "Good morning, Mr. Chadwick. May I come in for a few minutes? I'm following up on some new information that may have some bearing on Ms. Martelli's attack. Oh, here's your paper," he said, handing the dripping water-logged newspaper to Chad through the door. "I rescued it from the reflecting pool as I walked through the courtyard to the house. A new feature, isn't it? I don't remember any pool or courtyard being here in March. Gorgeous, absolutely gorgeous landscaping. Your paper boy could use a little more practice though, or do you think he was actually aiming for the water feature?"

Chad frowned, taking the dripping wet paper and throwing it onto the decorative concrete walk in front of the door where Owens stood, purposely spattering the detective's trouser leg.

"Lieutenant, I thought I made it plain, you can drop in at the office if you need to see me, but my personal residence is off limits. This is an invasion of my privacy," he complained with such evident belligerence that the detective thought he just might slam the door in his face. However, the door swung open. Owens stepped inside, feeling the animosity.

Dressed in a Japanese-style blue-and-white printed bathrobe, Chad turned and led the way into the contemporary domain of the kitchen. "What is it *this* time, Lieutenant? I'm in a real hurry this morning, got about five minutes." Looking annoyed, he poured himself a cup of coffee from the stainless steel coffee maker installed in the wall above the granite countertop, then gestured with the pot towards Owens.

90

"No, thanks. Got me a cup on the way over." Owens decided to drop the bomb before Chad had a chance to prepare himself. Watching for the reaction, he asked, "Actually, I came to ask about your head office gal, Susan . . . er, Ms. Farrell. Does she happen to have a brother named Sean O'Malley?"

Chad abruptly turned away, refilling his mug while he answered with his back to Owens. "I've heard her say she has a stepbrother. Can't remember his name though. Why do you ask, Detective?"

"Well, you see, Sir, we've had an anonymous tip about a person by that name recently booking passage to Paris. When I checked our data base, Sean's only living relative is a person by the name of Susan Farrell. I thought I would check it out to see if he's indeed related to *your* Susan. If so, it does seem more than a coincidence that someone, with what our data base listed as this O'Malley person's background, would up and fly to Paris for pleasure, which is what he put down as the purpose of his trip . . . especially when Ms. Martelli just *happens* to be there also. Mind you, it's just that I've got to check all the angles. Wouldn't be doing my job if I didn't. You see, Sir?"

"First of all, Lieutenant," Chad said, turning back to face the detective. "Let's get one thing straight right now. Ms. Farrell is not *my* Susan. Just an excellent employee who I'm lucky to have running the front desk and handling the secretarial load. I appreciate her capabilities. Secondly, if this Sean O'Malley person *is* her stepbrother, there's no reason to suspect any connection between his comings-and-goings with Susan, or with Claire in Paris for that matter. I think you're way off base on this one. I know you want to get this case wrapped up, but you're making a leap in trying to connect this guy with the burglary, and Claire's attack, through Susan. Is there any actual evidence to tie all the pieces together? You know it looks to me like the police are jumping to conclusions with this theory."

"Not really an official theory, Sir. Not yet anyway. Though, it's real interesting the way you've stated it. I'll put some thought into that scenario. Just wanted to find out if Sean O'Malley is related to Susan Farrell and, if so, how."

"Okay, Lieutenant, you do that. Time to go. I've got clients coming in town today and I'm late as it is, thanks to you," Chad said ushering the detective from the kitchen toward the front door.

As much as Chad tried to hurry him, the detective took his time, sauntering through the living room that opened to the balcony on the gallery level, half a flight up. The place looked pristine, a far cry from that night in March. He noticed the replacement artwork in the gallery niches. He also noticed the door to the master bedroom close quietly as a red-headed woman surreptitiously ducked out, heading toward the other end of the corridor where the detective had noted a back stairway on his original visit the night of the attack. Owens stopped to look at a large painting that took up most of one wall in the main living area. It was a contemporary canvas depicting a circle of women, in various states of dishabille, dancing in a sunlit meadow.

He turned to Chad, dryly voicing his surmise. "You've certainly got a good eye for beautiful things, Mr. Chadwick. That's a new acquisition, right? Since Ms. Martelli's attack in March. Let me guess, insurance money?"

"Detective, get out. Now." Chad shouted, losing patience. "I have no intention of discussing artistic merits or personal financial matters with you. And you are not to come back here. Ever. Understand?"

Owens apologized, "Sorry, no hard feelings. Right, Sir?"

He left the house, smiling, having gotten what he'd come for. The pieces were falling in place nicely. The detective leisurely followed Susan's route to the Cherry Creek offices of the Chadwick+Martelli Design Group.

Paris—The Saint-Germain garden

It began like a muffled drumbeat, persistent and vaguely familiar. Claire gradually came to an awareness of her surroundings. She was in the Saint-Germain garden, securely grounded by the ancient Paulownia tree, its feather light petals floating down from the limb overhead. She listened for a few seconds, eyes closed, unwilling to give up the last vestiges of the peaceful state she'd just experienced. The strange thrumming continued, more annoying than threatening. She opened one golden eye, fixing it on the source of the noise. The shaggy black creature stretched out beside the lounger lay watching her, head resting on its paws, tail beating a steady tattoo onto the weathered bricks.

"Penelope . . . I should have known. How long have you been here, girl?" Claire yawned, opening both eyes, and stretching. The big dog eagerly rose to the temptation of the outstretched hand, coaxing Claire to pet her with a happy lick of wet pink tongue.

"About five minutes." The voice came from somewhere behind her, causing Claire to sit up and whirl around to see the speaker. Malcolm smiled, straightening from his lounging position against the frame of the French doors.

"Penelope, down girl. Sorry, Claire, She seems to have a problem behaving herself when you're around. But did you have a nice nap? You looked so peaceful, we didn't want to disturb you," he said, dropping onto the other chaise lounge a few feet away. "Mmm, this does feel great. No wonder you fell asleep, I may never get up again."

"Malcolm. You mean you were just standing there watching me? Don't you have anything better to do?" But Claire was too relaxed to take umbrage for longer than a second. "Besides," she added in her own defense, "I wasn't asleep. I was meditating. And how did you know I was out here anyway?"

"Let's see. Yes, yes, and . . . I believe you if you say so, about the meditating that is. And as far as knowing you were out here in the garden, I didn't. It was Penny. She made a beeline out here as we came down the hallway on our way back from a trot in the park. Whew, do you always talk in clusters of questions?"

Claire tried not to smile, ignoring his question by asking one of her own. "Well, if you have something better to do, why aren't you doing it?"

"Because I was waiting for you to wake up. Or rather, now that I know you weren't asleep, to finish your meditation, so that I can ask you to accompany me in my 'something better to do'. Now that I'm in a reclining position, I may jolly well change my mind. I may not have anything better to do after all."

Claire dangled one arm over the side of the chaise to rub Penelope's ears. She looked over at Malcolm. His lean muscular frame stretched the full length of the lounge. The collar of his white shirt was open at the neck exposing a steadily beating pulse. She liked the way his dark hair tended to fall across his forehead and his absent-minded habit of running his fingers through it. There was something about the way he looked at her that was disconcerting, the sapphire blue eyes fairly glowed out of the tanned face. She looked away first.

"You must be tired," she said, referring to the topic of the afternoon, but more to dispel the sense of intimacy that had crept up around them.

"I am, and I'm not. Not too tired to take you to dinner."

Claire looked over at him again, but she couldn't see his eyes. He appeared to be studying the canopy of blossoms overhead. She thought carefully about *Category A* before answering.

"Could I have a rain check, Malcolm?" The barest pause, then the first excuse that came to mind. "Guess I'm just not in a going-out-to-dinner mood. In fact, I'm really not very hungry. The Marie-Claude thing, you know. It's still too fresh. I hope you understand."

There was a brief silence, then, "Claire?"

"Yes?"

"Do you dislike me?"

94

"Dislike you? How could I? I hardly know you."

"My dear lady, I've been trying to remedy that since I met you. You know, I ran into your mother in the neighborhood while I was out with Penny a little while ago. She decided to walk with us instead of continuing her run. I think at least one member of the Martelli family likes me a little better now."

Claire chuckled at the thought of her pint-sized mother keeping pace with the gigantic Penelope and her master. "I wouldn't take it to heart, Malcolm, Abbie always has a soft spot for people in the medical profession. After all, you speak her language. Just don't get on her bad side though. It also works the other way. In spades. And watch out for her *Columbo* routine," she continued, "as in the classic 'Columbo' crime fiction series?"

Malcolm nodded his head. "I do remember seeing reruns of the original series that cast Peter Falk as the Columbo character who became an icon as the underestimated detective. Right? But what does that have to do with Abbie?"

"Well, Abbie has the same abilities, disarmingly cordial, yet very perceptive. She's quite good at it, I'm afraid. She can worm information out of a tree stump."

"Thanks for the words of wisdom. I'll remember that," Malcolm remarked, a dry tone entering his voice. "Well, she's really first-rate in my book. I saw how she handled the situation with Emilie Fontaine today. The woman was in a state of hysteria. But I was too busy tending to Marie-Claude to do anything about it. Then, Abbie took over, and presto, *La Fontaine* was calm and rational. Not many people, nurse or not, have that ability. And as you will undoubtedly recall," he said, chuckling, "I have also seen her in action when it comes to running interference for her offspring. You're lucky, you know," he added, his voice becoming pensive.

Claire wished she hadn't sounded so flippant a minute ago. She was only trying to keep the conversation on the light side. She sobered at the wistful note in Malcolm's last words.

"What's your mother like, Malcolm," she asked, suddenly curious.

"I really can't remember her very well. Or my father. They were killed in a rockslide that propelled their auto off a mountain road when I was three."

"Oh, how terrible. I'm so sorry. Please forgive me. I didn't mean to pry."

"No, it's okay. It happened so long ago. Some time I'll tell you about my Granny Anna. If you're interested that is. She's the grand old lady that raised my brother and me. I couldn't have asked for a better surrogate mother."

Claire was decidedly interested. She would like to hear his story, but she didn't feel right about delving into his personal life. Or did she? *Category A* meant keep it light. As she formulated her thoughts, Penelope lifted her head, pricking up her ears as she turned toward the open French doors of the mansion.

"Claire, are you out here? Oh, there you are," said Abbie, stepping down onto the terrace. "Dear, I'm leaving for the reception now. Do I look all right? I feel like I'm just thrown together. Is Miranda down here somewhere? She's not upstairs."

Claire looked at her watch and started up like a guilty child, realizing with a twinge of conscience she hadn't given a thought to Mandy, or her mother's conference engagement, since Malcolm had joined her.

"Now I see where Claire gets her conversational skills," Malcolm said, chuckling as he extracted himself from his reclining position to greet her. "Hello, Mrs. Martelli. I think you look quite bonny. Can you join us for a few minutes before you leave?"

"Now I understand why Claire hasn't been up in our rooms," Abbie quipped in turn, indicating the healthy glow on her daughter's cheeks. "And, hello to you, Malcolm. But I thought we agreed you would call me Abbie, or Abigail, whichever you prefer. And thank you for the compliment. As for joining you, I must say no. I just wanted to let Claire know my ride is here, and to be on the lookout for Miranda."

"Your ride? Mom, I thought we discussed this. You were going to take a taxi there and back," said Mandy, coming out onto the terrace to stand beside Abbie. "This wouldn't have anything to do with the very distinguished gentleman I passed on my way through the lobby just now? Who is he?"

It was Abbie's turn to blush. "Oh, thank goodness, you're finally back, Miranda. Now I can relax and enjoy the evening. I won't have to worry about either of you. About the man in the lobby," she began, reaching out to take both daughters' hands, her face angelically innocent.

"Malcolm, would you mind excusing us for a moment, please? It won't take long," Abbie said with an unmistakable lilt in her voice. "There's someone special I want the girls to meet who indeed is waiting in the lobby. Dr. Benjamin Weston. You see, I was once engaged to Ben, our wedding date set, but then I met the man I recognized as my soul mate on first sight. Wedding date reset, grooms changed. The rest is history, as they say. But by the quirk of fate, or maybe Divine Providence, Ben might have become the girls' father."

Paris—The Saint-Germain kitchen

Mandy straddled one of the heavy turned-wood legs of the restored French butchers' worktable centered in the middle of the Saint-Germain kitchen. She had pulled her *Provençal* stool—a charming mismatch to the other three wooden stools lining the eating side of the worktable—to the end, as close as she could get to view Etienne's culinary demonstration.

Behind him, a sauté pan sizzled on the front burner of the beautiful brass and black enameled French range. A functional display of polished copper pots, big and small, hung in profusion from the copper and iron rack above Etienne's work area. Square glazed ceramic tiles girdled the walls, surrounding the diners with a buttery-hued atmosphere as well as providing an attractive contrast to the light and dark checkered tile floor. The bleached pine open cabinets and wall

97

shelves lent a soft background patina for the stacks of simple off-white earthenware plates and dishes stored within.

"*Oui,* in preparing the classic French omelet, it must be tender and creamy inside," Etienne instructed his audience of one, as he demonstrated the technique of tilting the hot pan in a circular motion to enable the uncooked liquid to flow away from the center.

"Then, we fold it over into a smooth, slightly swelling oval, using the *gruyere* and *boursin* cheeses to melt inside with the fresh herbs, like so. And now, we add a small amount of *garnishee* on top—a grated cheese, *parmesan reggae* in this instance. And, *voila!*"

Mandy inhaled the delectable aroma of the cheese spiced with *fines herbes de Provence* as Etienne expertly slid the last omelet onto a heavy earthenware plate. "This smells heavenly, Etienne, I can hardly wait. Are we ready to eat yet?" she asked, sampling the melted cheese that clung to the side of the empty pan with her fingertip.

"*Non,* Mademoiselle Man-dee, not quite. Please to be careful. The cheese is very hot," Etienne cautioned her. "Next we will lightly run all four omelets under the hot broiler for a mere instant," he said, opening the door to the oven and sliding the plates inside, "until the *garnishee* begins to brown slightly." The grated cheese turned golden almost instantly. Etienne slipped into the heavy oven gloves and rescued the hot plates of bubbling cheeses. He bowed formally in his best waiter's manner, "Supper is served, Mademoiselles, Monsieur. *Omelettes Giraud de Provence.*"

Mandy grabbed two hot pads and helped carry the omelets to the table where Claire and Malcolm were putting the finishing touches on the freshly picked mixed greens of Dom's afternoon harvest.

"Chow time," Mandy announced, setting the hot plates down on the heavy wooden mats used to protect the old marble top of the iron-based table.

"Oh, this looks superlative," said Claire. She savored her first mouthful of omelet. "Not only looks, but it is. Etienne, you are a wonderful chef. But you are certain, aren't you, that your aunt won't mind us helping ourselves to dinner in her kitchen like this?"

"*Non,* Mademoiselle, it is as I said before, *Tante* Emilie called a little time ago and invited us to, as you say, 'raid the icebox'. She would have liked to have cooked for you herself, but she has made arrangements to stay at the clinic tonight with Marie-Claude. *Tante* is very grateful to all of you for your help this afternoon and, by way of thanking you, she is planning on asking you to a much grander meal. One that she will prepare when Marie-Claude is better.

"Ah, that's what I've been waiting to hear," said Malcolm, breaking off a crusty hunk of the *baguette* to eat with his omelet. "How is Marie-Claude doing? I intended to ask as soon as we sat down, but this omelet captured my complete attention. My compliments, Monsieur, I have never tasted better. It's delicious."

The younger man beamed. "*Merci, Docteur,* to answer your question, *Tante* said Marie-Claude is displaying signs of coming out of the catatonia. *Docteur* Marchand is with her now. They are very encouraged. That is good news, *oui*? *Cousine* will be home soon, *oui*?"

Malcolm didn't answer right away. One by one, the other diners turned to look at him.

"*Docteur*?" Etienne inquired.

Malcolm's face was sober as he put down his fork. "It is very good news that she is coming out of the catatonic state this soon, Etienne." He paused, his next words carefully expressed. "Unfortunately, full recovery from a schizophrenic regression requires a little more time. The drug used to control this disorder is a psychotropic medication and must build up in the patient's system. And, until it has, well, let's just say it's in Marie-Claude's best interest that she remains at the clinic where she can be under constant observation and professional care."

He looked around in the stillness that followed to see shock and sympathy registered on their faces, their appetites diminished to simply toying with the few bits of omelet and salad remaining on their plates.

Mandy broke the silence first. "Malcolm, what exactly causes schizophrenia in the first place? It isn't a genetic factor, right? I mean, Madame Fontaine seems perfectly . . . perfectly normal," she stammered. "I'm sorry, Etienne, I don't know what I was thinking. I didn't mean to insinuate . . . ," she broke off lamely.

"It's okay, Mandy," said Malcolm, his tone gentle. "Etienne knows you weren't trying to embarrass him, or to insinuate anything about his family. Right, old chap? But to answer your question, I'm afraid I really can't tell you how schizophrenia originates," he said, looking at each one of them in turn. "That issue has been the subject of many years of ongoing research and several schools of thought. There is a drug intended to keep the symptoms in check as I mentioned, but there is no known cure.

"After we found Marie-Claude today, Madame Fontaine asked for my advice with regard to which hospital or clinic I thought Marie-Claude would be given the best care. I recommended the Edmond Marchand Clinic, instead of a regular hospital. This clinic is well-known in the psychiatric field and has an outstanding reputation for the excellence of their programs. When we arrived at the clinic, I was able to talk with Dr. Marchand himself, as I wanted to describe Marie-Claude's critical symptoms in person, psychiatrist to psychiatrist. Know that she is in good hands. Now, we'll just have to wait and hope for the best."

What Malcolm couldn't tell them, of course, was the privileged information divulged by Emilie Fontaine in the ambulance on their way to the clinic. She'd surprised him by revealing that her daughter had previously been seeing Dr. Marchand on a regular basis, but then added somewhat defensively that Marie-Claude had recently stopped those visits over her mother's strenuous objections. Tears streaking down her pallid face, Emilie went on, saying that her daughter was no longer taking the medication that Dr. Marchand had prescribed for what she simply termed, 'Marie-Claude's condition'. There was nothing to do about it, the poor woman lamented, as Marie-Claude was now of legal age. However it was her final disclosure that sent Malcolm reeling. Emilie said her daughter seemed so much better lately—since he'd arrived at the Saint-Germain to teach at *universite*.

Claire and Mandy began collecting the dishes from the table. Etienne broke the silence that had each of them speculating inwardly on Marie-Claude's future prospects. "*Non,* Mademoiselles, please to not worry about washing these up," he said. "Just be so kind as to stack them over by the sink, *s'il vous plait.* It won't take me long to do these in the morning," he added, stifling a yawn behind cover of his napkin.

"No, Etienne. I'll be happy to help you with these tonight. It will be all the worse to face in the morning. Claire, there's no need for all of us to stay, why don't you and Malcolm take off. Didn't you say you had to get the antique houses mapped out for tomorrow?"

"Well, *if* I get the overnight delivery from the office in the morning, I intend to visit the auction houses tomorrow," Claire answered. "But that's still a big *if.* Are you planning to photograph at Notre Dame tomorrow?"

"Planning on it. We'll fit it all in somehow. Maybe you and Abbie can meet me there after the antique houses, if you go that is. Let's coordinate in the morning."

"Okay, you silver-tongued devil, you talked me into it," Claire said, giving her sister a hug, then turning toward the back door that led out to the kitchen garden. "Thank you so much for dinner, Etienne, I enjoyed it. We'll catch up with you tomorrow for news on Marie-Claude."

"Claire, hold up. I'll walk you back to your rooms," Malcolm offered, smiling the smile that sent vibrations down her spine. "Etienne, you saved the day, or the night at least, with your culinary skills. Best omelet I've ever eaten."

Etienne nodded to both Claire and Malcolm. "It is the least I could do for you, *Docteur,* and the Mademoiselles," he acknowledged. "But, once again, it is I who must thank you for your aid to *cousine* and *tante* today."

Claire stopped in the open doorway before stepping out into the dark shadows of the garden wall. "Oh, Etienne, one more thing, a question, actually. Do either you or your granddad smoke cigars by any chance?"

"*Non,* Mademoiselle," he answered, a puzzled look on his face. "Why do you ask?"

"Well, er . . . no, never mind. It's nothing. Forget I asked. See you," she called, disappearing through the door with Malcolm right behind her.

"You want to wash or wipe, Etienne?" Mandy asked, wrapping the proffered chef's apron around her waist.

Paris—The Saint-Germain garden

Outside the bright kitchen, the garden slept in darkness, the path all but invisible. Malcolm fell in step beside Claire, taking her arm. They proceeded at a vigilant pace.

"Well, are you going to tell me . . . about your question to Etienne? What was that all about?" he asked.

"What was what all about?" She countered. "Oops. I just hit my shin on something. What was that? Can you see anything, Malcolm? I didn't realize just how difficult it is to navigate by starlight alone, did you? And the crescent moon isn't much better. I thought there would be lights out here. In fact, I know I saw some post lights earlier today, along this very path."

"Maybe Etienne forgot to turn them on. Stand still a minute, Claire. I think you must have bumped into one of those teak garden benches Emilie has placed around the garden. Yep, that's what it is. Anyway, in English gardens, this type of bench is considered quite necessary to congenial conversations, and the like."

"And the like? What does that mean?" Claire inquired, as his hand slide down her arm, warming her through her light blouse sleeve.

"Let's sit down, and I'll show you," Malcolm said, moving one arm up to wrap her shoulders, while gently guiding her down to sit beside him on the slatted wooden bench.

Claire's heart pumped a little harder, her thoughts racing in time with her body. *Got to remember . . . Category A . . .*

She inhaled his scent, the notes lingering between fresh lime and a light woodsy fragrance. He tilted her chin up and softly pressed his lips against the pulse thrumming at the base of her neck, slowly moving upward. Claire shivered at the sensation his lips created, like the wings of a butterfly fluttering across her neck, to the softness of her earlobe and onward to her eyelid. The trail of his kisses on her skin was immediate and heated. With deliberate slowness, he drew her arms around his neck. Her heart hammered as his fingers brushed her lips lightly, causing her to shiver once again. He touched his lips to hers, parting them slightly. She breathed in the warmth of his heady scent, completely losing her train of thought. She couldn't even remember how to exhale. Once again a totally unexpected current pulsed through her veins, this time ending in the pit of her stomach.

"Breathe, Claire," he whispered, his face close to hers. "Now, open your eyes."

She took a jagged breath, opening her eyes to his heart-stopping smile, framed by a circle of light coming from one of the post lights situated behind their bench.

"Etienne must have found the light switch after all. And I think I heard a door somewhere nearby open and close just now," Malcolm said, gently untangling Claire's arms from around his neck. "Probably should get you back to your suite, before anyone comes this way, like your sister or Etienne. Claire, are you all right? You're trembling."

The concern in his voice was obvious and served to clear her mind, bringing her back to the moment. She nodded at him and slowly stood up, murmuring under her breath what sounded like, *"Category A . . . Category A . . ."*

Paris—The Martelli's Suite at the Saint-Germain

"Ben Weston," said Mandy in a dreamy voice. "Who would have thought they would meet again after all these years. And in Paris of all places," she continued, handing Claire a wet cool washcloth. She had walked into the suite a few minutes before to find Claire already in bed with another of her headaches. And it was barely ten o'clock.

"And why do you suppose we are suddenly surrounded by people in the medical profession? Abbie, Malcolm, and now Ben. He's a well-known doctor too, you know, and much sought after as a lecturer in the pediatric field, his specialty. He takes a month off from his practice every year to work as an unpaid volunteer for that world-wide No Borders organization, in whichever third-world country needs his skills the most. He's in Paris as the keynote speaker for the IN conference, and to urge the nurses to establish some kind of international network to handle adoptions of children orphaned by the civil wars in Africa and the countries that have broken away from the Russian bloc . . ."

"Mandy, stop," Claire interrupted. "How do you know all of this," she demanded. "Mom has never mentioned him before, and they left as soon as she made that bombshell introduction. And she's still out, right? I have to think you're making all this up simply to entertain me. Right?"

She re-folded the damp washcloth to a cooler position and placed it back on her forehead.

"Claire Martelli! Of course I'm not making it up," said Mandy, an annoyed look marring the classic features. "If you didn't have that headache, I would leave your non-appreciative company and go write postcards to people who don't accuse me of storytelling." Mandy flounced up with an injured sniff. She began to pick out articles of her clothing that were still draped around the room, fastening them onto the hangers Etienne had somehow managed to provide for them before dinner.

"I'm sorry, Mandy. I'm just not myself tonight. Sit down and talk to me. This headache is making me cranky," Claire admitted, massaging her temples. "It's vibrating up the back of my neck and across the top of my head. Come on," she wheedled. "Please? The suspense is killing me. How *did* you find out about Ben?"

Mandy was only too happy to comply and to put off the boring housekeeping task for a little longer. She crossed a leg under her and settled back into the chair. "Do you remember when I walked Mom and Ben out to the taxi? No? Well I think you had already started to the kitchen with Malcolm after we all jumped at Etienne's impromptu dinner invitation. Anyway, I waylaid Abbie before they got to the taxi. I made up an excuse that I needed to talk with her in private, about our schedule for tomorrow. When I got her aside, I whispered that I wasn't about to let her get into that taxi with a man I knew absolutely nothing about, except that he and she were once engaged." Mandy stopped for breath, and effect.

"And? What happened next? Mandy?"

"I'm getting to it, Claire. Hold your horses." Mandy exclaimed, trying to spin out her scoop a little longer. She knew Claire would do the same if the roles were reversed, especially in this instance. "Well, you know our Abbie. She looked me straight in the eye and rattled off all the info that I just told you about Ben. Out loud. With him smiling at her from the curb."

"Sounds like Mom is over her jet lag and back in form again. What did Ben do while all this was going on?" Claire again re-folded the washcloth and placed it over her eyes.

"He just stood there smiling. And, well, he more or less *devoured* her with his eyes."

"Come on, Mandy, now you're telling . . . er, laying it on a little thick. Aren't you? No? He really *devoured* her with his eyes, huh? That's pretty strange."

105

"Well I wouldn't talk, Claire. Speaking about someone right here in this room as the subject of *eye-devourment*." Mandy peered under the folded washcloth to see the blank look on her sister's face. "You mean you really haven't noticed how Malcolm looks at you?"

Drawing herself up to a sitting position, Claire set the washcloth aside. She sighed. "Malcolm? No, this time you're wrong, Mandy. I would think you might possibly be right, after he walked me back to the suite through the garden tonight. Until, that is, we got to our door. He bent down to pick up the key I dropped. A folded paper fell out of his pocket and I picked it up while he unlocked the door for me. I couldn't help noticing the unusual drawing on the outside of the fold. He reacted at once. As soon as he saw the paper in my hand, he snatched it away. He appeared ashamed and embarrassed at the same time. I didn't know what to say, and evidently he didn't either. He stalked off down the corridor with just a gruff goodnight. Nothing else."

Claire turned to face her sister. She continued, "You see, I recognized that drawing. It was the same design as the medallion the police found at Chad's house after the attack. Malcolm might be watching me, Mandy, but not for the same reason you're thinking."

"Claire, you don't really think . . . come on, silly, you *are* getting paranoid. Malcolm isn't part of this medallion thing, whatever that may be."

"Well, if he isn't, then how do you explain that drawing? It did drop out of his pocket, you know. And he did scramble to get it away from me after I picked it up. It can't be a mere coincidence that it showed the exact same design as was on that gold pendant, or medallion thing. The one Lieutenant Owens showed me the very same night that loony tried to kill me."

"Be reasonable, Claire. Malcolm lives in London. What would he be doing in Denver last March? I suppose you would have me believe that he flew all the way to Denver to steal Chad's artwork, poison Duffy, and then attack you? Besides, you told me the guy had crazy icy blue eyes. Malcolm's are deep blue, and sexy maybe, but definitely not crazy. Claire, I believe you think the design on the sketch is the same as on the pendant the police found that night, but there has to be a logical explanation. You know it could be very similar, but not *exactly* the same. Why don't you just ask him, Malcolm I mean, about the sketch?"

"Ask him? Right, Mandy," her voice dropped off to a tired croak. "Should I ask that same man who most likely was hiding in the dark of the garden last night, and who is more than likely watching me? And don't ask me why. I don't know the answer to that. Yet. And he could have gone to Colorado to ski, you know, so I don't think that it's beyond possibility."

She turned onto her side, curling into the fetal position. "Malcolm is staying here, isn't he? He has perfect opportunity . . ."

Her voice dropped off to a soft murmur that caused Mandy to lean forward to catch what she was saying. It sounded like, *"Category A."*

Hearing Claire's even breathing; Mandy tucked the cotton throw from the end of the bed around her sleeping sister and turned out the lamp. She would have liked to ask about Claire's earlier reference to Malcolm in the garden. She tiptoed from the room, satisfied there was an explanation for the medallion drawing in Malcolm's possession. She just hoped her sister would give him the chance to explain. And, he'd take the opportunity.

And whatever is Category A about?

VICTORIA MASTERSON

5

Day Three

Paris—Claire's Journal, 16 May

I don't think I'm paranoid. Someone <u>is</u> stalking me. Yesterday, while we were walking along the river and again at the cafe, I had the feeling someone was following me. Watching, but hanging back just beyond my line of vision. I kept it to myself and made an effort to act as if everything was normal, so I wouldn't ruin Mandy's photo session, though it gave me the heebie-jeebies. I'm sure Mandy thought I was just being difficult while she was directing that hat shot. But the feeling seemed to go away after a while, around the time her card case went missing after lunch.

And the night before, someone <u>was</u> in the garden. There again I felt whoever was down there in the dark was keeping watch on me. Just like in my bloody dreams, which are really scaring the hell out of me. It's not just my imagination.

But I absolutely refuse to let this spoil our Paris sojourn— for me, or for Mandy and Abbie. Don't want to worry Mom any more than she already is. She thinks the pressure on me is over-the-edge stressful, what with leaving Chad and moving to the carriage house. Then, the attack in March, the nightmares, the headaches, those phone calls, let alone all the divorce proceedings and the meetings with the lawyers. At least that part will soon be over. Hopefully, the divorce will be final in just a few more days. And today, Mandy bought a bottle of French champagne, now waiting in the Saint-Germain's kitchen cooler, to celebrate the occasion.

Paris—The Martelli's suite at the Saint-Germain

"So the plan is to meet up with Mandy today at the Cathedral, after I check out the antique houses and Abbie's conference sessions have concluded. Around two o'clock. Right?" Claire queried, waving the courier envelope from Denver for all to see.

"Right. Well, open it, Claire. Has Chad sent everything you asked for?" Mandy challenged with a just-you-wait-and-see-look on her face.

"Let's just take a peek . . . oh ye of little faith. Here are the checks, my schedule, some change orders to review for the New Orleans project, with some comments from Lupe, and notes from both Chad *and* Susan," Claire answered, perusing the contents of Chad's note. "He says hello to all, he hopes we're having a good time, and info about the Crown Resort clients increasing the antiques budget to add some larger pieces to the project. Hmmm, that's really a surprise. I had to talk them into the idea of using antiques in the project in the first place."

Claire sorted through the rest of the contents in the packet. She shared the small desk in the sitting room with Mandy and her lap top, while her sister opened the shots of the cafe from the memory card she'd slipped into her pocket the day before.

"Okay, ready when you are," Mandy said, "but I'll fast forward where necessary as there are many shots of the same subject, using different combinations of f-stop settings and aperture openings. We start with some general shots along the Left Bank . . . moving on to the lovers wrapped around each other on the banks of the Seine . . . then to the book stalls lining the river walk . . . and finally we'll proceed to Claire's starring role at the sidewalk café."

Abbie laughed when she saw the photo featuring her with a Parisian book seller, each gesturing at the other with gusto. "I was only trying to bargain with him on the price."

"Good try, Mom, but you were bargaining in English. He probably didn't understand a word you said, or what price you offered," Claire said, chuckling.

Abbie only smiled. "Well Ben really liked the book, so that's what counts. He even reads a little French. He said the book dates back to the early Thirties, with illustrations of Parisian children from that era. He said the vintage drawings alone were worth the price I paid for the book. He's going to frame the illustrations and hang them in his reception area."

"Speaking of Ben, is he going to be in Paris for long?" Mandy asked.

"He said he wanted to take a few days to, um . . . "really feel the heartbeat of Paris", as he put it," Abbie responded, fiddling with her earring and looking away. "He's arranged for another doctor in the practice to be on call for any emergencies and his office has re-booked his appointments. Heaven knows," she said, dropping her gaze to the photos on Mandy's computer screen, "the man deserves a little time away from the daily pressures. It's easy to burn-out in the medical profession. By the way, girls," Abbie said, looking up again, this time with a clear gaze, "Ben has invited us all out to dinner tonight. His treat."

"Is that because you want us to get to know him better? And vice versa? Is there something you're not telling us, Mom?" Mandy asked, studying her mother's face closely.

"If or when there is something to tell, I will do so," Abbie answered, a peculiar tone entering her voice. "At the moment, simply consider it a very thoughtful gesture on Ben's part. He knows how special you girls are to me."

Claire and Mandy sandwiched their mother in a hug. "Okay, Mom. You just caught us by surprise with your little bombshell announcement yesterday," Claire said. "If he's important to you, he's important to us."

Mandy nodded her agreement. "And he's *very* distinguished-looking, I would like to add. I guess I'm not the only one who can pick 'em, as Claire has said. And don't look at me like that, sis. You can sure pick them too. Malcolm?" Mandy stepped back and focused her gaze on Claire's face.

Claire dropped her arms from around her mother and sighed. "Mandy, I feel the same as I did last night. So please, don't bring up that subject again. There really isn't anything to talk about."

"Well, I don't have any idea what either of you are talking about," Abbie chimed in. "What happened with Malcolm last night, Claire?"

"Nothing, Mom. Could we all just forget about Malcolm, please?" Claire fidgeted, retying the belt on her robe.

"You're wrong you know, Claire. But I'll drop it, for now. Who wants to see the rest of the photos from yesterday?" Mandy asked, changing the subject.

"Okay, I'm ready. I think. Bring on your *Woman in the Vermillion Hat* series," Claire replied, effectively burying her memories of last night's kiss with Malcolm in the garden. But not without effort.

Mandy flipped through the river walk shots to where the sidewalk café photos began. "Oh, Claire, just see how great you photograph? And that hat is fabulous on you. I just knew it would be. And look," she said, slowing down the progression of shots, "here you are with Etienne, close-up . . . closer-up . . ." She advanced the shots quicker now. "And here's where I changed lenses to get a wider angle of the café as backdrop behind you."

"Mandy, don't go so fast. You may be able to follow that quickly, but I can't. Go back to your first wide angle shot, I want to see something," Claire prompted her sister, a curious expression on her face.

"This one? What is it you want to see?" Mandy asked, studying the shot.

112

"Yeah, that's the one. Can you enlarge it? Yes, there, just in front of the *maitre d'* . . . the guy in the bomber jacket and cap who appears to be looking for someone. That's odd, you know he seems familiar somehow. It's almost like I've seen him somewhere before. Is that all the further you can enlarge it? I'd like to see more of his face." Anxiety colored Claire's voice.

Mandy frowned. "What is it, Sis? You look upset. Do you recognize this guy? I know I've never seen him before. Sorry, it won't help to enlarge it anymore, that's one of my favorite techniques, using a soft-focus effect in the background with the foreground in sharp-focus. I usually take some with sharp-focus both foreground and background though, just to cover my bases. Let's see what I can find." She began forwarding the images quickly. "I think probably about here . . ." she trailed off, stopping at one of the shots. "Just need to enlarge it . . ."

The knock at the door made all three women jump.

"Who could that be?" Claire asked irritably, while making a beeline for the bedroom, the only one of the three still in pajamas.

"I'll get it," Abbie volunteered, "it may be Ben. He offered to give me a ride to the conference this morning. But he's a little early."

Only it was Malcolm who stood in the hallway when Abbie opened the door. He carried a huge bouquet of pink roses. "Good morning, Mrs. M. Is Claire around?"

"Malcolm, please come in. What gorgeous roses," she exclaimed. "For Claire?"

"Yes, is she here? I would like to speak with her. Oh, good morning, Mandy. Didn't see you over there," Malcolm said, coming further into the room.

"Hi yourself, Malcolm. I'll tell Claire you're here, though I know she's getting ready to go to some kind of antique exhibit that's going on in the Saint-Germain area. Why don't you sit down, I'll just be a minute," she said, smiling as she softly knocked and entered the bedroom she shared with Claire.

"Not to be inhospitable, Malcolm, but my ride to the conference will be here in a few minutes. I'd best be waiting in the lobby so he doesn't have to climb all three flights of stairs," Abbie explained. "I'm guessing you would like to speak with Claire privately anyway. Sit down, it may be a few minutes until she's ready."

Malcolm threw Abbie a look with gratitude all over it. "Thanks, Mrs. M. If you don't mind, I'm a little too nervous to sit. I'll just stand, but thanks."

Abbie whispered a soft, "Good luck," as she left the suite.

When Mandy didn't return soon after Abbie left, Malcolm began pacing the room. His path took him back and forth in front of the Directoire-style desk, and on his next pass, the bouquet he carried brushed into a stack of papers on the desk top, knocking them to the floor. He bent to pick up the papers, tidying the pile as he placed the pages back on the stack, but something caught his eye on two of the papers he'd set on top of the rest. He picked up the top pages—notes to Claire from her office, he supposed. He studied them thoughtfully, and then looked around as Mandy entered the room, his face turning red with embarrassment.

"Sorry, Malcolm, but Claire's still dressing. She asked me to tell you she has some scheduled appointments at the antique houses that won't allow her time to meet with you this morning. She has to leave shortly," she said, her eyes going from Malcolm's red face to the pages still in his hand.

"I accidentally knocked these papers off the desk. Just putting them back." Then he faced her, saying, "Truthfully, Mandy, I didn't intend to violate Claire's privacy, but I couldn't help but notice the handwriting on these two pages. I would like to make copies to evaluate further, but I suspect both of the persons who wrote them have very real problems. Psychological problems. I know you probably don't want to hear any of this, but you must believe me. I'm saying this because the essential nature of my expertise as both a psychiatrist and graphologist has to do with behavioral characteristics, which include handwriting. It comes with the territory. If these persons are close to Claire in a working situation, I would definitely worry about her safety. Even more if she's involved with either of them in a more personal way."

Mandy put her finger to her mouth to shush him, as she glanced around to see if the door to the bedroom was still closed. "Okay, we need to talk, but not here. Let's go out to the hallway," she said in a low voice.

Malcolm nodded his agreement, depositing the large rose bouquet on the desk, next to Mandy's open laptop. The all-but-forgotten enlargement was still on the screen—the café scene with Claire sitting at a table in the foreground, while a smiling Etienne poured a glass of wine from a carafe. Behind them, stood the *maitre d'* and a few other patrons waiting for a seat, their faces easily recognizable in the enlarged version of Mandy's shot.

"What the . . ." Malcolm did a double take on seeing the clear image of a man hovering near the *maitre d'* in the background. He was plainly searching for someone in the crowd of café patrons. The man was dressed in a leather bomber jacket, jeans, and wearing a brimmed cap with an over-sized green shamrock woven into the gray woolen plaid just behind the leather brim.

"Malcolm, whatever is the matter?"

"Mandy, can you enlarge that guy's face any more? The one with the shamrock on the cap . . ." Malcolm broke off, afraid Claire might hear them, and simply pointed to the figure in the background.

"Yes, but it will knock out the foreground though. There. How's that? Do you recognize him?"

"Unfortunately, I don't know his name, but I know his face. I've seen him before. Here at the Saint-Germain. It was the morning that your mother and Dom got into it over the peeping episode, and the old man found that medallion thing in the hallway. This character," Malcolm said, pointing to the guy staring out at him from the enlargement on the lap top's screen, "passed Penny and me on the stairway, in a big rush. *Very* rude, even surly. He was dressed the same way as in your photo. Same leather jacket, and the same cap with the green shamrock."

"Wait a minute, back-up please. What did you say about finding a medallion in the hallway? You mean like a gold pendant?"

Malcom nodded, then asked, "Mandy, can we go somewhere and talk about this? I'm afraid Claire could be in great danger."

"Okay, where can I meet you? This is pretty serious stuff. I was planning on shooting at Notre Dame today. Can we meet somewhere near there?"

Malcolm thought a minute. "Why don't I just drop by the Cathedral after my class at *universite*? It would be the easiest. Around one o'clock or so? Will you still be there?"

"Yes, Claire is supposed to meet me there after she finishes up at the antique houses. She thought it would be around two, so the timing works. Just look for a lady with a camera on a tripod."

"Wonderful, I'll see you there. Oh, and Mandy, can you get a print made of this photo with the same enlargement as what you've done here?" Again, Malcolm indicated the photo on the screen. "And I'm going to make copies of these two notes on Claire's stack. Do you think she'll miss them?"

"She'll probably think they got mixed in with the other papers in the stack. Can you give them back to me this afternoon, so I can get the notes back on the desk?"

"Right. And please give her the roses for me. Tell her . . . just tell her I'd like to drop by later. Hopefully she'll hear me out. About last night."

Denver—Offices of the Chadwick+Martelli Design Group

Susan hurried to her place of command in the office's tastefully designed reception area. She'd taken an extra-long lunch break today, doing some research on Chad's business holdings behind his back.

Good, she thought, when she saw his office door still shut. She began listening to the numerous voice messages on the office phone, and was about to put her purse away in its normal place in the credenza behind her desk, when her cell phone began playing the theme to The Stripper. On seeing the identity of the caller, she checked Chad's office door once again to make sure it was still closed.

She wondered just where he was, behind that closed door, or roaming around the office suite ready to appear at her desk any second now? Susan eased out from behind the reception counter and then hurried down the inner office corridor to the ladies' room, where she knew she couldn't be overheard. She pushed the door open. It was empty.

"Sean? What's happening over there? I've left you several voice messages. Why haven't you called me? Have you finished the job we spoke about?"

"Slow down, Sis, you're cutting out on me. Can you call me back on a land line?"

"No, I don't want Chad to see a call from Paris on the phone bill because he has the carrier company break-down the time, so he can bill for minutes on calls to and from clients. It's just too dangerous. I'll call you back on my cell phone when he leaves the office in a little while. It'll be about an hour, he has a late afternoon appointment out today. Sean, did you hear me?"

"Got enough to understand. I think I'll have good news for you by then, Susie. Gotta run to church now. Call back when you can talk."

Paris—In front of the Saint-Germain

Already deep in thought regarding Malcolm's concerns about her sister, Mandy negotiated the three flights of stairs to the lobby in record time, her camera and equipment bundled inside the unfathomable canvas bag slung over her shoulder. She waved at Etienne, who held up a slip of paper, attempting to get her attention, but she was out the front door before he could rise from behind the desk. She didn't have time to stop and chat at the moment; she wanted to get to Notre Dame and begin photographing those spectacular flying buttresses on the east end of the Gothic-styled cathedral while she still had the morning light.

On the curb in front of the Saint-Germain, Mandy automatically began signaling for a taxi as they sped by, while mentally engaged in ticking off the views she would photograph at the cathedral. She had done her homework, reading about Notre Dame's majestic situation on the *Ile de la Cite*, the isle in the Seine known as 'the cradle of Paris'. Also on her list of must-have shots was the octagonal marker placed in the ground in front of the cathedral—Point Zero, from which all distances are measured in France. And she hoped to have time to climb the three-hundred-eighty-seven steps up the circular staircase of the north tower to the *Galerie des Chimieres* to photograph the legendary gargoyles and the magnificent views of the city from the height of that large upper gallery.

She knew she could shoot the grandeur of the high-vaulted interior at various times of the day as the sun made its arc around the imposing edifice. The enormous forty-three-foot-diameter north and south rose windows, and the slightly smaller one which centered between the two high towers on the west-facing façade, were known to illuminate the interior space while flaunting the glories of thirteenth-century stained glass in those medieval windows.

So much for studying the Cathedral in advance, Mandy thought. Before I can actually get there, I need to concentrate on the task at hand. She was batting zero at summoning a taxi.

"One. All I need is *one* of these over-hyped 'ten thousand taxis operating in central Paris'," she muttered, quoting the guide book in disgust. She inadvertently stepped off the curb into the street as her efforts to flag one down went unheeded from her position on the sidewalk.

They're totally ignoring me, she thought, thinking she should've left earlier and taken the underground Metro system. But then she wouldn't have had the benefit of Malcolm's expertise regarding the handwriting on the note from Chad, and then his recognition of Shamrock Man in the café photo.

But the question, Mandy considered, is whether Claire will think he looks familiar when she sees the blow-up of the Shamrock's face. Mandy felt there was a chance that it just might spark her sister's memory. She just may have seen him somewhere before.

One thing was certain. It was beginning to look like Claire might still be in danger, even in Paris. And she'd been so looking forward to the trip and getting away from Denver, besides having the divorce finalized. Mandy knew it would be hard to remain focused today until Malcolm got there this afternoon, even with the masterpiece of Notre Dame in front of her lens. She hoped between the two of them, they could put a plan together to protect Claire. But, the point at issue remained. From whom?

The driver leaned on his horn while his dark blue taxi zoomed to a stop with very few inches to spare between Mandy and the front bumper. She was quickly shaken out of her soliloquy in the process.

"Hey lady, stay on the curb. Don't you know you're fair game in the street? Leave it to an American to stand in the middle of morning traffic. You're a real nut case, sister." A manful head of dark auburn hair popped out the open window, looking fixedly at Mandy from behind a pair of Ray-Ban sunglasses.

Pulling his head back into the taxi, he leaned forward to talk to the driver, putting money into the cabby's outstretched hand. He emerged from the back seat trying to shake out the wrinkles in the chino sport coat he threw casually over his shoulder. By his accent, and attitude, Mandy identified him as a New Yorker, and guessed that he was probably a graduate from one of the east coast Ivy League schools. A battered olive travel briefcase hung like an appendage growing out from his left arm.

Mandy's knees finally stopped shaking in response to the close call. She smiled, deciding to take the 'high road', *if* she could resist the urge for instant gratification by not trading insults with this yahoo, who she classified as a number-one-card-carrying macho member of the masculine sex.

"Look, buster, I've got better things to do than stand here and exchange pleasantries with you this morning. I just want your taxi. So, let's agree that fate has determined we are *not* destined for each other, we'll swear undying love, and go our separate ways," Mandy said in her best jocular manner. She reached around him for the back door of the taxi.

He caught her elbow before she could find the handle. "Look lady, you don't make my motor race any more than I thrill you. But do me a favor, go *your* separate way in some other conveyance. I've asked the driver here to wait while I meet up with the guy I've an appointment with, whose probably already in the lobby here," he said gesturing toward the Saint-Germain.

"Then I plan to continue on *my* way, in this very taxi, out to breakfast with the gent."

Mandy feigned a sigh. "Okay, *New York*, this must be your lucky day. You win. I'll just walk down to one of the taxi stands and grab one there." She turned, sauntering in the general direction of the corner. He watched her for a few seconds, then shook his head and made his way through the front door and into the lobby.

Out of the corner of her eye, Mandy saw him disappear into the Saint-Germain. She quickly backtracked the few steps to the curb where the taxi waited, pushing a wad of Euro currency through the front window and into the cabby's hand, thus effecting his direct response. She loaded the canvas bag with her camera equipment into the back seat first, and with a triumphant grin, Mandy followed without delay. The driver pulled away and into the mainstream of traffic. He appeared not to care who his fare was, as he mumbled something about being paid to drive somewhere, not idle at curbside. Mandy was in a taxi and on her way.

Paris—Notre Dame Cathedral

When Malcolm reached Notre Dame shortly after one o'clock, he found Mandy pacing back and forth over Point Zero in front of the center portal, one of the three archways spanning the width of the west façade, the main entrance into the Cathedral.

"Sorry I'm late, Mandy. Got held up with a student consultation after class."

"Oh, Malcolm, that's okay, you're here now," she answered, relief evident in her voice. "I decided to wait for you here at the main entrance. Thought you might not find where I was photographing, and you'd give up and go back to the hotel. It's later than we originally planned to meet, and I'd rather Claire doesn't see us together if she shows up early," Mandy said, slipping her arm through his. "Let's take the walkway along the south façade, close to the river. It leads to a peaceful garden square dedicated to Pope John XXIII. I found it this morning while I was shooting those super-impressive flying buttresses on the east end of the Cathedral. I doubt even Claire would look for me there."

"Where did the two of you plan to meet up?"

"Well, that's the problem. We didn't discuss an exact location. I told her *what* I planned to photograph, and guess I just assumed she'd look for me in one of those areas. I did tell her the flying buttresses were going to be my first shot, so I could catch the morning sunlight. But now you ask, I should've realized once I got here this morning that she might not be able to find me inside the Cathedral because of the sheer size of the place, and the crowds. It's been a real test of patience to get set up for a shot and then have to wait till the tour guides herd along the groups of day-trippers. That's why I decided to wait outside for you."

"Was Abbie planning on coming along? In which case, if neither of them can locate you, what do you think they'd do? Oh, this is a pleasant walk," Malcolm complemented, when they got to the path that skirted the river. "Good choice, Mandy."

"Actually, I'm not sure what Claire and Abbie would do at that point. Both are very resourceful. Could be they'd join one of the tour groups, or maybe just explore on their own. I don't know, anything's possible with those two. Let's get started, Malcolm, I'll never hear the end of it if either of them decide to go back to the hotel, only to discover I haven't returned yet. They're sure to wonder where I was, since I told them I'd be photographing here most of the day. And, well, I'm afraid I'm a terrible liar, and I certainly don't want Claire to know that you and I met behind her back."

"Okay, Mandy. We can always meet again if need be," he said, following her to a spot along the wall that separated the garden from the Seine. The leafy limbs overhead created a modicum of shade, and the view was remarkable. They sat down on the bench, their attention captured by the sheer scale of Notre Dame's high-flying buttresses.

"A most spectacular view. I believe the word you Yanks would use to best describe it is, WOW. I've never seen them from this angle," Malcolm said, squinting up at the fifty-foot spans.

Mandy turned her gaze from the Cathedral to Malcolm. She placed her hand lightly on his arm, forcing him to look directly at her.

"Before we begin, I feel I must ask for your word of honor as a gentleman that I can trust you never to divulge any of the information I'm about to share with you to anyone, including Claire herself. I wouldn't be telling you any of this if there was some other way to help her. I do agree that it appears she is in danger. Or rather, *still* in danger."

Malcolm had been smiling at Mandy's choice of overdramatic phrasing, but as her last words sank in, he felt a cold wave plunge over him. "What do you mean? Claire is *still* in danger? Mandy, I need to know." But he suddenly realized, he did know. Not *what* the danger actually was, but that she *was* in danger. He had known all along, from the very first moment he'd met her—thanks to Penny's exuberance, when he'd seen fear as he looked into the depths of those topaz eyes, though he'd ignored it when he felt her response to him. And again, he knew by the distance she'd tried so hard to keep between them, until he'd broken through her resistance with that kiss in the garden.

"Mandy, please tell me, I must know. But first, be assured you can trust me. Whatever you choose to share with me will be considered a privileged confidence, by my oath as a physician. And, please realize, I'm only trying to help her, same as you. And you must believe me when I say I'm beginning to discover that I care both for and about your sister. And, yes, I realize I've only known her for several days now, which is why it would seem quite unlikely I should feel this way. But, strangely enough, I do. So there it is. And, I'd very much appreciate it if you didn't tell her any of what I've just shared with you.

"I actually guessed you felt that way about her. Why else would you want to help someone who can be so blasted pigheaded at times? Can you tell me what happened last night to make Claire so upset? I promise to keep it in the strictest confidence. And of course, that goes for everything else you choose to share with me."

Mandy crossed her heart with an X and then held up two fingers just above her eyebrow, palm facing out. "This gesture," she solemnly informed him, "is the special sign Claire and I concocted long ago as a pledge of confidentiality when sharing secrets with each other. It is my word of honor. There is no higher assurance I can offer."

"Okay, Mandy, I get the message. Save the dramatics, I'm a believer. Let's get on with it before Claire shows up. I'll go first. About last night, Madame Fontaine had given me a couple pieces of paper while we were discussing a break-in with the police in her office. This was just before the Marie-

Claude incident happened. When your mom came in to tell us how you'd found her on the floor outside the office door, I folded them up and put them in my shirt pocket. Then I forgot about them, as I didn't have a chance to return to my rooms until after Etienne fixed that excellent impromptu meal for us.

"After dinner, I walked with Claire through the garden and to your door. She rummaged through her purse to find the key to your suite; it dropped out of her bag and onto floor. When I bent over to retrieve it, the papers fell out of my pocket. I tried to pick them up, but she was faster. And you might know it, I had inadvertently folded the papers so that the front of the pages were on the outside. I thought Claire was going to faint; she looked like she'd just seen the devil himself. Her face drained of color and her eyes went cold when she saw the drawing of the design of a medallion or pendant of some kind, the one that old Dom found outside your suite the morning after you all arrived. By the way, that's what was stolen during the break-in. The gold medallion that Emilie had placed in a locked box to keep it safe.

"Too late, I realized something was terribly wrong. I was so embarrassed; I lost my head and grabbed the papers out of her hand. I couldn't take it. The expression in her eyes was like someone had just driven a stake through her heart. I muttered something inane like 'goodnight' as I turned away and almost ran down the hall to my rooms. I was, and still am, terribly ashamed and embarrassed by the incident."

Mandy could only stare at him, appalled by his revelation. "The peeper thing . . . Dom actually found a gold medallion outside our door? Then that's what he was trying to show us when we saw him hold something up. Actually, Claire and I were so busy trying to get Abbie calmed down, we didn't think to take a closer look at it. Then, Penelope raced in to save the day, and you know the rest. But you say someone broke into the hotel and stole the medallion thing-a-bob? No wonder Claire is so upset. I'm almost afraid to ask. What was on the other piece of paper?"

Malcolm sat with his torso hunched forward. Head down, he rested his elbows on the top of his thighs, his hands clasped together. The light breeze blew the stubborn lock of dark hair that habitually fell over his forehead. He spoke quietly. "The other piece of paper was a copy of Claire's business itinerary in Paris. Yes, I already know what you're about to ask. According to her mother, Marie-Claude made a copy of it after receiving a fax from Claire's office in Denver. Although she doesn't know *why* her daughter made the copy, nor do I. But Emilie asked me if she should tear it up or give it to Claire. Since it was only a copy of the original, I thought I might be able to keep an eye on her if I knew where she would be, and when, on business dealings at least. So I volunteered to take care of it. End of story."

"Well, now that I know, I'm not at all surprised she's acting this way. You really need to explain to her what you've told me, Malcolm. You've done nothing wrong, outside of being a little on the dense side when it comes to dealing with a woman like Claire. The trick will be to get her to listen. She can be rather a stubborn old thing."

"I know that. She's still not talking to me after last night. But now I understand why, and it's my fault entirely."

"She's been getting a little irrational at times, but it's because of what and who she's had to deal with in the last eight months or so. Frankly, I marvel at how well she's coping and wonder that she's not a total wreck." Mandy hesitated for a second, then continued. "And, there is something I need to ask you, Malcolm, of a personal nature."

"Let's have it, Mandy. What's your question?"

"I know this really isn't any of my business, and please forgive me in advance. But, as Claire is very dear to me, I definitely don't want to see her hurt again." Mandy turned toward him, searching his face for assurance of his sincerity as she continued. "Are you married, Malcolm? Or involved with a significant other?"

He looked at her, not knowing quite how to answer. "Mandy, the simple answer is no, I'm not married, and as for

VICTORIA MASTERSON

whether I'm involved with someone, I was at one time, but not now. I presume a 'significant other' is the Yank way of saying, a steady, special girlfriend. Am I right?"

"More or less. Thanks, for answering. I was halfway expecting you to tell me it's none of my business. And actually, it really isn't. It's just that . . ."

"It's just that Claire is your sister, and you want to keep her from getting hurt again. I think you need to fill me in on what she's been through to this point and what's going on now, Mandy."

"Okay, you're right. I'm going to give you the short version, the synopsis. You'll have to buy the book for the whole story."

Mandy stood up and moved to a spot next to the low wall overlooking the Seine. She leaned against the wall and gathered her thoughts, her eyes fixed on the boat traffic sailing the river, but not really seeing it. She turned to look over at Malcolm, who had joined her at the wall.

"I guess the best place to begin is with Chad. One of those notes you found in Claire's papers, although unsigned, was from Chad. You seemed concerned that she could be in danger if it was from someone she is in close contact with. Well, he's pretty darn close to her. Too close in my book. He's an architect, her business partner, and her husband. Though, soon to be ex-husband. Claire's the interior design part of their business, which mainly focuses on projects in the hospitality sector. She's a literal phenom in that field. Her work has won many awards. I know she wants to stay involved in the business, after the divorce, but that part is still up in the air. It is half hers, and she's at least half the reason for their success, if not more, due to her work.

"She separated from Chad and began divorce proceedings some months ago, moving out of the house they've shared for the last seven years. The divorce will be final in a few days' time. Personally, I couldn't be happier about it. Forget I just said that. And please don't let my feelings color your analysis of Chad's handwriting. I'll just say that it hasn't been a particularly happy marriage.

"Last March, Claire was brutally attacked when she went to pick up Duffy, her dog, at her former house, now Chad's place. She found Duffy poisoned and in bad shape just as a masked madman attempted to rape, if not actually kill her. Thankfully, she was able to fight the guy off. By the way, Claire is a first degree brown belt in *karate* and *jujitsu*. She used a kick to the knee, and a choke hold to take the guy down. And the vet was able to save the dog. The loony got away, however there's a police detective, who is pretty darn sharp, working on the case. He keeps us informed on the progress. And here's where your drawing of the medallion comes in. Oddly enough, the police found one exactly like your drawing, on the patio behind the house that same night."

"Wait a minute, Mandy. How do you know it was exactly like the one in the drawing?"

"Well, you have to understand, Malcolm, she and I are good friends as well as sisters. When I came in last night, I found she'd gone to bed with another headache, but was still awake. I sat down to see if she wanted someone to talk with, hoping to take her mind off whatever was bothering her. She was so distressed over what had happened with you in the hallway, she told me about the drawing of the medallion in your possession. She was absolutely positive the drawing was the same as the actual medallion the police found at the scene of the assault. Now I think you see what her take is on the fact that the drawing fell out of your pocket. And it certainly didn't help that you acted like a guilty person who'd just been found out.

"But, to be fair, she doesn't know . . . none of us knew, about the *other* medallion. The one you say Dom found outside our door. What do you think this all means, Malcolm? That someone definitely has Claire in their sights? Who would be doing this? I confess I'm all out of ideas regarding who might be the culprit. Even though I would be happy to throw Chad under the bus, if the situation warranted, he was in Vail the night of the Denver attack, and in Denver the morning after we arrived in Paris. Aside from him, do you think 'Shamrock Man' could be involved someway? And, for heaven's sake, why would anyone want to hurt Claire?"

"I can't believe all three of you Martelli's talk in questions, Mandy. First Claire, then Abbie, now you. It must run in your genes. Let's walk around to the front. There are still some issues you might be able to clear up regarding Claire's present state of mind. Abbie told me Claire was having terrible nightmares, and something about anonymous phone calls playing frightful music. If you don't mind I'd like time to mull over the whole scenario. Maybe an outsider's view will help to answer some of your questions and point the way as to how we can best help her."

The taxi driver let Claire and Abbie off at the plaza in front of Notre Dame. They walked through the large square leading to the Cathedral, staring up at the impressive facade while keeping an eye out for Mandy amid the throng of tourists and Parisians heading in the same direction.

"I'm sure she's inside photographing some special feature," said Claire, as they stood in front of the Portal of the Virgin, looking at the fine composition of thirteenth century statues depicting saints and kings surrounding Mary, the mother of Jesus.

"I certainly hope she got shots of this entry," Abbie enthused. "I want a copy of this and whatever other shots she's taking here, for my photo album. Since Ben will be here shortly to tour with us, I'm sure he's going to want a set of photos too. Do you think Miranda will mind?"

"Well, if she does, we'll just have to steal her computer and download the shots we want," Claire answered, craning her neck upward, trying to see the upper gallery. "Let's go in and find her. I'm dying to climb the circular staircase to that upper gallery where the stone gargoyles are perched atop that openwork railing. As legend has it, they're watching over

Paris. See?" Claire asked, pointing upward. "You can just barely see the openwork railing if you look for it. The views are said to be phenomenal from up there. If we can't find Mandy on the main level, she's probably up there because she said that was one of the highpoints of Notre Dame she particularly wanted to capture."

"Why don't you go ahead and do that Claire," Abbie interjected. "I don't think these old legs of mine can take the trip. Running is one thing, but climbing stairs quite another. Didn't she say there are almost four hundred steps? I think I'll just dally around the entrance here. Ben should be along in a few minutes. And I can appreciate these wonderful carved statues on each of the portals while I'm waiting. When he gets here we'll start looking for Mandy and send her on up if she hasn't already gotten those shots. But don't worry, we'll stick around until you come back down and then we'll tour the rest of the interior together. Does that work?"

"Sounds like a plan to me. Are you certain you want to be by yourself until Ben comes along?"

"Claire, I'm not without my faculties, you know. I'll be fine. Go on, scoot now."

Claire patted her mother on the shoulder and bounced an air-kiss off her cheek as she departed. She headed toward the north tower, where the centuries-old circular stone staircase was designated by a sign that read: North Tower—One-Way Only—UP, in French, Italian, Spanish, German, and English. She understood from that indication that she would be using the south tower, with its identical circular stone stairway, as her one-way route down.

She knew why the one-way directions were indicated as soon as she entered the north tower's dimly lit staircase. The width of the stone steps spiraling from the center column to the wall, was at most thirty inches, which although minimally ample for a straight run, was altogether cramped when cut into pie-shaped treads of stone. Claire kept to the outside of each step, her shoulder brushing the smooth periphery stone wall of the staircase, unable to place her whole foot on the stone treads at their deepest point.

She decided she must be one of an elite group of brave souls to make the climb that afternoon. The only sounds she heard were vague traffic noises coming through the occasional slit openings that provided a modicum of daylight for the stairwell. She wondered how Mandy had made the climb with her ever-present voluminous bag of equipment slung over her shoulder.

She proceeded no more than a few dozen stairs when she heard footsteps coming toward her from above. The meager light afforded by the generously-spaced string of bare bulbs spiraling along the center column flickered once, twice . . . then went out completely.

Oh, great, she thought, just my luck. No lights and some idiot, who must be from Outer Mongolia, as he or she can't read directions in English, or in any of the other four European languages, is coming *down* the up-staircase.

Claire knew there was no way that two people could pass each other in these narrow confines without one of them being knocked down the stairway.

"Hey, you up there, she called out. "You're coming down the wrong way. This is the one-way *up* staircase." But the footsteps kept coming towards her at an even faster pace now. Maybe the stone walls are insulating the sound of my voice and the jerk can't hear me, she thought.

"Okay, okay. You win. I'm going to head back down to let you by. I'm not that far from the bottom. Just slow down a little and I'll be out of your way in a few minutes," Claire yelled up as loud as she could. She changed direction, and carefully began making her way down, feeling along the stone periphery wall in the dark. She knew one false step could cause her to trip and she would end up crashing down to the main level with only a broken bone or two—if she were lucky.

Claire began to panic as claustrophobia set in. She wondered how the fool could move so quickly in the dark. She pushed herself to a faster pace, but had to stop to catch herself as she tripped over a large chunk of rock that came ricocheting down from above, turning her ankle in the process. And all at once she knew. This wasn't some clueless tourist who had made a mistake and taken the wrong way down. Some maniac was stalking her. Again.

How many more steps to the bottom? Claire didn't think she'd possibly climbed up as many as she was negotiating down. She tried to ignore the sharp pain stabbing through every movement of her ankle, and determinedly focused on getting to the bottom before the person coming down from above could catch up with her. She thought she saw a faint light ahead, and hoped it wasn't just her imagination. She put all her energy into making it down to that light, trying to ignore the footsteps getting closer from behind.

Suddenly something heavy slammed into her from behind. She plummeted forward in a headfirst dive. Claire felt a searing pain in her shoulder as she landed on the jagged edge of one of the stone steps. Her head collided with the wall, and she plunged into the heavy wooden door of the North Tower. She'd made it to the ground level. The door was flung open by someone who clambered heavily over her, then raced off in hasty flight, leaving the tower entrance wide open.

Claire wasn't aware of feeling any pain in her body. She tried to lift her head out of the sticky fluid beginning to pool onto the floor. With her cheek lying against the wet stone, she could see the substance was a bright crimson color. She vaguely wondered if it was blood, and if so, whose blood?

Can't do it yet, she thought. I'll just rest a minute . . . then I'll get up. Her range of vision dimmed. Someone screamed, and she gave in to the darkness swirling over and around her.

Denver—Offices of the Chadwick+Martelli Design Group

"Susie, no, of course I'm not a hundred percent sure. But I'd lay odds on it. I couldn't stick around to see if she ever woke up, but she was laying there in a heap at the bottom of the stairs when I took off. I'm sure the French police would have been happy to answer that question, had I asked, with a few of their own. Just as I'm sure a whole lot of people in the general vicinity of that place could identify me as a *person of interest*. Are you reading me, Sis?"

"Yes, loud and clear, Sean," Susan said into her cell phone, as she one-handedly stacked the papers she'd been working on into piles. "But you're going to have to find out for sure. It's important, Brother, *very* important to my future, and yours, I might add. You're the one who said you wanted to hobnob with the rich and famous marks, didn't you? Well, then go over to her hotel and . . . Oh, hell, I think he's back!"

"Susan, in my office. Now." Chad snapped, coming to stand behind her with his arms folded across his chest.

She felt her heart sink into the pit of her stomach. Her hands shook so badly, she needed to use both of them to get her cell phone turned off and back into her bag. She pasted a smile on her face and looked up.

"Hi, Chad. I thought your breakfast meeting would last later," she said, nervously handing him a stack of phone messages from the day before. "I'm glad you're here though. I came in early to get caught up on a few things. But, I was just thinking about how busy you've been lately. You know how much I miss you when we don't see each other for a couple days, lover," she purred. "How about I rustle up some steaks at my place tonight? Afterwards, we could open a bottle of champagne and watch a sexy flick on the adult channel."

Chad merely crooked his finger for her to follow him and headed into his office, reading the phone messages in his hand.

"Okay, Chad, I'll be right there, give me a second or two. I just need to straighten my desk top," Susan stalled, while she thought up answers to the questions she knew he would ask. She also knew her best defense with Chad was to entice the hell out of him.

She sauntered into his office, just as he was leaving a voice mail to one of the firm's clients. Walking around to his side of the desk, she sat down on the corner, crossed her legs and leaned toward him. She wanted to make it easy for him to appreciate how well she filled out the décolletage of the form-fitting silk sweater under her suit coat. But strangely, Chad wasn't taking her up on any of it. He abruptly motioned her to toward one of the upholstered chairs facing him, in front of his custom copy of Frank Lloyd Wright's prairie-style desk.

Susan gave a little pout, but sat down as directed, showing as much leg as possible while sending him her special *come-get-me* look from across the desk.

Chad leaned back in his chair, steepling his fingers. "Forget it, sweet lips. This is not the time or place. Was that Sean you were talking to just now when I came in?"

She took a deep breath, about to try out one of the fairly believable stories she'd thought up.

"I can tell when you're lying, you know. Give it to me straight. Your credit card privileges hang in the balance."

One look at her face gave him the answer. "Susan, what in devil's name are you thinking? We discussed this several times now. Or are you too stupid to see that Sean is a way-too-hot potato just now? I've told you Lieutenant Owens came to see me about the case and that he's identified Sean as your stepbrother. Owens knows all about Sean's past criminal activities, his arrest record. Everything. He's traced your stepbrother to Paris and now he's trying to connect him to Claire's case."

Chad shook his head. "What do I have to do to get your attention? I simply asked that you not have anything to do with Sean at present. A simple request, right? And here you are talking to him. In Paris. Did you know that mobile phone calls can be picked up now, tracked, and even recorded? But here's the big question. What is Sean doing in Paris?

"Owens may act like one, but he's no fool, Susan. He's trying to add one peg, plus one peg, plus one peg, to get to what he thinks is the logical answer. Right now, he's got Sean pegged as the . . ."

Chad's voice trailed off on hearing the light knock as the door was pushed slightly open. Lieutenant Grady Owens leaned his head around to peer into the office.

"Ah, just the two people I was hoping to catch. I saw both your cars in the lot as I was driving past. Took a chance that you were open early this morning. No one else seemed to be here, but then I heard voices coming from this office," Owens said, advancing to stand in the open doorway.

"Why don't you come all the way in, Detective," Chad said, somewhat peevishly, though he got hold of himself in time to play the part of the genial host. "We were just talking about rearranging the schedule for the week. Until Claire gets back.

"You know, Susan, we can do the schedule later, and I've kept you from your errands far too long," he said, looking at his watch. "I really need you to deliver those plans. ASAP. I laid them on your desk. Here, take my car," he said, handing her the keys.

"Right, Chad. Be back as soon as possible. And a good morning to you, Lieutenant Owens." Susan gave him an impersonal smile, sliding around him to get to the door.

"Sit down, Detective," Chad said, indicating the chair Susan had just vacated.

"I prefer standing. Thanks anyway. But before you leave, Ma'am, I need to ask if you've had any contact with your stepbrother, Sean O'Malley, in the last two weeks?"

"With Sean? Why, no, I haven't, Lieutenant," Susan answered, hoping he wouldn't catch her in the lie. "It's been quite a bit longer than that, maybe a month or so."

"Next question, Ma'am. Do you know the whereabouts of your stepbrother at this moment?"

"Once again, I'm afraid I can't help you. I really don't know where Sean is."

"Detective," Chad interjected, "Susan has answered your questions. If you won't tell us what the problem is, there's nothing more to say on the subject."

"I came here to tell you both that Europol has a warrant out for Sean O'Malley's arrest. A partial fingerprint was found at the scene of a break-in and burglary, at the same hotel where Ms. Martelli is staying in Paris. The police had enough of the print to identify it as belonging to your stepbrother, Ms. Farrell. It would appear, according to the hotel owner that the only thing stolen was a gold medallion, which was taken from a locked box in the hotel's office. The burglar could have had an inside source, or possibly, he discovered where the key was kept as the box wasn't broken into." Owens paused to let the information sink in. Chad's face was a mask; Susan avoided looking at him altogether. "Do either of you know anything at all about this?"

Chad answered immediately, afraid of what Susan would say if she were to answer, and Owens would know for sure that she was lying. "No, Detective, afraid we can't help you. But tell us about the significance of the gold medallion. I assume you feel it's relevant to the case somehow, right?"

"Do you happen to play poker Mr. Chadwick?"

"Actually, chess is my game. Why do you ask?" Chad gave Owens a cold smile, while pushing his glasses back up his nose. "Detective, is Susan free to go? Or are you going to arrest her because of what you assume her stepbrother has done?"

Owens bowed to Susan. "Please, Ma'am," he said, indicating the door. "On second thought, hold up a second. If you happen to think of anything that might help us track Sean down, maybe some small clue or insight into his present whereabouts, I'd appreciate it if you'll give me a call."

He started to leave, hesitated, and then turned back, looking significantly at Susan. "I can put in a good word or two on your behalf, you know, where it will be the most beneficial. And that goes for you also, Sir . . ." Owens let his voice trail off.

He tipped his hat to Susan, and then to Chad. "Good day, Ma'am, Mr. Chadwick," he said, making his way out through the door without looking back.

Paris—Residence Saint-Germain

"Claire, you really lucked out," Mandy said, watching Abbie and Ben bandage the gash they had just closed with stitches on her sister's shoulder. "Just a little ole bump on the head, a turned ankle, and your shoulder there. It could've been a lot worse, you know." Mandy gently brushed Claire's wayward curls away from the swelling just above her hairline. "And, luckily, no one will be able to see any of your injuries while they heal. They're all hidden. But, you must have the hardest head in the world, Sis. No concussion this time, either."

On seeing the look on Claire's face at this pronouncement, Abbie cleared her throat. "Miranda, could you grab Claire's nightie and robe? I think they're hanging on the backside of your bathroom door. She needs to get some rest as soon as we're through here."

"Mandy, no, not my nightgown. Please get my pajama bottoms and my old sweatshirt. They're folded up on one of the shelves in the armoire. I'm *not* going to bed, Mom. Just let me rest on the settee, here."

Ben finished taping the bandage on her shoulder. He looked down at her. "Claire, we don't know each other very well, so please don't think I'm trying to tell you what to do. But since you refused to go to the emergency room when the police ambulance arrived at the Cathedral, you're my patient now. And, as your doctor, I agree with Abbie. You need to get some rest. You'll be much more comfortable in your bed, not here on a short sofa or sitting upright in a chair. You need to sleep. Go," he said pointing toward the bedroom she and Mandy shared. "I'll be back to check on you in a little while."

Claire hobbled to the bedroom favoring her taped-up sprained ankle. She went unwillingly. The bed did look inviting, but she soon found out that simply stretching out and closing her eyes didn't necessarily cause her mind or body to relax. Her thoughts were doing a fast track.

Is someone really trying to kill me? It was definitely not an accident today. Someone deliberately pushed me from behind. Why would anyone want me dead? Or, maybe I should be questioning who might have something to gain by my death?

She heard Abbie come to the door and pretended to be asleep. Right now, she didn't want to talk about the incident to anyone, much less her mother. She didn't want to scare her. As soon as the door quietly closed, she was out of bed. She found a pair of leggings on the shelf in the armoire and pulled them on with her favorite sweatshirt. Old and faded as it was, the logo advertising the Rockies was still readable.

Her shoulder hurt, her head ached, and her ankle throbbed, but Claire decided she would chance the trip down to the Saint-Germain's garden. Somehow she thought she'd feel much better lying under the flowering branches of the venerable blooming tree in one of the chaise lounges on the courtyard. She checked the mirror, and admitted the image she saw there wouldn't win a beauty contest. However, the patchwork of bruises beginning to color a good portion of her body remained well-hidden by her choice of costume. Though, maybe black and blue would be a definite improvement over her chalk white face. The word vampire came to mind, not that she'd minded sexy Edward Cullen's' bloodless face in the Twilight movies.

Claire crept to the door, listening for voices that might be coming from the sitting room. All was quiet. She inched her way along the short hallway leading to the door of the suite, while checking over her shoulder to see if she'd been spotted. Her fingers reached for the handle, her escape all but achieved, when the door suddenly swung open and a very surprised Mandy stopped just short of running her down. Claire shot her sister a glance that pleaded for understanding.

"Is that you, Miranda?" Abbie's hushed voice came from the direction of the *bergere* chair in the sitting room. "Be very quiet, dear, Claire is finally sleeping."

Mandy mouthed the words, so her mother wouldn't hear. "Claire, stay right here while I go in and say a few words to Mom so she doesn't get suspicious. If you're gone from this spot when I get back, I swear I'll raise the alarm. Got it?"

Claire silently nodded, making their private sign for a promise, by crossing her heart and following up with the two-fingered salute over one eye.

"Okay, I'll be right back," mouthed her sister.

"It's me, Mom," Mandy said softly. She tiptoed into the room where Abbie sat alone.

"Where's Ben?"

"I thought he needed to rest, there's been so much going on, and now this. So he went back to his hotel. He promised to stop by later to check in on our patient, besides treating us to 'take-out' tonight from one of the local bistros Etienne suggested."

"Mmm . . . sounds like party time. So, why not take a short snooze yourself? I've got to re-take shots of the hotel and garden, and think I'll do it now while everyone is resting. Come on, Mumsie, get up before you fall asleep. You'll thank me later when you're not kinked and stiff. I'll keep an eye on Claire," she said, crossing her fingers behind her back.

Mandy waited till her mother shut her bedroom door, then returned to the corridor where she'd left Claire. "You know, Sister dear, you really need to have your head examined. Okay, what gives? Why are you out here instead of where you're supposed to be, in bed?"

"Thanks for not blowing the whistle on me, Mandy. Look, I wasn't able to sleep at all in the bed, so I thought I'd get some fresh air, to clear my head, which by the by, doesn't need examining, but sure could use a sturdy helmet. Anyway, I couldn't resist the thought of lying on one of the chaise lounges in the garden. And it's private. No need to feel everyone is gawking at me because of the way I look right now. I've always had the place to myself when I've been there before. Besides, I need to get back on my feet; I'm scheduled at the Simon Boulle antique house tomorrow."

"Claire, I don't think that's such a good idea. What's to stop whoever is out there that has you in his sights from having another go at you? That's right, nothing. Now, I'll make you a deal. I'll help you downstairs and try to cover for you as long as I can, *if*, and it's a big if, if you agree to give Malcolm the opportunity to explain why the drawing of the medallion and your Paris schedule were in his possession. Please do this for yourself, Claire, not for me. I think you'll find that Malcolm is actually on your side. And that's my final offer, take it or leave it.

"Otherwise, Ben and Abbie will probably tie you to the bed, or give you a shot of something. I've heard that there's a new drug that can knock you out in five seconds flat, by the way."

"Okay, okay. But, all I agree to do is listen, Mandy. I'm not promising anything else. Remind me to tell you what happens to little sisters who think they can get away with calling the shots for their older-and-wiser sisters. It goes something like, 'Vengeance is mine . . .'"

"Threatening retaliation now, are we? How about what happens to those older-and-wiser sisters who tend to be pig-headed and foolhardy at times?"

"What say we leave the dire threats until later, and just get this show on the road? I'll put my arm around your shoulder. You put yours around my waist. You can be my crutch."

"Let's try it. Just please keep your weight off that ankle, Claire. If you overuse it before it heals, it'll take forever to mend. Besides the fact I'd be in trouble, big time, with Mom and Ben."

The two of them hobbled to the top of the stairs. Claire grabbed the stair rail with her free hand, the other arm still across Mandy's shoulders. They slowly descended, step by step. When they reached the first landing of the three stair flights, both were out of breath and shaking.

"Whew . . . I need to rest a minute, Mandy." Claire sat down on the step above the landing, wiping drops of perspiration from her forehead.

"Now what, Sis? I don't know if we can make it down two and a half more flights of stairs this way. Sorry, I know how much you wanted to relax in the garden. I wish I were strong enough to carry you, but I'm afraid I'm just not up to that."

"But I am, Mandy," said a voice with a definitive English accent that held just a hint of the Scottish burr. Malcolm had come upon them from behind, just as they were traversing the last couple steps down to the landing. Not wanting to startle them or cause them to lose concentration and possibly fall, he'd simply held his breath and willed them safely to the landing.

"If Claire will allow me, I'll take it from here," he said gravely, making his way around to face both of them as they rested. He bowed and held out his hand to Claire, giving her the smile that never failed to send currents pulsing through her body.

Claire looked fixedly at Malcolm's smile. He's doing it again, she thought. Can't even stay resolute in distrusting the bloody man. She hesitated for a second, and then placed her hand in his. Mindful of her ankle, Malcolm pulled her upright while supporting her weight, and gathered her up in his arms in a single motion.

"Am I hurting you anywhere?" He questioned, turning his head to scrutinize her golden eyes with his own direct sapphire gaze.

Claire broke the look with a little sigh. She nodded her head. "My left shoulder is a little touchy yet. Don't want to tear out the stitches."

Malcolm carefully set her down, balancing her weight as before. "Let's try this," he said, picking her up again so she faced the opposite direction in his arms. "Is this better? Claire, if you're too tired, or if you're hurting too much to go down to the garden right now, it's okay. You don't have to prove anything to anybody. Just tell me which way, up or down?"

"I don't want you to have to carry me all the way down and then three flights back up, Malcolm. But I just can't go back to the suite yet with Abbie hovering, and Ben coming back to hover later on. I know they're only doing it because they care. They mean well, but they're treating me like a child." Claire's eyes welled up, a tear slowly rolled down her cheek. "Now, you'll all think I'm overreacting," she sniffled.

Malcolm tightened his arms. "You're allowed. How about a neutral place to hide out for a little while?" He asked, looking over at Mandy who'd been sitting on the stair tread quietly watching the scene between her sister and Malcolm.

"Guess I know when I'm not wanted," she said getting up. "I've got photos to re-take anyway. Sounds like a plan, Malcolm. I know you two have things to discuss. I'll just go back and leave a note for Abbie so that when she wakes up she won't freak that you're not there, Claire. But it probably would be a good idea if you come back to the suite before Ben gets here. He's planning on bringing in dinner for everyone."

"Right. Thanks, Sis, I owe you one."

"And I've got a witness to remind you of that when you conveniently forget to remember."

Malcolm nodded at Mandy and headed back up the stairway with Claire in his arms.

"Where are we going? You surely haven't had second thoughts and are about to take me back to the suite?"

"Wait and see, and *no* to the question on second thoughts," Malcolm teased. "Quiet," he whispered, passing her suite, "We don't want to be found out now." He went on down the hallway and up the five steps to the alcove set back at the end of the corridor, where he gingerly stood her on her one good foot while he unlocked the door to his quarters. A tail-wagging monster met them at the door.

"Our chaperone," he said, indicating Penny and picking Claire up again.

"Malcolm, put me down. I can walk now, no stairs."

"Yes, stairs," he said, carrying her in and down the five steps to the sofa in the main sitting area of his rooms. Still wagging, Penny came to plop down on the floor at Claire's feet.

"Malcolm, this is charming," she said. "And here I thought all the suites would be alike in that the residence has undoubtedly been updated and made-over several times through the years."

"True, however it's been in Madame Fontaine's family since it was constructed as a mansion over two hundred years ago. I always stay here, and in these very quarters, when I'm in Paris. My rooms once belonged to the housekeeper from back to the time of the manse's beginning. There's even a small kitchenette, updated with current appliances, on the upper level where we came in. And the entrance to the bedroom is on that level also, except you go up a couple more steps to get into the room."

"Why all the levels?" Claire asked. "The suite we're staying in is all on one level."

"The proprietress related the story to me the first time I stayed here, about five years ago. It appears the areas under the upper levels in these quarters were once used for storage when the manse was originally built. It was the housekeeper's responsibility to keep control of the linens, feather beds and pillows, towels, and that kind of thing. So the storage areas for these were built into her rooms, where she could control both the quantities and the usage by the rest of the staff.

"Besides that, the original owner who built the house always remembered the time in the century before, when Roman Catholic priests were hunted down by Protestants. This is all according to Emilie Fontaine, by the way. The priests were once hidden in sections of the mansions of that era where they felt no one would find them. Priest-holes, they were called. Over there, in the area behind the built-in book shelves, below the kitchen level, is the original owner's idea of such a priest-hole, in case he or his family ever had need to hide. And it certainly came in handy during the French Revolution, when nobles were hunted down and beheaded.

"In the back of that book shelf," he continued, "there is rumored to be a secret panel that springs open with a hidden lever. I've looked for it, but never found it. It's evidently quite an ingenious design, but then, again by way of *la Fontaine*, there are secret passageways all over this old manse. And she should know. She has the history of the house in letters and journals dating back to the beginning cornerstone."

"What an amazing story, Malcolm. Do you think Madame Fontaine would tell us if there are secret passageways to and from our suites?"

"If there are such passageways, I'm not so sure she would tell us. But I'm not being a good host. Can I get you something to drink, Claire? Some wine, perhaps? I've found an amazing red table wine, on the fruity side, but dry. Can I get you a glass? It might help you to relax, so you can rest. Totally open to your discretion, of course." he hastened to add. "Or would you prefer water or a fruit juice?"

"I believe I'm going to choose the wine. And you're right, I think it's exactly what I need right now. Thank you, Malcolm."

He nodded at her. "Good choice. I'll just be a minute," he called over his shoulder, wending his way up to the kitchenette level to open the wine.

Claire looked around the room, analyzing the décor as was her wont. She decided it fit Malcolm to a tee, more masculine than their suite, almost like a library with the built-in book shelves lining the room. There was a carved wood mantelpiece, in typical eighteenth-century French styling to her left, several comfy over-stuffed chairs across from the sofa with a delightful short table in the Empire style sharing the space between. A beautifully carved wood railing with turned wood balusters ran the perimeter of the upper level, opening the space and making it appear even larger. Over it, she could see Malcolm working to open the wine in the kitchenette.

Via the open French doors down the wall from the bookcases, a smallish balcony boasted pots of blooming flowers, alive with an artist's palette of color. Through the wrought iron railing beyond, she could tell the balcony oriented in the general direction of the walled garden below, but from a slightly different angle than hers.

Malcolm set the tray with the stemmed glasses of wine onto the table. He picked up both glasses, handing one to Claire, and held his up in a toast. "Here's to you Rocky," he said with a smile and nod toward her sweatshirt, "you are without doubt the strongest woman I've ever known. And I don't mean in terms of muscles," he said, touching his glass to hers. "Here's hoping our friendship will continue to grow. And now, I owe you an explanation."

"About the other night, at your door, the pieces of paper that dropped out of my pocket and you picked up . . ." Malcolm stopped, thinking just how to tell her so she wouldn't think he was assuming too much in their short acquaintance, lest he frighten her away for good. This wasn't the time to declare his feelings for her, the ones he'd only discovered himself, a mere twenty-four hours ago.

He looked over at her, saw her eyes drop to the glass of wine in her hand. She took a sip and set it down on the tray. That's when he noticed her hands clenched together in her lap as she waited for him to continue.

"Okay, Claire. There's only one way to say it. I've been interested in finding out what old Dom was doing outside your door the morning after you arrived, when Abbie accused him of peeping. I know the man and he simply isn't the type that would do something like that. So, I asked Emilie Fontaine about the incident. I've gotten to be friends with the Fontaine's in the past several years I've been coming here. Emilie explained how Dom had found something on the floor in front of your door. He'd knelt down to pick it up just as Abbie came up the stairs. And then the fun began. Dom is barely able to understand English, let alone speak it. He attempted to show everyone what he'd found, but by then Penelope came bounding onto the scene, and, well, you know the rest."

Claire looked at him doubtfully. "What has that got to do with the drawing and my Paris itinerary, Malcolm?"

"Hold on, Claire. I'm getting to that. The drawing of the object was made by Emilie, from memory. You see, the real

LEFT OF THE LEFT BANK

article, a medallion of sorts, was stolen in a break-in the other night."

"That's impossible, Malcolm. I'm the only one who's seen the actual *article*, as you call it, in person. Which *is* a gold medallion, or charm of some kind. You see the reason I know it can't have been a drawing of *that* medallion is because of the fact it was found *in Denver last March*, after I surprised a burglar who tried to kill me. It was found on the scene after the attack, and is now a piece of evidence in the possession of the Denver police."

"Well, I can only surmise there are two medallions of the same design, and the person who lost it at each scene, is very careless, or perhaps there are two people with two medallions. I suppose it could also be a symbol carried by members of some kind of group or organization as a token of identity. Claire, you don't have to take me into your confidence of course, but if you would like to share anything that's happened, or anything that's bothering you now, I'd welcome the opportunity to be of help," Malcolm said, moving closer to her and taking her hands into his large warm ones.

She deliberately pulled her hands from his and moved further away. "You don't seem surprised to hear about the attack in Denver, since you appear to take it in stride. Should I wonder why? Or do I see Mandy's fine hand in this? But do go on. You were saying that you had the drawing in your possession, because?"

Malcolm got up and moved to one of the upholstered chairs across from the sofa. Go easy, he said to himself. She definitely wasn't comfortable knowing he was aware of at least some of what she's going through. He picked up his wine glass, twirling the stem absently.

"Because I intended to stop by the Saint-Germain office after my class to take a look at the medallion Emilie had locked away. However, that was before she told me it had been stolen sometime in the wee hours that morning. She invited me into the office to listen to the discussion of the break-in and theft with a police officer who'd come by with some follow-up

145

questions, and she gave both of us copies of the drawing in lieu of the actual medallion. I would think that she gave me a copy as I'd shown so much interest in the incident involving Dom and Abbie, and had asked to see the medallion.

"After the police left, Emilie showed me a copy of your Paris itinerary saying that Marie-Claude had evidently made the copy from the fax that arrived from your office in Denver. Emilie was upset as to the intent behind making the copy. She asked me, since she knew how her daughter enjoyed talking to me, if I would try to find out from Marie-Claude the whys and wherefores. And that was the exact moment, you three, along with Etienne, came in to find Marie-Claire in a state of . . . shall we say, distress? In her condition, there was no way to question her as to why she copied it, or what she intended to do with it. I had it in my hand when we rushed out to see what the problem was. I must have folded it up with the drawing and put them both in my pocket, intending to take them out when I went to my quarters later. But that didn't happen, as we were treated to Etienne's cooking skills that night. Then I walked you to your door, and, well, you know the rest. I was so embarrassed. I could tell after seeing your face that you'd jumped to conclusions of your own. And it was probably not the best time to offer explanations. So I ran off. Not very sporting of me, I know. Can you forgive me for being a stupid ass, Claire?"

She turned the full force of her molten gaze on him, pushing the curls out of her face. "That depends, Malcolm. First of all, I don't consider you stupid, or an ass. But if we were to try and patch things up between us, I'd need to know I can trust you implicitly. And I don't mean that lightly. There are only two other people in my life right now that I can say I trust that way. You've met both of them, however I'm having a few doubts about one of them."

Malcolm smiled in his disarming way. "Claire, I can assure you the one you're talking about is as true to you as ever. She is simply overwhelmed by her desire to keep you safe. Frankly, we've joined forces to try to protect you. Is that such a bad thing? Especially after the occurrences that are happening here in Paris. Evidence, the incident at the Cathedral today."

Tears welled up in the golden eyes. "I know, I shouldn't have said that. Why do you want to help me, Malcolm? What's in it for you?"

"Maybe I'll answer that someday, just not right now. Can you accept that, Claire?" He asked, refilling her glass. "Just know it's important to me that you are safe and whole, both physically and mentally."

"I'll accept that," Claire said, smiling just a little. "But seriously, I am afraid." She paused. "I'm not trying to be melodramatic when I say this, but I am afraid for my life now. My entire belief system regarding my vulnerability is in jeopardy. Ever since I started studying the martial arts five years ago, I kind of thought I was invincible. Thankfully, I was able to use my knowledge in *jujitsu* during the attack in Denver, and I survived. Just bruised and banged up a little. There was no way I could have used *jujitsu* today in that dark staircase. I've always thought my knowledge of the martial arts would keep me safe, that I could protect myself from anything. It's scary to know that isn't the case anymore."

"I hear you loud and clear. Let's just get you healed up. You won't be alone, Claire. I'll be there with you. And I'm certain you can count Abbie and Mandy in also. You three women are rather exceptional in my view. Oh, and Penelope will be on the team also, right old girl?"

Penny lifted her head and gave a woof. Claire smiled and scratched behind her ears. "My dog, Duffy, likes to have his ears scratched too. He'll be mighty jealous when I get home and tell him about you, Penny."

"Oh, oh. That's probably Mandy," Malcolm said, hearing the knock at his door. "She was to let me know when it was time to get you back to your suite." He left the chair and headed up the stairs.

"Come on in, Mandy," he said opening the door. "Claire's relaxing on the sofa. It must be time to get her back, right?"

147

"Right. Should I throw my hat in first?" Mandy asked with a grin.

Malcolm chuckled. "It's safe. She's not gunning for you, if that's what you're asking."

"Hey, Sis," Claire called up the stairs. "What's going on?"

"Oh, nothing special. Abbie's up in arms because I let you sneak out, and Ben just called to say he was on his way up with the food, that's all. So, I thought it would be a good time for you to come back to the suite and act like a good little patient."

"On our way," said Malcolm. "Hope Abbie doesn't mind when I carry Claire into your suite. *Deja vu*," he said with a wicked little grin. "She didn't think too highly of me then. Hope this time is different."

"How did you manage it, Ben? This dinner is excellent. Just like we're eating out in one of the best French restaurants," Abbie remarked, balancing her plate of food on her knees in the *bergere* chair.

"Oh, I have my ways," Ben remarked, eyeing Abbie's rather full plate from his position on the cane-seated bench by the fireplace. "It really has been too many years; I'd forgotten how much food you can put away," he teased.

Malcolm sat cross-legged on the floor, leaning back against the loveseat where Claire was ensconced, surrounded by pillows, her leg propped up on the footrest belonging to the *bergere* chair, with a bag of ice covering her ankle.

"The food is great," Malcolm said, between forkfuls. "Thanks for inviting me to stay, Abbie. And Ben, I think whichever restaurant you obtained this kind of a take-out meal deserves to be touted in a guidebook. Let me guess, that superbly smart *brasserie* down the street? Right?" At Ben's smile and nod, he grinned up at Claire, trying to draw her into the conversation. "What do you say, Claire?"

But Claire remained silent, toying with the food on her plate.

"Well, I'm sure Mandy will agree," Malcolm said, getting up for a second helping.

"Hmm, what was that?" Mandy asked, deep in concentration at the desk, her empty plate next to her computer. "Sorry, I guess I wasn't paying much attention. I'm looking for the photo taken with sharp focus on the guy in the sidewalk café. I want to enlarge his face to the point that Claire can take a look. She thought he was somehow familiar in soft focus, when we reviewed the café shots before you dropped in this morning, Malcolm."

"Has it only been this morning that I stopped by? Seems like it's been much longer than that. With all that's happened today, I feel like I've aged at least a year, not just a matter of eight hours or so," he replied. "If I hang around you Martelli's much longer, I'll be an old man before I'm fifty," he said, again attempting to rouse Claire out of her brooding reflections. And he succeeded.

"If that's the case, I don't see why you think *you've* grown older. I didn't see you at the Cathedral today," Claire shot back.

Mandy looked up sharply at Claire's comment. Malcolm realized he couldn't catch her eye in time to warn her off from saying what he was afraid she was about to tell Claire.

"Who do you think found you lying at the bottom of the stairs, in a pool of blood, and out like a light, Claire? And who do you think carried you to the ambulance and consulted with the medics on your injuries, refusing to leave until Abbie and Ben arrived on the scene? Before you woke up and declined to be taken to the emergency room? And if he won't tell you because he doesn't want you to know he was at the Cathedral, in the middle of a discussion with me on how best to protect you, I will. I was a few seconds behind him in getting to the stairway, and quite frankly, I didn't know whether you could be moved, or even if you were alive. You were laying in such a frightening position."

"Easy, Mandy. I only did what any other trained medical person would've done," Malcolm said, intent on downplaying

149

his part at the scene. "I saw the guy running away through the crowd and I really wanted to go after him. I only caught a glimpse of him from behind. And I think I'd have beaten him silly, if I'd caught up with him. But Claire, you were my first concern. An injured person requiring aid always takes priority at the scene of an accident. Or in this case, a cold-blooded assault. Right Ben, Mrs. M.?" Malcolm asked, again intent on making his role at the church into the action any responsible physician would take, and therefore less personally intimate to Claire.

Before either could open their mouth to answer, Claire pointedly remarked, "Why didn't anyone tell me that Malcolm once again saved the day? You know you're getting to be a regular hero to damsels in distress," she said looking down at him with a feigned smile. "I must confess, maybe I *am* getting paranoid, because I'm beginning to feel I'm always the last to know information that affects me personally.

"Besides today's incident, what about the fact that I didn't know that Dom found a gold medallion in front of the door to our suite, identical to the one found at the scene of the burglary-slash-attack in Denver? And, who is the person you call 'Shamrock Man', aka the Shamrock that I overheard the two of you talking in whispers about, once again behind my back, just this morning while I was in the bedroom getting dressed?"

Mandy stared at her sister for a second, suddenly understanding why she felt the way she did. Then she turned her laptop toward her and pointed to the close-up image. "Claire, meet the Shamrock," she simply said.

"Shamrock Man," Malcolm pronounced, on seeing the enlarged image again.

"Sean O'Malley," Claire said, the words imploding into the conversation like a sharp shooters bullet.

"Who or what is a Sean O'Malley?" Abbie asked, seeing the color drain from her daughter's face.

"Susan's stepbrother," Claire stated quietly.

"Susan at Claire's office," Mandy explained for everyone's benefit. "She is mostly Chad's Gal Friday, though she also manages the reception desk."

"Are you certain, Claire?" Malcolm asked. He made his way from the floor to sit beside Claire on the sofa. "How certain?"

"One hundred percent certain. I had a casual dinner with him after Chad and I officially separated, and I'd filed for divorce."

"And? Did you have any more casual dinners with him after that?"

"It was only the one time. We ran into each other at a small café where I'd gone to pick up a quick meal to take home. I'd met him before on several occasions, from when he'd stop by the office to see Susan. He suggested that we share a table for dinner rather than both of us eating alone. We did. But there was something about him that bothered me. Oh, he was a gentleman, but it was like he put on an act to impress me. And he didn't, or maybe couldn't, look me in the eye when we were talking. The second time he offered to take me to dinner, I made up an excuse. And I haven't seen or heard from him since.

"Oh, Good Lord, now I remember!" Claire exclaimed, her hands trembling to the point of nearly spilling the uneaten food onto her lap.

"What is it, Claire?" Malcolm demanded, saving the plate of food just in time.

"The tattoo. Sean was wearing a short-sleeved shirt the night we had dinner together. I noticed a tattoo on his arm, a little above the elbow. It was the same depiction as the design on the medallion! I knew I'd seen that design somewhere before. Just couldn't place it the night of the attack. I've got to let Lieutenant Owens know," she said, patting her pocket and looking around the room for her phone.

"And there's something else you should know, speaking of the detective," Abbie said, breaking into the conversation. "As a matter of fact, Lieutenant Owens called from Denver while you were out this afternoon, Claire. That's why I knew you weren't in your room. Miranda didn't tell me, she kept your escape a secret. Anyway, when I told him you weren't in, he asked me to give you this message. "Very important," he said. There it is, under Mandy's plate." Abbie got up and went to the desk. "I'm sorry, I was actually waiting for you to come in, intending to give it to you right away, but then Ben arrived with the food, and I guess I let my stomach take over."

Claire took the folded piece of paper and opened it. After reading it herself, she handed the message to Malcolm. "Please read it out loud, so everyone will know."

He scanned the note, then read: *"Claire, I believe you already know Susan Farrell's stepbrother. He's been traced to Paris. There's a warrant out for his arrest for breaking-and-entering, and theft. His fingerprints were identified at the scene, placing him at your hotel on this charge. Please be careful. He's a very dangerous character. If you see him, call the Paris police without delay. Will fill you in later."*

Malcolm looked down at Claire's white face. "Do you think it could have been Sean who shoved you down the stairs this morning, Claire?"

"It was pitch black in that staircase, Malcolm. And whoever it was, didn't speak. I couldn't identify anyone. I suppose it could've been Sean, he's evidently been following me," she said, nodding toward the face on Mandy's laptop screen. "I'm getting goose bumps just thinking it could be him," she said, her voice flat and expressionless. "But, what possible reason would he have for wanting me dead?"

Day Four

Paris—Residence Saint-Germain

Etienne looked up from the newspaper he was reading with his morning coffee at the reception desk. "Bonjour, Monsieur, what can I do for you this very fine and so pleasant a day?"

"I'm here to see one of your guests, M. Martelli. Not sure of the first name."

"You will have to wait, Monsieur, until I call the suite to see if Mademoiselle Man-dee is available."

"Look, it's not a mademoiselle I'm supposed to meet. It's a *Mister* M. Martelli, must be Michael or Mark, something like that. This is the hotel where he's supposed to be staying, and I've left several messages over the last two days, with no word in return. Just tell me what suite or room he's in and I'll find him on my own. I'm not leaving another message that doesn't get to him." He turned toward the stairway, then turned back to face Etienne. "I suppose this Man-dee person could be his wife?"

"One moment, *s'il vous plait,* Monsieur, I will call the Martelli's suite to see if you are expected. And your name?" Etienne asked, reaching for the phone, his expression smoothly masked behind an assumed *savoir-faire.*

"Just tell Mr. Martelli, I'm here to talk with him about the guidebook."

"*Merci,* Monsieur, I will dial."

"*Bonjour*, Mademoiselle Man-dee? It is Etienne. There is a person in the lobby who has said he is attempting to meet with a Monsieur M. Martelli about a guidebook."

"*Oui*, Mademoiselle, I will tell him," Etienne said, hanging up the phone.

"Monsieur, I have been asked to have you to wait. Someone is coming to speak with you."

"Well I hope this Martelli person doesn't take too long, I've got a taxi waiting outside."

"We will see, Monsieur. We will see."

Mandy flew down the three flights of stairs as quickly as possible, so anxious was she to meet the free-lance writer the publishing company promised would be a leading name in the travel magazine industry. She would be collaborating with the writer to create a unique section planned for the guidebook called Paris By-Ways. The standard tourist sights she'd still photograph without collaboration, having previously met with the art director and gotten her vision and blessing prior to leaving for Paris.

Who would it be? Mandy could hardly wait to get down to the lobby to see. She rounded the corner into the lobby and stopped short.

"You!" She hissed, looking at the man with a full head of mahogany hair, wearing rimless Ray-Bans, and leaning casually against the walnut-paneled wall.

"Right back at you, sister. Say what kind of joke is this? More of your little games?" He straightened up and walked over to stand in front of her, taking off his dark glasses. "So, let me get this straight. You're M. Martelli? Wait, don't tell me. Of course. Man-dee Martelli, alias M. Martelli, taxi thief. I should have seen this coming."

"It's Miranda Martelli. Mandy for short." Her voice was strained, she forced herself to look him in the eye, recognizing him instantly without the Ray-Bans.

"Is everything okay, Mademoiselle Man-dee?" Etienne waited nearby, listening to their exchange. "If you require someone to show the monsieur out, I would be happy to comply."

"No, it's all right, Etienne. Just a case of mistaken identity."

"Couldn't be more mistaken," the visitor said. "Perhaps I should introduce myself, Mademoiselle Man-dee," saying her name as Etienne did.

"No need. I recognize you now without the sunglasses. You are Neal Ross Kincaid, I've seen your picture with your byline in several travel publications."

"Right on, my little taxi thief. And you are the photographer hired to work with me on the Paris By-Ways section? Don't you think it ironic that fate really did intend for us to be together after all?"

Mandy flushed. He was throwing yesterday's words right back at her. Was it only yesterday? If she had only heeded that little voice in the back of her head. Common sense tried to warn her she wasn't exactly proficient at stealing taxis. But she'd ignored the voice. Her desire to stand up to any challenge always got her into trouble. Delaying instant gratification was definitely not her best suit.

Neal Ross stood there, swinging his dark glasses by one of the stems, glowering at her. "No, I don't think this arrangement is going to work. Destiny or not. I'll call New York and see who else they can come up with."

"Look, Mr. Kincaid, I do apologize for yesterday, stealing your taxi and all. I was simply tired of being totally ignored by the cabbies. And I needed to get to Notre Dame as I'd planned to shoot the flying buttresses before I lost the morning light. Could we talk about the special By-Ways section, at least? I really want to hear your ideas, and perhaps you'd like to hear mine. You see, while I've been shooting the usual Paris landmarks, I've discovered a few sites that you might want to take a look at. Maybe some of those shots could work into what you're thinking of for some out-of-the-way scenes and places that would appeal to adventurous tourists who want to see more than the usual sights."

155

Mandy stopped chattering, out of breath. She knew she'd been talking way too fast for fear he might not listen. And for just a second, she thought he might be wavering. But then, he put the Ray-Bans back on and held out his hand to shake hers.

"Good luck, Mademoiselle Destiny. I will admit it's been real." He headed toward the door, but then turned back to her. "Martelli . . . that name is ringing a bell, now that I see you are not *Mr.* M. Martelli. But where have I run into it before? Hmm . . . something to do with a woman. A woman, and . . . a restaurant. That's it. By chance, are you related to a Claire Martelli?"

"You know Claire?" Mandy gaped at him. "She's my sister."

"Well, I won't hold it against her, Destiny. So she's your sis, huh? A very attractive five-foot-six blonde with long curly hair, gorgeous tawny gold eyes . . . a face that you wouldn't easily forget?"

"Yes, I guess you could describe her that way. How do you know her?"

"Well, I was in Colorado around the holidays, skiing at Vail. I took my last run just as the mountain was closing for the afternoon. I skied down to a restaurant called Lord Jim's Table, and I happened to meet your sister at the bar. She was waiting for a friend and I was waiting for a table. When I asked her what she did, she told me she was a partner in a firm that specialized in designing within the hospitality industry— as she put it. Then the owner came over to greet her and I found out your sister actually designed the interior of that restaurant. We ended up having dinner together as her friend never showed."

Mandy leaned nonchalantly against the newel post supporting the stair railing. "Claire is here in Paris, also, Mr. Kincaid. We have a suite here at the Saint-Germain."

"Really? I'd like to say hello to her. Maybe I could take her to dinner. I know some great restaurants here that she'd enjoy seeing the interiors as well as the food. Is she in now?

"Unfortunately, no. Claire left earlier to visit some of the antique houses in the area. She's in Paris looking for some unique pieces to use as accents for a French-themed project she's doing in New Orleans. I'll tell her that I ran into you, though. Anyway, nice to meet you. I hope you find someone you feel you can work with on the By-Ways piece."

Mandy turned toward the stairway and took the first step when he spoke. "Just a minute, Destiny, perhaps I'm being a little too hasty. It wouldn't hurt to take a look at some of your shots. After all, I might be able to give you some pointers. I like to photograph when I visit a place that I'll be writing about. Not to brag, but I'm pretty good at it."

Mandy smiled, saying an inward "*gotcha*" before turning back around. "Really? I'd like to see some of your photography work sometime, Mr. Kincaid."

"Mr. Kincaid is way too formal for Claire's little sis. How about you call me Neal Ross? Oh, and grab your laptop. We can do breakfast and look at some of your stuff at the same time. Maybe your sister will return before we get back."

Mandy fervently hoped she wouldn't, realizing she'd just dangled Claire like a carrot in front of the man who could be holding her future in his say-so. She'd done it again, ignored that little voice that cautioned her to think before opening her mouth. Once again she hadn't been able to ignore the challenge that presented itself in the person of Neal Ross Kincaid, premier travel writer and globe-trotter. And to think Claire had once playfully called *her* a gypsy.

Paris—Simon Boulle's antique shop

The tasteful hand-lettered signage simply stated—*Simon Boulle, Antiquities*—on the glass display windows. The name alone proclaimed to the world that this was one of the most reputable antique houses in the *St-Germain-des-Pres* area on the Left Bank. Malcolm arrived a little early for his appointment with the owner. This wasn't the first time he'd been called by this particular antique dealer to determine the authenticity of questionable pieces. Using his expertise in graphology, Malcolm searched for traits of deceit and fraud in the *provenance*, the handwritten history of ownership and origin that accompanies a valuable antique when purchased.

He strolled through the artfully arranged furnishings and *objet d'art* pieces, fascinated by these archaic remains of bygone eras. The exhibits dated from the more recent past—in the neighborhood of around a hundred years old—to those items going back through the past several centuries. On a previous visit, the antique dealer had even revealed a few treasures from the Renaissance Era, now locked away for viewing by appointment only. The French pieces, typical of the various periods of France's history were represented in abundance. Though there was also a stunning variety of furnishings and objects collected from all of parts of Europe, and Russia as well.

Malcolm headed in the direction of Simon Boulle's office. Generally, in all the times he'd been in Simon's shop, he could count on both hands the number of lookers in the store at any one time. Today, he was surprisingly confronted by several large groups of people looking over the assortment of antique furnishings. He excused himself a number of times as he made his way around and through the crowd to Simon's office in the back of the store, deciding the upcoming auction was the reason for the traffic this day. He continued down the corridor leading to the owner's private work domain, to the consultation area where they were to meet.

Out of courtesy, Malcolm stopped some twenty feet away from his goal, on seeing Simon talking to a woman, most likely a potential buyer, just outside the open door to his office.

As Malcolm waited, he watched the antique dealer shake hands and heard him call one of his staff to show the woman to the section of the spacious shop where the French antiques were displayed.

The woman pivoted, walking slowly in Malcolm's direction. Her head inclined, she was deep in conversation with the young man Simon had assigned to her. Malcolm couldn't help but notice her. She was striking, walking with a barely noticeable limp that only added to her mystic. He took in the total view, from the sexy, strapped heels on her feet, to the top of her deep-rose ruffled hat that completely covered her hair. He thought he'd seen that particular designer hat somewhere before, but brushed it off, reasoning that it probably was a copy, not an original. Her glance came about, golden eyes gazed towards him. Those eyes . . .

Not believing his own eyes, he looked again. It was Claire.

He stood there for a moment, stunned by her smart appearance, particularly in view of the injuries she'd suffered yesterday; and the fact she was here, in Simon's shop. After Ben's take-out dinner party last night, Malcolm had asked her to wait for him today, worried that Sean O'Malley would concoct some new *accidental* mishap of the lethal variety. When he got back from his appointment, he'd told her, he would personally escort her to some of the antique houses in the area. And he thought she'd agreed to that.

"Claire, what are you doing here?" Malcolm looked at her face for some sign denoting a twinge of guilty conscience or at least a hint of surprise on seeing him here.

She smiled. "*Bonjour,* Malcolm, I'm taking care of business, of course."

Simon came up to them. "*Bonjour, Docteur* Sutherland. Oh, so the both of you know each other? Mademoiselle Martelli has come to my humble shop from Colorado to purchase antiques for a restaurant project. Wonderful. *Oui?*"

Claire smiled again, turning to the young man at her side. "Just point me in the direction of the Country French section, Philippe. I will roam around and write down the pieces I'm interested in, and you can give the list to Simon for me. *Oui?*"

"But of course, Mademoiselle."

She nodded at Malcolm. And the last he saw of her was her straight back following Philippe down the aisle, looking around at the displays, and stopping now and again to admire an individual piece.

"That one, she has a good eye." Simon shrugged his shoulders. "I will probably end up very sorry for the deal I will make her. But talented and attractive women like that are deserving of my attention."

"Attractive yes," Malcom agreed, shaking his head. "But how do you know she's talented, Simon?"

"Because she said she wanted to set up a business relationship for future projects where she will also be using antiques. She showed me some photos of the work she does on that device she carries in her portfolio. Very impressive. But I have a feeling *mon ami* that you are in for a merry chase with that one. Come, let's get our business attended to. *Oui?*"

Malcolm followed the antique dealer into his inner sanctum. He sat down at the gorgeous Louis XV antique that was used as a conference table and waited while Simon gathered together the papers of *provenance*. If there were any antique-look-alikes coming in with the rest of the shipment from the Provence area, he would be able to ferret out the perpetrator from his or her handwriting. Then when the shipment arrived, it would be an easy task to take those pieces, identified by the handwriting on the *provenance*, out of the group of furnishings scheduled for the auction. Simon and his people wouldn't have to burn the midnight oil to visually study every piece on the shipment to determine if it was authentic, as they would only have maybe a day at most prior to the auction.

As he waited for Simon, he thought about Claire. Without a doubt, she was fast becoming a totally perplexing enigma. Was she trying to prove something to him, or herself? She knew the danger, but came out alone anyway. Why? Did she think she could handle the O'Malley character through her knowledge of the martial arts, if he attacked her in broad daylight? Malcolm could only hope she would re-think the situation and decide it was too dangerous to leave herself open to possible consequences, daytime or not. Besides, it wasn't as if he hadn't volunteered for bodyguard duty.

A loud crash sent vibrations through the French seeded glass panels the antique dealer had customized into his office walls. Then Malcolm heard shouts and the sound of many feet scrambling over the wood parquet floor of the antique house.

Philippe came running into the consultation area. "Monsieur Boulle, come quickly. A man, American I think, is running through the shop with the police chasing after him. The mademoiselle is okay though, she was not injured when that large Provençal painted armoire came crashing down. But, Monsieur, it was so close!"

Malcolm was out the door before the man had finished. He ran to the front of the building looking for Claire, just in time to see her run across the street and jump into a taxi waiting at one of Paris' for-hire stops, then take off. The police milled about. The ones inside the shop, dressed in street clothes to look like antique buyers, were combing through every display for the American. While others, in uniform, were out on the street looking up and down for the man. Malcolm could have told them it was already too late. Sean O'Malley was very good about disappearing into crowds, down stairways, and what seemed like, at times, thin air.

Simon came up to stand next to Malcolm who was still looking out the door. The antique dealer shook his head. "That could have been a nasty business. According to the police, and my staff, that large *armoire* was pushed over deliberately, very nearly crushing Mademoiselle Martelli. A few more inches, and . . . poof!" He raised both hands with a look that said it all.

"Who called for the police, Simon? Seems like they had to have known something was about to happen as they were already in place."

"I don't know the answer to that, *mon ami*. But I must go now and talk with the inspector. I left the letters of *provenance* on the worktable in my office. Do you think you could take a quick look at them before you leave?"

"If you wouldn't mind, I'd prefer to take them with me, Simon. I'll study them tonight and plan on getting together with you tomorrow or the next day. Then we can discuss whether any of the handwritings point to the person responsible for the sudden influx of fake antiques you say has been coming out of the Provence area recently. I'd rather not just leave a report without going over my findings with you personally."

"*Oui,* that is a better plan. I'll look forward to seeing you soon. Just call the shop to set an appointment." They shook hands and each turned in separate directions to take care of immediate concerns.

Just as Malcolm made his way out the front door, the antique dealer rushed out and called to him. "Monsieur, wait. Mademoiselle Martelli evidently dropped this leather portfolio. One of my staff found it as they were hauling the damaged *armoire* to the back room. Will you be seeing her this night or tomorrow? If not, I can send a messenger with it to the hotel where she's staying. In fact, do not worry. I have changed my mind. I want to send her flowers and a written apology for not seeing to her welfare after the accident, though according to the police, she wasn't injured, and she left under her own power. So, I will have the leather case delivered with the flowers. That is probably a much better idea."

"No, no. I'll be happy to take the portfolio to her, Simon," Malcolm insisted, taking the sleek little case from the antique dealer's hands. "She may need it before you can get it and the flowers delivered. I'm planning on seeing her tonight anyway."

And besides seeing her, he wanted to hear her narration on how lucky she was that both the uniformed *and* plain-clothes members of the police department were already in this vicinity at just the right time—staked out, and tipped off that someone of interest would be entering the antique house just after her arrival. Setting a trap was one thing, making herself the bait quite another.

Claire was unable to keep her teeth from chattering during the taxi ride back to the Saint-Germain. She wrapped her arms across her body in an attempt to uproot the bone-chilling fear that had taken possession of her when the heavy armoire came crashing down, barely missing her. But it was well worth it, *if* the police were able to catch Sean and take him into custody, thereby taking him out of her life forever.

She didn't think she could ever bring herself to explain to anyone why she'd done what she just did. But one thing Claire knew for sure, she was proud of herself for doing it.

Denver—Residence of E. Forde Chadwick

The clock on the night stand on the other side of Chad's bed read five o'clock. It was early, but Susan was used to getting up around this time when she stayed over. She usually waited until Chad was through showering before she went down to fix a light breakfast for the two of them. On week days, she would then head to her condo to shower and dress, usually getting into work around eight. But she didn't have to hurry this morning. The weekend was finally here.

Just now, she lay there thinking how happy she would be when Claire was no longer in the picture and Chad was single once again. She'd already planned on how she would get him to marry her after he was free to do so. The problem, as she identified it in her mind, was that she would only get a diminished portion of Chad's money if the divorce court decided on splitting his net worth down the middle, awarding half to Claire, as well as splitting the business itself between the two partners.

And Chad's "we'll just have to wait and see" didn't help, because Susan didn't want to share the wealth. She wanted it all. She'd even figured out a way she could be rid of Chad, in time. Then she'd have all the money. Satisfied her game plan would work, she plumped the down pillows behind her and patiently waited for Chad to get out of the shower.

Her cell phone pulsed on the night stand next to her. She frowned, not recognizing the number on the screen.

"Hello?" Susan said, tentatively. Thank God the shower was still running.

"Suze, it's me, listen up. Don't say my name over the phone, use the name you called me when we were kids. Okay? And this isn't my regular cell number. I'm using a *burner,* so I can throw it away after we talk. And one more thing, from now on, I don't want you to call *me.* I'll call *you.* Got that? There's been some trouble over here. I'm going to have to lay low for a few days. And I can't talk more that five minutes right now, Suze. Gotta keep moving. But what's happening back there?"

"Now hold on just a *freaking* minute. What's happening back here? I'll tell you what," she said somewhat shrilly, agitated by his announcements, but then determinedly lowered her voice.

"There's a warrant out for your arrest, Buddy boy. For breaking-and-entering, and theft. Once again, it's that stupid medallion you can't seem to keep around your neck. That's what. And, Lieutenant Owens is hot on your trail. He asked if I knew where you were. You've *got* to be more careful. He suspects you and is trying to tie you to the attack last March on you-know-who. Is . . . is the job taken care of?"

He cut her off. "No. The job's not over. Not yet. It's going to take a little longer than I thought. Ran into some unexpected problems."

"We're running out of time you know."

"Cripes, Suze, I'm aware of that. I just need to let things cool off a little. I'll get the job done. Don't worry."

But how can I get hold of you?"

"What did I just say? I'll call *you.*"

"But what if I need to reach you, Buddy?"

"Look, I've got to disconnect now. Don't know exactly when, but I'll keep in touch. Do *not* call me on my cell phone. You hear? Not for *any* reason. Bye for now."

Susan listened as the line went dead. Her nerves were so on-end from Sean's call, she almost wet the bed when a towel-wrapped Chad came out from the shower and slid into the empty space beside her.

"It's Saturday you know, sweet lips, and I'm up for twofers this morning," he whispered in her ear, not knowing it was the absolutely last thing Susan was up for.

Paris—Residence Saint-Germain

Malcolm commanded Penelope to a down position and then added "stay", before he rapped on the door to the Martelli's suite. "Good girl, Penny." He reached down and ruffled her ears.

When Abbie opened the door, the big wolfhound wagged her tail which sounded a bit like a muffled drum solo on the carpeted floor, though she stayed in the down command.

"Malcolm. How nice to see you," Abbie said, looking down at Penny with a questioning look on her face.

"Hello, Mrs. M. Is Claire around?"

"No, she's not here at the moment. Was she expecting you? She and Mandy were invited to dinner by that freelance writer Mandy is collaborating with for that guidebook. Ben and I were just about to go out and grab a bite. We'd enjoy your company, can you join us?"

"Thank you, but I'm on my way to the Saint-Germain kitchen. I've been invited by Emilie and Etienne to prepare one of my special one-dish recipes. And, to answer your question, no, Claire wasn't actually expecting me. One of the reasons I stopped by was to invite not only Claire, but all of you to a home-cooked meal, instead of eating out again. I guess I'm a little too late for Claire and Mandy, but would you and Ben care to join us? I bought enough food this afternoon to feed the whole French fleet.

"And I have excellent news concerning Marie-Claude. She is now officially on the road to recovery, completely out of the catatonic state. She's on a course of medication under her doctor's supervision. If her system handles the medicine in good order, she might be allowed to come home for a day or two on a pass basis, but will be expected to return to the clinic to finish the full course of therapy. How about that?"

"Oh, that's wonderful news, Malcolm. Isn't it, dear?" She said, turning to Ben, who was standing behind her in the late afternoon shadows of the room. "I told Ben about the Marie-Claude episode," she explained to Malcolm. "I hope you don't mind."

Ben came into the doorway. "Sounds like you've had your hands full these last few days, Malcolm. Frankly, I'd love to have dinner here in the old manse's kitchen. It would be an experience I might not have another chance to partake in. What do you say, Abbie? And I promise that Malcolm and I won't talk shop *all* evening."

"Looks like we'll join you and Emilie and Etienne, Malcolm. You go ahead, Ben and I will be right behind. I want to leave a note for Claire and Mandy where we'll be. And I volunteer to be your *sous chef*, Malcolm. Just tell me what you need chopped, diced or sliced. I'm plenty experienced."

"Thanks, I'll take you up on that, Mrs. M. Oh, I almost forgot one thing. I've trained Penelope here to guard the door to your suite. Thought I'd bring her here after you're all in each night, then come and get her early in the morning. I'd rather Claire didn't know about it right now. But it would make me feel better with O'Malley still free and roaming at will, especially after the incident at the antique house this afternoon."

The way Abbie's face drained of color told him that Claire hadn't shared today's episode with her mother. "Uh, oh, guess you didn't know? I promise to tell you the whole story while I'm fixing dinner, if you wouldn't mind waiting till then, since I can assure you, she's fine. I was there. He missed. Again. But he's still on the loose. The police were there in force, though he seems to be adept at eluding capture, just like in the other instances.

"And would you give this to Claire for me?" he said handing Abbie the leather portfolio she'd left at Simon's in her hasty leave-taking. "She, uh, dropped it at the antique shop today, and I told Simon I'd return it to her."

Abbie forced a smile, putting on a semi-convincing stalwart persona. "Okay, I'll give the portfolio to her, Malcolm. And I'll wait until dinner to hear the whole story. But I also want you to know how much I appreciate your thoughtfulness in offering your Penelope to guard our door through the night. But I won't tell Claire, if you prefer she not know about this." She bent down to pat the big dog's head. "We'll get along just fine, won't we, Penny? And I'm going to make sure you get some treats to keep your strength up."

"Mrs. M., not to be unappreciative, but Pen here has to watch her weight, don't you big girl? She works best for a pat on the head once in a while. But you probably won't see her, as she will be late coming on duty, and early going off her shift. She's happy to do it for all of you, though you've witnessed how taken she is with Claire."

After being introduced to Penny, Ben gave her some attention also. "Malcolm, how will she know whether someone walking down the corridor is friend or foe? For instance this O'Malley person, what will she do if he were stupid enough to come to the door?"

"Good question, Ben. You see, Penny and I have run into Shamrock Man on the stairway a couple of times without knowing him as the bad guy. Penny sensed it however. The fur on the back of her neck stood on end, and she growled at him. So, she can identify him from his smell. Penny is very good at identifying people as good or bad by smell. I've never seen her get it wrong. Besides, I seriously doubt whether any patron of the hotel will be out and about during the time of night she will be on duty. Penny won't attack someone just for walking past, though I am planning to leave my door ajar so that I can hear anything that might sound as if she's in her protective mode. And I'm a very light sleeper. But it's up to you, Mrs. M., Ben. What do you think?"

Abbie took Ben's hand. "Nothing to think about. We agree Penny should be hired as night guard, right dear? I for one, trust your wolfhound's abilities to protect Claire and the rest of us during the night. So, even though it will be a heavy burden on you, Malcolm, I'm all for it. When can she start?"

7

Day Five

Paris—The Saint-Germain garden

"Wouldn't you know it . . . the beautiful and mysterious lady in the rose hat. Actually off-stage and without an audience, are we? Or are you about to resume your role as bait again? Will the Saint-Germain *jardin* come alive with plain-clothes police costumed as gardeners, or maybe as gnomes hiding out among the flower beds? Good God, I've been around you Martelli's too long. I'm beginning to talk in questions, just like the three of you."

"And a good morning to you, too, Malcolm. And Mademoiselle Penelope, of course. Do I detect a measure of sarcasm and disapproval in that tone?" Claire put down her book as the big dog came up to where she relaxed on the cushioned chaise with her ankle propped up and covered by an ice bag. She absently scratched Penny's ears while looking up at the figure lounging against the gnarled trunk, his right arm thrown around one of the heavily blossoming limbs of her favorite tree overhanging the terrace.

"I would have to say it's more like disappointment, with a little frustration thrown in."

"Let me get this straight, you're disappointed and frustrated with *me*?

"Claire, I'm trying my best to understand where you're coming from, and quite honestly, even as a psychiatrist I'm failing miserably." He unwound his length from the ancient tree and moved around to sit on the chaise next to hers.

She studied him thoughtfully. "Well, how hard can it be? I'm willing to take a stab at listening to *your* problems if you want to be the patient. Do you remember Lucy's sign in the Peanuts comic strip? 'The psychiatrist is in—five cents'? Cough up a nickel and I'm *in*."

He reached into his pocket and pulled out some coins. "Here," he smiled as he handed her a small brass coin, "will the French equivalent of a nickel's worth, five centimes, be acceptable, Doctor?"

"Yes, Mr. Sutherland, that will be sufficient to cover our first session," she said, taking the coin. "Now, just lie back, close your eyes, and relax. Tell me . . . when did you first notice these feelings of disappointment and frustration?"

"Well the frustration part began about the time I met an American woman in Paris. At the Residence Saint-Germain on the Left Bank, to be exact. That was perhaps only a handful of days ago, although it seems much longer when I think about it. The disappointment part comes later."

"Go on."

"Well, Doc, it has to do with this same lady. She's a very special lady. Bright, tasteful and cultured, unusually independent, brave beyond belief, and she's been blessed with perfect genes, hence her gorgeous eyes and hair. All in all, she is the total woman. And totally stunning. Or like the Yanks would say . . . 'the whole enchilada'.

"And according to the portfolio she left at Simon's yesterday, she's also very creative and capable in business. Now, you would think with all these glowing attributes, she would have the world, or at least *her* world, at her command. Unfortunately, it seems she's in a predicament that requires her to accept help from others around her. Physical protection, for sure, and perhaps aid in restoring her emotional balance, as well. But she's keeping those who would readily help her at arm's length."

Malcolm opened his eyes and looked over at Claire, who was looking away, toward the fall of white wisteria covering the stone wall. A tear rolled down her cheek.

"Can you help me?" He phrased his words slowly. "Because I really do need your assessment of the situation, my very dear Doctor. You see, this lady has captivated me. From the very moment I untangled her and Penny from the floor, and picked her up in my arms, I've fallen under her spell. You see, I just discovered that I'm in love with her." His heartfelt words sounded a quiet conviction as he moved to sit on the edge of his chaise, facing her. He took her hand. "What should I do now, Doc?"

"Oh, Malcolm, you *can't* love me. I'm a total wreck. You deserve someone who is as steady and strong as you are. Not a wretched wimp with hang-ups, who is afraid to go to sleep at night because of demon nightmares. Who looks over her shoulder for the bogeyman. And, to be perfectly honest, who really isn't capable of loving again, that is, fully in every respect, until she can put a failed marriage and the past seven years in order. Besides, it's way too dangerous for you to be anywhere near me. The so-called *accidents* Shamrock Man dreams up could backfire and then you, Mandy, Mom, and even Ben could get hurt in the process—just because all of you have so unselfishly offered to be there for me. I couldn't live with myself if something terrible were to happen. Besides, if Sean gets his way, I may not be around very much longer, anyway. So it's a moot point, isn't it?" Having said that, Claire burst into tears.

Malcolm moved over to her lounger and gathered her into his arms. With his chin against her tousled curls, he cuddled her close, rocking her gently while she sobbed against his chest. He held her, soothing her while the weeping turned into sniffling, then just an occasional quiver. She sat up and pulled away from him, embarrassed that he'd seen her lose control.

She searched the pockets of her hoodie for something to mop the bucket of tears that had spilled from her eyes, tracking down the front of his white shirt.

"Oh, now look what I've done to your shirt. Sorry, Malcolm. I don't know what came over me to break down like that. See, I told you I'm a wimp."

"Here, use this." He offered her a folded handkerchief, embroidered with a crest and his initials. "Don't worry about the shirt, it'll wash. And, Claire, I never again want to hear you apologize for allowing yourself to release some of the emotional pain that you've kept locked inside, behind that stout-hearted front you put on for your family and my benefit. Crying it out is a good way for you to be able to move forward from this point. And, one more thing. I promise not to say any more about my feelings for you, until we get the Shamrock mess cleaned up. After that, you're fair game."

Claire knew her eyes were swollen and red. But she turned toward him and smiled anyway. "I'm truly honored by your declaration, Malcolm, but please understand that right now, I can't promise to reciprocate your feelings. I value your friendship, and maybe that's the first step in loving someone. At this point, I'm not able to take that next step until I find myself again. I need to determine answers to the why's in my life. And, obviously that necessitates getting closure regarding my failure of a marriage and my feelings regarding Chad. And it's not fair to keep you dangling while I sort out my life."

"Fair or not, I'm in it for the long haul, Claire."

Totally immersed in trying to have him understand her current state of mind, Claire unconsciously placed her hand on his arm. "And I'm damned tired of being a victim in whatever game Sean O'Malley is playing. But I'm no longer afraid. You see the person who is trying to kill me now has a face. I *know* him. Believe me when I say I was scared spitless when I didn't know who was behind all of this. And now it's not so terrifying. Malcolm, I must take an active roll in my own protection. As much as I appreciate you wanting to help me, no one else can do this for me.

"Well, how about a helping hand? I'm here for you, Claire. Get used to it. If I can help you through the rough spots, why not take a chance? And I'm truly a good listener. Sometimes it's all that's needed. To talk it out. And I intend to be a damned good bodyguard."

"Don't you see, Malcolm? *I don't need a body guard, and I can't accept your help in that respect.*" She emphasized each word to make her point. While inwardly, she struggled to hide the fact that her renegade body was making *its* need known in the most convincing way as a warm rush invaded her senses, leading downward to her essential core.

Whether I do or don't need him, she thought, I'm not going there.

"Claire, I'm asking you to listen to where I'm coming from. I really don't see why you think you can't accept my help. It's not every day that the woman I love is in mortal danger. It's only natural to protect the person who is the object of that love. And, don't tell me you're afraid I'll get hurt, or worse, in one of the Shamrock's schemes. I'm a big boy. I can take care of myself, as well as you. Like it or not, I will protect you. So you might as well accept it. Please trust me, Claire."

He gently lifted her chin, looking into her eyes, then leaned forward and placed a soft kiss on her lips. She leaned into his kiss as her body went rogue on her. So much for not going there, she thought as he pulled her onto his lap. His arms tightened around her, pressing her very willing body to his chest. He deepened the kiss.

"Oh, there you are, Claire." Abbie said, pausing at the open French doors before she walked out onto the terrace after seeing that her daughter and Malcolm were oblivious to anyone and everything, except themselves. She waited while the couple broke apart and returned to a semblance of normality. "Just look at that gorgeous wisteria trailing over the fence," she said, pointing it out to Ben, who had tactfully lagged a bit in following her out to the garden.

"I didn't know where you'd gotten off to, Claire. You've been gone quite a long time. Had I known you were with

Malcolm, I wouldn't have worried. That was certainly a wonderful dinner you prepared for us last night, chef. I must get your recipe. Do you give it out?"

"Hi, Mrs. M., Ben." Damn, he thought, willing his breathing back into a normal rhythm while trying to focus his mind back to reality. "Er . . . glad you enjoyed it. I'll write down the ingredients for you. It's a fairly easy meal to make."

Abbie glanced at Claire's face, seeing the red swollen eyes. "Are you ready to come back upstairs, dear? Ben wants to take us to that *brasserie* where he got that delicious 'take out' the other night. You probably want to change into something a little less casual. And, Mandy isn't back from showing that writer the places she's scouted for him to take a look-see for the travel guide. I thought we'd leave her a note and invite her to bring him along."

"Can you join us, Malcolm? The women have us outnumbered, so we men have to stick together. Besides, I'd like to talk to you about the symptoms that might make identifying psychosis in juveniles easier to diagnose. That's part of your field, right?" Ben queried, coming forward to shake hands.

"Uh, sure. I'd be happy to join you. And, shop talk or not, I've always had a keen interest in that subject." Malcolm gave Claire a wry look, finding her watching him over her mother's shoulder, while nodding at something Abbie was saying.

Malcolm turned to Ben. "Are you planning on an early dinner? It will take me about thirty minutes to shower and change. Claire may need a little longer though. How about if you two go ahead and enjoy a private cocktail or two. Then I'll wait to escort Claire, and we'll meet you at the bistro in about an hour. Does that work?"

The others nodded in agreement, and all four headed toward the interior of the hotel just as Etienne came to the French doors with a message in his hand. He bowed, saying, "Madame, Mademoiselle . . . I have good news, and not so good news."

"I think we would definitely prefer hearing the good news, Etienne," Claire suggested.

"*Oui,* Mademoiselle. The good news is that my *Cousine*, Marie-Claude, will be home tonight on what *Tante* Emilie calls a pass. She is to return to Doctor Marchand's clinic in two days. Then *Tante* says to tell all of you that she will prepare a wonderful celebration dinner on tomorrow evening. She hopes you will all attend."

"What wonderful news, Etienne."

"I'm so happy for Marie-Claude, and all of you."

"Tell Madame Fontaine we will be honored to attend the celebration."

Etienne nodded at them all in turn. "You have all been so kind, and so generous with your time. You are to be celebrated as well.

"And now, for the not-so-good news. Mademoiselle Man-dee called just several minutes ago, from the airport, and asked me to give this message. She is returning to the States tonight, because of a meeting in the morning with the publisher of the guidebook she is working on. She said to say to you that she only had time for one very quick call, if she was to catch her flight. Mademoiselle Man-dee said to tell you she was running? And that you would understand. She will call you from New York, after she has met with the publisher. She did also say that when she couldn't get hold of either of you while she was traveling in the taxi to the airport that she left a message on Mademoiselle Claire's phone.

Abbie and Claire looked at each other, the shock on their respective faces quite evident to Malcolm and Ben.

"What in the name of Saint Michael is going on? Claire, did you know anything about this?" Abbie wavered, as she tried to process the news. Ben caught hold of her to steady her. With Malcolm's help, they got her to a lounge chair. "Claire? Tell me what you know. It's just not like Miranda to go off like this without talking to either of us, personally."

Claire put her arm around her mother's shoulders and gave her a little squeeze.

"Mom, I didn't know anything about her taking the night flight back to the States until just now, same as you. But after seeing the way that Kincaid character treated her last night at dinner, I'm really not surprised. What an arrogant ass. He thinks he's such a hot shot because his articles, *and* picture, *and* byline, appear in all the major travel publications. The only thing she told me was in the Ladies' Room at the restaurant. Evidently, he and Mandy got into it over a taxi of all things, the day before yesterday . . . the Notre Dame day. And, he's holding the incident against her as she evidently bested him and stole the taxi out from under his very macho New York nose. Of course, neither of them knew who the other was the day of the incident. He only had the name of the person he was to meet, as M. Martelli, who, for some reason, he thought was a man. The way Mandy tells it is that it wasn't until the next morning, when they met in the lobby, that he took off those dark glasses, and then, of course, she recognized him. And that's when he began needling her.

Abbie gave Claire a whatever-are-you-prattling-on-about look. "I truly don't know how any of that taxi business could possibly tie in with the publisher demanding she be in New York for a meeting tomorrow morning. I know why she couldn't get a hold of me as I forgot to charge my phone last night. It's dead. What about yours, Claire?"

"I don't have it with me. I left it in the suite. It's charged though. And, Mom, the tie-in is that Neal Ross Kincaid probably threw Mandy under the bus with the publisher because of the affront to his ego over her winning the taxi contest. He probably said something to the effect that he can't work with her because she won't cooperate with him. Or, perhaps he insinuated that she's not a big enough name as a photographer. I'm afraid to say it, but my thought is that the publisher called her back to New York to break the contract because of Kincaid's demands. And, if so, he's also very likely to tell her if she comes back to Paris, it'll be on her dime. Bye, bye expense account."

Ben, who had been standing behind Abbie's chair, listening to the conversation between the two, bent and kissed the top of Abbie's head. "Don't worry, my dear, I can help. Claire, where did you leave your phone? I know it's in your suite somewhere, but exactly where? You can't go hopping up those three flights of stairs with your ankle just beginning to heal. And, Abbie is still a bit shaky. So, it's between Malcolm and me. What do you say, old man? You may have to carry Claire up those three flights when we get back from dinner. So, I'm volunteering to go up and retrieve the phone."

Malcolm nodded. "I hear you, Ben. But I can do both, you know . . . carry Claire *and* retrieve her phone."

"I have a marvelous idea that will solve all our problems," Abbie said coming out of her funk, and saying it twice to be heard over the men's discussion. "Thank you, Ben, and Malcolm, for your kind offers, but why don't we all go up? We need to change for dinner anyway. No sense in someone going up to get the phone, bring it back down, go back up to dress, and, well, you get the picture. Except for you, Ben. Are you going back to your hotel to change? You look fine, you know. No need to get a taxi and all that entails."

"Well, actually I'm not going back to my hotel. I have a little announcement," said Ben, nodding at Etienne who had been standing to the side, while listening to the Americans and the Englishman discuss who was going up and down. "Tell them, Etienne."

"Yes, *Docteur*. You see there was a smallish suite with a parlor, and a bedroom and bath that became vacant just this afternoon. I mentioned it to *Docteur Ben*, here . . ."

"And all things considered," Ben cut in, "I decided to take him up on it. I love this old mansion. I'd rather be here with Abbie and the rest of you. And, of course, it will save a lot of back and forth time, as I'll be in Paris another couple days," he said, giving Abbie a special look.

"That's great, Ben. I'm glad you'll be with us," Claire said, smiling at the only man her mother had ever shown interest in since their father's passing.

"Well, Claire, besides being happy about staying here, I thought maybe I could help Malcolm keep an eye out for that demented piece of trash who's been stalking you and causing those so-called accidents. My rooms are on the third floor, so I'll be watching and listening to anything that doesn't seem normal. We'll catch this Shamrock person."

"*Oui, Docteur,*" Etienne said in agreement. And, I also am watching for this very bad person, Mademoiselle Claire."

"You are all being very kind, but please, I don't want to spoil anyone's vacation . . . Ben. Or, cause anyone to neglect their work . . . Etienne. And, Malcolm, we've had this discussion just this afternoon, and you are aware of my feelings. I refuse to be a burden, and I definitely refuse to act like one. Enough of this, shall we start up? I for one am very curious about the message Mandy left on my phone."

"Oh, yes. I'm so anxious for Mandy's sake. I certainly would like to hear her message with my own ears, if you wouldn't mind, Claire. You can tell so much from a person's voice what's not being said out loud. Kind of like reading between the lines. And unfortunately, she's going to be all alone when she finds out why the publisher called her back to New York. I just know its bad news. You don't insist that someone jump on a plane and travel for eight hours across an ocean, just to have a meeting, unless something drastic is about to happen.

Claire gave her mother a hug. "Don't worry, Mom. I know Mandy. At first, she'll be devastated if we're right about what the meeting with the publisher is about. But, perhaps it was meant to be. Kincaid called her Mademoiselle Destiny all evening during dinner, and also kept referring to something about fate. I didn't ask, just thought he was needling her with some personal barb having to do with the taxi incident. But you know what? He just may be the catalyst that propels Mandy upward. And, *her* destiny may include fame and fortune to a degree that quite possibly could overshadow his. Wouldn't that frost him?"

Prior to dinner, Claire had turned on the speaker element on her cell and pushed the voice mail button to play the message for all to hear. Now, hours later, Claire and Abbie were finally alone in their suite.

Claire showed Abbie which buttons to push to replay Mandy's message. And, tired from the emotional trauma of the day, Claire went to bed, asking her mother once she was finished listening to the message, to recharge the phone by plugging it into the cord which was already plugged into the outlet. Abbie promised to do so, but felt she needed to listen to her youngest daughter's voice just one more time. She pushed the voice mail button on.

"Hi Claire. It's Mandy. I'm leaving you and Mom this rather long message as I tried both your phones a little earlier with no luck. I'm certain you've already gotten the message I left with Etienne, just as I'm certain it came as a shock to both of you. Anyway, I'm hoping this will update you as to why I'm in a taxi on my way to the airport right now, to get on a plane heading to New York. Unfortunately, there was no time to come back to the Saint-Germain and tell you in person what's going down. I've left straightaway from today's photo shoot, so I can get on that overnight flight knowing I will have to make a run for it as it is. But, nothing new. Right? So, I will try to explain.

"The publisher of the guidebook who contracted me to shoot the Paris photos called me as I was just finishing up my session today. He didn't mince words. Although he did stop just short of coming right out and telling me he's breaking my contract, but I got that message from what he didn't say. I'm pretty sure I already know what's about to take place when I get to the meeting at his office tomorrow morning. He's going to tell me that Neal Ross Kincaid has complained about my attitude, and has also expressed the desire to team with a known photographer he's worked with in the past. And, since he thinks Neal Ross has the name readers will follow on the pages of his guidebook, he will honor that request. It will be

179

Neal Ross, not me, who will find out-of-the-way places of interest in Paris and it will be his photographer who will be taking the shots for the new By-Ways feature of the book.

"I can hear it now: "Thank you very much for understanding, Ms. Martelli. There is really no alternative for me to take in this case."

"Well, guess what? I don't care to work with Mr. Neal Ross Kincaid either. I've seen places in Paris in the few days I've been there that are off the beaten track, and would photo beautifully, and I know I can find more. So, here's what I'm planning on doing, if I'm right about my hunch. I'm going to contact some other travel publishers while I'm in New York, and show them some of my Paris shots. I've got my memory cards with me—nothing else, like clothes—just camera equipment and memory cards. Anyway, I might be able to sell the idea of doing an on-going feature in a monthly travel publication, with myself as the photographer or maybe the writer-journeyer as well. I'll try to push the concept from a personal point of view, for the adventurous traveler who has already seen the major tourist attractions. And not just Paris, but other interesting places, wherever they're located.

"I don't know how long this will take, but I feel I must try to get another publisher before I come back to Paris. And I realize it's a long shot. Hope you understand.

"Anyway, I'll be staying at my friend Jesse's place while I'm in New York, so not to worry. Send me prayers and luck. Love you both. Take care of yourselves. Claire, I want to hear that the police have caught the Shamrock when I call after the meeting. I feel like I've let you down. Please be careful and stay safe. I'm certain Malcolm is standing by. Talk to you tomorrow. Bye for now."

Paris—In a dark room

Claire forced her eyes open, feeling the steady vibration of her phone resting on the pillow next to her head. Why was her phone on the pillow? She didn't remember putting it there when she went to bed. Since she'd been in Paris, she normally plugged it in to recharge the battery at night and set it on the table between the beds. And from what she could see in the semi-darkness, the room was totally unfamiliar. Intuition told her she should stay still until she could recognize where she was, and why the phone was on her pillow. A chill prickled up her spine causing the fine hairs on the back of her neck to stand up.

She thought she was alone, although she was fairly certain there had been someone else in the room when she fell asleep. But who? Mandy was in New York. She was fairly certain it wasn't Abbie. Even as she dredged her memory, there was a blank where the face should have been.

The vibration stopped. The message on the lighted screen read "Missed Call." Keeping herself as still as possible, she looked at the number listed there. She didn't have a clue if it was someone she knew, or someone she didn't want to know. What she did know was that the number wasn't in her call directory, or a name would have come up. And then came the beep telling her someone had left a message.

She'd just worked up the courage to listen to the missive when she heard what sounded like scratching from the other side of the door. Claire cautiously sat up on the bed, listening intently, hoping to identify the noise and what was causing it. Just as suddenly as it started, the clawing noise stopped. There was only silence in the room, as well as from the other side of the door. Quietly and carefully she made her way through the gloom to what she hoped was the door, where she'd heard the scratching noises. She painstakingly turned the knob so that the noise wouldn't transfer through it. The door wouldn't open. She turned the knob in both directions and pushed, then pulled. Nothing. She felt along the edge of the door to see if there was a separate key lock or dead bolt. Again, nothing. She was a prisoner.

Afraid to make any noise lest whatever had clawed at the door would hear, she returned to the bed where her phone's small aperture glowed. The only light in the room. She tried walking outward from the side of the bed, holding her phone in front of her, to see what was in the room that might help her in some way. When she hit her shin on what she thought was a second bed, she almost cried out, but stopped herself in time.

Why couldn't she remember either the room or how she'd come to be there? She speculated that Sean had somehow found her alone and had used some kind of a knock-out agent. Then kidnapped her. Already shaken, she was now just the slightest fraction away from full panic.

I need to get out of here. Before he comes back to finish the job with some new hellish 'accident' he's dreamed up. Her mind scattered in a myriad of possibilities. Of course, why didn't I think of it right away? I'll use my phone to call for help. What an idiot!

The only excuse she allowed herself for this oversight was to suspect that whatever substance he'd used to knock her out was still in her system.

Picking up what she now considered her lifeline, she took care to precisely dial her mother's number. A woman answered, but it wasn't Abbie. An impatient voice told her she must have the wrong number. With shaky hands, she quickly punched in the number for Mandy's mobile, and got a similar response, but in a man's voice this time.

What's happening? This is really weirding me out.

Afraid time was running out and she would soon see who or what was on the other side of the door, she sat on the bed, head hanging, wondering who she could call next. And whether every phone number in her list of contacts would have similar results as the ones she'd just made to her family. And quite simply, why had she neglected to put the Saint-Germain's number into her list of contacts? Or ask Malcolm for his mobile number? But she hadn't.

Claire finally pushed the quick-dial number she'd added to her contacts when she'd arrived in Paris—the SOS English language crisis line, the only recourse remaining to her. She hung up when no one answered on the tenth ring, questioning herself as to why she hadn't found out the hours the line was available. Besides, how could she tell any of them where she was, when *she* didn't know?

Desperate to find another solution, the darkness that permeated the room was relieved by the merest hint of light. Taken by surprise, she turned roundabout to look in all directions, seeing obscure shapes as dark shadows silhouetted against the soft light that seemed to emanate from no particular source. She peered into the faint glow, attempting to identify the objects in the room, hoping they would give her a clue as to where she was. Or how to escape. The rectangular shapes of several windows became apparent on one wall of the room, however there was no light coming into the room from outside the bare glass. Instead, all she saw was solid black, unrelieved by moonlight, street lights, headlights, or even neon signs.

Claire puzzled over this fact, as she gingerly made her way toward the window wall, around the shadowy form of the bed she had grazed her shin on just a few minutes ago. Although she couldn't be certain in the dim light, when she moved past the bed, she thought she saw what appeared to be the still shape of a body, lying on top. She froze, swearing inwardly that the form had moved slightly. Goose bumps raised on her arms. Carefully watching the dark outline atop the bed, she rocketed past as if demons pursued her. She made it to the closest of the windows and couldn't help glancing back over her shoulder. But all was still. And quiet. Obtrusively quiet.

Reaching her arm out, Claire touched the black emptiness of the glass with a shaky hand. It felt cold and clammy as if it sweated. She put her face to the glass, squinting to see through the blackness for some sign of movement or light. It was as if there was nothing but a vacuous void beyond. Despair gripped her. Futile tracks marked the glass where her fingers limply slid down the blank surface.

Her spirit became as lethargic as her body. Gotta get a grip, she thought, leaning against the glass, feeling the window sill pushing against her knee. She knew it was dangerous to give in to those kind of feelings. She slowly dragged herself up to one knee that once again came in close contact with the sill.

That's it, she thought . . . the window sill. She knew that, usually, when a sill jutted out as far as this one did, it meant that the window was traditional, and traditional meant casement window. It opened by sliding the bottom portion upward, over the fixed portion of the upper glass.

Energized once more, she quickly glanced around her, looking for something to stand on. In the gloom, she could just make out that the ceilings were high in the room, and the sizable window came close to matching in height. She wasn't tall enough to reach the top of the lower window which, if luck were with her, would have a lock on the top of the wood frame that encased the glass.

There appeared to be the form of a table and chairs a few feet away from where she stood. Groping her way, she dragged one of the chairs to the window, and climbed onto the seat. With her arm outstretched, she reached to where she could feel the top frame of the lower window. She ran her hand along the center area at the top.

Nothing. Her disappointment was dizzying, almost sending her crashing to the floor. She straightened her back and stretched up once again, this time exploring the whole top of the frame. Her fingers came in contact with a metal lever. She almost swooned in delight. There was no center lock. Instead, the window fabricator had installed *two* locks, each one splitting the top width of the window into thirds.

Of course, she reasoned. One lock wasn't sufficient for this size window. This must be a very old building. Windows just aren't built with this kind of craftsmanship these days. Live and learn. The thought brought a smile to her face, remembering how Abbie always turned it around—learn and live. Claire actually preferred it that way. Especially now. Thinking about her family gave her the extra impetus she needed to find a way out of the room before Sean came back for her. Hopefully, the window would prove to be her ticket out.

She pushed upward with both hands clenching the top of the window frame. It wouldn't budge. Stuck fast. She almost cried in her desperation, but forced herself to calm down.

Probably hasn't been opened in a very long time, she considered. And, having been coated through the years with layer upon layer of paint didn't help.

Turning over in her mind the possibility of prying it open, she scouted around for something to use as a crowbar. Her eye fell on what looked to be a large bucket with a handle. She felt the handle. It was made of metal and seemed to be heavy enough for her purpose, if she could get it loose from the lower portion of the wooden bucket.

For the first time since she woke and found herself a captive of the room, Claire realized she'd lucked out. The bucket was old, made of staves of wood, encircled by several metal bands to keep the wood slats together. The wood had dried out sometime in the past from lack of moisture. She was able to pull the handle off with just a sharp tug and straighten it out by stepping down on it with all her weight.

Using the handle as a crow bar, she attempted to work the bottom frame loose from the sill. No luck. It was unyielding.

Got. To. Get. It. Open. She focused on the thought, knowing the window just might be her only way out.

Standing once again on the chair, she strained from the center of her being, using all of her concentration and force to push up on the top rail. And, little by little, it inched upward.

When she first felt a breeze coming through the opening she'd made at the bottom, she breathed easier. The air in the room was stagnant and smelled of must and old wood. And, although she still didn't know *where* she was, she now knew the room she was in was used as a storage area for odds and ends of furniture. Was this some backroom at the Saint-Germain?

Claire stopped for a moment to rest her arms. She got down from the chair and peeked out through the three-inch space she'd been able to achieve thus far as an opening at the bottom. What she'd thought was a black void through the glass, was really black paint in a heavy layer on the backside of the glass itself. Although the vacuous space was still dark as it was nighttime, it now glowed with streaks and spots of street lights, headlights, and neon signs. She would need to lift the window further to see what floor she was on, but could already see it was not street level.

Please . . . she prayed. Let it be no higher than the second floor.

But she was still in Paris. The lights outlining the Eiffel Tower sparkled in the distance.

She wondered whether her mother or Mandy were even aware that she'd been kidnapped. Were they looking for her? Or did they think she was with Malcolm? And was it possible that he was already searching for her at this very moment? She pondered these questions uneasily. What if no one realized she was missing, until it was too late?

Claire climbed back up on the chair and redoubled her efforts. Just need about a foot more and hopefully I can make it out of here, she kept telling herself.

But she was interrupted in her work, startled by a noise coming from the other side of the locked door. The scratching had resumed. She jumped down from the chair, panic washing over her. After the attack last March, Claire knew she'd been letting fear get the best of her, even though that time she'd been able to choke out her assailant in a *jujitsu* move. Though she'd trained in the martial arts, she knew the element of surprise was all too important when it came to facing down an attacker. Especially for a woman who couldn't compete with a man when it came to weight and muscle in a stand-and-fight encounter. And if there were a gun or knife involved, the cards were definitely stacked in favor of the person with the weapon.

She concentrated on breathing slowly and deeply, determined to confront her phobic apprehensions head on. By dint of sheer willpower, she refused to allow them to control her, jacking up her confidence level considerably. She picked up one of the wood staves from the now defunct bucket and began to make her way to the door.

186

Okay, Sean, if you're out there, bring it on.

The obstacle course of left-over furnishings caused her to move cautiously in the dim light, steering a path around shadowy forms indiscernible as to their usage or identity. Claire came to the vague shape contoured much like a small bed that she had knocked into on her earlier exploration of the room.

She stopped short on hearing a low animal-like sound coming from within the bundled semblance of a body laying atop the mattress, the same dark silhouette that she'd sworn had stirred slightly on her way to the window. Its position shifted again. In the same instant, a deep red glow lit the shadows filling the room. A crimson light swirled around the ragged form. An iron grasp locked onto her wrist.

"Claire."

Her name came out of the form in a guttural whisper, not fully human.

"You must pay," continued the hoarse whisper.

For just a second, Claire froze in place, mesmerized by the red chaos eddying around her. Now she came to life, realizing it was now or never. She tried to pull away, all the while hitting at her captor with the wooden stave that she still held in her other hand. Again and again she struck.

Obviously enjoying her dilemma, snorts came from the ragged form in what sounded like a bass version of a hyena's laugh. She was pulled down onto the bed, her wrist suddenly released. But before she could extricate herself, boney hands enfolded her neck, slowly and deliberately applying more and more pressure. She tried to scream. Nothing came out but a pain-filled croak.

She was strangling.

There was a rushing in her ears. All sounds in the room seemed to be coming through a wind tunnel. Except for the increasing uproar at the door. For some reason those sounds turned into a furor of extreme proportions. The scratching became wild clawing, now intermingled with clamorous pounding and barking. Shockingly, she heard her name shouted over and over, as from a great distance.

The hands suddenly disappeared from around her neck. She was able to draw in air once again, but her chest hurt from the effort. She lay on the bed, gasping. The ragged form became a slack and shapeless bundle of rags.

The outer door to her private hell burst open. Something grabbed her shoulder and shook her.

"No . . . no . . ." she protested, fighting off the hand on her shoulder, her whole being focused on making her way to the open door. Anywhere away from this new threat would do.

"Please. Let me go." She stumbled up from the bed and collapsed on the floor.

"Claire. Claire, it's all right now, honey. Just one of your nightmares. Wake up, Claire. You're safe now."

Claire opened her eyes to see both her mother and Malcolm leaning over her. She was on the floor, next to the bed, in her striped silk pajamas. The sheets were wound around her legs, and beads of perspiration dotted her forehead. She looked at them, staring vacantly, but didn't speak. She turned her head in both directions to see the rest of the room, but there was no outward sign of recognition that she was in the bedroom she shared with Mandy, in their suite at the Residence Saint-Germain.

They untangled her from the sheets, and Malcolm picked her up gently. He laid her on top of the bed and covered her with the light weight feather comforter.

"There, that's better, Claire honey," Abbie said. "Will you please sit here a minute, Malcolm, while I get her some water? I don't want to leave her alone."

"Of course. I'll keep watch. Besides, I want to see if I can get her to come back from wherever she was in her nightmare. She's still in a half-dream state. I don't think she's totally aware that she's no longer dreaming." He sat down on the side of the bed, and smoothed the wayward curls out of her face, then took her hand.

"Claire, its Malcolm. I'm right here with you, babe. It is definitely okay for you to come home now. Abbie and I are here. Even Penny. We'll keep you safe. Come back to us, Claire."

Abbie returned to the room carrying a tray with a glass and a basin of water, and towels over one arm. She placed the tray and towels on the bedside table and pulled up a chair.

"Hi honey, its mama. I have some nice cold water for you to sip, and a cool cloth for your forehead. Can you sit up?"

Abbie looked across the bed at Malcolm. "Could you lift her up a little, please? Just lean her up against these pillows. I think she'll be more comfortable with her head elevated."

Abbie adjusted the pillows as he lifted Claire and settled her so that she lay with her head higher than the rest of her body. "There, honey. Isn't that better? Now, I'll just put this cold compress on your forehead." She placed the folded washcloth so that it covered the area on Claire's forehead that was already swelling from hitting her head when she collapsed onto the floor. Wringing the water from a second washcloth, she began lightly patting her daughter's face and arms with it.

Claire began to tremble when she felt the cold water on her heated skin. She looked up, recognized her mother, and whispered, "Mom, I'm cold . . . so cold."

Malcolm jumped up and grabbed a thin blanket lying across the foot of Mandy's bed.

"I'll be right back, Mrs. M. I can heat the blanket up in the oven in my quarters. Send Penny for me if you need something before I get back." And with a look on his face that read his world was right side up again—Claire was back among the living. He raced from the room, commanding the big wolfhound to "stay" in her position on the floor at the end of Claire's bed.

Malcolm stooped to pick up the telegram lying on the floor just inside his door. He threw it unopened on the wooden counter, the prep area of his small kitchen, before turning the knob for the oven to 'on', and selecting a low temperature. He re-folded the blanket so it would fit in the limited space inside the totally dated but uncommonly serviceable appliance.

While he waited for the blanket to warm, he decided he was interested enough to open the telegram. He wasn't sure what he was the most curious about: *who* the telegram was from, or *why* send a telegram in the first place, when the sender could simply call him on his mobile instead of going to the trouble and expense a telegram incurred. He decided the only way to find the answers to these questions was to read it.

"Arriving Paris on Monday. Stop. Pick up at Gare St-Lazare station at three in the afternoon. Stop. Bringing a surprise. Stop. Signed: A.W."

Malcolm shook his head, musing aloud, "Should have known. A.W . . . Anna Worthington. Or, more formally, the Countess of Rosemore Grange. What scheme have you cooked up now, Grandmother? And what problems are you bringing with you? I wonder," he questioned softly, folding the telegram and setting it back on the counter. He opened the door to the oven, finding the blanket heated to a pleasant warmth. Turning off the oven, he headed back down the corridor to the Martelli's suite, blanket in hand.

"Oh, that feels so good, Malcolm," Claire sighed, reveling in the warmth of the blanket snugged around her, and feeling both the chills and the tenseness slowly recede from her body. "Thank you for going to the trouble of heating the blanket, it's much appreciated."

"No problem. If it cools too soon, I'll be happy to reheat it." He took her hand, sitting down in the chair next to the bed, his elbows leaning on the mattress. "Where did Abbie get off to?"

"I told her that outside of being a little chilled, I'm doing well, thanks to your combined efforts, and suggested she get some shut eye. I also told her that there was nothing more she could do that she hadn't already done. I had to insist at first, but she finally saw that I'm indeed back in reality. She went to her room saying she was going to try and get hold of Mandy, but Sis is probably at the meeting with the publisher about now. I heard Mom's cell ring just before you came in, and I'm pretty sure she's talking to Ben now. At least I think so. If she'd been able to reach Mandy, I know she'd would've let me know."

Claire rescued her hand, and shifted to a sitting position, wrapping the still-warm blanket tightly around her shoulders and torso. She smiled at him, and continued. "However, now I'm telling you the same thing I told Mom. I'm afraid I've caused both of you to lose sleep this morning. Thank you once again, Malcolm. Now please, you needn't worry about me anymore, either. You need to get some sleep as well."

Malcolm looked at her for a few seconds, slowly shaking his head as if he didn't hear her correctly, and then abruptly got up and walked from one end of the room to the other and back again, apparently engrossed in his thoughts. Claire knew he would speak when he was ready, though she quietly followed his restless pacing. Finally, he sat down on the edge of Mandy's bed, facing her across the aisle between the two beds. Penny came over and laid her head on his knee, as if she knew and was in accord with whatever he was about to say. He idly messed the top notch on her head and rubbed behind her ears for a few seconds, then looked over at Claire.

"Please allow me to get something off my chest that's bothering me, because I know it has to be affecting you more so. Even though it's only been a matter of days since we met, I think I know you fairly well, at least the part of you that is having dreams about someone trying to harm you, and the cover you hide behind to protect yourself and those around you. I know you've said you aren't afraid anymore, because now you know who is behind these lethal incidents. More than likely, you think it's that madman, Sean. And I'm not saying it isn't him, but someone else may be involved, someone who's helping Sean."

She shrugged her shoulders to indicate she wasn't going to allow herself to be bothered by the reality of what he was saying.

"Please listen to me, Claire, this is a very serious business. A triple threat—the very real intent on someone's part to kill you, the freaking accidents themselves, and what it's doing to you on a mental and emotional basis. I'm trying my damnedest to protect you. And Penny and I may be able to guard you physically, but how can I preserve your innermost safety when you keep all your feelings and fears bottled up inside while hiding behind that stoic façade? I would like to help you further, if you will allow me. I really think a little therapy would open your eyes to what your ongoing nightmares are trying to tell you. What I'm suggesting is a session or two of hypnosis."

Before he could say anything further, Claire spoke up. "You think hypnotizing me is going to reveal the person who is doing this? From my nightmares? I'm not into your field of expertise, Malcolm. And, quite frankly, I don't think your therapy can possibly help me understand what is really taking place in the nightmares. As of this last version, it's even changed from the way it normally begins. It was very different from all the others."

Malcolm perked up his ears. "What was different about it? Would it bother you to talk about it, right now, while I'm here and you're warm and safe? I'd like you to fill me in on what takes place in those dreams"

"I suppose it wouldn't hurt to just talk about it, but *no way* on the hypnosis therapy. That's my condition for letting you in on my dreams. Okay?"

He gave a nonchalant what-do-I-care shrug. "It's your call, Claire. Go on."

"Well, the nightmares started right after the attack, this last March. But you already know what happened. From Mandy.

So I won't repeat everything. But, there's a part you don't know because I've never told her.

"From my attacker's actions, I'm certain he intended to rape me at knife point, and quite possibly, kill me afterward. Luckily, I was able to get a choke hold on him from behind. So, after trying to break the hold and make an escape, he fell against the glass sliding door, and ended up on the floor, passed out. Unfortunately, I was still on his back when he crumpled against the patio door. I happened to glance through the glass on my way down to the floor, seeing complete blackness beyond it, with one exception. I thought I saw a face peering in just for a fleeting second, but decided it was only a reflection of my face, or my mind playing tricks on me. And then, I passed out also. When I came to, the police had just arrived, and Mr. Wonderful was gone. End of episode one."

She'd told the story while concentrating on finger combing Penny's ears. The big wolfhound had moved to lay beside her bed. Claire looked up to see Malcolm's reaction. He was staring at her, the look in his deep blue eyes somewhere between concern and outrage.

"My very brave and resolute lady," he said simply, picking her up in his arms, blanket and all. He carried her to the amply-sized wicker rocker in the corner of the room, where he sat down with her on his lap. He gently smoothed the fly-away soft curls away from her face, while rocking her slowly. "You should never have been put in a position that required you to fight for your life. How I wish I had been there for you. And if it means anything to you, I completely understand where you've come from and what you're doing to protect yourself now."

Claire sighed, and leaned back against his shoulder.

"Only, don't get too comfortable, my dear. You were about to continue to episode two, the ongoing nightmares."

"Okay, okay," she said, yawning. "Where do you want me to begin? And please don't say, at the beginning or I'll be forced to find a new shrink, *Doctor* Sutherland," she threatened, but with a tell-tale smile as she laid her head on his shoulder and closed her eyes.

"Ahh . . . well then, I can't lose my favorite patient. Why don't you start with what form the dream has been taking prior to the one this morning, then tell me what changed in this last one. After that, you can sleep to your heart's content."

"But I don't have a nickel on me, Doctor. Can I owe you?"

"I'll put this one on account, Ms. Martelli. So, tell me, how do these dreams start? And what takes place in these dreams? The doctor is *in*."

"You just call them dreams, as if they were pleasant little fantasies. But I call them fiendish," she said, opening her eyes, but leaving her head on his shoulder so she wouldn't have to see the expression on his face. She told him how the nightmares always started in black-and-white, and how she gradually discovers she's in a threatening situation.

"Suddenly, the black-and-white erupts into red. Not *just* red, more like a swirling deep red maelstrom out of which a shrouded figure appears. Actually, I'm not really sure what name to give it; a feeling of evil always permeates the dream when it comes forth, like some kind of soulless apparition. Anyway, it comes toward me, reaching out for me with boney claws for hands. The face is always hidden by a hood, and all I can see is red turmoil surrounding it. At that point, fear always possesses me. No, fear isn't really the right word. I'd have to say the better word would be *beyond* fear to panic. In this state, I can't run or move any part of my body. I can only stand there, terrified, and wait for it to come for me. And, that's when I always wake up, just before it gets me." She shuddered, remembering all too well.

"Claire, that's only human. Self-preservation if you like. See, in your dream, you are threatened by an evil too terrifying to *have* a face, or identity, or for you to actually see through the fear surrounding the evil to *identify* it, which would seem to say that somewhere in your subconscious, you do know the evil that is facing you. Also, you are in what you termed the 'red maelstrom', which again translates to being in a state of fear, confusion, and possibly self-denial. But, let's continue with the changed dream you just witnessed this morning before we get too far into dream meanings. But, I see you have at least a thousand questions," he quipped, aiming for a jocular note to divert her, and adding a very non-professional smile. "Could you possibly hold them until you finish with the next episode? Then we'll discuss both."

"All right, I do have a lot of questions, though thankfully not a thousand." She wriggled around until she had unwrapped herself from the blanket in an attempt to find a cooler position. She was plenty warm now, with her body pressed close to Malcolm's.

"Yes, and I'll answer every one of them. Afterward. Claire, would you be more comfortable in your bed?"

She looked at him ruefully. "Sorry, it is rather warm in here now. At least you got rid of my chills. Good job. But *you* are going to have a rather uncomfortable time sitting in that straight chair by my bed."

"What if I borrow Mandy's bed? Seems like that would resolve the comfort problem. I only want to borrow the top part, if you think she wouldn't mind. And, I'll arrange to have the duvet as well as the sheets changed before she gets back."

"Perfect. I'm sure she won't mind, especially if she gets clean bedding out of it." Claire climbed back into her own bed and punched the pillows until she found just the right degree of incline. She yawned, thinking how she wouldn't mind having clean sheets and duvet cover as well, after wrestling them in her dream all night. She propped herself against the pillows. Surprisingly, she felt an intimacy creeping around her that she wasn't expecting, as she watched Malcolm remove his Nike's, take off the cotton V-neck sweater he'd thrown on over his tee-shirt, and settle himself on top of Mandy's bed.

"Comfy now?"

"Yep. Just hope I don't fall asleep," he said, attempting to stifle his own yawn. "Just give me a shove if I do,' he said with a wide grin. "A gentle shove, please. Now, go on with your account of this morning's episode."

Claire gathered her thoughts and began. "You see, what's so surprising, is that the whole complexion of the dream changed. I thought I was here in Paris when it began. It was so realistic. Like I actually thought Sean had kidnapped me and that's why I didn't find it weird that I woke up in a strange and dark room, even with my cell phone pulsing on the pillow next to my ear. I remember being afraid to answer it, and even more afraid to listen to the message that was waiting."

She proceeded to tell Malcolm the context of the dream she'd suffered that morning with the unique differences that stood out from the pattern of her former nightmares. He mentally noted the dissimilarities she said made it so plausible. First and foremost, that she actually thought that Sean would kidnap her, if given half a chance, and that he would lock her in a room that, at first thought, she couldn't find a way out. Secondly, the fact that she didn't recognize her surroundings, or where the room was located, or how she'd gotten there, were all very telling in Malcolm's mind. In his professional reference, they stood for the unknown. And in her perception, the reality that Claire had come to know since the attack, she was indeed smack dab in the middle of uncharted territory.

As Claire continued on with further details from the nightmare, he began to see a pattern forming that indicated her subconscious was manifesting details from the night of the Denver attack. The fact that she was looking for a way out of the room, for instance, her attempt to escape through one of the windows into what she'd described as a black void, but was actually black paint on the back of the glass, symbolized the glass patio doors which called her attention to the blackness beyond.

Also, her expectation that Sean would kill her, meant she may be identifying Sean as the masked person who actually attacked her that night. Again the dream allowed her subconscious the freedom to work out these substitutes for the real thing which were terrifying to her psyche.

But now she was telling him about the rag-bundled form that grabbed her wrist, and of the chaotic deep red colors that began to swirl about the room, one of the few matches to her previous dreams. He didn't want to miss anything she was saying, so he put this information on the back burner for further reflection, listening intently to the next element of the dream.

In her nightmare, when she talked about the frantic clawing and heavy pounding on the door, Malcolm realized her subconscious had intensified Penny's soft scratching and sporadic whines from her guard position at the door to the Martelli's suite, into demons clawing and wildly barking.

However, what he remembered as actually taking place was that he'd heard Penny's scratching through the open doorway of his quarters, and had gone down the hall to the Martelli's door to make sure everything was all right. Penny seemed on edge, pacing in front of the door, and giving it a little scratch with her paw every so often, though Malcolm couldn't hear any sound at all coming from within the suite.

"What is it, girl? Should we check on Claire? I'm with you. I'd rather be certain she and Abbie are okay, rather than worry until it's time to get up. Well, let's make a go of it, then."

When no one answered his tentative rapping, he decided to knock a bit louder to get their attention, but not loud enough to wake up other guests in the hotel. Abbie had finally opened the door, surprised to see Malcolm in the hallway. Then Claire began screaming and all three had rushed to her bedroom, finding her on the floor beside the bed. He put that episode on the back burner also.

At the moment, he noticed goose bumps travel up and down Claire's limbs as it became evident she was re-living her feelings of terror at the part of the dream she was in the process of describing.

"Then, it started talking to me in a raspy hoarse whisper that I'll never forget. It called me by name, and said something like 'You have to pay'. . ."

"Claire, you're trembling. If talking about it is causing you to experience the same panic-stricken feelings over again, we must stop. I know you've already said no to hypnosis, but please, I'm asking you to reconsider. You see, one of the good things about hypnotherapy is that you wouldn't either relive or remember the intensity of your frightening feelings. Your psyche would allow you to talk about them without the emotional connection."

"Claire? I thought I heard voices. Are you all right?" Abbey pushed open the door to see Malcolm sitting on the side of Claire's bed, holding her hand in both of his, comforting her. Claire was sobbing quietly.

"Malcolm? What's happened? And please tell me why you're still here. Not to be unthankful for all you're doing for her, but she really does need to sleep right now."

"Sorry, Mrs. M. I thought it would be best to hear from Claire's own perspective about her nightmares. I know I can help her through the emotional and mental issues affecting her. I just wanted to get a better understanding of those dreams that are tormenting her.

"I'm okay, Mom. It isn't Malcolm's fault I started crying. It's just . . . *everything!*" With that, Claire broke into large alligator-sized tears.

Abbie quietly motioned Malcolm to the door. Seeing the extreme frustration reflected on his face, she whispered to him as he passed. "Get some sleep. Doctors need it, too. Contrary to what some of you think, you're human also. And thank you from the bottom of my heart for all you're doing to help her."

"You're right. We probably all need some sleep. It's just so hard to leave her when she's like this. Is it okay if I come back later in the day? Just to make sure she's okay."

"Malcolm, you never need to ask. You're always welcome here."

8

Day Six

Denver—Residence of David Kessler

Kessler relaxed in the hot tub that had just been installed that same morning on the deck jutting off the master bedroom suite on the second floor of his house. He picked up the snifter he'd placed on the rim of the tub and took a healthy swallow of Napoleon brandy, then lay back to better view the heavens on this very clear spring evening. He'd read in the morning's paper that tonight was one of the best times to watch for meteor showers. And he looked forward to seeing one or two arcing across the sky, just as he had as a boy, when he used to call them shooting stars.

It had been a dilly of a day. And he'd wanted to relax in his preferred manner, which generally meant having sex. So, he wasn't happy when Margo told him he had the tub to himself as she had an appointment with a new client to discuss catering a large wedding event. Okay, so they'd been married for twenty-five years. And maybe he wasn't in the same shape as when they'd married, but neither was she. They both had begun to droop a little, here and there. He was definitely dispirited by his almost non-existent sex life these days. He'd thought that maybe the hot tub might work a little magic in that department.

It seemed as though nothing was right since Claire filed for divorce from Chad, and moved out of the house down the block. When she still lived there, he would see her at least once a day, whether she saw him or not. Like when he'd stealthily crept down the alley and hid by her garage to watch through the wrought iron fence as she bent and stooped in her little athletic shorts and halter top while out gardening on weekends. Or like when he'd hired her to remodel and update the furnishings in the second story's master suite, as well as his office on the first floor at the rear of the house. As he'd known in advance, there had been no problem with his easy-going wife on that score. She and Claire got along famously, and it was really not something Margo felt comfortable doing anyway. Her bailiwick, the kitchen, was also remodeled and refurbished by Claire, to Margo's wish list and specifics. The end result had proved to be an instant success—Margo's Specialty Catering really began to flourish after the new kitchen was installed.

After Claire left Chad and moved away, Kessler found the only way he could get it on to have sex with his wife, was to imagine it was Claire he was making love to. And although he'd repeatedly made indirect insinuations to Claire during the time they worked together on the remodeling and new furnishings for the house, it had all been for naught. Totally ineffectual. Or at least she pretended not to understand his meaning.

The night of the attack, last March, was a date he would always remember. He'd carried through on his end of the bargain, but never again. How could he ever forget the picture of Claire that night as he sat beside her on the sofa, assuring her that Duffy was out of danger? It had been pure agony to look at her face and see those eyes, ordinarily a very sexy shade of gold—tiger eyes. But on that night, one was swelling shut and the other was dark with fear and suffering. He'd seen up close and personal the bruised face, colored an angry shade of purple. His own part that night made him wonder what kind of monster he'd become. And all because he'd wanted to get back at her for spurning his advances.

He'd only seen her once since then, when he'd delivered Duffy to her the next day. She was so stiff from the injuries she'd suffered in the attack, she could barely walk. But she'd flung herself down beside the animal and gathered him in her arms. Crying and petting him at the same time, she assured him repeatedly in a low voice that she would never leave him with Chad again.

Margo broke his introspection, calling up the stairs, "David, I'm leaving now. Oh, thought you'd want to know that you have a visitor on the way up."

"The hell you say, I'm in the hot tub, Margo—naked. For Pete's sake, what are you thinking, woman?"

"She's thinking we've known each other a long time and that you would want to see me, friend."

Water splashed in all directions, drenching the virgin wood of the newly constructed deck, as David quickly turned around in the tub to see a shadowy figure standing in the open doorway to the bedroom. "Oh, it's you. Go to hell. I'm not playing your game anymore. That detective is already on my trail."

"Just one more teensy little favor, David. I need you to get Duffy for me. One of the women in Claire's department at work is taking care of him while she's in Paris. I understand that the woman, Loupe, keeps him in her fenced backyard while she's working. Shouldn't be too difficult, he knows you. And then bring him to me."

"Why?" David asked. Anymore, he'd become suspicious around this long-time acquaintance.

"That, my friend, is none of your business. Here's the address. I'll just leave it here on the table. Just call when you've got the dog. Oh, and that's a very nice hot tub, friend. I'm glad to see you'll get much enjoyment from my generous gift, for doing that *last* little favor for me. I'll leave you now. Have a good night."

Turning his back on his departing visitor, Kessler looked up just in time to see the meteor show begin, as a shooting star soared across the night sky, arcing down and disappearing into the horizon line. Somehow it didn't delight him like he thought it would.

VICTORIA MASTERSON

New York City—Jesse's Residence

Mandy sat forward in the taxi, eagerly watching out the window at the lights and the numbers of people walking in the neighborhoods she passed through. She'd directed the cabbie to take her to the address of Jesse's loft, over the pizza shop in the Village. At one time, she'd wanted to live in New York and was curious to see if she would've liked it. And she couldn't wait to get together with Jess again. He'd told her that his lady-love, a model, lived with him now, and they were planning on getting married when he felt he could support her and a future family. Although deep down, Mandy still experienced a small tug on her heart strings, the good wishes she felt for her friend were sincere. She only hoped the woman he loved was good enough for him. In Mandy's eyes, Jess deserved only the best.

The cabby leaned on the horn in response to another taxi pulling in front of him and turning at the oncoming corner.

Well, that's New York for you, she thought. The lights lit up the night. But, she would've preferred to see the Village when it was daytime.

Upon meeting with the guidebook publisher that morning, she'd guessed correctly. Her contract was formally terminated, thanks to Neal Ross Kincaid who sat through the meeting with a smug look on his face. Afterward, it had taken her most of what was left of the day to call some of her photographer friends and question them as to other possibilities in the publishing field.

She'd contacted a few of the ones they'd recommended, and luckily found interest and, more importantly, she scored two confirmed interviews for the next day. Now, if she only had time before her appointments to purchase an appropriate outfit at one of the department stores. She was wrinkled beyond repair from her all-night trip, as well as having worn the same outfit throughout the day.

She was glad she'd taken the time when they landed early that morning, to shop at the airport for necessities that she hadn't had time to pick up at the Saint-Germain before her wild dash for the plane. So, thankfully, she had a toothbrush and the other toiletries that one requires when traveling. Surprisingly, she'd even discovered a small lingerie shop, where the buyer profile for the goods offered was the traveling businessman who was expected to bring home a little something for the little woman, be it wife, mistress, or girlfriend. Mandy found the prices exorbitant, but a gal has to do what a gal has to do. And, hopefully, after meeting Jesse's girlfriend, just maybe, she wouldn't mind if Mandy borrowed one of his shirts to sleep in, as the nightgowns, even the ones on sale, were definitely out of her league.

The taxi driver pulled up mid-block, in front of a rather typical Village neighborhood pizza spot. Above the entrance was a blazing red and yellow neon sign proclaiming 'Johnny's Rendezvous', and flashing the words 'Pizza Anytime' below. Mandy got out of the cab, surprised at the number of people she saw through the front window, who were obviously enjoying Johnny's fare. She headed toward a glass door to the side of the restaurant which she hoped lead up to Jesse's loft. Inside, she noticed an intercom system on the wall beside the door, and decided to take a chance. Granted, it could be any number of things besides a loft up there, given the red painted bead board on the stairway walls; her first guess being a gambling parlor or, on second thought, maybe a fortune teller. She took a deep breath and pushed the buzzer.

"Yes?" A woman's voice, clear and self-assured, came over the speaker.

Oh, great, Mandy thought. Am I just supposed to say, "Hi, I'm Jesse's old girlfriend? Can I come up?" But before she could think of a way to reply, she saw Jess approaching the entry. Opening the glass door, he practically knocked her off her feet as he pulled her into his arms.

"Mandy! How great it is to see you again. How French you look, woman." He engulfed her in a bear hug as the door opened at the top of the stairway. A beautiful tall and willowy brunette in a stylish at-home caftan looked down.

"Jess? Is this your old friend? Bring her up so I can welcome her, too."

"We're coming, Gia. Let's go up, Mandy. Wow, I can hardly believe you're really here. After you, my friend," he said, bowing her up in front of him.

They got to the top of the stairs, out of breath, but laughing in their happiness on seeing one another after such a long time. Mandy smiled as she came face-to-face with Jesse's new love.

"Gia, this is Mandy Martelli, the photographer I've talked so much about. And Mandy, meet Gia. Her first name is actually Giacomettina, her last name is as long, and close to being unpronounceable, if you can believe it. So she's decided to build her modeling brand using only her first name. You know how popular one word names are these days."

"Welcome, Mandy Martelli. Come in, please. It's true that Jess has done nothing but talk about you since he found out you were coming to town."

Mandy followed Gia into the living space, impressed at how well the eclectic scheme worked in the small loft. The furnishings were spare, basically contemporary. However, a couple beautiful antique pieces were precisely placed in the room, looking almost sculptural and adding to the ambience. The basic color scheme was a neutral palette, mixed with brown tones, salmon pink and deep peach accents. There were a few touches of black, splashed here and there, which charmingly played off the mixture of deep and soft hues. And, thankfully, no red.

Mandy mentally approved her friend's taste. Good going, Jess, she thought, looking around the impressive loft. And a beauty for a fiancé as well. She looked up just in time to see him watching her with a sentimental look on his face.

"Gia," Mandy said quickly, attempting to break the mood before his beautiful girlfriend could see the look on his face, and possibly be jealous. "You're so kind to let me crash here with you guys. I hope Jess told you why I'm in New York.

Sorry for the last-minute notice, by the way. This trip was completely unplanned as of yesterday. And now here I am, with just a necessaries kit and my camera equipment."

"We're happy to have you stay with us, Mandy. Let's put your equipment bag in our little closet that we call a guest room. Then we can sit down, have a glass of wine, and chat. Sorry, but I'm going to have to call it an early night, though. I have a six o'clock modeling gig in the morning," she explained, "and the camera finds every little line and under-eye circle when I try to cheat and don't get a full eight hours sleep before a shoot. I hope you and Jess will not think me impolite. You two can stay up and talk about old times. In fact, I'll be upset if you don't."

"Well, I'm going to have to get up early in the morning also, in time to stop in at one of the department stores and find an outfit to wear on my way to my first interview tomorrow. So, I won't be far behind you."

"Wait, Mandy that's not necessary. You can borrow whatever you think will be appropriate from my closet. We're about the same size, I'm just a little taller."

Mandy's mouth gaped open, looking at the gorgeous model. "You must be joking, Gia. I thank you for your generous offer, but I'm afraid there isn't any way your clothes will fit me. I'm not as tiny as you are."

Gia looked at Jess, who shrugged his shoulders. "She's probably right, honey. You are pretty thin. And please don't tell me again. As a photographer, I know the camera adds ten pounds. But as your significant other, I still say you're flirting with danger to be this thin."

"What size do you wear, Mandy?" Gia wouldn't give up.

"I'm an eight, Gia. What size are you? About a four?"

Gia laughed, delightedly. "No, of course not. But thank you for flattering me. Actually, we're the same size. Depending on the cut, sometimes I can wear a six, rarely, a four. But I have many pieces hanging in my closet that are eights. It's just that I'm a good deal taller than you. It's only an optical illusion that you think I'm smaller than I am. So if you were to choose one of my shorter skirts or dresses, they should fall about the right length on you."

An hour later, Gia was in bed for the night. Mandy had tried on and borrowed a stylish outfit that would definitely impress the publishers she would meet the next day, which true to Gia's foresight, did indeed fit her very well. And, now she and Jess were relaxing with a glass of wine on the cubed sectional sofa.

"Looks as if things are going well for you, Jess, and you deserve it. Gia is an angel, how did you two meet?"

"Wouldn't you know, on a photography shoot, of course. I needed a model for some shots I was hired to take last winter at the Rockefeller Plaza skating rink, for a NYC tourist brochure. The gig called for a model that could actually skate, as well as look beautiful for the camera. The agency sent Gia, and that was the start of it. Well, after that, everything more or less fell into an easy pattern of us becoming a couple. And here we are."

Jess poured her another small glass of wine, even though she waved her hand over the top of the stemmed glass. "It's just to relax you for your big day tomorrow. But enough about what's going on with me. Tell me how Abbie and Claire are doing. You said on the phone you were all three in Paris, until you got called back to New York for that meeting this morning.

"Well, when I talked with them earlier today, they had already guessed the outcome of this morning's meeting. They felt better about the fact I'd be staying in New York for a couple more days when I told them you and your fiancée were putting me up while I pitch the Paris Byways concept to other publishers. However, the news of the day regarding Abbie is that she has a new beau, her former fiancée from before she and my dad became a twosome. Actually, they only recently met again, in Paris. He's a doctor, a pediatrician . . . and never married after Mom broke their engagement way back when.

"And as for Claire, she's finally filed for divorce from Chad, which I feel is a good and positive step in her life. I

206

don't think those two were ever meant to be together. But, she's been going through some very anguishing episodes since last March. There have been a few incidents, actually attacks that have taken place, except they've been planned to look like accidents. Like she isn't the intended victim. And, quite frankly, she's very lucky to have survived. Even the police haven't been able to capture the guy they think is the maniac, who is now in Paris doing his evil deeds. And no one knows why. Is he just a psycho after Claire? Or is there some other motive?"

"My God, that's terrible, Mandy. Are the French police protecting her?"

"Well, the detective on the original case of the Denver attack, has notified the French authorities with the suspect's name, including a description and previous history with the law. He's actually been arrested several times for assault and robbery, but no convictions. The Paris police are cooperating, but this guy seems to be an escape artist. It appears he has the most fascinating ability to disappear into thin air. On the good side, Claire has met a terrific Englishman, a psychiatrist, who appears to be in love with her. He's trying to protect her when and where the police can't, especially since we're all staying at the same hotel. Evidently, no other *planned* accidents have taken place from the time I left. Knock on wood. Though, I feel as if I've deserted her since I had to leave Paris so abruptly. It's rather imperative I get back there as soon as possible."

"Mandy, please promise me that you'll watch out for yourself as well. Just thinking about you being caught in the crossfire, as it were, is enough to send me into a tailspin. I just don't know how I could cope if you were hurt. Or worse. You see I've made my peace with the fact that you don't love me the way I love you. The way I'll always love you. But I need to know you're alive . . . somewhere in the world."

Mandy looked down at her wine glass, shoulders slumping, totally disheartened by his revelation. "But Jess, what about Gia? She's a wonderful person, so giving, so gorgeous."

"Yes, she is all that. And I do love her, just not the same way I love you. It was touch and go there for a long while, then when Gia came on the scene, I found it's possible to love more than one person at a time. Just differently. I know you don't want to hear this, but you'll always be in my heart, Mandy, just know that. And know also that I wouldn't, or couldn't, do anything to ever hurt Gia."

Denver—Residence of E. Forde Chadwick

Susan sleepily rolled over. She was in Chad's bed, though his side was empty. It was early morning, just before dawn, and the room was in shadows. Still groggy, she peered around, wondering where he'd gone. There was no sign of him in the room. She forced herself to get up, throwing on the robe she kept in his closet, and made her way out to the catwalk that overlooked the living room. As she leaned against the railing, studying the shadows in the lower level, she noticed light spreading out from under the door of the kitchen and heard what sounded like lowered voices coming from within. Barefoot, she padded down the stairs, stopping when she came to the closed kitchen door.

A very odd time of the morning to have a visitor, she thought. However, on hearing soft whining sounds, she began to put two and two together. It had to be Duffy. But how? Susan knew that Claire had taken Duffy on a full time basis after the attack incident. And, she also knew that Loupe was taking care of the animal while Claire was in Paris. She put her ear to the closed door, listening, to see if she could hear who was with Chad. Somehow she was certain he wouldn't appreciate her knowing who he was talking with. But Duffy heard her, investigating on the opposite side of the door, and sniffing at the small space that allowed the light to seep under. The door to the back terrace closed softly, and she heard a motor start up and move off down the alley.

208

Uh oh, she thought, better hightail it back upstairs. But the door suddenly opened, allowing both Chad and Duffy to catch her in the act of spying.

"Susan," he said, greeting her amiably, "after you, my dear." Chad ushered her into the kitchen and toward the table. "You probably want to know what's going on. Well, you're about to get your wish. Cup of coffee? No? It is a little early for you," he said, accepting the shake of her head as an answer. He poured himself a mug of fresh-brewed and sat down at his usual place at the table.

Susan sidled past him, taking a seat across from him. "Chad, I woke up just a few minutes ago, and you weren't there. I was worried, so I came looking for you. Then I saw the light from under the kitchen door. That's all. Just lil' ole' me, worried about lil' ole' you."

It was as if he hadn't heard her, apparently lost in his thoughts. He absently tore a corner off the paper napkin at his place and wadded it into the general size and shape of a spit ball, rolling it between his fingers until it was solid. Susan had only noticed this mannerism appearing since he and Claire had separated. After deciding it was a nervous habit, she'd recently observed that he seemed to be doing it more and more often. She waited for him to speak, petting Duffy while trying not to be obvious about staring at the paper ball he was rotating between his thumb and second finger.

"Susan, I need to know I can trust you implicitly. Can I?"

"Of course, Chad. Why do you even ask?"

He glanced across the table, giving her a thin smile while pushing his glasses back up his nose. "Let's just say I've had my doubts lately. Mostly due to the actions of your stepbrother, especially since I found out he's in Paris. I've asked you several times now to keep him on a tight leash. Yet, Detective Owens maintains a swinging door in and out of my office, while reporting some new escapade of Sean's making, almost all of which involve *planned* accidental mishaps with Claire as the target. And according to Owens, the incidents are escalating. Call him off, Susan. Now. Is that plain enough?"

"But, Chad, I thought . . ."

"You evidently thought wrong. Or, put more bluntly, didn't think at all."

"Chad, please listen to me. I can't reach him on his regular cell number. He's got that phone turned off. When he wants to talk to me, he buys a cheap, no-contract phone. And then throws it away after the call is over."

"Susan, I don't care how you do it, just get it done. At once. And don't come running to me if he gets caught by the Paris police. I'm washing my hands of your stepbrother, as of this, your second, third, and *final* warning.

"Oh, and I'm going up to Vail for a couple days, leaving as soon as it's light out, and taking Duffy with me. I've missed the lad," he said, ruffling the Springer's ears. "It's going to be an all-male bonding trip. Right, Duff? And one last thing, my pet, you are not to divulge the fact that Duffy is with me. Not to anyone. And that includes Loupe."

Paris—Residence Saint-Germain

Marie-Claude looked around when she heard the "ssst" coming from somewhere over by the stone wall of the Saint-Germain garden. A voice she remembered drew her attention away from the selection of fresh salad greens and herbs she'd picked for the dinner her mother was preparing in the big kitchen.

"Marie-Claude, over here."

Looking around to see if anyone else had heard, and seeing no one, she casually moved toward the wall with her basket of greens. If someone were to see her and ask, she intended to say she decided to pick some cucumbers for dinner. Fortunately, these were growing up the wall on a trellis not far from the kitchen door. When she got there, she saw it was indeed who she thought it would be. The American was hidden in the cascade of white wisteria not far from the cucumber vines.

"Hello, beautiful, where've you been? I've come around to see you several times, but that young man, the one they call

Etienne, is now manning the desk in the lobby. What happened? Did you lose your job?"

Marie-Claude self-consciously brushed a dark tendril behind her ear. She smiled to hide her nervousness. "I didn't know you would care, Harley. You see, I . . . I went to help take care of a family member, *La Cousine* Odette, who lives in a small town in the country. She is so very much better now. So I am back."

"Well, I missed you. A lot in fact. And I really missed the conversations we had, you know where you kept me laughing about the anecdotes that happened with some of your hotel guests? Like those annoying Martelli women, that bothered the heck out of you? I thought maybe later on, we could meet for a bite at one of the small out-of-the-way cafes around here. You name your favorite, and I'll be there. Who knows, since writing is what I do, maybe we could collaborate on a book of Parisian anecdotes. I bet you know a good many from being in the hotel business and all. And when we finish with dinner, maybe you could show me what Paris is like after dark. What do you say, beautiful?"

The door to the kitchen opened, as Emilie looked for her daughter and the produce she'd sent her to pick. Marie-Claude quickly called to her, "I am here, *La Mere*, almost finished. I will come in just a minute or two." Then in a whisper to Harley, "I'm not sure I can get away tonight."

He whispered back, "I'll be in the storage shed waiting for your answer. Don't disappoint me, okay?"

She gave him a quick nod. Oh, how she'd love to go. She'd show Malcolm. Since she'd come back on her two-day pass from the clinic, her mother had warned her that Malcolm and Claire were what she called, *ami/amie*, and to expect him to act differently. She'd even rubbed the hurt in by saying "not that there was anything between you and *Docteur* Sutherland in the first place."

She really didn't think her mother would allow her to go out with Harley. In fact she already knew she wouldn't, as she'd advised Marie-Claude if she wanted to come home for good, she would have to prove that she could live day by day in a condition of emotional stability. Equilibrium, *Docteur* Marchand had called it. And moreover, she would have to convince them she could be trusted to keep herself in that mental state of balance and composure, by taking the medication prescribed by the doctor. Marie-Claude groaned just thinking about the *forever* of it.

She busied herself with twisting the cucumbers off the vine, while she thought about how she could work this her way, without causing a problem with her mother, the doctors, and even Harley, himself. Just before her *interlude*, as she was inclined to call it, he'd expressed the necessity of keeping his presence a secret. He'd said that he was on a classified operation for the U.S. government, and no one was supposed to know his whereabouts or it could compromise his assignment. She remembered when he'd originally asked her to help him by giving him the location of the locked box containing the gold medallion. And, then again, when he'd asked for her to leave the key under the box so he could recover the medallion and deliver it back to its rightful owner. He'd assured her it was part of his assignment, and that no one need be the wiser if she did as he asked.

Marie-Claude carried her basket into the kitchen and set it on the worktable. Her mother, the head chef for this celebration dinner, directed her to transport the greens to the sink, and to plunge them into the cold water bath she'd readied for that purpose.

"*Merci*, Marie-Claude. But where are the onions?" Emilie queried while washing the dirt from the other vegetables. Didn't I ask you to dig a few of the purple onions, also?"

"*Oui, La Mere. Pardon*, I will go out and get some for you right away."

"And hurry, *s'il vous plait*. I need you to prepare the greens into a big salad and then set the bowl to chill in the cooler. Also, call Etienne and ask him to leave a sign on the desk that he will return in twenty minutes. I would like him to cut off an amount of beef hanging in the big cooler for the

LEFT OF THE LEFT BANK

Sauté de Boeuf a la Bourguignonne I am making for the dinner tonight. And when you come back with the onions, you can go to the wine cellar and bring up several bottles of our best Bordeaux. It's in the rack straight ahead as you cnter."

Marie-Claude hurried out to dig the onions, by way of the tool shed, set against the side of the old manse, in a niche created by the stone wall. It was cool inside and smelled of cigars. Sean, alias Harley, stepped out from behind the door and gave her a hug, placing a chaste kiss on her forehead.

"Mmm, you smell good. So, have you decided where we're going for dinner, my little mademoiselle?"

"Harley, I will not be able to go out tonight. *La Mere* is having a dinner for some of the Saint-Germain's guests. I guess I'm lucky that only two of those awful Martelli's will be attending. The youngest one that Etienne calls Man-dee is not in Paris right now, something about her being in New York City for a couple of days, before she is to return. But *La Mere* expects me to be social with these visitors. There is nothing I can do about it. I have the idea that you could come to my room while the others are eating. Maybe if I played like I was sick after a little while, I could get out of the dinner early. I would have the bad headache, you understand. No one would see you if I told you a secret way into the manse, from right here in fact, and also, another way into my room. I could lock the door so we could be private. She wants me to go the cellar to get some bottles of wine for dinner, so it would be easy to bring to my room one more bottle for us. But I must get back to the kitchen now. Will you come?"

"There is a secret way into the house, you say?" Sean could hardly believe his luck. Here he thought he'd have to wine and dine her to get any information as to Claire's schedule, and when she might be alone, without that Englishman and his dog to protect her. But if Marie-Claude delivered on what she promised, he wouldn't have to take the risk of the police stumbling onto him at a restaurant. "Where is it?" He looked around, curious to find what could be the way in. "The next thing you'll tell me is that there are secret passageways running through the house."

"*Oui*. There are. But will you be coming, or not, Harley? *La Mere* said never to tell anyone about the passages, but you are not just anyone. Especially if you agree to come to my room later."

"Okay. I'll be here later on, about nine. Will that work? Good. Now, show me the way in, and then where to meet you."

"The entry is hidden in the side of the mansion, over here. You must press in on this stone. See, it's up this many," she said pointing to each one, "and this many over from the corner. And this is the particular spot." Again she counted by touching each one, then pressed hard on the top left corner. There was a low grating sound as the rock foundation of the mansion shuddered slightly, like someone dragging a too-heavy weight across bedrock. The stones slowly moved inward, leaving a smallish opening to crawl through, if one were stout of heart and limb.

Sean, a.k.a. Harley, stuck his head into the gap but could see nothing in the utter darkness behind the hole except the copious moldering of cobwebs highlighted by the late afternoon rays of sunlight streaming through the shed's single window across from the wall. Imagined or not, his ears registered water dripping somewhere ahead and the skittering of small feet, thankfully running away from him, toward the further end of the tunnel. The envisaged sources of the sounds provoked a shiver in response and he quickly jerked his head out of the hole.

If Marie-Claude noticed the spasm of aversion, she did not voice it, but only continued on with her instructions. "Bring a flashlight, there is no light in the passages. At the end of this one, there is another wall, with another hidden opening that leads into the wine cellar. I will be in that room at nine o'clock. Just hit the wall twice with a rock. There are plenty of those laying around the floor down there. I will let you in, then we'll go together to my room. I must get back now, Harley, before *La Mere* begins to look for me." Marie-Claude stood on tip-toe and planted a wet kiss square on his mouth before she quickly turned and left him standing there, staring after her.

"Little sister, little sister, just what do you have in mind?" Sean whispered as he pressed on the corner of the stone, allowing the opening into the mansion to close. He waited a few minutes to make sure no one was watching, then left the shed and climbed back over the stone wall. He walked down the shady streets, keeping out of sight as much as possible. He was looking for a quiet neighborhood bar that he could hide in until it was time to go back to the Saint-Germain and its secret passageways. But first, he planned on calling big sister, Susan, to tell her the good news.

The tantalizing aroma of the *Bourguignonne* sauce spilled over them as soon as they entered the kitchen by way of the garden door, Abbie in the lead and Ben just behind her. Claire and Malcolm arrived a few minutes later, taking the time to amble through the raised beds of the culinary garden, remarking on the lush smelling herbs, before they made it into the manse's big kitchen. Malcolm set Penny on guard duty outside the door, promising her a bountiful plate of scraps as a special treat. He wasn't taking any chances, having been privy on very recent occasions regarding Sean's propensity to appear and disappear out of virtual thin air.

Once they were all inside the big kitchen area, their attention focused on Marie-Claude, who appeared to be her natural self once again, aside from a rather subdued demeanor. Malcolm had pre-warned them that this would be a possible side effect of the medication she was taking. It was the first time they'd seen her since her breakdown and they were quick to congratulate her on her speedy recovery.

Emilie Fontaine was in her element, happy to have her daughter home, even though it was only for a couple nights at present. And as the aroma of the wine-based sauce mingling with the excellent cut of beef, assailed everyone in the kitchen,

215

she was pleased to hear the unanimous approval voiced by her guests on her excellent choice of the classic French entrée.

Both Abbie and Claire offered their help in last minute preparations; however they needn't have. Their hostess graciously thanked them, but said nothing further remained to be done, except to sit down and eat the delicious repast she'd created. The only incident that in any way marred their enjoyment of the dinner, which was pronounced "marvelous," was the fact that Marie-Claude begged their understanding for a painful headache. She asked to be excused from their company and planned to go to her room and to bed, predicting that a night of sleep would cure it. She was certain to be well in the morning, she said.

Both Ben and Malcolm offered to escort her, but were told it wouldn't be necessary, as the manse's kitchen, was connected by an interior corridor to their private quarters, and kept locked as it was located just off the lobby. Her mother explained that it was the best of both worlds. They had a small kitchen in their suite, one that was adequate for normal, everyday meals. And then this grand one, as she called it, for the breakfast buffet of Parisian rolls and buns, as well as for large dinners, holiday celebrations, or when their guests chose the very expensive all-inclusive plan, which meant they were served a *haute cuisine* dinner on an everyday basis.

Marie-Claude thanked them all for their well wishes, as well as their help during her so-named *interlude,* and hurried through the door that connected with the interior corridor to their quarters. She returned in a matter of seconds, popping her head back in to say, *"Bonne nuit, La Mere,"* and telling her mama not to do the clean-up chores, that she would do them in the morning when her headache was gone. As she turned to leave for the second time, she saw Etienne standing just outside the doorway. *"Pardon, Cousine,"* she said politely, and slipped past him into the corridor.

"Come in, Etienne. Did you close the desk for the night?" Madame Fontaine asked, as she prepared a plate for him.

"*Oui, Tante.* Everything is good—entry door secured, intercom turned on for those certain guests who are out late, desk cleared and the office door locked."

Malcolm pulled out Marie-Claude's vacant chair. "Come sit, Etienne. You are very lucky there's some of the *Bourguignonne* left over. I know I devoured it like I'd never tasted such an excellent meal, and come to think of it, I haven't."

Etienne agreed. "No one makes this dish like *Tante* Emilie does. Not even my family in Provence. It is her much appreciated specialty. And to think I was so afraid there might not be any left over," he said, smiling guilelessly at Malcolm.

"Well, I think the rest of us also did proud justice to it, Etienne." Claire added, speaking for Ben and Abbie, who were enthusiastically nodding their heads.

"And now, dessert," Emilie announced, pouring champagne into tall flutes that she'd set at their places. "Etienne, you will have some after you finish your dinner."

"Oh, my," said Abbie. "I didn't know, and I don't think I've left room for dessert."

But when the *Gateau de Crepes a la Normande* was carried in, Abbie decided she could make room. As did everyone else at table.

"Please give me the name of this in English, Emilie, so I can make everyone jealous in my office back in the states." Ben laughed, as he actually took out his cell phone and photographed the cake-like mound of flaming crepes.

Emilie was delighted by the reception her *gateau* received and continued spooning the flaming liqueur over the dessert until the fire subsided. She began cutting portions from the mound as from a cake, while explaining her creation. "It would translate into English, *Docteur* Ben, as a mound of crepes with apples, flambé. When the crepes are cooked, according to the classic French recipe, they are layered, instead of stuffed individually, with sliced apples cooked with sugar until it becomes like a thick applesauce. The fresh apple filling also is layered with a liqueur flavored whipped cream, and then sprinkled with crushed macaroons and slivered almonds. Of course the authentic presentation requires warmed Calvados, an apple brandy from Normandy in this case, poured over the top and then lit, although nowadays some chefs use any brandy, cognac, or even a dark rum.

"Bravo, Emilie, this is one dinner I'll never forget. Thank you for going to the trouble of making it for us." Malcolm toasted her with the champagne.

"*Merci*, but it was nothing compared to what you did for Marie-Claude when she had the breakdown. Though, I'm afraid she prefers calling it, the *interlude*. Do you think that means she isn't able to face reality, yet?" Emilie looked at Malcolm, studying his reaction to her question, the reflection of a mother's hope shining in her eyes.

"No, not at all, Emilie. It means she is trying to adjust to what happened. She's facing it, her way. It would only be a reality problem if she denied the breakdown ever occurred. It's only natural that she make it more palatable by responding with a descriptive word that makes it easier to live with right now. And, since she *is* facing it, from what I've seen tonight and what you've told me, I would suggest you allow her to claim the self-assurance she's seeking. She's looking for your understanding and acceptance, both of which are, again, completely normal. I'm certain Dr. Marchand will get in touch with you, when Marie-Claude goes back, asking you to come in for an appointment to discuss the success of the pass."

Just as he finished making his suggestions, Penelope's wild barking outside the door alerted them that something was happening that shouldn't be happening. Malcolm did a full-stride sprint, arriving at the door a couple seconds before Etienne, and the rest piled into them from behind. Many hands went for the door latch; someone jerked it open. They rushed out, looking for Penny, who they spotted around the corner in front of the tool shed, still furiously barking.

"What is it, girl?" Malcolm couldn't see into the shed, as the door was closed. He went up to the small window, next to the door, but still couldn't see in because of the darkness.

"Ben, Abbie, please don't let Claire out of your sight, not even for a second. Etienne, you and I are going inside. Could be an animal, I suppose. But somehow, the way Penny is barking, I don't think so. Does anyone know where we can get a flashlight, quickly?"

Emilie ran back toward the kitchen door, yelling over her shoulder, "I know there is one in the drawer under the sink. Hold on." She came hurrying back a few seconds later, holding a flashlight and a lantern. "Here, take them."

Malcolm switched them both on, handing the lantern to Etienne. "All right, everyone. I know you want to help, but I'm asking you to go back inside and lock the door until we investigate. When you hear us knock and give the password, then and only then, do you open the door. The password is the name of our dinner entree, in French. Got that? Claire, can you please stay with Ben and your mother. I can't worry about you and figure out what's going on at the same time. Emilie, you might want to check on Marie-Claude while you're in there."

Claire spoke up in a quiet but insistent voice. "No, Malcolm, I'm coming with you. I don't want to hide. And I don't want either of you in danger because of me. Maybe Madame Fontaine should call the police."

Malcolm shook his head. "I think we should wait to see if it's something to do with the Shamrock before we call the police. And, if it is, you'll be in danger out here, Claire. And time's a wasting. Who knows, there may be a way out of that shed, and whatever it is that caused Penny to set up that ruckus, will be long gone. And besides, she'll warn us if something's wrong. We'll be fine. Please, Claire?"

With a look between them, Ben and Abbie each put an arm around her. "Come on, honey," said Abbie, "let Malcolm find out what's going on before we jump to any conclusions on whether it's Sean, or just a small animal that was startled by Penelope here."

Claire reluctantly allowed them to take her back into the kitchen. Ben locked the door, turning the dead bolt with a key he found hanging on a hook above the door, while Emilie sped down the corridor to check on Marie-Claude.

Meanwhile, outside. "Are you ready, Etienne? I'm going to open the door quickly, then I'll use the flashlight to see if anything's hiding in there. You wait out here, and hold the lantern up in the doorway for general lighting. Be prepared. If something rushes out, be it man or beast, get out of the way fast," he instructed. "Penny will chase it down. Don't try to be a hero. Okay, my friend?"

Etienne nodded his assent, his eyes round as saucers.

Seeing this, Malcolm remarked. "Your first time in the line of danger? You'll do fine. Just stay calm. Use your common sense. Here we go." He grabbed the leather thong that served as the handle and gave the old wooden slab a hard shove. The door creaked open inward. They were met with complete darkness as well as silence. Even the crickets that had provided a constant background noise since they came out of the kitchen, stopped chirping.

Malcolm cautiously stepped into the shed, shining his light into and around stacks of folding chairs, trellises and gardening tools. Over in one corner stood a potting table, under and beside which, numerous clay pots were stacked upside down. He studied the shed's structure. Although ancient, it had been built of solid stone materials, except for the roof, which looked as if the timbers creating the open beamed ceiling had been recently replaced. He wished that some of the storage sheds on his grandmother's country property back in England were as well-constructed. The floor was made of stone, as were the walls. It blended in well, with one of its walls being the actual stone wall that outlined the property, and the one directly adjacent was actually the stone wall of the back side of the mansion. There was no way anything could get in or out except through the heavy timbered door, held together at top, middle, and bottom by thick iron braces.

Seeing the way Penny was sniffing at the floor in front of the one wall of the mansion, Malcolm thought that something, or somebody, must have been in the shed recently. Inhaling the stale smell of a cigar in the air, he amended his thought to a somebody. Penny started whining and scratching at the same place on the wall she'd been sniffing.

"Bring your lantern over here, Etienne," he said, indicating the stones where Penny was single-mindedly engaged in pawing. "What do you know about the hidden passageways inside the mansion? Your aunt Emilie told me about them some time ago. There would have to be a way in and out. Do you know if it's somewhere here in the shed?"

Etienne looked his amazement at Malcolm. "Long ago, when *Cousine* Marie-Claude and I were younger, maybe ten years of age or so, we would play in the wine cellar and one day when we were roughhousing, we got tangled up and accidentally fell against one of the walls. A hole opened up in the stone wall down there, but we were afraid we'd get in trouble if our parents found out. Also, as a child, I remembered the darkness on the other side of the opening. It was full of cobwebs and looked most scary. I think we were frightened there might be skeletons in there, or that the stones would move back into place and we would die in there because no one would know where to look for us. But, to answer your question, I have heard stories about these passageways, but I have never known exactly where they start and where they lead to, except for that time in the wine cellar where it opened by way of accident. Do you think someone knows the way to get in and out of the Saint-Germain using these passages?"

"The thought does cross my mind, especially now that I see how Penny is reacting. And it couldn't possibly be an animal, unless it's a trained ape, or Dracula. Let's try to see if we can find the secret of opening the stones, being that it's actually the outside wall of the mansion. It would be in this vicinity, somewhere, if there is an entry through the shed."

Together they pushed and pulled up, down, and to each side. But the secret entry, if there was one, remained elusive. It wouldn't open for them.

"Etienne, if we went to the wine cellar, through the house, would you be able to remember where the hole opened?"

"Oh, *Docteur*, it was so long ago. I cannot promise, but I will try."

Before Malcolm and Etienne could make their way into the kitchen, Emilie Fontaine came flying out that door, nearly hysterical.

"What is it? What's happened, Emilie? Is Claire all right?" Malcolm tried to calm his fear for Claire, as well as the sobbing woman, so he could find out what had upset her. Etienne put an arm around his aunt's shoulders.

The others followed the distraught women into the garden, Ben and Abbie right behind Claire, who lead the way. She went straight to Malcolm's side. "Did you find anyone in the shed?" She asked, putting a hand on his arm.

"No, there is nothing in the shed, but stored items." Malcolm looked at Etienne over Claire's head, telling him with his eyes not to say anything about the passageways or Penny's interest in the stone wall of the manse. "Claire, why is Emilie crying?"

"Well, you suggested she check on Marie-Claude, to make sure she was okay. So Madame Fontaine went to her room and knocked. She said there was no answer, so she turned the handle to find it wasn't locked, and opened the door quietly in case her daughter was already asleep. Turns out, Marie-Claude's bed was empty; the quilt covering the bed hadn't even been turned back yet. In fact, she was nowhere to be found in their quarters. Madame doesn't know what to think. Was she kidnapped? Was it Sean? Did she sneak out of the manse? Where could she be?"

"I see. Let's go back inside. Etienne and I will look for Marie-Claude, once I get you back to your suite, Claire. And before you say anything, I'll let you know as soon as we know what's happened. Okay? Etienne, is your grandfather on the premises? He might be of help in our search," Malcolm said, looking at the younger man significantly.

"*Non. Grandpere* left this morning to visit family in Provence. He will be back soon, perhaps at the end of the week. But, *Docteur*, I would call him to come back now, if it is important."

Ben spoke up, "Malcolm, while you and Etienne are looking for Marie-Claude, I'll take Madame Fontaine, and Abbie and Claire, up to the Martelli's suite. I think it's best if I stay with the women until you give us the 'all clear'. What do you say?"

"Great idea. We'll go up with you and check out that floor first. And, I'll leave Penny with you to be your second in command."

By the time the little party reached the fourth floor, an argument had ensued between Claire and Malcolm. "You know I'm not going to hide my head in the sand while you and the others put yourself in danger for me. I need to do this for my own self esteem."

"Claire, be reasonable, we don't even know if it was Sean who Penny was barking at. He may not be around at all. If he's got any sense, he'd high-tail it out of Paris and lay low for a long while."

Abbie walked into their suite, followed by Ben who promptly searched the rest of the suite. Donning his best calm-in-the-face-of- emergency look, he moved to stand next to Malcolm, saying quietly so as not to alarm the ladies, "You need to take a look in here, Malcolm. There's no one in the room now, but it looks like someone *has* been here. And not long ago."

But Claire and Abbie had heard. Both followed Malcolm, who whistled in surprise when he got to the bedroom door that Claire and Mandy shared. He attempted to block the scene inside with his body while both ladies tried their best to peer around him. He couldn't quite keep his comment to himself, "Holy Hell! What war happened here?"

"Oh, no," cried Claire, who'd ducked under his arm to get into the room. Now she stood dumbstruck, rubbing her forehead with one hand as if she couldn't believe the scene that met her eyes upon first glance. Abbie went around Malcolm, following Claire into the bedroom. She, too, could only stare at the sight that faced her. The doors on both wardrobes in the room were wide open, as were the drawers inside, but all were empty. Everything that had once been inside, was now strewn randomly throughout the bedroom in jumbles of tattered remnants of clothing that had been ripped and cut to shreds.

Claire could only manage to ask one question. "Why?"

Abbie pulled herself together and took charge as she'd always done, when she'd held the position as supervising nurse responsible for the newborn nursery. She moved to stand beside her daughter, placing her arm about her and giving her a little squeeze.

"I know, I know. It just doesn't make sense. We're all shocked, but thank the good Lord it's only clothes. They can be replenished. You, dear one, cannot be replaced. So it's a good thing we weren't here when Edward Scissor hands arrived. Do you carry any insurance for this kind of incident, Emilie?" Without waiting for an answer, she glanced at her daughter once again. "Claire, tomorrow, we're heading out to do some serious shopping."

She turned and eyed the three men who appeared to be surreptitiously studying the architecture of the room, looking uneasily at each other, but keeping their thoughts to themselves for Claire's sake. "So, gentlemen, we need to know *how* whoever did this, got in and out of our suite. The entry door was locked when we arrived, there was no indication of a break-in. Of course, that would be *after* you find Marie-Claire. Now, if you'll help me, Emilie, Claire, we'll have this mess cleaned up in no time."

Marie-Claude restlessly paced the dimly lit wine cellar, turning at once as Sean opened the heavy timbered door, the hinges of which desperately needed oiling. She held her breath in fear someone would hear the loud creaking noise the door made as he entered the low-ceilinged chamber.

"Harley, where have you been? I thought you said to me that you would bring back the key ring as soon as you unlocked the door to *Grandpere's* quarters. What has taken you so long a time?"

"Take it easy, beautiful, I had to wait until your mother and her guests were safely out of sight. They were all over the place. Besides, I thought I'd check out grandpa's rooms to see if there was another way out before I stayed there overnight. That was a great idea, Marie-Claude. Now we can spend more time together, at least until the old man returns. You take the key ring back, just in case your mom decides to come looking for it, and then meet me in grandpa's quarters. But before you leave, show me where the passageway from the tool shed opens into this room. Okay?"

For a fleeting few seconds she looked at him with suspicion, but then decided she needed to trust him. He was her last chance to get out from under what she'd determined was her mother's life-long control, knowing she would never be strong enough to do it on her own.

She went to the cellar wall that had been built parallel to the outside wall of the manse, which formed one wall of the shed. Counting out loud in French as she moved along the wall from one corner, she placed her hands on two of the lower stones, one directly above the other, and pushed in on the lower of the two in a practiced manner. Then she pushed in on the upper stone, exactly the same way. The stones slowly slid back as a unit, forming a squarish opening just large enough to crawl through.

She'd learned the two-step process as a young teen, after attempting many different methods to get the wall to re-open. The memory of the accidental opening, when she and Etienne had caused it to do so as children at play, still vivid in her mind. The combination of steps had taken her several years to learn, in a try-and-try-again process. But after her father left them, it had become an obsession. She'd been completely absorbed in the challenge, sharing her compulsive exploration with no one, not even her *cousine*.

Finally the day had come when the rock and mortar panel had finally opened to her touch. Surprisingly, it had taken all of her determination and many more days, before she had the courage to use the flashlight she'd hidden in the cellar to investigate where the tunnel led, knowing nothing of the outside entry through the shed prior to pursuing the pathway of the tunnel.

Sean, alias Harley, had already climbed through the recess in the wall. He stuck his head back out, brushing spider webs from his hair. "Dark as a tomb in here. Got a flashlight handy? I'm going to crawl through to see how far the outer wall is from here, and if I can figure out how to open the portal from the inside. You stay here, beautiful. If I don't come back, you'll know I'm stuck in there somewhere. Come find me. Okay?"

"Harley, wait. It's been many years ago, but when I first figured how to open the wall from this chamber, I also crawled through the shaft to where it ends at the wall of the shed. I was in panic when I couldn't count to find which stone would open the access. So I shut my eyes and made myself think brave to become calm. When I opened them, I saw a small ray of light coming through a chink in the stone wall, which I figured had settled through the years. But luckily, it was daytime. So I pulled down on the top corner of the rock just over the crack of light, and by chance, it was the right one. The group of stones began to move slowly toward me at once. But, first, you must back up and press yourself close to the right wall or the panel of stones could crush you. And if there is no light coming through the window of the shed, I don't think anyone would find which rock opens it."

"So it's pull down, not push in, when you're inside the passage and trying to get out, huh? That's important to know. Uh, oh, sounds like someone is looking for you, beautiful."

Voices calling, "Marie-Claude," could be heard coming nearer as what sounded like more than one pair of feet descended the stone stairway from the main level. "Quickly now, is there any way to get to your room or grandpa's from here, by way of the tunnel?"

"Yes, there is a way. But there is no time to tell you how. Why?"

"I'm going to stay in the tunnel right beyond the opening here until you think up some reason to be in the wine cellar. Then after they escort you back to your room, I'll come back into the cellar here and make my way to grandpa's room. Meet me there. Got it?"

With that said, he disappeared through the opening and the wall began to close, secluding him on the other side. Marie-Claude barely had time to sit down at the table and put her head down before the timbered door to the wine chamber burst open with a screech.

"Marie-Claude, *Cousine*, are you okay? What is the trouble?" Etienne rushed into the room, looking around to make sure she was alone.

Malcolm followed, eyeing the corners of the room and the areas behind the shelves, then looked down at Emilie's daughter who was staring at them in wonder. "Marie-Claude, can you tell us where you've been? You weren't in your room, and we've been looking for you everywhere in the hotel. Etienne, go tell your aunt that we found her. I'll take her back to her room. Tell her to meet us there."

Marie-Claude rubbed her eyes, sitting up and looking around. "Why, is there a problem? I'm really not sure what has happened. All I remember is that I was dizzy from that terrible headache when I left the kitchen. I remember falling down in the corridor. And then nothing until just now when you came in. Why am I in the wine cellar?" She looked around her with a bemused expression on her face. "I told *La Mere* that those drugs they have me take are not good for me. This is proof of it."

"Nice try. I'm certain Dr. Marchand will be interested to hear you're having hallucinations. It might go better for you if you tell the truth, you know. We've already seen Claire

227

Martelli's bedroom. Someone was not in balance either emotionally or mentally when they destroyed all her and her sister's clothes. Are you saying you don't remember doing it?"

This time fear replaced the bemused look on Marie-Claude's face. "Destroyed their clothes? *Non, Docteur*, I know nothing about it. You must believe me. I have not been anywhere near that floor. *Oui*, it must have been someone else. *S'il vous plait, je ne comprends pas*," she said, breaking into French. "*La Mere. La Mere.*" She sank to the floor, crying, "*La Mere*", over and over again.

Malcolm could see she was visibly upset and prayed this wouldn't bring on another catatonic state like before. But he was sure she was stronger now because of the medication, and he was inclined to believe her. But if she wasn't the one responsible, who was? Everyone else was accounted for. He continued mulling it over in his mind, as he picked her up and carried her up the stairway to her room.

By the time they got to the apartment, Marie-Claude was crying hysterically. Her mother, waiting at the door, indicated for him to put her on the bed, where she curled up into a ball and continued to sob. Malcolm asked what medication Dr. Marchand had sent, in case it was necessary to calm her. Emilie found the small bag of medication from the clinic and handed it to Malcolm, who read the labels and took out one, recommending to Emile that she give one to her daughter right away. After Marie-Claude had taken the pill, she settled down, but repeated her mother and grandfather's names over and over, interspersed with a name that sounded like "Harley." After quietly filling Emilie in on the little he'd learned from her daughter, he went on to explain there was something he felt she was holding back about the evening, but that he believed her when she said she didn't destroy Claire and Mandy's clothes. He left mother and daughter on the bed, Madame Fontaine holding Marie-Claude who was curled up like a little girl, while she patted and soothed her.

Etienne waited for him in the hallway. "Where to now, *Docteur*?"

228

"I'm thinking that we need to get that shed locked tonight, Etienne. Is there a keyed lock on it, like a deadbolt? If so, let's go out and check inside once more, then lock it for the night. I want to make one final search of the ground floor and the wine cellar, then we'll call it a night. By the way, where do you stay when you're here? I didn't hear you say anything about which room was yours when we checked earlier."

"Well, sometimes I stay in *Tante* and *Cousine's* suite, like when both of them had stayed at the clinic, or when they go out of town for a few days. Other than that, I stay with *Grandpere* in his quarters. There is a second room that is not his own bedroom. That is the room I use mostly. *Tante* Emilie had a bed and other furnishings brought in for me, so I would feel at home. We did not go into *Grandpere's* rooms when we made our early rounds. They are just off the kitchen along the corridor that leads to *Tante's* suite and the lobby. I had better get the master key ring if we're going to lock doors, and unlock others."

Malcolm nodded, and sat down on a bench around the corner from the lobby while he waited for Etienne to retrieve the keys from the office. He rubbed his temples. He couldn't remember when he'd been this drained. Then again, he wasn't sure what had drained him the most—the emotionally charged evening after Penny started barking, the clothing incident, or the search mission that had taken him up and down three flights of stairs for the past hour or so. He knew there something he was just not getting, something that would make sense of all the incidents tonight. He just couldn't get a handle on it at the moment. But he was certain that it had something to do with Claire and Mandy's slashed clothes, and Marie-Claude's denial of having done it. The peaceful quiet was a welcome tranquilizer and he leaned back against the wall and closed his eyes, waiting for Etienne to return.

The next thing he knew, he was being shaken awake. Etienne had returned and was pointing to the floor. "*Docteur,* look there, at the floor. Those muddy tracks go all the way to the lobby and into *Tante's* office. I found the ring of keys on the floor, not locked in the drawer of the desk where I left them. But no one was around. You must have seen someone go by while you sat here, because, you will remember, there were no tracks when I left you. But *Tante* called to me as I was going by her door, saying she heard noises coming from outside. So I stepped out the kitchen door to check for her. It was just the wind, I think, blowing the limbs of the trees against the manse and rattling the glass in these old windows. I'm sure you've heard it, as you have stayed here so often. But I did want to tell you that I found the key to the tool shed's deadbolt on *Tante's* ring, and I locked it before I came back in. And I locked the kitchen door to the garden as well. So that is taken care of for this night."

Wide awake now, Malcolm listened closely to Etienne's recital of the muddy tracks and the noises Emilie had heard outside. "Did you check inside the shed before you locked it?"

"*Oui, Docteur.* There was no one."

"Where did the muddy tracks lead after you followed them to the office?"

"That is what is so strange. They just stopped at *Tante's* desk. Of course there was very little mud by the time the person who made the tracks came down the corridor to the office. I did backtrack to see where they started. I was surprised to find them coming up the stairway from the wine cellar."

That's it, Malcolm thought, the light dawning. There definitely is a passage from the shed into the house, and it must lead into the wine cellar. And from the wine cellar, our late caller could now be anywhere inside this old place. Or out by now. But what did he want with the keys? Of course, that's the link with the clothes. It has to be Sean. He went up to the Martelli's suite and let himself in with the key, destroyed the clothes, probably to keep Claire on edge, all the while knowing Marie-Claude would be blamed. He must have tricked her into showing him the secret passageway into the manse. But how did he get to her? It's not that she'd been easy to meet up with, even before her collapse. But, he must

230

become invisible so the police can't find him. And now that he knows the way in, he can come and go as he pleases. One thing is sure, he needs a safe house to keep out of sight—where his intended victim is within his reach any time of the day or night. Good Lord.

"Etienne, let's go. We need to check out the one place we neglected to look in before. Where you're staying. *Grandpere*'s quarters. And I think it would be a good idea to get hold of Dom and see if he would be willing to come back as quickly as possible. I'm hoping he knows about other secret passages and their location throughout the mansion."

When they arrived at the rooms Etienne and his grandfather occupied, they unlocked the door and entered, on their guard as to what they might find. Etienne picked up an umbrella from the stand in the entry, while Malcolm was satisfied with the long-handled flashlight he carried.

They had agreed prior to entering that one would go through the unit while the other stood guard at the door, so in case the elusive Shamrock was actually in the unit, he couldn't escape as he'd done on so many other occasions. Malcolm indicated he would stay by the door as Etienne was familiar with the layout of the apartment, while he waited for the chance to deal with Sean both for Claire's sake and to appease his own sense of justice.

But once again, they came up empty-handed. Although Etienne was certain something had been disturbed in his *Grandpere*'s bedroom. It just didn't look right, he'd said, but he couldn't remember what was out of place. They left the apartment, locking the door and headed toward the kitchen end of the old mansion, to check the doors once more, and turn out the lights. However, the sound of glass shattering, coming from within the rooms they'd just left, caused them to stop dead in their tracks. Retracing their steps, they unlocked and cautiously entered the apartment again. A rush of wind coming from Dom's bedroom showed them where to look. The glass in one of the windows of the old man's room was broken, indicating the Shamrock's way out. They could hardly ignore the fact that he had indeed been in the apartment while Etienne searched and Malcolm stood guard. But where?

Malcolm carefully leaned out the broken window, shining the flashlight around the grounds of the garden outside. He saw no one, and heard only the chirping of the crickets. "No one out here now. We'll have to get this window boarded up before we turn in. Do you know if there's a sheet of plywood around? Or better yet, is there a glass company that makes house calls this time of night?" He thought, if not, he could ask Etienne to sleep in Dom's room tonight, as a last resort. Because it would be just like Sean to sneak back in through the broken window. He shuddered to think of that possibility.

Etienne wasn't certain if there was any material to temporarily cover the window. He was about to leave the room to call a glass company, when he stopped and excitedly pointed to the wardrobe which was angled out from the wall it usually stood against. "That is it. That is what didn't seem right when we were here the first time. But I could not remember its exact place on the wall. He must have been hiding behind it."

"Well, yes and no," Malcolm said, examining the wall behind the skewed wardrobe. "Look at that."

On the backside of the *armoire* was a panel that had been lifted off, showing a small space, just big enough to stand in, between it and the back panel of the wardrobe's interior.

"He must have hidden in here until we left, and he thought the coast was clear. So he made his escape out the window. He evidently didn't know the secret to opening these old windows, or else this one was stuck. But I'd give a tuppence to find out how he knew that hidey-hole was there."

Day Seven

New York City—Jesse's apartment

"Mom . . . hi. It's Mandy. Is Claire there with you? Yes? Okay, put me on speaker so you both can hear. Got it? All right, here goes. You're never going to believe this, but as of today, the publisher of that new travel magazine, JOURNEY, has contracted me to do a feature article for each of their bi-monthly issues, starting with five this year. And the contract is renewable on a yearly basis if both sides are in agreement. You've probably seen their first issue on the newsstands recently. No? Well it's a knockout premier edition," she said, pacing the living room of Jesse and Gia's apartment in her eagerness to give her family the good tidings.

"Thanks, Claire. What did you say, Mom? One at a time! I can't understand either of you when you're both talking at once. How did it happen? Well, amazingly enough, I was able to get an interview with them earlier today, and I pitched the idea of doing an on-going feature, kind of a take-off on the By-Ways idea, with yours truly as photographer and writer-journeyer as well. And they loved it! We're going to plan an itinerary to take in places in Europe to begin with. And it can go on and on—Alaska, South America—any city or country that we all agree hasn't been thoroughly covered.

"I'm to meet with the publisher and others in the top echelon again tomorrow, to firm up all the details. But we're going to start with Paris. I showed them some of the shots I'd taken and saved to the memory cards, and they were impressed. I'm so excited, I can hardly stand it. Of course, I'll have to go back and re-shoot with a different focus the ones I've already been paid to do for my former assignment for the guidebook. But that's no problem. There's always a new angle for any particular subject."

Mandy listened for a few minutes, nodding and looking pleased with the praiseworthy remarks that were being showered on her from across the sea. From the apartment's open kitchen came the satisfying pop of a cork. And then a cheer went up.

"Oh, that? Jesse and Gia just opened a bottle of Prosecco to celebrate. You know . . . my favorite Italian bubbly? What was that, Mom? Yes, I'm reserved on the overnight flight tomorrow evening. I'll take a taxi to the Saint-Germain. It'll be early morning when I get in, so I'll just ring the buzzer and wake Etienne up to unlock the front door. Okay? Anything new with the Shamrock?"

"Say that again?" The look on Mandy's face went from complete elation, freezing into an anxious frown as she listened to a brief description of the happenings centered on Claire since she'd been called to New York by her now-former travelogue employer.

"Claire, are you serious? That's monstrous. Let alone frightening. You know, it's getting way too dangerous for you in Paris, and for Abbie as well. I know you don't have all the antiques purchased yet. But listen, Sis, you can always leave your requirements for the items you're looking for. You know that antique dealer you met with before, Simon something . . . Simon Boulle, right? I'm certain he'd locate them, and take a few shots from different angles. Then all he has to do is attach the photos to an e-mail, along with the dimensions. How

234

simple is that? He can also take care of having the pieces shipped to the States. That's all part of what he offers those customers who purchase antiques at his shop, right?"

Mandy's face went completely colorless as the seriousness of what she was listening to hit home. "Claire, for God's sake, please don't do that. Replacing the clothes is a small matter compared to what you're talking about doing. Please don't do it. Offering yourself as bait at Simon's shop could be extremely dangerous. What do you mean, you've already done it once? And he got away again? You know when you tell me you're going to do some dumb stunt like that, I have to think you've gone absolutely stark-raving mad.

"Okay, okay. Calm down. You know I didn't mean that. I understand you want it all to end and go away. Just, please, do me one favor. Wait until I get there before you do anything more. Promise me, Claire. Listen, what about this idea? Now hear me out before you say it won't work. Lieutenant Owens can probably get the French police to give you some protection until this Shamrock guy is caught. I can call him tomorrow morning, before my appointment. How does that sound? Now will you promise me?"

Mandy listened again, this time for a couple minutes, her shoulders drooping by the second. "I see. And they couldn't catch him either? He just disappeared into thin air again. Well, what about Malcolm? He's trying his best to protect you, isn't he?

"Okay, forget I asked. Claire, the guy's in love with you. What's so unusual about him wanting to take care of you? So, let's not argue. Can we talk it over like big kids when I get back there?

"Fine. And, Sis, remember that what you do or don't do can also affect Abbie. Just think about that before you do something rash that may have consequences for her also.

"Yah, okay. You too. Watch yourselves. See you the day after tomorrow. Love you. Bye"

She clicked her phone off, her festive mood ruined. To their credit, Jessie and Gia asked no questions. They simply

235

waited for her to join them in the kitchen of their open loft plan.

"Here, sit yourself down, Mandy. Let's toast your new undertaking. And what a plum. When your story and photos are printed and the magazine distributed, the Paris project will definitely establish your talent and abilities to your new publisher, but more importantly, to the readers of JOURNEY." Jesse paused, picking up his glass. "To Mandy. To Paris. To JOURNEY and its readers." They clanked their stemmed flutes together.

But Mandy, worried about what was happening with her family in Paris, lost her desire to celebrate. "Thanks, both of you. You've been great. And I owe you big time. Please, and I'm serious about this, I will happily reciprocate if either of you, or both, ever need a favor, and I have it in my power to do, it's already a done deal. Now, if you don't mind, I think I'll hit the sack. If I get through the meetings they've scheduled for me at the publishing offices tomorrow sooner than expected, I might try to get an earlier flight than the midnight special. Will I see you tomorrow, Jess?"

"I'm sure you will. You're not getting rid of me quite so easily. I'm taking you into the city to your appointment in the morning."

"Well, thanks for the thought, but that's way too much trouble. I'll just get a taxi."

"Sorry, Mandy. Not a chance. Besides, now that you're such a hotshot, I've got to keep on your good side. I've always heard it's who you know." He winked at her.

"Whatever. And thanks again, Jess. What about you, Gia. Will I see you before I leave?"

"I have another early morning assignment, so I'll give you a hug tonight. And Mandy, I found several more outfits you would look great in that I never wear for some reason or another. I would consider it an honor if you would be kind enough to adopt and enjoy them. I certainly can use more hanging space in my closet."

On seeing Mandy's look of suspicion, she added, "It would please me, my friend. Look, I put them in your room, along with a carry-on bag. However, what with having to take your camera equipment on with you, I would suggest you check the bag.

"One of these days, Jess and I will show up at some unique out-of-the-way place you're shooting for the magazine, and I'll get the bag from you then. Okay? Now, quit fretting. I'll stay up fifteen more minutes so I can see how wonderful you look in the clothes."

Paris—Shopping and the Opera Quarter

The day after finding her clothes ripped to shreds, Claire, along with Abbie and Ben who insisted on accompanying her, took advantage of the bright sunshine to go shopping for lingerie and a few changes of clothing. She'd decided to try to get everything she needed for the next few days at a department store that Emilie Fontaine suggested. However, her mother urged her to look at the smaller specialty stores and boutiques that offered more in the way of high fashions. But, Claire hesitated. She knew Mandy would also need to shop and figured her sister would prefer doing a tour of the boutiques and maybe even hitting an *haute couture* shop just for the fun of it. So, *Au Printemps*, one of Paris' premier department stores, would do nicely for today's shopping expedition.

It was also located near a Metro stop on the Right Bank, the Boulevard Haussmann in the Opera Quarter. And she was looking forward to riding the underground rail, even though Abbie and Ben had suggested a taxi would be safer and quicker.

Claire had placed the Opera Quarter on her 'must see' list, and felt she may not have another chance to visit it except for today. The famous nineteenth century *Opera de Paris Garnier* structure had been designed for Napoleon III. She'd read that the building boasted a mixture of materials and styles ranging from Classical to Baroque, complete with sumptuous columns, friezes and sculptures on the exterior.

She knew she needed to persuade her mom and Ben, who were so nervous about the possibility of the Shamrock showing up, they'd tried to curtail everything she wanted to do. As an inducement, she offered to buy lunch at the *Café de la Paix*, built opposite the opera house and also designed by Charles Garnier. It was said to have retained its old-fashioned ways and nineteenth century décor. And to her relief, Abbie and Ben finally agreed to lunch there.

Prior to entering *Au Printemps*, Claire paused, fascinated by the crenulated glass and metal canopy projecting over the main entryway, thinking it a French fashion statement in its own right. She whipped out her camera, glad she remembered to bring it along today. Generally, when traveling with Mandy, she simply asked her sister to get a shot of something she wanted to preserve for her design-muse files.

Besides the visit to the opera house, the expedition was a definite success in terms of shopping for clothes that were distinctly designed in the latest Parisian styles. Claire tried on and purchased a variety of smart separates for daytime, straight off the rack. It took a little coaxing on Abbie's part, but in the end, she splurged on a chic little black dress that she wasn't sure just where she would wear it, but it called to her from the hanger. She'd finished off in the lingerie and accessories departments, investing in a number of fashionable adornments that would emulate the Parisian style on a more moderate budget.

The three of them now sat at an outdoor table at the *Café de la Paix*, surrounded by shopping bags. Glad of the chance to rest their feet, Ben and Abbie at first insisted they take a seat inside the cafe, worried that the Shamrock might try something in the outdoor venue. However, Claire convinced them that it was far safer outside, people-watching the crowds passing by in the *Place de l'Opera*, which was one of Paris's busiest intersections. There were so many people around, he wouldn't dare attempt another so-called accident here, she said. And besides, she'd pointed out, the opera house was situated across the square from their vantage point at the cafe, and would provide them with an all new view of the exterior.

The waiter appeared to take their order. Abbie and Ben opted for one of the café's *plats du jour*; while Claire decided on a light omelet and a salad. Then, on seeing Ben eye the fresh fruit tarts on the desert cart close by, she ordered a plate of tarts for the table to share to complete their meal.

As they waited for their food to arrive, Claire took her camera out to show them the pictures she'd taken at the opera house. It'd been all she'd read about, and more. "Look at this one, the Grand Staircase. Just see the way that white marble is set off by the red and green marble balustrade. Remember how the stairway takes you up to the auditorium? I tried to get all five tiers in this shot, but there was never a time without other tourists on several of the flights. What I wouldn't give for the same shot during an actual performance with women dressed in their opera finery parading up and down the tiers. And just look at this one . . . with the plaster cherubs blazing gold leaf against all that red velvet. A real dichotomy of styles though, even though I love the false ceiling painted by Marc Chagall in the mid-sixties." She stopped for breath before showing her mother photos of the domed ceiling covered with mosaics in the Grand Foyer.

"Well, you can have all those fancy styles and materials," Abbie said. "For me the small lake hidden beneath the structure was the most interesting feature."

"I can understand your preference for the lake, Mom, especially given the fact that it provided the inspiration for the phantom's hiding place in the stage version of *Phantom of the Opera*. The lake adds to the romantic mystique and historical notoriety of the building. However, that place really gave me the willies, it felt like the phantom was still down there, hiding in the shadows. Watching. Did either of you get that impression?" She asked, turning to Ben when her mother shook her head. "Look how dark it is around the other side of the lake," she said, "everything is in shadow." She held the camera so they could see the photo she'd taken of the lake and the surrounding area.

Hearing his name, Ben guiltily turned his gaze back to the two women. He appeared to be only paying attention to their discussion with one ear, Claire thought, seeing his full attention focused on studying the passing crowd. She knew Abbie had made him promise that he would be on the lookout for the Shamrock during their outing today. But on hearing her comment about being watched, he simply gave a tight-lipped smile and shook his head. His manner caused Claire to wonder if he'd seen what she'd seen—a shifting shape in the shadows. Or was it only a movement of the shadows on the surface of the lake? It had been so dark in the deeper recesses around the lake, she couldn't be certain what she'd seen. Waiting for his reply, she noticed the evident relief on his face as the waiter saved him from responding, setting their lunch selections in front of them.

Their little party was seated in the front row of the outdoor tables, facing the *Place de l'Opera*, so that all three could view the throngs passing by. Behind them, between their table and the façade of the café was another row of tables, one of which had just emptied. The one directly behind them.

Before Claire realized what was happening, someone began shoving the bags containing her purchases further under her chair and the table, presumably to give the new occupants more room. She turned around with a smile, intending to apologize for the many shopping bags and to ask if they were still in the way.

Ben frowned and started up from his seat, until he saw who it was.

"*Excusez-moi*," Claire began, and then stopped as recognition hit home for her also. She stared up, open-mouthed, at the dark-haired man who was also staring at her, albeit red-faced, while helping to seat one of his female companions. That's what prompted her to look over the two women in his company—one sleek and beautiful, and the other, already seated, a well-polished elderly woman with the proud bearing of a matriarch.

Abbie shifted around to see what had attracted Ben and Claire's attention. "Malcolm." She exclaimed. "I didn't see you come in. Please join us, there's plenty of room," she said signaling the waiter before staring at the two women seated at his table.

"Oh, I am sorry, I didn't know you were . . . ah, otherwise occupied. We've been sightseeing today, and shopping, as you see from the evidence. And I'd say it's been quite a successful outing." Abbie looked straight into Malcolm's eyes as she continued in a more formal manner. "But, don't let us keep you from your companions. So good to see you again, Doctor." She turned her head slightly to observe her daughter's reaction as Ben leaned across the table to shake hands with Malcolm, adding his pleasantries.

The shadows around the opera's underground lake forgotten, Claire's curiosity piqued. Upon studying Malcolm's face she decided it was as if he was in another world—or perhaps caught up by some experience or emotion from the past. She suddenly realized how little she knew about his previous life. Deciding to wait him out, she lowered her eyes, but continued to watch him through thick lashes. A few seconds later, he appeared to come back to the present with a purpose. He straightened his shoulders, flashed her a smile, and began introducing his guests to her table.

"Countess, I would like you to meet some very special friends of mine . . . Claire Martelli . . . her mother, Abigail Martelli . . . and Dr. Ben Weston. They're all from the States, and are also staying at the Saint-Germain. This is my grandmother, Lady Anna," he explained, fondly putting a hand on her shoulder, "who has come to Paris from England to visit me. And, this is her companion . . . Cerian Bradford, whose family owns the manor adjacent to Rosemore Grange, my grandmother's home."

Taken aback that Malcolm had never mentioned his grandmother was a peeress of the realm, it instantly struck her that he could also be titled, if not now, maybe one day. Her mind in a fog, she tried to assimilate the information. Vaguely, she heard Abbie ask the countess where they were staying.

Lady Anna, as Malcolm called her, replied. "We generally lodge at the Ritz in the Tuileries Quarter. But, as my grandson's accommodations are in the St-Germain-des-Pres Quarter, Cerian and I are at the Hotel d'Angleterre there. However, we are hoping he will stay at our hotel while we are in town. Cerian has been looking forward to him showing her around Paris as she's been away for the past few years, living in Italy," she explained. "I told him I was bringing a surprise. They've known each other from childhood, you see, and were affianced at one time," she finished, patting her grandson's hand still on her shoulder.

Claire felt her heart do a flip-flop. She stared blankly at Malcolm, again trying to process the information that he'd previously been engaged to Cerian, the beautifully tailored English woman who was now smiling up at him. She placed her hand on his arm in what Claire deemed to be a possessive gesture geared to communicate her intentions to Claire.

Okay, got it. Message received, loud and clear, Claire thought. She smiled at her new-old rival. *Game on.*

"Lady Anna has been wonderfully kind to bring me with her on this visit. I've been so looking forward to seeing Malcolm again. I just couldn't wait until the university session was over for him to come home from Paris," Cerian said. She blushed with charming effect.

On seeing this, Malcolm instantly directed a glance at Claire, who was unabashedly staring at his ex-fiancée who, in turn, gave Claire a smugly triumphant smile. "Ceri," he said, taking her hand from his arm, and moving into his chair, "the waiter is here for our order. Have you decided?"

"Oh, just order me my usual, Malcolm."

Claire couldn't help herself. She was completely absorbed, watching as Cerian flirted outrageously with Malcolm, tossing back her straight, almost black, fringed mane, and batting dark, sexy eyes. A little overdone, thought Claire, noting Cerian's heavy eye make-up, but I have to hand it to her, the whole look definitely boasted high Italian style.

Fascinated by the show Cerian was putting on, Claire studied Malcolm's reaction to his ex-fiancée's calculated efforts. To his credit, he appeared uncomfortable with the situation. How characteristic, Claire thought, knowing he was too much of a gentleman to make a scene.

Okay, stop it, Claire chided herself. *Quit with the catty thing. I'm sure he was very surprised to find his once-betrothed traveling with his grandmother when he met her train at the terminal.*

But, in truth, this incident also surprised Claire, in relation to her own feelings for Malcolm. Just a few days ago, he'd expressed love for her while they were sitting on the terrace in the garden. She'd told herself then that she needed to wait until she was herself again. Once the divorce was final, and the Shamrock incidents hopefully ended, she'd be able to clarify how she felt about him. She'd found out all right, and sooner than she thought. This afternoon was indeed an eye-opener. Surprising herself, she'd just discovered she was just as much enamored of him as he said he was of her.

Okay, Cerian, we'll duke it out, but I think you've already drawn the short straw. You had your chance.

Somehow that thought made her day.

While Malcolm and his grandmother were busy eating and listening to Cerian's stories about her time in Italy, Claire and Abbie conversed quietly. But Claire wasn't comfortable with the display Cerian was putting on for her benefit. She found it impossible to ignore the tinkling laughter emanating from the table behind her. It's definitely time to leave, she thought. She wanted to get her purchases back to the privacy of the Saint-Germain where she could relax and think through this new situation. Claire waited for the waiter to bag the rest of the pastries, then paid the bill and began gathering up the bags. Ben flagged down a taxi as there was no way they'd be able to carry everything back to the Saint-Germain on the Metro.

As they attempted to control the results of the shopping expedition, Malcolm came around to their table and began taking the bags from Abbie and Claire. She smiled her thanks and whispered the offer of a private fashion show that night. "Unless you're busy, of course . . ."

He grinned as he placed the bags in the taxi, whispering close to her ear. "You're on. I'll make my escape after dinner. And Claire, I won't be changing hotels."

Paris—Hotel d'Angleterre

As Lady Anna remarked earlier, the Hotel d'Angleterre was indeed a close neighbor to the Residence Saint-Germain. While the old aristocratic mansion situated in the *St-Germain-des-Pres* was purely eighteenth-century French, the Angleterre's background was strictly English. It had at one time been the premises of the British Embassy and even now it retained some of the original features, including its fine old staircase, an exquisite terraced garden, and the mantelpiece in the salon. There were only twenty-nine bedrooms, but all were uniquely and stylishly decorated. And many of these boasted original beams and gorgeous hand-carving on the upright supports of the antique four-poster beds. All in all, it was noted to be a most charming and utterly civilized hotel.

At least that's what everyone who stayed there generally remarked, everyone, that is to say, except her ladyship, the Countess of Rosemore, a peeress in her own right—her late husband, Sir Thomas Worthington, holding only the lifetime rank of Knight.

Malcolm stopped by his grandmother's rooms to collect her for dinner. While waiting for Cerian to join them, the countess took the opportunity to talk privately with her grandson.

"Malcolm, we'll be moving over to the Ritz tomorrow. This hotel is not satisfactory. You must join us, as it's not in close proximity to the place you're staying now."

"Grandmother, I can't do that. First of all, I've booked my rooms through the end of the month, until the graphology course is completed for this period at *universite*. And, besides, you know I brought Penelope with me. The Ritz would never allow an animal her size. May I ask what is wrong with this hotel?"

"There is simply no elegance here. Beams and four-poster beds. Really. The only thing impressive about the place is the mantelpiece in here, and as I understand from the hotel's *concierge*, that is true of the mantelpieces in all of the rooms. So this room is hardly unique.

"But, after seeing you with the American girl today, I think I know the real reason why you don't wish to change hotels. It's that little blonde with the wild curly hair, isn't it?"

Before he could answer, she went on. "You know, Malcolm, I'm not going to live forever. We've talked about this before. My title will rightfully pass on to you, my oldest grandson, through your mother's lineage, she being my only child. The estate as well. I want you to come home and take your rightful place as the future Earl of Rosemore."

Malcolm stood up and paced the room. Stopping in mid-stride, he faced his grandmother. In his eyes, she was the wonderful woman who'd taken his brother and him in as orphans after their parents, Lady Anna's daughter and son-in-law, were killed in a rock slide while driving in the mountains on a visit to the family's winery in Italy.

"Grandmother, you must know that I deeply appreciate your very generous offer and your confidence in me. The fact is, I've never wanted the title. This is the twenty-first century. The way of life you knew in your younger days is no longer possible. The landed aristocracy is fading away. The old estates are expensive to maintain in today's economy. Many are being turned into luxury hotels and tourist attractions, charging an excessive rate to stay there to see how the other half lived in centuries past, and even into the present."

"I do understand what you're saying Malcolm. But I trust you to lead the family into the future. I wasn't going to tell you this, I was actually going to wait until you finished lecturing at the university and came home. However, I think you should know that Jack is back at the Grange house. He has apologized to me for his actions that caused the break-up between you and Cerian. I have taken him at his word. And then she returned also, but just recently. You need to forget the past, Grandson. Marry Cerian and be happy at Rosemore.

"I need you there to run the family business. I'm ready to retire the responsibility. Jack knows I have chosen to leave you the title and the estate, and that you are my choice to head the family's winery in Italy. He understands and is perfectly comfortable with that arrangement, even suggesting that he be your number-one man at the winery. But he said he'll work at whatever and wherever you need him. Also, he's already made his peace with Cerian, and wants you to marry her and put the gossip to rest. Give him a break, my dear. He wants nothing more than for you to come home so he can beg your forgiveness . . ."

Malcolm began pacing at the same time Lady Anna began talking about his brother and Cerian. "Grandmother," he broke in, "I don't wish to discuss Jack at the moment. But you must know that I have no feelings left for Cerian. Surely, you've realized that by now. I can forgive them, but forget? I'm afraid not. If you brought her here in the hope that we would take up where we left off, you've wasted your money. Not a chance. Ceri is part of my past. Call her an historical event in my life, one that took me some years to make my way through. But it's over. If she is the condition for which I would inherit the title and estate, and the family's business in Italy, I'm asking you to entitle Jack instead of me. I'm definitely not interested. I know you, Grandmother, and you will always do what you think is right. As I must. Please know, whatever your final decision . . . I will always love and honor you, just as I do now."

"Grandson, this American girl is not part of our social class. She has no links with our way of life, or our ancestry. Given time, you would understand that. She just won't do as your wife."

Blue flames blazed in Malcolm's eyes as he stopped pacing to stand in front of his grandmother. "How can you say that? Claire is someone worth getting to know. Before you make a blanket assessment about her, just because she comes from the States, you might try giving her the time of day."

Grandson and grandmother glared at one other, each deadlocked in their own personal view of the matter.

Lady Anna broke eye contact first. "All right, Malcolm, if she means that much to you, I will *try* to get to know her. But on one condition. That, in the meantime, you keep an open mind. Please think seriously about giving Cerian another chance." On seeing the look on his face, she added, "A person *can* change, you know."

As if on cue, Cerian appeared in the open door that adjoined their rooms, posing before she made her grand entrance. She was dressed to entice, in black silk—high fashion to the nth degree. "Oh, Malcolm. I didn't know you were here yet. Am I worth the wait?"

Denver—Offices of Chadwick+Martelli Design Group

Lieutenant Grady Owens waited patiently in the reception area of the Chadwick+Martelli Design Group's office for Susan to show up. When she did make her appearance, she was out of breath, and the look on her face said she'd rather be anywhere but at the office right now. And when she saw the detective, her body language expressed a textbook defense mode.

"Chad is out of town for a couple days, Lieutenant. But I'll leave him a message that you stopped by when he calls in today."

Owens got up from the comfort of the tastefully upholstered chair he'd chosen, the only seat that gave a clear view of the entry door, Chad's office door, and the reception desk.

"I wish I had your hours, Ms. Farrell. I'd be in hog heaven. Did you even get lunch today, Ma'am? If not, I have a bag of donuts left over from morning," he said, holding up a crumpled and greasy brown bag. "I'll share with you."

"Lieutenant Owens, I make it a habit to stay away from donuts. They're nothing but sugar and grease." She eyed the bag with distaste. "But, thank you for offering to share. Now, what is the purpose of your visit? Or is there a purpose?" She walked to the desk and set her tote bag down, fishing in it for the five-inch-heeled stilettos that she only wore when she didn't need to walk very far.

Owens admired the fashionable foot-wear. "Very nice, but how do you walk in them?"

"Lieutenant. What do you want?" Susan snapped.

Owens noted the irritation transparent in her voice. He watched her effort to paste the mask of cool efficiency back on her face.

"Sorry. I'm sensing your annoyance with my visit today. This office just seems so interesting, at least it's been true in the several times I've stopped by."

"And you find my stilettos interesting, Lieutenant?"

"No, Ms. Farrell, not your stilettos. What's interesting is that Mr. Chadwick just leaves the office to run by itself for a few days, without Ms. Martelli here to take over. She's his partner, right?"

"True, but you forget that as Chad's assistant, I'm next in command when Claire's not here. And, FYI, I'm quite capable of running the office. Anyway, Lieutenant, it's just for a few days. And I can call Chad if something comes up that he needs to know about."

"Do you think he would need to know if I were to take you down to the station for questioning, as an accomplice in the attack on Ms. Martelli back in March? If so, you'd better call him now."

Susan eyed him, disbelief showing on her face, her long red hair moving back and forth as she shook her head slowly from side to side. She gradually backed away from the side of the reception counter, where she'd been standing, obviously waiting for Owens to leave.

"What are you saying? You think I had something to do with the attack on Claire? Lieutenant Owens, I can't believe you actually think that. I really can't go down to the station, I *must* be here. Chad is counting on me."

Still backing away, her legs hit the seat of the chair at her desk. She sat down abruptly, looking both shocked and scared at the same time. It came as a surprise to her that the detective evidently thought he'd found something that might prove that she'd taken part in the so-called burglary-turned-attack that night.

Nobody knows, she thought. Nobody knows *for sure*, she amended. And, of course, Sean didn't count. The fact of the matter was she hadn't heard from him for several days now. And she had no way to get in contact with him and needed to do so, badly. On top of everything, including the very revealing conversation she'd had with Chad, now she was in the hot seat with the police, and there was no way to reach her stepbrother. And even Chad had taken off. In her mind, that meant she now had the full impact of the detective's attention.

Just then, a distraught Loupe, Claire's assistant, hurried into the reception area from the interiors department. "Susan? Excuse me, I don't mean to interrupt, but I'm expecting a delivery of wall finish samples for the New Orleans restaurant. Has it come in yet?"

"No, nothing has come in, Loupe. I'll let you know when it arrives," Susan said, while mentally hoping she'd be there to receive the package. Because, if not, she'd be in some small closed room being questioned while who knows who was standing behind the one-way glass, watching and listening in on the interrogation.

Owens turned toward Loupe. "Excuse me, Ms. Guadeloupe Smith? Right?"

"Uh, yes?" Loupe turned, eyeing the man's rumpled jacket and the scuffed shoes.

"Sorry, Ma'am, don't mean to be nosy. But I heard Ms. Farrell here, say your name just now. And I happen to have a treat for Duffy somewhere in one of my pockets. Tried to give it to Mr. Chadwick when I last saw him, but he told me you were taking care of the pup while Ms. Martelli is in Paris." Owens searched his jacket for the rawhide bone he hadn't taken out of his pocket since he'd last worn the coat. "Here it is. Would you give it to Duffy, please? With the compliments of the Denver Police Department, of course. By the way, how's the pup doing?" He offered the plastic-wrapped bone to Loupe, who accepted it with a shaking hand.

"Thank you, er . . . officer? But I'm afraid Duffy is missing." After admitting that fact, the words poured out. "He simply disappeared from my fenced back yard. I discovered he was missing when I got home from work the day before yesterday. Since then, I've talked to everyone on my street, who also helped me look everywhere in the neighborhood for him. I also called every shelter in and around the whole city.

"I even made up 'missing notices' on the computer, from some pictures we took of him playing in the yard. And, I offered a reward for his return, as well. My son helped me tack up the posters. I feel just awful. Claire trusted me, and I let her down. I'm hoping someone will call saying they've found him, or he'll come back on his own, before I have to tell her he's missing."

"Loupe, I'm certain Duffy is okay. He's a friendly dog. Someone probably took him in. I'm sure he'll be back, safe and sound," Susan said, feeling sorry for the distressed woman, all the while knowing that Duffy was with Chad. At least she hoped he hadn't lied to her when he'd promised her that he would see to it that the dog was safe and well.

Noticing how keenly the detective studied her reaction just now, Susan knew she'd made an error in judgment by showing empathy to Loupe. She suspected that her few words of comfort would probably start him thinking that somehow she knew the dog was all right. And that would probably give him the clue—find Chad, find the dog.

Whatever Owens's thoughts, he turned his attention back to Loupe. "Ma'am, we haven't really met. I'm Lieutenant Grady Owens of the Denver police department, like I said before. Maybe I can be of help. First, I need to know if there was any way he could've jumped the fence, or tunneled underneath, or maybe gotten through a small space."

"No, I'm sure of that, Lieutenant. Duffy was secure. I checked the fence myself before I said yes to Claire when she asked me if I would keep him while she's away. It's an eight-foot-high cedar enclosure with a padlocked gate. When I discovered he was missing, I checked to make sure all the cedar boards were in place. They were. And there was no space to get under the boards as I have a stone foundation for the fence.

"But here's the odd part. I asked my neighbors if they noticed anything strange going on near my fence that day. One of them, my neighbor directly to the south, said she heard Duffy barking up a storm, but didn't see anything out of the ordinary. Just some kids from the neighborhood playing, and some guy out walking his dog along the north side of the fence. I have a corner lot, you see. She said Duffy stopped barking and wagged his tail when the man and dog came even with where my neighbor last saw him. So she didn't think anything more of it."

"Interesting," was all Owens said, glancing over at Susan, who was busily sorting some papers on her desk. "Could your neighbor describe the guy who was walking his dog yesterday? Or the kind of dog he was walking? Just in case Duffy was taken, you see."

Loupe shook her head. "I asked her that because I think that's what had to have happened. Though I don't know how he could've accomplished it. Unfortunately, she said it was all so normal, she didn't have reason to study the man. But she thinks the dog was of medium-size and had a tannish coat."

"Well, I'm willing to bet your efforts will prove successful, Ma'am. And, I'll tell the car patrol in that area to keep an eye out for Duffy. You live in the Bonnie Brae neighborhood, off University Avenue, right?"

"That's right, but that's astounding you know where I live. But I do thank you for the offer, Lieutenant. I need all the help I can get. I certainly don't want to tell Claire that Duffy is lost," Loupe gulped, "or stolen." She turned to go, calling back to Susan, "Let me know as soon as the package arrives, please."

After Loupe retreated back to her department, Owens walked to the high reception counter that formed Susan's command post. He casually leaned his elbows and forearms on it, looking down to where Susan had started to work on her computer while he talked to Loupe. Shaking his head, he said, "You know, there are times I almost feel sorry for you. I know all about the way you and Sean grew up. But the keyword here is *almost*."

He straightened up, becoming the detective again. "Well, Ms. Farrell? Do you have something you would like to say? Or would you rather go down to the station and we do it real formal-like?"

"Detective, if you want to ask me questions, I'll be happy to answer . . . that is, if I know the answer. I have nothing to hide. Other than that, I don't have anything to say." She looked him in the eye as if daring him to call her a liar. The only thing that indicated she wasn't being entirely truthful was the slight tic in one eye.

That, coupled with the way she jumped when her cell phone began to play a tune, announcing an incoming call, was markedly suspect to Owens. Especially as she made no move to answer it. She did pick it up and look at the number displayed, but then clicked the phone off.

"You were about to ask me something, Lieutenant?"

"Okay, first question. Was that Sean calling just now, and you didn't answer because I'm standing here?"

"Sean? No, it was a friend, that's all. I'll call her back later."

"Oh, right. And I'm Santa Claus come early. You don't make it very easy for yourself, do you, Ms. Farrell?"

"And what is that supposed to mean, Lieutenant?"

"It means you're being foolish to protect Sean the way you're doing. Who else are you protecting? Never mind. It would be a waste of time to listen to your denials. Again. I'm going to forego our date at the police station for now. But I want you to seriously think about the offer I made a few days back. About maybe getting you a deal with the DA in return for the right information."

The lieutenant departed after repeating his advice to think about it, and giving her a meaningful look with one eyebrow cocked.

She was left staring thoughtfully at the glass door he'd just closed on the way out. The immediate reaction to the detective's warning caused her to make a beeline to her desk for her phone. What if Sean didn't leave a message, she thought. Panicked, and feeling sick at heart, she went to messages on her cell, wondering what had gone wrong. How had her plan gotten her into this predicament? It had all seemed so easy.

Seeing a communiqué waiting for her from Sean, she promptly played it back.

"Hi, it's me," he began. "Just wanted to fill you in on what's happening here. I have great news. I've reconnected with the little French girl whose family owns the residence hotel where you-know-who is staying. I found out from the girl that the hotel actually was built as a mansion way back in the eighteenth century. The present family that owns it are descendants of the rich guy who built it. And here's the best part; she told me about some secret passageways—in, out, and supposedly, running through the place. Can you believe it? How lucky is that? Of course that means I can come and go through those passages and be inside the place where your *competition* is staying, without anyone knowing I'm there. Sweet, huh?

"Look, I'll call you back in a couple hours, from inside the mansion. Bye for now. I'm burning this one. Be somewhere you can talk when I call back. Okay?"

Susan's spirits were definitely lifted on hearing Sean's message. Fortified by the news, she dismissed Lieutenant Owens' offer from her mind entirely.

She had no way of knowing that the foregoing message had just been recorded, via a mini 'bug' which had been placed inside her cell phone by her employer.

Denver—Susan's Apartment

Susan's phone rang several times between the time she got off work, and the time she fixed herself a late dinner at her apartment. Every time it played the Stripper, the silly song that she'd used as a turn-on for Chad, she jumped a mile, grabbing the phone in the hope it was Sean. But every time, it was too late. Chad called, according to the ID showing his name and listed number on her smart phone. But he didn't leave a message any of the times he called. She hadn't returned Chad's calls in case Sean happened to call at the same time, which seemed to be the way her luck was running. Her nerves felt like they were tangled into knots and someone was pulling them tighter and tighter.

Her stepbrother's call was over-due. He said it wouldn't be but an hour or so in his message earlier today. That had been at lunch time. She was beating herself up that she'd ever asked him to help her. Now, she felt something had gone wrong, and it would be her fault if he was in the custody of the French police right now—or, worse. If something happened to him because she'd gotten him into this mess, she'd never forgive herself. Susan crossed her arms on the kitchen table, and pillowed her chin on her arms. She stared at the face of the phone she'd placed directly in her line of vision, willing Sean to call.

She knew he'd do anything for her. It had been that way since they were kids, when her druggie father got himself arrested for attempting to mug an old woman and steal her purse.

They'd never heard another word from him, though they'd tried to find out if he was in jail or prison. But when the police started questioning about who was responsible for them, they stopped asking.

Their mother had long since ceased to care about anything, even them. And one night when she got so drunk she couldn't turn a trick, they found her, blood pooling from a gash in her head, just down the street from the boarded-up house where the three of them existed on food stamps. Her pimp had beaten her until she'd fallen down, hitting her head on the curb. He'd left her amidst the garbage in the gutter. Susan and Sean called the police anonymously, hiding behind a trash bin while they watched the coroner put her in a body bag and take her away.

After that, it was just the two of them, ragged and skinny. They made a pact that they wouldn't let any agency or official, no matter how well-meaning, put them in an orphanage, or worse yet, split them up. When the weather was too cold for them to stay in the abandoned house, they walked to one of the missions that serviced the poor, for a hot meal and a place to sleep for the night. When asked, they fabricated stories about why they were alone.

For a long while, they simply begged on the street, Susan dressed as a boy with her flaming tresses covered by a cap. She saved all the money they collected, tying the coins in a handkerchief she kept tucked into a special inside pocket she'd sewn into the waistband of the much-too-large pair of jeans that once belonged to her mother. Every so often, when some generous soul donated paper money, Susan stuffed the bills into an old vinyl make-up bag, also once her mother's, and secured it into another special pocket inside the jeans.

However, they soon found they'd get more *donations* if thirteen-year-old Susan would let down her long red hair and dance like a gypsy, while ten-year-old Sean accompanied her on the harmonica—the only thing of use his stepfather ever taught him.

Susan's reverie ended as she found herself falling asleep, still waiting, and wondering what was keeping Sean from calling. She moved from the table to the sofa, trying her best to stay awake.

The notes of the Stripper began to fill the apartment. Susan had turned up the volume on her phone, and the loud melody startled her out of sleep. She jumped sharply, scurrying to the table where she knocked the phone to the floor in her haste to answer. She grabbed it up from where it had fallen, surprised to see she'd slept for a couple hours.

"Please, please, let it be Sean," she prayed out loud, looking closely at the number on the little screen. Chad must have given up, she thought, clicking the green on-button. "Buddy? Oh, my God. I've waited hours for your call. Are you okay? Why didn't you call sooner?"

"Calm down, Sis, I'm fine. I just couldn't take a chance and call while I was exploring the secret passages behind the walls. This place is strung with narrow pathways and stairways that go all the way up from the first floor to the top floor. And, well, I didn't know if my voice could be heard through the walls. Didn't want to take a chance on that. So I waited to call until I left the mansion.

"I'm covered with years of cobwebs and dust, along with a few spider bites, but it was worth it. I located the stairway to the floor where the Martelli's are staying; and discovered where it opens into their suite. Anyway, I had to wait until it was safe, until I didn't hear voices anymore through the walls, which meant they'd all gone out. Then I opened the panel on the inside wall of the passage. It's been built to look like it's the back part of the armoire in one of the bedrooms. I also found that the narrow corridor actually continues beyond their place, to a panel in the wall at the far end of this wing. I think that's the suite where that English guy with the humongous dog is staying."

Susan's anxiety increased the more she listened to Sean's description of the mansion's secret passageways, monster dogs, and Englishmen. She'd been pacing through her small apartment all the while he talked. But now she forced herself to sit down at the table again. Taking a deep breath, she made her decision. It wasn't too hard after all, she thought, as the choice was between the money and her stepbrother. And he was her only family.

"Buddy, stop. Stop right there. Listen to me for a minute. This is getting way out of hand. And that detective is creeping me out. From what he said yesterday, I'm certain he suspects you were involved in the attack last March. So this has got to stop right now. Please come home. It's just not worth your getting arrested, or possibly hurt. I was wrong to involve you.

"And besides, Chad has insisted that "I call you off," his words. And to do it now. That's the way he said it. He's been acting strange lately. In fact I think he's likely to throw me, you, or both of us, under the bus in a heartbeat. I'm sure he feels Lieutenant Owens on his heels, too."

"Don't panic, Suze. It's all going to be okay. Owens doesn't have any proof. He's just trying to make you squirm. If he had hard evidence, he'd have arrested someone by now.

"So now, listen up. Here's the way it's going down. It's quite simple from here on out. Now that I can get into and out of the place with no one being the wiser, I can have the job done in the wink of an eye. Then maybe I'll lay low for a while before I come back there. I've been thinking of spending a little time with our Irish contingent. See what I can drum up with them. I'll be safe enough hiding out in Ireland. And they can probably fix it to get me back to the States when things cool down. Just trust me, okay? I know what I'm doing.

"Look, Sis, I've got to burn this one now. I'll let you know when everything is wrapped up. It's payback time for the early days when you watched out for me. And don't let that Owens character scare you, ya hear? He doesn't have any concrete evidence. How could he? He's only zeroing in on you because he thinks you'll crack given enough pressure. Those detective

257

types are masters at the divide-and-conquer ploy. Just be cool and businesslike, but don't give him the time of day. I've never seen anyone better at doing that than you, Suze. Bye for now."

"Buddy, wait. Don't hang up. Buddy?" But he'd already turned her off.

10

Day Eight

Paris—Residence Saint-Germain

Claire awoke in an entirely new frame of mind after spending a totally wonderful evening with Malcolm. Knowing that Mandy would arrive sometime late today, or at worst in the early morning, also added to the effect. And she couldn't wait to tell her sister the news. Would Mandy believe her? She herself could hardly believe it, but knew it was all too true. Her positive mental attitude was due to her newly discovered feelings for the tall Englishman she'd been holding at arm's length since the first time she looked into those stellar indigo eyes.

A wide yawn proliferated into a luxuriant stretch, from her neck to her shoulders and down her arms. She leaned back onto the pillows piled against the *toile* upholstered Louis XV-styled headboard, her thoughts dreamy and abstracted.

Claire didn't want to admit it, but yet discerned she'd never be able to set her failed marriage behind her without owning up to past illusions and oversights on her part.

I wonder. Am I beginning to see my way out of the mess I had a hand in creating . . . tacking on the phrase that now sent chills up her spine . . . *by marrying Chad?*

259

She hoped she'd made the right decision last night. By allowing Malcolm to hypnotize her, she'd thought it might help to untangle the meaning of the recurring red dreams and perhaps even expand awareness on her personal agenda to get herself straight on the deterioration of her marriage. And she readily admitted this also meant her relationship with Chad.

She'd finally consented as Malcolm explained away her last fear, that a hypnotist could control a person's mind and free will.

"Not so," he'd replied, and went on to say that nothing would be divulged that her psyche wasn't ready to make known. Besides the fact, he'd agreed that they would concur in advance on what area of past experiences she wished to recover.

When the session was over, Claire felt lighter inside, like she'd just flung off a heavy burden that had been weighting her down for years. She was finally okay about owning up to the guilt that she'd tried unsuccessfully to bury. She'd married Chad on the rebound after the three-year relationship with her fiancé had fallen apart. Although formally engaged with a ring, and with the wedding date only a few months away, Claire was advised by a friend that her espoused, Adam, had taken his old flame to a Mexican resort for a weekend's stay. Adam had told her he was attending a business conference in Phoenix at that same time.

After the shock of discovering Adam's duplicity and lack of commitment, Claire had cancelled the wedding, uprooted her life, and moved to Denver from Chicago. She'd heard about an opening to head a newly-planned interior design department at the architectural firm Chadwick & Associates, as it was known at that time. Claire interviewed with Chad, the corporation's owner-president. Subsequent to studying her impressive portfolio and upon receiving a sterling reference to his phone inquiry at the Chicago design firm where she'd worked for the last five years, he'd hired her on the spot.

Shortly upon joining the firm and getting the design studio up-and-running, she'd received a premier assignment. Chad asked her to design and furnish the interiors of his personal residence, proudly showing her the newly completed architectural plans for the house. Claire relished the assignment, aware of what it represented—a stamp of approval for her expertise and performance since joining the firm. She worked closely with Chad for nearly a year, the time it took to complete the construction and interior finishes of the residence, along with the furnishings and final touches.

On the evening of the official open-house reception for Chad's new residence, he'd surprised Claire with a public proposal and a ring. Put on the spot and still glowing from his open appreciation of her talent in designing the striking interiors of the new house, Claire had impulsively said yes. It was only after they were married, she'd looked back and realized that she'd misinterpreted her feelings of professional friendship and a successful partnership of their individual design abilities, with love.

Chad's wedding gift to Claire had been the partnership in the firm, though it was what everyone except Claire had expected as her proficiency in the interiors department had already grown the firm's profit by a healthy measure.

Immersed within these thoughts, Claire lost all track of time. The sound of voices coming from the sitting room caused her to jump up and fling aside the feather quilt, suddenly remembering that it was the weekend and Malcolm was picking her up for breakfast. No lectures at *universite* today.

She headed for the bathroom, concentrating on a quick wash-up, realizing as she did so that she would soon be sharing the tiny space with Mandy again. She missed the comradery she shared with her sister, but was glad at the moment that the time-share wasn't in effect. Claire did the best she could with her naturally curly mane, parting it in the middle and letting the curls free-fall over her shoulders, and finished with a light touch of make-up. Heading for the armoire that now held the semblance of a new wardrobe, she quickly dressed in a gray straight skirt, detailed as only the

French designers delight in doing, and added a silk top under the gray and aubergine pin-striped jacket. The outfit from yesterday's shopping expedition modishly displayed her trim figure in an enviable manner.

A low admiring whistle and a definite all-male appreciative gaze met Claire at the doorway of the sitting room. The pair left with Abbie's wish for a good day ringing in their ears.

They'd scheduled a full day together, beginning with a stop at one of the sidewalk cafes that served freshly-baked rolls and other breakfast offerings. Afterwards, Malcolm would escort her to some of the exhibits being held at the antique houses situated in the same quarter as their hotel.

Very diplomatic on his part, Claire thought, knowing it was not only tactful, but a direct answer to her recent grumbling about not getting her business concluded in all the excitement that had taken place since her arrival.

After that, the plan was to come back to the hotel for another hypnosis session, to be held once again in the relative privacy of his quarters. One part of her was excited about the possibility of putting an end to the nightmares that had plagued her since the attack. Though at the same time, she was more than a little apprehensive about what else the session would reveal from her subconscious mind.

But she was certain of several things. She felt alive once more, the first time since her decision to file for divorce from Chad. And the second certainty was the promise she'd made to herself, her intent to rid herself of all the deep-seated mire surrounding that decision.

Paris—Simon Boulle Antiquities

As it turned out, Claire happened to be in the right place at the right time. The annual antique exhibit, known as the *Carre Rive Gauche*, was taking place in the *St-Germain-des-Pres* district. She found it a 'smashing' success, to put it into

Malcolm's manner of expression. With his knowledge of the streets in this district, they shopped most of the dealers in the exhibit. They ended up at Simon Boulle Antiquities, where she confirmed her choices from her previous visit, which had been one of her more criticized activities, the *Claire-as-bait* incident.

But now, she couldn't believe her luck. In fact she was immensely pleased that she'd found all the antiques she planned to purchase for the resort project, including those she intended for the upscale French restaurant which had been formulated from the design stage to be a drawing card for the hotel.

At Simon Boulle's, Claire photographed her selection of antiques which she would attach in her e-mail to Loupe, directing her to have quality photographs made of these, along with the pieces she'd purchased at other exhibits, and send them off to the New Orleans' clients. She made arrangements for crating and shipping the chosen pieces to the States, certain that the furnishings would excite everyone involved in the enterprise. The antiques were prime examples of country French and classic Provence styles, perfect for the French-themed project.

Claire finished her business arrangements and decided to take a look at some of the other antique genres while waiting for Malcolm to conclude his own business with Simon.

Malcolm, who'd deliberately saved this antique house for their last stop, was now closeted in Simon's office going over the graphological report he'd been retained to compile by his old friend and sometimes client.

"So, Simon, I've determined what disparities appear in the handwritten letters of provenance for that group of antiques coming in from southern France, as you requested," he said, passing the veteran antique dealer a lengthy report enclosed within a business folder.

"My analyses identifies which pieces are likely to be fakes and which are authentic, based on the handwriting of the individuals who made out the papers tracing the origin and lineage of each piece. And as you mentioned earlier, there are indeed more than a few counterfeit antiques coming from that area, both in this batch, and I would not hesitate to make a pretty accurate guess, in the past as well. Assuming, of course, the same people who have written these provenances have also written them for the copycat antiques you've been sent in previous shipments."

Simon nodded, he set his reading glasses on his nose and scanned the report while Malcolm continued. "After studying the handwriting on the letters, I'm certain that the authorities in Provence, who've been shuffling around the paperwork for the pieces in question, are more than likely involved in the hoax. The auction takes place on Monday evening, the day after tomorrow, right?"

Simon nodded again, looking at Malcolm over the lenses of his glasses. "And the shipment is overdue. Though I've been guaranteed that it will arrive that morning."

"That leaves precious little time for you and your crew to carefully examine each piece before the auction, which is most likely how they've planned it."

"If only I would have known in advance that the shipment would be held up this long, I would not have advertised the Provence antiques to be available at this sale. But, *mon ami,* you have once again done a great favor by going over the letters of provenance to discover which pieces on the shipment are dubious. And these I intend to personally inspect."

Simon always marveled that Malcolm could study a person's handwriting and see elements of dishonesty and deceit, forgery in this case, among other things. This time, Malcolm's findings revealed that six out of the twenty-some pieces due to arrive early Monday morning, were open to serious doubt regarding their authenticity.

And, as Simon had commented a few years back when he'd originally sought help in this area, "*Docteur* Sutherland, expensive antiques are big business these days, especially the ones that because of their rarity or styling command prices of five-figures and up."

At that time, Monsieur Boulle had cited an example that had taken place a few years back, in which a friend of his, also a dealer in antiques, sold what was reportedly a fourteenth-century hand-carved trunk, supposedly owned by one Robert the Bruce—the famous warrior Scot who murdered his rival on the altar of a church known as Greyfriar's Kirk, and then went on to be crowned king of Scotland.

The rare trunk was purchased at the then unheard-of-price of eighty-five thousand pounds by a wealthy peer of the realm. However, upon delivering it to the new owner's estate, one of the men carrying it held up a bloodied hand that he'd caught on a half-buried staple prong sticking out from the bottom. On further examination the trunk was found to be a fake. The half-pulled staple had evidently been missed, once part of a series of staples that originally held the bottom boards together while building the piece using twentieth-century methods.

"C'est la vie," Simon couldn't help but adding.

Claire's watch read six o'clock. Upon leaving Simon Boulle's shop, she and Malcolm stopped at a sidewalk café for a pick-me-up of Kir, the classic French *aperitif*—white wine mixed with a small amount of *crème de cassis*. But now, after relaxing over the *aperitif*, Claire's feet were tired and she was hungry. Thinking about the hypnosis session she'd planned with Malcolm for later that night, she decidedly preferred an early dinner on their way back to the Saint-Germain, rather than going back now and then going out to eat later, after the session.

"Malcolm, I know this is an American thing and certainly not as cosmopolitan as Paris, but bear with me, please?" She couldn't help but smile as she looked at him across the table. Even in her weary-to-the-bone state, she definitely liked what she saw in the warm and expectant look he gave her.

"Certainly, Claire. But I am curious . . . what can be so American and yet so unsophisticated? Of course it can't have anything to do with the fact that the emergence of your country as a unified and cultured nation is not even a quarter-of-a-century-old," he teased, covering her hand on the table with his warm one.

"I can see where we are going to have an enlightening discussion on what makes up the culture of the USA at a later time when I'm not so tired. But would you concede for right now that it wouldn't be such a terrible thing if we were to eat dinner earlier than usual? I'm completely done in from the day's antiquing and don't think I'll be able to stay awake to eat at a more cosmopolitan time later, especially after a session of hypnosis."

He squeezed her hand and smiled. "It's totally up to you. I can go either way."

Interpreting the look on her face as his answer, Malcolm asked the taxi driver to stop at the Hotel Ritz. He told Claire he wanted to see if Lady Anna and Cerian would like to join them for an early dinner at a fine restaurant on the fabulous seventeenth-century *Place des Vosges* in the *Marias* district, not far from their current location. After hearing about the place, Claire's stomach growled and she perked up, looking forward to eating outside under the fabled vaulted stone arcades. The fact that it was open now was also appealing, as Malcolm said so many of the better restaurants in Paris closed after lunch and didn't reopen until around seven to eight o'clock at night.

She wondered how the Parisian women were able to eat so late and still remain slender. She hadn't seen very many overweight women in all the time they'd been here, saying as much to Malcolm, as he disembarked from the taxi in front of the Ritz. "Well," he replied, "it's a closely-guarded secret, but I will let you in on it when I get back." Leaning back in, he gave her a quick buss on the cheek, and told the driver to wait. "I'll only be about five minutes. Hopefully," he said, over his shoulder, and disappeared into the interior of the hotel.

Paris—Residence Saint-Germain

Earlier that day, Etienne had promised Malcolm he would call his *Grandpere* to see if he could possibly cut short his visit to the family holdings in the flower growing region of southern France. But Dom had replied it was impossible to come back before later in the week as he was helping with the planting of trial species in the new field the family had recently acquired. Even after Etienne explained the importance of knowing the layout of the passageways running through the mansion, Dom could not be budged, repeatedly saying, "*No demain, dans quatre jours.*" As Etienne hung up the phone, his thoughts were totally absorbed in finding another way to unravel the secret of the passages—today or tomorrow, not in four days' time.

He had his suspicions regarding the muddy footprints on the stairs coming from the wine cellar. And then finding Marie-Claude *in* the wine cellar, seemingly unaware of how she got there. Part of him refused to believe that she had somehow unlocked the secret of the passageways. But the night of his *Tante's* dinner pointed to this possibility. Besides Dom, there was no one else he could turn to. He decided to take a gamble and talk with *La Cousine*, knowing that tomorrow was the day Marie-Claude would return to the Marchand Clinic, where the success or failure of the two-day pass would be determined by her doctor. Etienne felt he may not have another opportunity. It might be a long while before his *cousine* was allowed another pass.

However, when Etienne arrived at the open door of the suite his two relatives shared, he quietly stepped back into the shadows of the foyer on seeing *Tante* Emilia tiptoeing into her daughter's bedroom. He was within earshot of the conversation taking place between mother and daughter after finding Marie-Claude awake from a nap, but crying softly into her pillow.

"My dear little girl, what is it? Why are you crying?" Emilie asked, sitting down on the edge of the bed, and stroking the dark mass of hair away from her daughter's face. Marie-Claude sobbed louder.

"You know, *ma petit*, you have seemed so very nervous since the celebration dinner the other night. I want you to know, whatever the problem, that I love you, and how much I've enjoyed having you home this weekend." Emilie tenderly wiped the tears away from her daughter's cheeks, adding in a whisper, "Marie-Claude, I promise you I will always be here for you. Please tell me what is making you cry. Perhaps between the two of us, we can do something about it."

"Oh, *La Mere*, I have been so stupid," Marie-Claude whimpered, tearing up again. "I thought he loved me, but it was all an act. He doesn't love me, he was only stringing me on."

"Who, *ma petit*? Who are you talking about?" Emilia drew a blank on what male acquaintance her daughter would mistake a buddy, or familial, kind of love, for the romantic love of a man and woman. She took a wild guess. "Etienne? He loves you like a sister, you know, even though you're cousins. He would never do anything to make you feel this way."

"No, not Etienne . . . Harley!"

"Marie-Claude, look at me," Emilie insisted, as her daughter turned her face to the wall and continued crying, louder now. "Who is Harley? And what has happened? This person, Harley, has he harmed you in any way?"

A knock on the open bedroom door startled both of them. "Who is it? Emilie asked, turning to face the doorway. "Etienne? What is it, Nephew?"

"*Pardon, Tante*. I heard sobs as I passed by in the corridor and came to see if everything is okay." He came into the room, and seeing Marie-Claude crying uncontrollably, he sat down on the other side of the bed, taking her hand. "What is it, *Cousine*?"

Marie-Claude simply shook her head, unable to talk through the sobs.

It was Emilie who answered, face and body tensed to hear the worst. "I am not sure. She mentioned someone with the name of Harley, and that he strung her along. Do you know anything about this, Etienne?"

He shook his head, but then his face lit up, and he became animated. "The muddy footprints tracking up the stairs from the wine cellar . . . Harley? *Cousine*, was this Harley person here in the mansion?"

Emilie Fontaine just looked from one to the other. "Etienne, you and *Docteur* Sutherland were searching the manse for someone that night. Someone who destroyed the clothing of Claire Martelli and her sister. And then he somehow escaped through the window in Dom's quarters. Is this the person she's talking about?"

It has to be, *Tante*. But, we know him as the Shamrock, and *Docteur* also called him by the name of Sean, not Harley."

Marie-Claude stopped crying. She listened to Etienne with an incredulous look on her face, as she pulled herself up into a sitting position. "Oh, I have been so foolish. *Non* . . . how do the Americans say . . . hoodwinked? Now I am discovering his true intentions. He told me his name was Harley, not Sean, and he seemed genuinely interested in me as a person. I met him when I was manning the reception desk, before the, er, *interlude*. Before I went to the clinic. Oh, what have I done?" She began to whimper, banging her head back against the painted iron headboard.

Her mother reached out to stop her. Framing her daughter's face with both hands, she waited until Marie-Claude was quiet again, though her color continued to drain to a deathly pale. She moaned, eyes closed. "I am the reason a monster is now loose in the Saint-Germain."

"*Cousine*, no matter what you think you did, he is no longer here, he is gone."

"You cannot understand, Etienne. Because of my selfish wishes, he now knows the way through the manse's secret passageways. He could be in here right now, and we would not know it."

Her mother and cousin looked at her in alarm. Emilie spoke first. "But, *ma petit*, no one but Dom knows the passageways' secrets. Not even me. In our noble ancestral line, Gerard de Bergeron planned the mansion and commissioned its construction back in the mid-eighteenth-century. I have always heard he put in secret passageways for the purpose of concealment and escape obsessed as he was with the history and use of the priest holes in the century before. Again, it is said he became neurotic over the notion that these passages would be needed in his century. And as it turned out, his foresight was correct. The Bastille was stormed in the year 1789, becoming the flashpoint to the actual revolution. Our ancestor literally kept his head due to these same passageways. He died of old age many years after the Reign of Terror ended. I have always considered the passageways part of an evil time in our history and deliberately chose not to learn their location, or how to get in and out of them, hoping the necessity that drove Gerard would die with Dom when he passes on, as he must . . . someday," she said, nervously making the sign of the cross in the air.

Etienne repeated her talismanic gesture to ward off the angel of death who might otherwise take notice of the fact that old Dom was still alive and kicking.

He stared at his cousin with a troubled frown. "Marie-Claude, I have a memory of a day, so many years ago, when we were children playing in the wine cellar. We got a little too rough in our game of capture the flag, and ended up falling hard against the wall that was constructed of stone, a common building material back then. I remember how we both grabbed for a handhold around the edges of the stones as we hit. And to our surprise, a part of the wall opened for a few seconds, then closed again as we scrambled up from the floor, again using the edges of the stones to pull ourselves up. I have the memory of that extraordinary incident in my head to this day, in a way only children recognize and become intimidated by the imaginary possibility of ghosts, vampires, and other nonhuman things lurking behind the wall. I thought we agreed then to never mention to anyone what had happened, but most important, to leave it be. We said nothing good could come out of exploring what was waiting within that black hole in the wall. Remember?"

Marie-Claude nodded, closing her eyes, shame and embarrassment fighting for dominance on her marble-white face. "I remember, Etienne. I remember very well."

"But you didn't leave it alone, did you?"

"I couldn't, *Cousine*, the urge to find the way to open the stones kept coming back, day after day, after day. I tried to resist, but then I would find myself down in the wine cellar, searching for the spot on the wall that would give access to the portal again." She opened her eyes and stared at him. "I became obsessed. It took me years, but I finally solved the puzzle. And then of course, I had to explore the passage behind the opening, where it led, how to unseal the stones on the other end. I saw no vampires, Etienne, but I did make it a habit to carry a silver crucifix in my pocket. After that, just for curiosity sake, I used the same method on the opposite wall, and found that the stones opened to another tunnel. This one lead to a number of wood-built passages that run out of the lower level and upwards through the entire mansion. In many more months' time, I mapped all the tunnels and ways through the walls."

Etienne's face lit up in his excitement. "Where is that plan, Marie-Claude? Now you can redeem yourself. It would be a very great service . . . keeping the Shamrock from attaining his goal. He is evil, you see? This is important, *Cousine*, tell me where the map is, *s'il vous plait*.

Emilia had been watching both their faces intently during Marie-Claude's confession. "But there is no such map. Is there, *ma petit*?" She asked, knowing the answer in advance.

"No, there is nothing written down. It is all up here," she said tapping her forehead. "I was afraid to put it on paper, afraid that someone planning something bad might find it and use it for evil purposes. Like Harley. He really is the person they call the Shamrock, isn't he?"

Her mother nodded, but assured her that everything would be all right, unwilling to admit it was possible things might not turn out in a positive way. She turned to her nephew who now wore a dejected look. "Etienne, could you please find *Docteur* Sutherland? Marie-Claude can give both of you the information you need to get into the secret passageways and where they lead. And right away, *s'il vous plait.*"

"Yes, *Tante,*" he said, hurrying to the door. "I will try his room, but I have not seen him since he and Mademoiselle Claire went out together this morning. If nothing else, I will try the Ritz, where his *grand mere* and her companion are staying, or Madame Martelli may know where they are."

Paris—Restaurant in the Place des Vosges

Malcolm and the three women, who Cerian playfully called Malcolm's Harem, were enjoying coffee and liqueurs, under the vaulted stone arcades of the restaurant's outside venue, having just finished dinner which had been pronounced excellent by all. In the midst of another story Cerian was telling about life in Italy, Claire's mobile began ringing. She fished it out of her purse thinking it might be Mandy informing her she had just arrived at the airport and would be at the Saint-Germain as soon as she could get a taxi. Instead, it was Abbie on the line, saying it was urgent that she and Malcolm come back to the hotel at once.

Claire was instantly on alert. "What's happened, Mom? Are you all right? Ben is with you, isn't he?"

"Yes, we're both fine, Claire. But Emilie has asked Etienne to find Malcolm and to request that he come back to the Saint-Germain as soon as possible. He came to the door just now and inquired if I knew where you both were, or if I could get in touch with you. I told him I knew exactly where you were and would call and give you the message."

"Right, Mom. But, a question . . . did Etienne say *why* Madame Fontaine wants Malcolm to come back right now?"

"Well, it has something to do with secret passageways and the Shamrock, so I'm sure it's important. Etienne also says Malcolm will know what he's talking about, however he's standing right here. Can you have Malcolm talk with him?"

"Yes, I'll put him on."

Malcolm had been listening with one ear to Cerian on his right side, who was not-so-slyly trying to negotiate an evening out.

"Just the two of us," she was saying, "to go dancing. Like we used to do before . . ."

But he'd already stopped paying attention and reached out to Claire, on his left, for her phone after catching bits and pieces of her side of the conversation with her mother.

"Etienne? What's going on?" Malcolm's full attention became riveted on what the young Frenchman on the other end of the line was communicating. A minute later, he switched off Claire's phone and handed it back to her. The look on his face was all it took to convey the import of Etienne's message. Without waiting for an explanation, Claire began to gather her things knowing she wouldn't find out what was happening until they were alone.

"Sorry to have to end our outing so soon, ladies, but Claire and I must head back to the Saint-Germain right now. It's rather a private matter." Without further explanation, he signaled the waiter for the check and paid the bill.

"Grandmother, Ceri, we can drop you off at the Ritz on our way."

Cerian's pout showed her extreme displeasure at the way the evening was turning out. "I'm not ready to go back to the hotel yet, Malcolm. It's still early. Unless you come in when we get back to the Ritz and have a nightcap with me at least."

"Not tonight, Cerian. Grandmother, ready? I will worry if you ladies stay out partying without an escort."

"Yes, Malcolm, we're coming. I'm way too old for partying till dawn in Paris. Come, Cerian. If you want a nightcap, we can get one in the bar at our hotel. But tomorrow, Grandson, I'm planning on everyone coming to the Ritz for dinner. My treat. Claire, please tell your mother and her friend that I won't take no for an answer."

Everyone turned to look at Claire who showed some hesitation in the silence that followed the invitation pronouncement. "I'm not certain if we can make it, Lady Anna. But thank you for inviting us. You see my sister had to fly to New York on business, and she returns to Paris sometime late tonight, or early morning. As it's been a few days since we've had a chance to talk, I'm thinking she'll probably want to spend the evening with Mom and me, to fill us in on her new assignment and, well, other family matters."

She glanced up at Malcolm to see his reaction, and found a quizzical look on his face. But it smoothed out into a smile when he saw her watching him. "We'll have to let you know tomorrow, Grandmother."

"Malcolm, if Claire doesn't care to accept my invitation, which I now expand to include her entire family, sister also, then I insist on you joining us at least. I've hardly seen you since we arrived," the Countess of Rosemore commanded her grandson, her face set in a peevish frown.

Claire looked to Malcolm for help in standing up against his grandmother's wishes. Seeing none coming from that quarter, she thanked Lady Anna once again for her generous invitation and suggested that instead of dinner, they all get together at the Ritz for cocktails with her mother, Ben, and her sister prior to the countess' dinner with Malcolm and Cerian. She made a point to say that it would be *her* treat.

Malcolm looked uncomfortable as his grandmother distantly agreed, though there was a definite chill in her voice.

"After you, ladies," he said, planning to talk to Lady Anna in private regarding Claire's situation with the Shamrock, which he was sure was the cause of her refusal of the dinner invitation. Wanting to get this part of the evening over as quickly as possible so he could speak singularly with Claire, he ushered the women toward the street in front of the

274

restaurant to the waiting taxi at the curb with Cerian hanging on his arm all the way.

Malcolm assisted his grandmother into the back seat of the taxi and tried to help Cerian in next, but that lady had other ideas. "Oh, Claire, you've had Malcolm to yourself all day. It's Lady Anna's and my turn now. Malcolm, you get in the middle. Claire, you don't mind riding up front with the driver for the short time it will take to get to the Ritz, do you, dear?" She pulled her ankle-length split skirt up above her knees, showing off as much leg as possible while sliding in next to him, knowing he couldn't help but notice. "Is there room for me in here?" She asked, using her best coquetry to squeeze herself as close to him as possible.

Claire counted to five under her breath and got in the front seat.

After dropping Lady Anna and Cerian at the Ritz, it was a quiet ride back to the Saint-Germain, especially when Malcolm remained vague in answering Claire's questions regarding what had happened that required Etienne to ask him to come back right away. Then it was Malcolm's turn. He attempted to draw Claire into conversation regarding his grandmother and her aristocratic mannerisms, but she pleaded off saying that the day had been tiring and she had a headache.

"Let's just call it a night, Malcolm. I'm sure it will all keep until tomorrow," she said, on seeing Etienne hurry toward them as they entered the lobby.

Halting midway at the front desk, Etienne diplomatically studied the reservation book kept there, knowing he must wait until Malcolm was alone before he could tell him about Marie-Claude and the Shamrock, and the map his *cousine* had hastily drawn showing the way through the hidden passages.

Claire paused at the bottom of the staircase. "Besides, Malcolm, I know you and Etienne are going to either search for Sean, or explore the secret passageways tonight. And since you aren't planning for me to come along, I'd just as soon turn in early since Mandy will be here sometime later tonight or early morning. I'm right, aren't I? You don't want me tagging along from some misguided sense of protective code of honor."

Commanding Malcolm's attention, Claire's topaz eyes were disturbingly perceptive. "Though in all fairness, I will say that I was certainly capable in defending myself when I was attacked last March. But then, things are different in the States, I have to think. For the most part, American women demand, and get, more independence and equality than many of their counterparts here in Europe. However I must admit, your grandmother apparently is blessed with an independent life style. Tell me, Malcolm, is it only women in the upper class, the ones that can trace their noble lineage back for generations that are allowed to be independent in England? Or can women of the middle class enjoy that distinction and acceptance also?"

Seeing as well as feeling the chill in Claire's demeanor, Malcolm moved forward to pull her into his arms, attempting to reassure her, but she broke loose and took several steps up the stairway.

"Claire, wait. Please? Can we take this discussion up again a little later on? But tonight for sure. I promise. Right now, it's very important that I talk with Marie-Claude before she goes to bed for the night. She's due to go back to the clinic first thing in the morning. So this is my only chance."

"I think it's a grand idea to call it a night, Malcolm. In fact, things are going way too fast. I suggest we take a breather. It's really like being on a roller coaster these past few days. You have your family to contend with. As well as Cerian, of course. And I have many things to sort out. But I do appreciate the help you've given me with regard to getting in touch with some of the things I've been trying to block subconsciously. I can take it from here. And maybe in a few months' time we can see if we still have feelings for each other, and decide what we want to do at that point."

"A few months' time? What are you talking about, Claire? And what about Sean? Do you think he's simply going to ride off into the sunset?" In his haste to make her understand, he started up the stairs toward her.

"There is nothing more to discuss, Malcolm," Claire said over her shoulder as she turned and fled up the stairway.

Claire reached the fourth floor in a flustered state, already sorry she had reacted in quite so intense a manner with Malcolm, which she now admitted to herself was a direct result of his grandmother's imperious bearing that evening. She entered the suite to find Abbie and Ben locked in a tender embrace on the sitting room's settee. Abbie reacted by pulling away as soon as she heard the door open, however Ben kept his arm around her in a show of support.

"Oh, my dear . . . I didn't think you'd be back from dinner so soon," Abbie began, patting her hair back in place. "We've been enjoying a bottle of wine that Madame Fontaine sent up from her excellent cellar. Here, let me pour you a glass. It's a fine burgundy and I believe it will become one of your favorites. You and Malcolm will definitely enjoy it. Why, Claire, whatever is the matter?" She asked, seeing her daughter's teary eyes. "Where is Malcolm?" Her obvious embarrassment over being seen by her daughter in Ben's arms turned to concern. She looked over Claire's shoulder as if she expected Malcolm to appear any second. "Did something happen tonight involving that Shamrock person? Is that why Etienne needed to get hold of Malcolm right away? And where *is* Malcolm? He knows how worried I've been about you since we arrived in Paris, but he gave me his word he would keep you safe."

"Mom . . . Ben . . . sorry, didn't mean to interrupt," Claire said, acknowledging both and hoping to get into the bedroom before her mother could ask any more questions. "Nothing to worry about, Mom. No Shamrock Man. And I don't know where Malcolm is at the moment. He's somewhere in the mansion, I believe. But it's no concern of mine. I'm glad I found out now that his grandmother has other ideas with

277

regard to Malcolm's life in the future's department. Or maybe it's just an attitude unique to the English upper class. The peers of the realm thing."

She pulled herself together, trying to come up with a plausible excuse to make good her escape. "It's been a long day, shopping all over the Saint-Germain sector at the various antique houses. I'm really exhausted and I'm going straight to bed. Mandy most likely will get here in the wee hours and I need to get some sleep before she arrives. Knowing my sister, we'll be talking through whatever's left of the night, catching up with everything. You lovebirds will excuse me?" Claire gave her mother a peck on the cheek as she attempted to navigate past them and into her bedroom. "Goodnight, Ben. Glad you're here for Mom."

"Goodnight, Claire. Thank you for allowing me to monopolize your mother. She's just as wonderful today as she was years ago," Ben said, getting up to give Claire a hug. "I'm here for you and Mandy too, you know."

"Thanks, Ben. I appreciate that. 'Night, Mom," Claire said, giving both of them a watery smile and turning to head down the corridor.

"Wait, honey, take a glass of wine with you. Things have a way of mending themselves after a good night's sleep," Abbie said, handing her the wine glass. "I'll come to your room later and we can talk."

Claire entered the bedroom and closed the door, securing it behind her. She took a sip of wine and then another, finding the rich flavor to her liking, before placing the glass on the bedside table. She knew it probably wouldn't do any good to lock the door, even as she turned the key. She flopped down on the bed wanting more than anything to have a good cry in private. But she knew that when Ben left, her mother, with all best intentions, would be knocking at the door. And she really couldn't handle any heavy explanations tonight. Her nerves were on high alert and her headache felt like some group from the seventies was rocking heavy metal behind her eyes. The talking could wait till morning. Claire hoped her mother would understand her need for solitude right now.

At first she couldn't move from the original position she'd collapsed in when she flopped onto the bed. She finally found the energy to get her mortal parts up and into the tiny bathroom intent on soaking a washcloth under the cold running water. She squeezed out the excess moisture and held it to her eyes, letting the cool cloth soothe the sting and swelling her tears had caused. After repeating the process several times, she retreated to her room again where she sat on the edge of the bed, finishing off the glass of fine old French wine, allowing the velvety smoothness to claim her completely. It was gone all too soon. She set the empty glass down and lay back on the bed, plumping the pillows against the headboard and positioning the cool cloth over her eyes. She didn't want to see, think or feel at the moment. She wanted only to be. In just seconds, she was incognizant. Her limbs turned flaccid. She fell into a state of nothingness.

Malcolm and Etienne left Marie-Claude in the care of her mother. They had a sketch that she'd drawn while giving them the information they would need to find and search the secret passageways. Now with flashlights in hand they headed down the stairs to the wine cellar, after Malcolm asked Emilie for phone numbers to reach both she and the police in case of trouble. Neither of them was armed, but Etienne picked up a cleaver on his way through the kitchen and Malcolm grabbed one of the sturdy canes Dom kept in the umbrella stand in his quarters. They had searched both areas prior to their descent to the cellar wine room hoping to find evidence as to whether Sean was hiding inside the mansion's living areas, or somewhere in the far reaches of the tunneled maze behind the walls.

"Where to begin? What say Etienne? Would it be better to start the search in the tunnel leading to the storage shed, the outside route, before we tackle the more intricate system of passages that lead in the other direction? Marie-Claude's map shows more places the Shamrock could hide if we go to the right . . . the inside track."

"*Docteur*, I am not sure which way it is better to start in, but according to *cousine's* map, there is a main tunnel and then branches. I am worried he could hide in one of those branches," Etienne said, pointing to several scribbled lines on the map. "If that were so, we could go right past him, and nothing would stop him from slipping behind us and getting out of the manse and away."

"Point taken, Etienne. So, in order to make sure that can't happen, one of us will have to stay on the main track at the point where the passages diverge. The other one will then proceed to check the way to where that fork ends, then double back to the main track. I propose we take turns so that neither of us gets the short end of the straw."

"*Docteur*, your plan sounds like it will work, but what is this straw you're talking about?"

"Sorry. Your English is getting so good, Etienne, that I forgot for a moment. It's just a figure of speech, old man. I'll explain later. Okay, let's get on with it. To the right then."

Etienne showed Malcolm the system that Marie-Claude had discovered on how to count and where to press the stones lining the wine cellar's walls that would initiate the opening to the tunnel. Malcolm noticed how quietly the two-hundred-some-year-old system opened. There was a slight grating sound as the stones forming the 'door' swung back into the tunnel, but nothing like what he'd expected. "Let's hope this level of craftsmanship is repeated in the rest of the passages," was all he said. He kept quiet regarding his main concern so as not to worry Etienne.

Marie-Claude told them the wine room tunnel connected into a maze-like series of passages built of lumber. The centuries-old wood used in the construction could possibly be rotted by now, or warped and skewed from their original connections, and they'd never know it until an integral piece gave way under foot.

The longer he thought about it, the more unwilling he became to allow Etienne to proceed without warning him of the possible danger. He switched on his flashlight. The beam of light shone bravely into the tunnel. He turned to the young Frenchman. "Before we proceed, Etienne, you should know this could be dangerous. I intend to go in there to search for Sean, but I want you to think carefully before deciding to accompany me. There are all sorts of possible scenarios that could cause serious injury, or even death. I'm not trying to scare you, just want to inform you that anything could happen. For instance, there are evidently stairs as Marie-Claude said the passages go up to the top floor. Being built of very old wood, these could give way at any time, or maybe already have, which could present a serious situation. And that's just one possibility, there are more. And I won't think any less of you if you decide not to go in. As I said, I have to do it. Claire is in imminent danger from this freak."

Etienne stood up from his kneeling position in front of the opening. Facing Malcolm, he held eye-to-eye contact even though the Englishman was several inches taller. "*Docteur*, this mansion and its secrets have been in my family for centuries. One of our present-day family has caused Mademoiselle Claire to be in danger through revealing the presence of the passageways to a stranger . . . this Shamrock person. I will accompany you. I have already realized there will be dangers, but it is both necessary and an adventure at the same time. Please do not worry about me. We must find him before anything else happens. I am ready."

Etienne held up his hand in a close imitation of 'high five', breaking the seriousness of their task. Malcolm laughed, giving back the gesture, and thumping the young man on the back.

"Then let's get on with it, Etienne."

It was after two o'clock in the morning when Mandy rang the late bell beside the Saint-Germain's front door hoping she wouldn't wake anyone but Etienne. There were some cars yet moving on the street in front of the mansion-turned-hotel, but as it was situated on a side street, it was mainly only taxi's that cruised by. From where she stood, she saw lights through the sheer drapery of the lobby windows on either side of the main door. That surprised her. She was about to ring the bell once again, when she heard a key turn in the lock. Finally, she thought. Etienne must be a heavy sleeper. She gathered her camera gear and the rest of her belongings the cabbie had haphazardly dropped near the entry. But it wasn't Etienne who opened the door. It was Madame Fontaine.

"Oh, I'm so sorry to wake you, Madame. I thought Etienne would answer the bell." Instead of acknowledging Mandy's late arrival or welcoming her, Emilie Fontaine simply stepped back and motioned for her to come in. Strange, thought Mandy. Then she saw Ben and her mother standing a little way behind the proprietress. "Mom, Ben . . . what's going on? Why are you down here this time of morning? And where's Claire?" She asked looking around for her sister. One glance at the serious looks on each of their faces caused fear to grip Mandy's heart in a stranglehold. "Where is she? Mom?"

Abbie's state of anguish and frustration was plain to see, although she roused herself to welcome her youngest daughter with a fierce hug. "Honey, it's so good to see you. Please forgive me, it's just that I'm so worried about Claire. Let's sit here a minute. We'll try to fill you in, at least with what we know."

Ben stepped forward and put his arm around Mandy's shoulders, leading her toward a sofa and placing her between Abbie and himself. Madame Fontaine took the chair across from the trio, her face set in a tired mask. Mandy wanted to scream as the movements and voices of those around her decelerated into slow motion due to her anxiety over her sister. She took a deep breath and forced her patience level back to normal. "Please, someone tell me this very second. *Where is Claire?*"

"I'm afraid it's not the answer you want to hear, Mandy. Quite simply, we just don't know," Ben responded as gently as possible. "She came straight up to the suite last night after having dinner with Malcolm and his grandmother, and his ex-fiancée. Evidently, something happened during the evening. She was upset when she came into the sitting room. Both your mother and I saw tears in her eyes. She said she was tired from antiquing all day and wanted to get some sleep before you got in. She accepted a glass of wine from a bottle Madame Fontaine had generously supplied from her fine cellar, and then went to her room. After I left your place, Abbie tried knocking at her door, but Claire didn't answer. So Abbie tried to open the door to see if Claire was okay, but it was locked. The key was still in the lock on the inside when we broke the door down about an hour ago. There was no sign of her anywhere in the room, or anyone else for that matter."

"What are you saying?" Mandy whispered in disbelief. "That she's been kidnapped somehow out of a locked room? That just isn't possible."

"Easy, Mandy. At this point, all we know is that she's missing. Malcolm and Etienne were already searching for the Shamrock in the secret passageways behind the walls, before, well before there was no answer to Abbie's knock."

"Then Emilie here," Abbie gestured towards Madame Fontaine and continued Ben's explanation, "called Etienne's phone and alerted them that Claire may be in trouble. In no time, they were out of the tunnels and up to the suite. Then all three men knocked the door down.

"We think maybe Shamrock Man found a way to get into that room in our suite, possibly through the armoire that was built into the wall, like Malcolm found in Dom's room. We've all searched for some mechanism that would open a way into an inner passage, but none of us were successful in discerning how to gain access.

"Malcolm even posted Penny as guard outside our suite as a precaution prior to resuming the search. He left the door open so Penny could let us know if she returned." Abbie choked up on her next words . . . "or was returned, if she was taken by force."

Seeing Abbie's discomfort, Ben took up the tale again. "Then Malcolm and Etienne went back to scour the passages hoping that she had somehow gotten in there on her own. He told us Claire was upset that he wouldn't take her with him when he and Etienne began their search for Sean. And since Penny's on alert upstairs, we've been waiting down here in case something happens on this floor, or for Malcolm to call saying they've found her. But so far, no word nor sight of her, or anyone else."

"This is unbelievable. You're actually saying this old mansion has secret passageways? That only happens in horror movies with haunted houses, vampires and the like. Good Lord. How incredible. But even so, how would Sean know about them?" Mandy asked. She sprang up from the sofa in an urgency to take some kind of action that would help her sister. "Never mind, I can see from your faces that somehow he found out about them and is using them to hunt her. So that has to be how our clothes were destroyed? Well, I for one am not waiting another second. We need to call Malcolm to see if they've found anything. Have they searched the fourth floor yet? Or another question, one I don't really want to think about, could Sean have possibly gotten her outside and away from the mansion without them knowing? Call Malcolm, Mom. If you don't, I will," she said, grabbing the phone out of her bag. "But before that, we're calling the police. What's that number, Madame?"

Before anyone could speak, a loud and urgent barking filtered down the open staircase, seemingly coming from the distant top floor. Stunned at first, Ben jumped up and started up the stairs, with Mandy a close step behind. She called back over her shoulder, "Mom, call the police, and then get hold of Malcolm and Etienne. Tell them Penny's barking her head off. They need to get to our suite as fast as possible."

"Mandy, stay downstairs with your mother. There may be trouble."

"You and what army is going to stop me, Ben? I'm coming with you, like it or not."

They were both puffing as they gained the third floor. Heads poked out of the occupied rooms along the way, complaining about the racquet made by Malcolm's wolfhound, even though Penny was a common sight around the manse. Many of the guests demanded to know what was happening. Not stopping to answer the litany of questions, the two hurried on. Penny raced down to meet them, almost flattening Ben in the process. Then the big dog bounded back up the stairs to the fourth floor, barking all the way.

Ben and Mandy followed as fast as they could, though they couldn't keep up with the excited animal. Breathing hard, Ben ran into the Martelli's suite with Mandy on his heels. The rooms were empty, though they still heard Penny barking—the ruckus coming from the far end of the hall.

"What the . . .?" Out of breath, Ben leaned against the wall, attempting to make sense of the unexpected situation. The decibel level caused by Penny's deep bark rose sharply as she galloped into the suite, and, just as suddenly, headed out and down the corridor again.

"She wants us to follow her, Ben! Let's go."

VICTORIA MASTERSON

11

Day Nine

Vail, Colorado—the company cabin

David Kessler took the winding mountain road slowly. He'd turned off the main highway outside of Vail that took him through a half mile of preeminent views to reach Chad and Claire's log home, snuggled as it was amongst pine trees, aspen, and rock formations. And the view from the front porch was incomparable. He looked off towards a cascading stream rushing down a nearby slope, from rock outcropping to rock outcropping. Well worth the drive.

Truth be known, he'd been trying to smother his nagging conscious for some time now, but to no avail. So he just stood there on the porch staring at one of nature's stellar achievements, letting the strength of the falling water seep into his resolve, helping to steel himself for the coming scene with Chad. He'd wrestled for several days with the whys and wherefores of the reason for his trip today.

"Oh, what the hell. It's not going to get any easier. Just get it over with," he muttered, forcing himself to act. He raised his fist to knock on the door. An urgent bark from inside answered his sharp rap. Duffy jumped up to look through the beveled glass panel of the entry door. But no Chad.

287

Kessler peered through the glass, seeing no movement other than Duffy's stub of a tail going ninety miles an hour as soon as the dog recognized the vet.

"Where is he, boy? Did he go into town and leave you here by yourself?" All he got in answer was more wagging tail as an excited Duffy pushed his nose into the glass and gave a friendly woof.

Kessler looked around the porch area, knowing Chad's propensity for always leaving a key hidden outside, resulting from the time he'd driven up to Vail without remembering he'd taken the key to the cabin off his ring to have Susan get an extra made. It had cost plenty, both in terms of time and money, to get the lock re-keyed by a Vail locksmith even after calling the locksmith he used in Denver who then assured the Vail locksmith he was the real owner and wasn't attempting a break-in. As Chad told the story, he could've driven back to Denver and then up to Vail again in the time it took to accomplish the whole process.

The only piece of furniture on the porch was a bench made of weathered aspen wood. Kessler carefully felt around the sides with no results. He looked carefully at the square post legs of the bench. One of them had a large knothole on the back side with a wood plug still in the hole but sticking out a fraction. Although there were many varying sizes of knotholes in the bench, something told him that Chad had found the one place that most people would never think to look.

Using the screwdriver he kept in his car, he was able to pop the knothole out into his hand. Inside the hole, he discovered a metal object wedged in the back of the niche. As his fingers were too large to grab onto it, he used the screwdriver once again to pry out the object, which was indeed a key.

An omen, he thought, a sign that today's mission was meant to be. He turned the key in the lock and entered the cabin.

Duffy was all over him. Overjoyed to see a friend, he jumped up on Kessler and licked his hand over and over.

"What's the matter, boy? You all alone? Where's Chad, huh?" He called out a loud "hello", but no answer. Checking the other rooms of the log home, he saw where Duffy had made a bed among the throw pillows on the rustic leather sofa, but no sign of Chad. In the kitchen area, he was dismayed to find that Duffy's food and water bowls stood empty. "Bet you're hungry. Shame on Chad. What could he be thinking to leave you here alone with nothing to eat or drink? Hang on, fella, I'm getting you some grub and some nice cold water," the vet said, filling the bowls as he talked to the excited animal. He sat down at the island, watching while Duffy scarfed down the dog food he'd found in one of the cabinets.

Kessler resigned himself to the fact that he wouldn't be facing off with Chad after all, which is why he'd made the trip to Vail in the first place. And lucky for Duffy that he had. But he'd faced down his own indecisiveness, and it felt right.

"I'm taking you back to Denver, Duffy my friend. Looks to me like Chad can't be trusted to take care of you, leaving you alone like this. Loupe is worried sick about you, boy. I should never have listened to Chad and taken you from her yard the other day. Let's make her happy—as well as yourself, of course. Okay? It's payback time, pal. But then you've never held a grudge, have you?"

He took one of his business cards from his wallet and wrote a note to Chad on the back side, propping it up against the island's prep sink faucet.

The smug glow of self-satisfaction lasted all the way back to Denver with Duffy riding shotgun in the passenger seat.

Denver—Offices of the Chadwick+Martelli Design Group

"Very smart of you, Ms. Farrell. I'm beginning to think there's hope for you yet," said the detective. Owens had been standing at the reception desk a few seconds without her noticing him, watching her hands speed across the keyboard of her computer. She jumped in surprise, turning her head to see him lounging against the high counter above her workspace.

"What? Oh, Lieutenant Owens, you startled me. Where did you come from? Certainly not through the entry door, or I would've seen you."

"No, you're right. I've been here a while, talking to Loupe in the Design department. You were out when I arrived. Powdering your nose, I presume. She called me a little while ago to tell me the good news that Duffy was back in her yard when she stopped home for lunch today."

"Yes, I know. She told me all about it when she returned from her noon break . . . how she checked him over to make sure he was okay and got him settled inside the house. She said she didn't want to take the chance that he might go missing again if she left him out in the yard."

"Yes, and I'm happy for her. And Duffy. Luckily, she said he didn't appear any the worse for his latest adventure, except that he seemed a little thinner. But you know all of that, of course. You're a very smart lady. That's why I complimented you. You realized I've suspected you knew who took Duffy, and it would be to your advantage to be instrumental in getting him returned. Although it's not always 'all's well that ends well,'" the detective pointed out, "especially if it's a situation where a law's been broken. Dog-napping, in this case. But to change the subject, is your boss back yet, Ms. Farrell?"

In a matter of seconds, Susan closed down. He could almost see her go inside herself and shut the door.

"No, he's not. And I had nothing to do with either Duffy's disappearance, or his return. So, if that's all you came for, please excuse me, Detective. I have plenty of work to get done before he gets back."

"Has he even called in to see if there are any problems? Or to let you know when he will be back?"

"Yes. As a matter of fact, Chad called me last night," she lied, in return. "And I told him how smoothly everything is going here. I am very capable at my job you know, probably to your amazement," she added. "As to your other question, he

290

said he was taking a few days R & R, and would be back in day or so. And before you ask, I do *not* know where he is. I asked him, but all he said was that he would fill me in when he returned," Susan said, her manner both challenging and curt. "Would you also like to know what I had for breakfast this morning, Lieutenant?"

Owens held up a crumpled grease-spotted bag. "No need for sarcasm, Ms. Farrell. I did bring donuts but Loupe and I ate them all as neither of us had a chance to eat lunch. Can I throw this in your wastebasket? And, not to worry, I'll take your cue and leave now. But first, I'm certain you'll want to know about an event that took place in Paris a few hours ago . . . regarding someone you care about."

Susan stood and faced him, her face ashen. "Okay, I'll bite," she said in an attempt at bravado. "And what event would that be, Lieutenant Owens?"

"Maybe you'd better sit down first. You see, the French police just notified me that your stepbrother, Sean, has been captured and placed under arrest. Ms. Farrell?"

Owens watched her guard go down. Her shoulders slumped. Body swaying, she fumbled for the back of her chair. Afraid she might faint, he hastened around the counter and caught hold of her before she lost her balance. "Easy now. Here, let me help you, Susan," he offered, unconsciously using her given name, and attempting to hold her up and bring her chair behind her at the same time.

But she pulled away from him and straightened up like a steel spring snapping back into place after being stretched to the breaking point. Waving him off with an impatient gesture, she positioned her chair to face her desk and slowly sat down, her back ramrod straight.

"Tell me . . . what was Sean arrested for, Lieutenant?"

He read the strain in her voice. Uncertain as to whether she'd entirely regained her control from the shock of the news, Owens debated whether to go around to the front side of the reception counter, or stay with her, not knowing how she'd react when he told her the whole story. Deciding on the latter choice, he settled himself, leaning against the partition at the far end of her desk—one leg casually thrown over the corner of the desk, the other leg braced on the floor so he could move quickly if she looked faint again.

"Why don't you relax a minute, Ms. Farrell, have a drink of water, or better yet, does Mr. Chadwick keep any . . . um, spirits in his office?" Owens asked, seeing how close she was to losing control again. "My sainted mother always recommended a little of the spirits now and then. For purely medicinal purposes, of course. Being Irish and all," he added, quirking an eyebrow.

"Lieutenant, please, just tell me what happened in Paris with regard to Sean's arrest."

"Okay. Here's the long and the short of it. At least what I know at present. Someone kidnapped Claire Martelli from her bedroom late last night. The police said that the discovery of secret passageways in the old mansion where she's staying was the venue, and probably the catalyst for the abduction. There was no other way she could have gone missing as the door to her room was locked from the inside with the key still in the lock. I understand they tore the place apart to find her. Which they finally did. She showed up, unconscious, in another guest's room. Again, no way to get in or out except through the secret passages. Thankfully, she's okay, but whoever did it, slipped her a knock-out drug in a glass of wine. She neither saw nor was able to identify her abductor."

Susan let out the breath she'd been holding. "She's alive then. So the police are holding Sean on what charges? Sounds like purely circumstantial evidence."

"Funny you should say that, Ms. Farrell. Sean admitted he had knowledge of the secret passages, but insists he knew nothing about Ms. Martelli being kidnapped. He was caught inside the walled property, though outside the mansion, in a kind of storage shed built into a wall of the manse. The police are saying he'd just left the mansion through the secret entry tunnel located there, but he claims that he'd just arrived and was about to *enter* the tunnel, not exit."

"So, basically, it's Sean's word against theirs. Right?"

"I wouldn't count on Sean going scot-free because of that, Ms. Farrell. They may not be able to prove kidnapping or attempted murder, but they think there's enough evidence to both hold him and try him. He hasn't exactly been the poster boy for the Boy Scouts. There's that little matter of a standing warrant for his arrest, as I told you previously, on charges of breaking and entering, and robbery of a certain gold medallion, valued at over a thousand French francs."

Susan dropped her eyes for a couple seconds, then raised her head and looked straight into his with determination. She hesitated for a split-second, then, "Lieutenant, can I ask a favor? I must talk to Sean. Can you help me get in touch with him? Most likely you think I don't deserve to ask, but I'd appreciate it nonetheless," her voice and eye contact never wavering.

Owens studied her face thoughtfully. He could see she was dead-set on trying to help her stepbrother. He knew she wouldn't desert Sean, no matter how difficult it might be to get to him in a Parisian jail. She was loyal, he would give her that. In his book, loyalty is as good a trait as they come. So why did that make him feel like he would be playing with fire if he started thinking about her good qualities? It wasn't his fault that she and her stepbrother had grown up on the streets, or that Sean had gotten in with the wrong crowd, besides the fact that both of them were easily manipulated. The detective was beginning to fit the various elements of the case together by piecing in bits of background information on all the players.

"That may take some doing, Ms. Farrell. But I'll see if I can add some influence in the matter."

Paris—Residence Saint-Germain

At first, Claire thought the low voices around her were part of a dream, but they didn't go away when she awoke, though she pretended she was still asleep. Her head felt like it was a

293

jigsaw puzzle, but missing some of the pieces necessary to complete it. She concentrated on trying to hear what the voices were saying, but it was impossible to hear because of a constant buzzing in her ears. The longer she lay there, thinking about why there were voices in her bedroom, the more certain she was that something had happened that she couldn't remember. Indeed, all she could actually recall was coming back to the room and lying down on the bed with a cold cloth over her eyes, subsequent to going out like a light.

Okay, concentrate, Martelli. The wet cloth? Because I was crying. Prior to that though? Abbie and Ben in the sitting room, offering me a glass of wine. Right. I conked out so quickly, it wasn't normal. Could someone have slipped something into my wine glass when I went into the bathroom? Sean? He certainly had opportunity . . . and desire, based on past experiences. But why would he just knock me out, instead of finishing me off? And I didn't see him, because . . . he was probably hiding in the room somewhere? I actually locked the bedroom door from the inside. He must have been in the armoire, no other place to hide. Of course. Then he had to have come through a panel of some kind located in the back of the armoire . . . from a secret passage that Etienne told Malcolm about. Everything is beginning to fall into place now.

Unwillingly, Claire thought back to the cause of her tears, admitting to herself why she had been so upset with Malcolm prior to coming upstairs last night.

Lady Anna . . . Malcolm's rather imperious grandmother. So domineering with regard to Malcolm's life. I'm evidently a threat to her influence on him. I don't doubt for a minute that she wants only the best for him. But the best, in her way of thinking, can never be an independent American whose way of life is so different from the landed English aristocracy. After meeting her, I'm certain Lady Anna will never rest until Cerian is back in Malcolm's life, as his wife, at the Rosemore estate where he will carry his grandfather's title, the heir apparent. Even though Malcolm doesn't appear to care about titles and ancestral lands, or Cerian for that matter, he does honor and respect the woman who raised him. As he should. Don't know why I expected him to stand up to his grandmother when she acted in such a superior and condescending manner concerning her dinner invitation at the Ritz. So why does it still hurt when he didn't?

"Mom, I think she's awake, her eyelids are flickering."

Her sister's voice was directly replaced by Abbie's motherly concern. "Thank the Lord. Claire honey, just take it easy. Ben and Malcolm both think you were slipped a . . ."

". . . Mickey Finn. Right?" Claire finished for her, sitting up with some effort. She blinked and squinted in the daylight that assaulted her eyes.

Mandy and Abbie both jumped to help adjust the pillows behind her.

"Thanks, that's better. You don't know how glad I am to see you both. It's all coming back. For a split second, before I blanked out, I thought I'd really bought it this time. That my luck had finally run out and no knight in shining armor would come to save me . . ."

Claire couldn't finish as she was suddenly enveloped in a double hug from her mother and sister, causing her to beg for mercy. "Please . . . I love you too. But I can't breathe," she gasped, attempting to draw more oxygen into beleaguered lungs that were just recovering from the knock-out substance.

"It's probably a side effect from your being doped, Claire," Mandy said. She drew back to give her sibling more air. "Malcolm called some of the hospitals for an antidote to various types of sedatives, his and Ben's choice of substance they think you were given. He found a substance abuse specialist in a hospital close by that after a thorough check of their credentials with their respective hospitals, was willing to provide them with an antidote, *if* it were necessary," noting her sister's face was just beginning to show some color. "You've been out for a very long time," she added. "But both our doctors have been checking on you.

"However, Mom and I've been talking, and not that we're trying to tell you what to do, Sis, so please don't take it that way. But, Abbie and Ben are ready to return to the States and we all concur that Paris is too dangerous for you to stay any longer. We think you'd be better off in Denver where Lieutenant Owens can provide some protection. You seem to think you're like the proverbial cat with nine lives. Even so, you've used up quite a few since we've been here." Mandy stopped for breath.

Claire took the opportunity to interject. "Let's leave that discussion till later, okay? Right now, I've got to finish piecing together what happened. For my peace of mind," she added, impatient to get on with it. "All I know for sure is that I put the wine glass on the bedside table, then went into the bathroom to run a wash cloth under cold water. When I came back, I finished the glass in a couple more sips and lay down on the bed, covering my eyes with the cloth, because . . . well, never mind the *because* for now. I really don't remember anything after that. Nada. Zilch.

"It was Sean. Right? He must have been hiding in the armoire and put something in my wine. I remember locking the bedroom door with the key. So he had to have gotten in through one of the secret passageways." She looked for confirmation from her mother and sister.

Abbie hesitated a couple seconds before answering, "Well, we know that's what had to have happened, however the police arrested Sean in the storage shed, where we've been told the entrance into the mansion is located, but. . ."

"Really?" Claire interrupted. "He's really been arrested? Then I'm not in danger anymore. Why didn't you tell me right away? *But what*, Mom? Mandy? I really need to know everything." Energized by the news, Claire moved to sit up on the edge of the bed.

"Okay, okay, Claire. Just take it easy," Mandy pleaded, attempting to get her sister to lie back again. "Please. Can you just hang-out until Ben comes in to give you a once-over? He said it's important to see if there are any toxic after-effects of the drug, so he'd know if you needed the antidote." She looked to Abbie for help.

"Honey, we thought it would be best to wait until you felt good enough to hear the whole story from Malcolm. He knows first-hand everything that went down when Sean was captured. In fact, Malcolm was the one who tackled Sean when he tried to run. But, if you're sure . . ."

The look Claire gave her mother was answer enough.

Before Abbie could answer, Mandy reluctantly picked up the story of Sean's arrest and the resulting outcome. "Okay. I know this will sound unbelievable," she began, "but please don't get your hopes up too high, Sis."

Mandy watched the anticipation fade from her sister's face. She rushed on. "However, Sean told the police he knew about the entrance and the hidden passages, but insisted that he was just getting ready to go *in*, not *out*. He claimed that he hadn't been in the mansion's vicinity since earlier that day. And, we can't prove otherwise because he was wearing gloves, so there goes the possibility of fingerprint evidence. The police bundled him off to jail until they can investigate further, but unfortunately, there's no hard proof that he intended to harm anyone, or you in particular.

"They've got him on trespassing, maybe breaking and entering, along with theft in reference to the medallion that old Dom found outside our door. Unfortunately, all charges are debatable as Marie-Claude admitted she was the one that voluntarily showed him how to get in and told him about the passages that run throughout the mansion. So all they've actually got right now is Marie-Claude's statement. But, again, it doesn't prove an attempted felony. He told her he wanted a way to visit her without anyone knowing. Said he didn't think her family would approve of clandestine meetings and that he couldn't openly see her, because, and, get this . . . he was an undercover agent from the States on a hush-hush mission. And regarding the break-in, there's no clear-cut evidence it was Sean, though Marie-Claude admitted she told him that her mother had locked the medallion in the security box for safekeeping. There was one partial thumb print on the bottom of the safety box, somewhat obscured by Madame Fontaine's, but the police have said they're sure it's a match to Sean's."

The look Claire gave her sister was one of complete dismay. "So, besides Marie-Claude, everyone else involved, including the police, fell for his con? So what's going to happen now? Are they just going to let him go free?" Claire nodded toward the armoire. "So he can come back and sneak into the mansion anytime he wants?"

Abbie picked up the story. "No, he only conned Marie-Claude. Of course, no one else believes that Sean is telling the truth. And, Claire, at this point we don't know what will happen concerning him. I know Lieutenant Owens has collaborated with the French police to strengthen their case so Sean can be tried here in Paris. However, he said it would depend on which country has the most evidence and could make the best case. If the detective has enough evidence to extradite him back to the States, to Denver, he will. It's all up in the air at the moment."

Visibly depressed by this last bit of information, Claire automatically reached for the carafe of water on the bedside table. Neither of her family spoke as she sipped the water her mother poured for her. Leaning back and closing her eyes, she mentally reviewed the ramifications in either case.

Abbie rescued the glass and put her finger to her lips giving Mandy the *shhh* sign. "She needs to rest," she mouthed.

But after a moment, Claire broke the silence. "That's definitely not good news. So, if the police can't make the charges stick here in the French jurisdiction, I'm still not safe from the maniac."

"Well don't worry about it until we find out that it's happened," Abbie said. "Let's not dwell on that possibility. Let's think on a more positive note. I really can't believe the Paris police would allow that to come about, but if it does I will have to say . . . 'they are so near-sighted . . .'"

". . . they can't pound Sam into a bean hole'." Mandy finished another of her mother's nonsensical 'Colo-isms', which made her sister smile.

"Claire, Lieutenant Owens is a smart cookie," Mandy went on, "as smart as they come. I'm sure he'll take charge of the situation if Paris isn't able to hold Sean for trial."

Claire felt the anxiety surrounding her mother and sister's attempts to downgrade the danger she was in. Though her spirits remained unsettled by this last bit of hopeful assurance on her sister's part, she fought for a more upbeat focus. Her gaze slowly moved around the room, stopping on the armoire. To get her mind off of the possibility of Sean free again, she couldn't help but think about her new wardrobe hanging inside.

"Mandy, you should see the new duds I bought the other day. They were hanging in the armoire as of last night. As someone had to come into the room from the secret passage that way. Are they still there? Or, I guess the real question is whether they're still wearable? If not, what a great excuse to go shopping again." She rambled on with a valiant show of spirit. "Oh, and did you find how to open the panel from the inside of the armoire to get into the passageway?"

"Now I see why Malcolm thinks we all talk in questions," Mandy quipped. "Okay, one at a time. I'm afraid most of your new duds, especially the silks, are pretty much beyond salvageable at this point. Some of the more fragile ones are past saving, torn and wrinkled. Though there are a few pieces that can be rehabilitated. I think there might be enough left to get you home when you've recovered, tomorrow or the next day."

Seeing the look on Claire's face, she hastily added. "Pertaining to the armoire's access to the other side, Malcolm located the place where it should be, from the hidden passage side of the wall, but we haven't discovered the secret of how it opens, from either side. While you were under the effect of the sedative, we all pushed, pulled, and even tried to move parts of the detail trims, but no luck. Either we just haven't found the right combination, or it's possible the mechanism got stuck when Sean closed it. After all it is a couple of centuries old."

"So I've been here on the bed the whole time? How long was I out?" Claire countered with more questions.

"Not exactly sure, but a fairly long time from all indications," Mandy said, answering the last question first. She continued with a frown. "Claire, please don't be alarmed, but you have to know. You see, you actually weren't in this room when the men broke the door down."

"You mean I was dragged into the passageway? And Malcolm or Etienne found me?" Claire shuddered, reacting to the realization that anything could have happened during the time she was out. And scary. She had absolutely no memory of the situation.

Impatiently, she looked to Mandy. "Okay, Sis, let me know the worst of it."

"Claire, we're not sure just how you got there, but you're right on one thing. Malcolm did find you . . . when he broke the door down to *his* bedroom. Strangely enough, it was also locked from the inside."

"What? I was in Malcolm's bedroom?" Claire couldn't believe her ears. "But how?"

"I know, dear, this whole thing is so perplexing," Abbie remarked. She sat down next to Claire on the bed. "When we get back to Denver, everything will be better."

"No, nothing is going to magically disappear, Mom. Unless Sean is tried here in Paris and found guilty of the whole list of attempts on my life, as well as the theft of the medallion, and the breaking and entering charge, I can hope they put him away for a long time, can't I? Even if I'm lucky enough to be rid of him while he rots in prison, I have a whole lot of other things to work out, beginning with the business and Chad. Unfortunately, those issues can't wait as long as it will take for the court system to see that justice is done in regard to Sean," she pointed out.

"I hope you also add Malcolm and your future onto that list, Sis. Seems like a couple of the more important elements to work out."

Claire ignored Mandy's remark. "Okay, please finish with the story. What else happened? How did Malcolm know where I was?" As soon as she asked, Claire's heart plummeted, suddenly realizing that he also had the same opportunity as Sean. But motive?

"It was Penny, she's the real hero," Mandy continued with the recital of events. "Malcolm left her outside our suite when he and Etienne went back into the passages. The rest of us went downstairs to wait for the police and for Malcolm's call telling us he found you. Then we heard Penny barking all the way to the lobby, down three flights of stairs. Ben and I ran upstairs, but found our suite empty. Then Penny raced into the room and, just as quickly, back out. So we followed her . . . to Malcolm's quarters. He'd left the entry door open and Penny ran straight through to the bedroom door, pawing and scratching on it, and barking her head off. We couldn't get in because it was also locked from the inside and Madame Fontaine doesn't have extra keys to the bedroom door locks. I called Malcolm to tell him what was happening. He and Etienne, and the police, all arrived at the same time. They knocked down the door to the bedroom. And there you were, for all intents looking like you were sleeping peacefully, snuggled in Malcolm's bed."

"Okay, got it. Mandy. Stop a minute and listen. Please?" Claire asked, seeing the dogged look begin to form on her sister's face.

"Claire, I think I know where this is going, and I just don't believe Malcolm is part of some plot to do you in. Wouldn't it be pretty stupid of him to kidnap you and take you to his room when he was the driving force to knock down the door? But, *someone* is, that's evident, and it pretty much looks like Sean at this point."

"Please, Mandy. Just listen. You, too, Mom," Claire added, looking up at her mother who had opened her mouth to speak, but closed it at Claire's meaningful look. "Let me get this out. Maybe I'm just naturally suspicious after all that's happened. But, what if Sean *is* telling the truth? Then that means

301

someone else was in the passageways. And we actually know who. Malcolm and Etienne. Yes, I know they were ostensibly there to find Sean, before Sean could find me. But what if Malcolm somehow purposely lost Etienne along the way and made his way to the fourth floor. Being the intelligent and astute person we know him to be, he could've figured out how to open the panel that leads into the armoire and into this bedroom and, a little farther down the way, another panel leading to his quarters, most probably his bedroom. He could have drugged me, carried me through the passageway and into his room very easily. Let's face it, he could have done all those things."

All three women turned toward the doorway at the same time as Penny came rushing in, skidding to a halt next to Claire's bed, where she demurely sat down, tail wagging furiously. Malcolm lounged against the frame of the broken door, arms folded, looking both stoical and bemused at the same time.

"Yes," he said. "I could have done all those things, Claire. But I didn't. And I can assure you, if I wanted to get you into my bed, I wouldn't have to drug you and carry you off. Believe me when I say you would want to come. I guess there's no way to prove it at this point, but the offer stands . . . if and when you want to try it."

Claire flushed a deep red at his suggestion that ignited a sudden fire within. Embarrassed by the unexpected reaction shooting through her body, she wished for nothing more than to wipe the annoying self-assured smile from his face.

She fumed inwardly. *Some nerve. For him to be so egotistical to suggest that I'd want to go to bed with him. He's really a superb actor if my qualm indeed proves correct and he's been a part of this all along. Has he really only been setting me up for Sean to finish me off?*

Inwardly, a little voice cautioned her to stop with the suspicions until she found proof that he was not friend, but foe. *Damn!* She knew how devastating that would be. Not that she'd ever admit it if it turned out that he actually was in

302

cahoots with Sean. To forestall her all too imaginable fears, she allowed her indignation to resurface that he could be so flip and grumbled something about him being the last person in the world she would go to bed with.

"Our sleeping beauty is awake," said Malcolm, without commenting on her muttered remark. He moved inside the room as Ben came up behind him. Mandy stood, taking Penny in tow, and offered her chair to Ben so he could get to his patient. Abbie rose and signaled Malcolm to take her station on the other side of the bed. He refused with a shake of his head, telling her he was fine where he stood, and adding it was mutually agreed that Ben would be Claire's primary physician. He explained in a low voice that he only wanted to satisfy himself that Claire was recovering without undue problems.

Ben set a small bag on the nightstand and proceeded to take Claire's pulse. "Forgive me for not being here when you woke up, Claire. How are you feeling? You certainly have good color, and an acceptable pulse rate given the circumstances," Ben added, noting his patient's sudden flush in answer to Malcolm's close scrutiny from the end of the bed.

"I'll survive, Ben," she responded. "Just a headache."

"I'll have to say she's much better than when she first opened her eyes," Abbie informed them. "And, thank the Lord for small favors, her mind seems clear."

"I'm guessing he used one of the sedatives from the Midazolam group, Ben," Malcolm said to his colleague.

Ben didn't answer, intent on his examination. He pulled a stethoscope from his pocket and listened to Claire's heart and lungs. Putting the instrument away, he moved to sit on the edge of the bed, looking into her eyes with his small flashlight.

"I agree with your prognosis, Malcolm. That would be my best guess also. That group of sedatives does have a low toxicity level, hence the clarity of mind."

Ben turned toward his patient. "After listening to your breathing, Claire, your lungs appear to be effectively working off the sedative. Nothing to worry about there. And with these kinds of sedatives, there is a rapid onset of action, which I would have to think caused you to lose consciousness rather quickly. Am I right?"

"Right. I only remember lying down. Then a few seconds later . . . nothing. But how did you know that?" Claire asked, impressed by his knowledge of the sedative's effects.

"Well, it's not such a hard thing to pin down after we found your empty wine glass on the bedside table here. When the police came on the scene, we asked them to test it for drugs. They sent it to their rush lab by special dispatch and will notify us of their findings. However, Malcolm and I have already discussed the possibilities that would explain what might have happened and we've drawn the same conclusion. Someone had to have slipped a drug into your wine glass, a sedative in this case, while you were in the bathroom. Abbie and I both drank the same wine without any ill effects. We heard water running in the bathroom after you went to your room, but not a sound after that. We have to presume that the someone was Sean, who we think was probably hiding in the armoire, which would also be not only the way in, but out, as well. Not so difficult to figure out after all." Ben stood up and closed his traveling medical bag.

"And now, I suggest we let Claire rest. The way she's recuperating, I anticipate she'll be up and around shortly, but no more excitement. Frankly, I don't think any of the rest of us can take anymore. In fact I'm going to my room to catch a quick nap myself. But you won't be alone, Claire. We'll all tag-team in shifts," Ben said, seeing her look of apprehension. "And I'll ask Madame Fontaine to send up a light soup. But I won't sleep a wink if you don't promise to let me know if for some reason your present condition changes. Okay?"

Claire nodded her agreement. "Thanks, Ben."

One by one they left the room. Mandy volunteered to go down for the soup so that Ben could get right to his nap. Abbie followed Ben out the door to talk to him privately. Only Malcolm stayed behind, saying he wasn't tired and would take the first watch so the others could rest.

"I know you need to rest, Claire, but I'd like to talk with you later after I get back from the dinner Grandmother is hosting at the Ritz. I've already sent her a note saying you're recovering from a mishap, so she won't expect you or the others to attend. I don't want to go, but for me it's a command performance. You do understand, don't you?"

Mishap, indeed. Claire wasn't sure if she even wanted to be in his company, let alone listen to whatever he had to say. She decided to reflect on it between now and then. If she needed an out, one of her family could make the excuse she was sleeping.

"I'd like that, Malcolm, as long as I'm feeling up to it later on. Check with Mom or Mandy on the way down to your suite when you get back. Okay? And, please give your grandmother our regrets." Claire closed her eyes. She knew nothing would happen to her on *his* watch. It would be far too dangerous for him to show his hand now if indeed he was somehow involved with Sean in the plot.

Claire pretended to sleep until Mandy came back with the soup.

Paris—The Ritz, Lady Anna's suite

The countess swept into the guest bedroom off the living room of the elegant suite at the Ritz without knocking. She found Cerian applying metallic bronze color to her eyelids while seated at the makeup counter that was part of the hotel's tasteful appointments.

"Lady Anna, this is a surprise," Cerian said, looking in the mirror to see her benefactress entering the room." I'm not late for our cocktail date with Malcolm and the Martelli group, am I?" She revolved on the tufted taboret to face her benefactress. "Didn't we say seven-thirty for cocktails?" She asked, checking the time on the diamond-studded watch encircling her wrist.

"Cerian, you're not late. I came to tell you the Martelli's won't be coming. Just Malcolm. He sent over a messenger with a note saying there was some trouble late last night after they returned to the hotel. I'm not sure just what that means. He didn't go into any further explanation, but said he would fill us in when he got here. It appears that Claire Martelli is not feeling well and is resting in bed." The countess tossed her head. "But, after her lukewarm response to my dinner invitation last night, I think Ms. Martelli is using this rather lame excuse so she won't be expected to come for cocktails . . . *her* invitation by the way . . . let alone for dinner."

Cerian rose from her perch. But Malcolm will be here, right?" She tightened the neckline of the silk robe she wore so that her generous bosom encased in lacy lingerie only just peeked out.

"Yes, Malcolm is still coming for cocktails and dinner, my dear." She scanned Cerian's décolletage noticing how the filmy fabric of the low-cut undergarment was meant to entice and invite further exploration on Malcolm's part during the evening ahead.

Lady Anna did not miss Cerian's intention. She was thoughtful for a moment. Then, her face lit up. "What are you wearing tonight, my dear? The low-cut deep red silk cocktail dress that we picked up the other day at that new couture shop?"

Cerian smiled. "Yes, Lady Anna. I think it's perfect for tonight. Don't you? It will certainly show Malcolm that his American girlfriend can never be our equal."

"And more. My dear, I have a plan in mind that will knock Ms. Martelli out of the running for good, and Malcolm will be yours again. . .as well as my heir to Rosemore Grange." She patted a place beside her on the lush velvet divan.

Paris—Residence Saint-Germain

Claire was tired of having Ben, her mother and sister as babysitters all day, even though well-meaning ones. So she convinced them that she was no longer in need of medical supervision—the effects of the sedative having worn off. She'd insisted they allow her some privacy. Now, she restlessly paced the bedroom, arguing with herself whether she should meet with Malcolm, 'to clear the air' as he put it, when he returned from his dinner engagement with his grandmother and Cerian. She was angry with him on the one hand for what she considered his crass 'offer' to go to bed with him. Besides that, a part of her still felt disquieted due to her former suspicions. She'd deliberated on it all afternoon and she'd moved on to think his questionable involvement was merely that—possible, like it would be in the realm of possibility that Paris could be hit by a snowstorm in July, but not probable.

Okay, let's face it head on, Martelli. You don't want to believe that he hasn't been upright and honest with you. Not only that, but you just can't get over your feelings for him, especially how you've come to think of him as much more than a friend, possibly a someone that could become a partner in a committed relationship.

Only a couple more days and the divorce will be final, she reminded herself. And what would it be like to be in a romantic relationship with Malcolm . . . to be lovers?

Am I ready for that? Stop it! Let's not rush into anything, Martelli. You can't have forgotten so soon how you rebounded into the relationship with Chad . . . after Adam. And how that turned out.

She sighed. Not that both her former fiancé and Chad's indiscretions hadn't torpedoed the trust factor in the marriage to one, or the commitment of the engagement to the other.

In another few days, I'll be returning to the States, so whether Malcolm's feelings, or my own, will grow stronger or fade over an ocean away . . . I'll just have to wait and see.

Besides, the fact that he wants to stop by to talk when he gets back may help clarify certain issues. And he did make a point of saying, "alone." Well, my friend, in this room we'll be alone, but Mandy, Abbie and Ben will be within earshot.

Claire stopped pacing. She felt better having put her nagging thoughts to rest. She looked at her watch, thinking Malcolm should be coming by any time now. A quick stop in the bathroom to freshen her face and hair, and she was ready. She made her way to the suite's sitting room where dinner was in full swing thanks to Ben's take-out order from the popular neighborhood *brasserie* nearby.

"Look who's here," exclaimed Abbie, delighted that her daughter felt well enough to join them. "Come sit down, honey, Ben brought your favorite, pork chops *charcutiere.*"

"Thanks, Ben. It smells wonderful. But first, let me check to see if Malcolm is back yet. He's planning on stopping by after his dinner with Lady Anna and Cerian."

"Let's just leave the door open, Sis," Mandy suggested, her mouth full of cheese-topped French onion soup. "I'm sure he'd have knocked on the way to his suite if he were back. He'll stop in when he sees the door is open. And you can eat while the food is still warm."

"Sounds like a plan," Claire said her mouth watering from the aromas coming from the containers. "You know homemade broth is great when you're not feeling up to par, but it never fills me up. This will be my first solid meal since dinner, let's see . . . it was the night before last. I'm still trying to get my time sequences in order. I'll have to say whatever was in that sedative left me with some gaps to fill in, along with a powerful hunger."

Abbie began to fill a plate for her from the containers, but on seeing the amount of food her mother was piling on, Claire shook her head." Thanks, Mom, but let me start with just a pork chop and a spoonful of mashed potatoes with some of that excellent sauce. I've been trying to figure out the ingredients for the sauce so that I can make it at home. I know it's tomato-based with finely chopped onion and dill pickle of all things. I think we can all agree on that, but I'm pretty sure there's wine and butter, and also a little mustard involved.

What ingredients do you taste, Mom . . . Mandy?" Much to her surprise, Ben answered before the others could comment.

"I'm with you on all those ingredients, Claire. However, I'm thinking you need to add just a small amount of aged white wine vinegar, maybe just a tablespoon or so. The sauce tastes so smooth, I think the vinegar is what's drawing all the flavors together. And if you simmer it for ten or fifteen minutes, the vinegar and the wine give up their essence, reducing the amount of liquid to make a thicker sauce. And then finish it, of course, by adding a little freshly ground white pepper and kosher salt to taste. Although I like to use French sea salt also."

The three women stared at him. Abbie was the first to speak, the others speechless, reflecting on what he just said. "Since we've been together here in Paris, I've discovered what an epicurean you are regarding French food, Ben, but I never dreamed you were also a gourmet cook."

"French food is one of my favorites, Abbie. I've taken some cooking classes at Le Cordon Bleu schools over the years, recreational only, not professional courses," he said modestly. "Actually, I enjoy cooking. It gives me an outlet from the less pleasant aspects of my practice and a chance to unwind from long hours at the clinic. Besides, like the esteemed Julia Child, I love to eat.

"So, I started taking evening and weekend cooking classes here and there, and found that I actually enjoyed learning how to prepare classic dishes in the French, Chinese and Italian vernaculars, my favorites. I make a mean *Ossobuco*, braised veal shank in a tomato-based sauce with vegetables that slow cooks for hours until the meat is so tender you can cut it with a fork. You are all invited. Maybe we can set a dinner date in the near future, after I've had a chance to catch up from being gone this week."

Mandy's face screwed up into a moue. "Sure, and I'll be the only one still in Paris after you all head back to the States. Guess that leaves me out, at least for now. But, don't you worry, Ben. As soon as I'm back in Denver, I'm going to take you up on the invite.

"Speaking of returning home, when are you and Ben planning on leaving, Mom? Have you made reservations yet?" Mandy took another pork chop and tore off a piece of crusty baguette to soak up the sauce. Before either could answer, she went on to defend her second helping, saying, "Don't anyone say anything, please. I know I'm piggin' out, but the food's so good, I can't help it. Besides, I'm still starved from the long flight and then the hullabaloo over Claire when I got here. Was that just early morning, *today*? Seems like an eon ago. This is my first full meal since I left New York and they say you're supposed to *feed* jet lag."

"Uh, I think you're confusing that with 'feed a cold, starve a fever,' Mandy. I've always wondered who *they* are who say all these things, but I think in this case they say you're supposed to drink liquids for jet lag." Claire set her sister straight with a smile. "So have a glass of the red wine Ben brought up from Madame Fontaine's cellar. It's another excellent vintage, but a little bolder than the one I zoned out on last night. Personally, I'm not letting the glass out of my sight this time," she informed them.

"Thanks for the dinner and the wine, Ben," she said raising her glass in a salute. "And I, for one, will take you up on the dinner invitation as long as I wouldn't be imposing on a private dinner for two?" Claire asked looking from Ben to Abbie, whose face colored to a becoming shade of pink.

Ben smiled and shook his head, "Of course you wouldn't be imposing, Claire. I look forward to your attending. We'll make it a threesome, but if you'd like to bring someone, that would work, also. I'll leave it up to you." He turned to Mandy. "You have a standing dinner invitation, Mandy. Whenever you're in town, you're welcome to dine at Doc Ben's place. But to answer your previous question, Abbie and I are scheduled on the flight to New York leaving the day after tomorrow, the overnight flight. I thought we all might go out for dinner tomorrow evening to celebrate our last night in Paris. How does that sound?"

Before anyone could answer, a commotion in the hallway outside their open door caught their attention. A hushed masculine voice could be heard urgently shushing a higher-pitched giggle that was definitely female.

Claire's heart did a flip-flop. The color drained from her face. She was certain she knew both those voices. And to make matters worse, the merriment and shushing were becoming more distant as they moved on down the corridor. The only suite in that direction, beyond the Martelli's, was Malcolm's. She had to know for sure.

Claire collided with Mandy, both attempting to get to the door first. Mandy won, and valiantly tried to keep Claire from seeing a familiar dark-haired man carrying a stunning brunette in a low-cut deep red silk dress down the hall. Too late, Mandy put her arm around her sibling for moral support. Both sisters watched as Malcolm carried Cerian into his suite, the door closing off her tinkling laughter.

Claire slumped against the door frame, her face showing utter disbelief at the scene she just witnessed.

Mandy tightened her hold on her sister, attempting to pull her away from the open door. "Come on, Claire, let's go back in. I'm as shocked as you are. You know this is entirely out of character for Malcolm to act like this."

Trembling, Claire allowed her sister to guide her back into their suite. Ben and Abbie jumped up to help Mandy on seeing Claire's distress.

Before they could get to her, Claire drew herself up and insisted she was capable of navigating her way to the bedroom on her own, saying she was just tired and wanted to go to bed. She turned to them before leaving the room. "Mom, Ben, would you mind if I traveled with you back to the States? I'll make my reservation first thing in the morning. Just leave the airline and flight number on the desk there. And, Mandy, do you want to do some shopping tomorrow? We haven't had much opportunity to do so since we've been here, and you probably won't be back in Denver for a while." At her sister's nod, she pasted a smile on her face, turned and made her way down the hall to the bedroom.

Denver—Offices of the Chadwick+Martelli Design Group

The rising sun crept up to illuminate the tallest peaks of the Rockies silhouetted against the promise of another intense blue Colorado sky. Yawning widely, Chad drove his Mercedes CLS Coupe into his reserved parking space. His was the first car in the lot this morning. He'd almost decided against coming into the office until later in the morning, after he'd had a chance to crash for a couple hours, but wanted his early presence to be noted by his employees as they arrived for work.

He'd been gone longer than he'd originally planned, and Susan was beginning to get suspicious. He'd decided just recently it was time to trade in their relationship, built on sex for carnal pleasure, to one that would once again present a new challenge in that arena. Being completely self-absorbed, he considered himself extremely lucky not to be inconvenienced by a personal conscience. His focus was strictly on putting together professional business dealings through his chosen field, architecture, in order to increase his monetary worth, and then again, on the more personal side, to inflate that most basic of all human instincts, his libido.

In general, his *modus operandi* was to plan ahead for what tact to take in any given situation, one that would place him in the best light for the sole purpose of personal aggrandizement.

He pondered his options on the dilemmas facing him in his current sleep-deprived state. Putting the Susan complication aside for right now, he needed to come up with an approach on how best to react if Duffy was found dead at his Vail home because he'd left him alone. Although he could rightly say he'd left a message on his mountain neighbor's voice mail to please stop at his place while he was gone, letting it be known he'd be *properly* appreciative if they'd feed and water the dog.

He'd also suggested that they give the spaniel a quick walk a couple times a day as he was "unavoidably detained." He had in fact left that message.

After all, Chad thought, since they lived up there year round and their cabin was just a little further down the road from his place, it couldn't have been that much of an imposition, could it? After all, what were neighbors for? He didn't really want to face Claire concerning the animal's fate if they hadn't gotten the message. Or, if perhaps they simply decided not to accede to his request for some reason.

Chad shook his head. The problem was he'd instinctually acted before he'd considered all possibilities of what course of action to take before leaving Duffy alone at the cabin. And now—after the fact—it was so very easy to come up with a better solution. For instance, he could've called Susan and sent her up to the cabin to get the dog. He could have made it sound like a casual request. And she could have stayed at his Denver home with the dog until he returned.

She was always at the house per his biding anyway, he thought, smiling as he remembered some of the more imaginative nights he'd spent with her at his place in the past. Of course, he wasn't kidding himself. It wasn't love. It was only passion. And passion alone was non-effective in attaining the state of mind required to love—a state of mind not in his vocabulary.

Chad chided himself for going down that road. Back to the problem at hand. The truth of the matter was that he hadn't wanted Susan to know he'd left the dog unattended because she'd probably begin to put two and two together. She wasn't stupid. He'd wanted her to think he just needed to get away for a couple days and took Duffy with him for companionship while Claire was gone. It wasn't a secret—the whole office knew Claire refused to honor their custody arrangement. She hadn't shared Duffy with him since the attack. But that was all right with him. He'd only requested that they share the dog after they'd separated for appearance's sake. But better than that, he knew it would be a source of frustration to Claire as Duffy really belonged to her for all intents.

Chad unlocked the double glass doors into the building and then the keyed door opening the private stairway to his own office. He'd planned this personal entry-cum-escape so he could come and go without being seen in the reception area or in the corridor in front of the elevator, which was the way everyone else reached the only suite of offices on the second floor. He'd designed it so that the elevator door opened onto a peerless pair of nine-foot-high glass and pierced metal custom doors, leading into the offices of the Chadwick+Martelli Design Group.

He debated as to whether to turn on the lights inside his office, but the opportunity to catch a few winks before anyone came in was far too great a temptation. Endeavoring to put a lid on his restive thoughts, he settled into the cushy luxury of the leather-clad sofa, the focal point of the very masculine, and impressive, conversation area at one end of his large work space. He was sound asleep in a matter of seconds.

Susan unlocked the office door and turned on the lights, then headed for her desk carrying her usual tote bag of five-inch stilettos she wore in the office. She'd decided to come in early to get caught up on work she'd put off after hearing about Sean's arrest from the detective. She'd noticed Chad's car parked in his usual spot this morning, and was both glad he was back, and angry with him at the same time. She couldn't help but wonder where he'd been all this time.

Soon to find out, she thought, glancing through the floor-to-ceiling glass wall that fronted onto the reception area to see he wasn't at his desk, and the office was still dark. She sat down on her chair, changed into her stilettos and picked up the thick pile of messages she'd taken for him while he was gone.

"Chad? Are you in here?" She called, after knocking softly and entering his office. She turned on the lights, and not seeing him, looked around, thinking he must be in his private washroom. However, a familiar snore sounded from the conversation area, compelling her to look in that direction. Chad lay on his back on the sofa, his jacket pulled up over his chest like a blanket.

"Chad," she said, shaking him. "Wake up, sleepy head. Time to go to work."

When Chad didn't move and the snoring continued, she tried another tactic. "Okay, my man, take your choice. Either you get up right now, or I'll join you. It's been so long, lover. I've missed you."

"Oh, excuse me, Ms. Farrell. I didn't know this was a private party." The voice of Lieutenant Owens came from the open door behind Susan.

Startled, Susan jumped up from where she'd been sitting on the edge of the sofa and whirled around to face him. "Lieutenant Owens! What are you doing here?"

As the sound of conversation made its way through his slumber, Chad woke with grumpy recognition. "Owens? Yes, what *are* you doing here? Can't a man get a little shuteye in private?" He struggled into a sitting position, running his hands through his hair and putting on his glasses, pushing them up his nose.

"Saw your car in the parking lot, Mr. Chadwick. Thought I'd pop up and welcome you home with some news," said Owens, lounging against the open door.

"Oh? And what news is that? Let me wake up a minute, Lieutenant. Susan make us some coffee." On seeing the look on her face and the sheaf of messages in her hand, he added a curt and thinly veiled directive. "Please. And, Susan, we'll go over the messages after our early morning guest leaves." So saying, Chad entered his private washroom, calling over his shoulder, "I'll just be a minute, Lieutenant, need to use the little boy's room."

Susan waited until he shut the door. Then, in a low and pleading voice, "Please, detective, is there anything new regarding Sean? I must know. How can I get in touch with him? He needs to know I'm here for him." She wrung her hands, trying to hide the fact that her eyes were tearing.

Owens put a hand on her shoulder to get her full attention. "Ms. Farrell, I'm afraid the Paris police have different policies than we do and they refuse to make your stepbrother accessible to you right now. They are in the process of uncovering more evidence in order to put Sean on trial there. You could wait and take your chances. If they can't make a good case for attempted murder and kidnapping, they will go with the lesser charges—breaking and entering, along with the felony theft charge of the medallion. You might be able to see him in a French prison after he's remanded into same. If you're willing to travel to France, that is, and then apply for permission. I really can't promise you how long that will take.

"The other option is as I've offered before. Are you ready to make a statement? If so, I can start the extradition procedure that will bring him back to the States, and to Denver. You'll be able to see him at that point. But, I must advise you, he will be tried for attempted murder in the attack on Claire Martelli in March," the detective explained, watching her face carefully. "The ball's in your court. Take your pick."

"But you said you would get us a deal if I . . ." Still undecided, Susan left the thought hanging. She flinched away from the hand resting on her shoulder.

"Not exactly. What I said was that I would get you a deal with the DA *if* . . . and I repeat, *if* you collaborated with me at that time." Owens kept his voice low, hearing the door to the washroom open. "The opportunity does have a deadline. Let's take this up later. I'll be in touch."

Chad walked to where they stood, looking thoughtfully at the two of them, and noting his mistress' tears. "Susan, are you quite deaf this morning? I hope this isn't indicative of how you ran the office while I was away. So let me be perfectly clear. Make the coffee. Now. Unless the Lieutenant here is paying your salary of course."

"Sorry. Right away, Chad." For just a split second, a marked look of rebellion showed in the cat-like eyes, but she composed herself quickly and left the room.

Chad turned to Owens. "Now, detective, what brings you here so early this morning?"

"Well, I stopped by to tell you the news a couple days ago, but found Ms. Farrell in charge who said you were gone and she didn't know specifically when you'd return." Owens held up a grease-spotted paper bag. "Care for a donut with the coffee?"

"Never touch those things, myself," Chad said, motioning Owens to the chair across from his desk. "If you don't mind, Lieutenant, could you be brief with whatever it is you are here to tell me. My schedule is pretty full today, as you can imagine, what with being gone a day or so."

"Yes, I can imagine, Mr. Chadwick. And, hasn't it been longer than that? More like three?"

"I didn't know you cared, Lieutenant. Keeping tabs on me now?"

Owens dug into his paper bag for a sugar-drenched donut, took a bite and set the remaining piece on Chad's desk, the sugar powdering both his coat and the desk top. Ignoring Chad's attempt to call for Susan to clean up the mess, he munched on the bite, reflecting. "I always forget to take the napkins when I get the donuts. Sure you won't have one Mr. Chadwick?"

"Detective, out with it. What is it you stopped by to tell me? As I've said before, I have a busy day, and you weren't on my schedule. So, I'd appreciate it if you would hurry this along."

"All right, Mr. Chadwick. I just thought you might like to know that while you've been away, both Ms. Martelli and Duffy, her dog, were abducted, but thankfully, both have been recovered with no serious effects from either incident.

"No one knows who the culprit is that took Duffy, but he's back safe and sound. As for Ms. Martelli's kidnapping, the French police have arrested Sean O'Malley and have charged him with that as well as intent to do bodily harm. Seems as though he insists that he didn't kidnap Ms. Martelli, that he was just coming to the hotel to visit the proprietress' daughter, through a secret passageway no less. As I said, just thought you might be interested. I realize you and Ms. Martelli are breaking up housekeeping, but she's still your partner, or do you even care at all?"

To cover his reaction on hearing that Duffy was indeed alive, Chad jumped up from his chair and attempted to put on a much maligned face after hearing what Owens had just said about Claire's disappearance.

"Detective, Claire and I have had our differences, but I'm not a monster, as I'm sure she would have you believe. Of course I care what happens to her. Thank you for telling me, I'll call her right away to see if there's anything I can do. I've been out of touch with her this last day or so. Poor Claire. You did say she's okay? And Duffy, too?"

Owens stood up. "Yes, they're both fine. Don't you even want to know the details of these incidences, Sir?"

"Of course I do, Lieutenant. I'll get the whole story from Claire. I'll put through a call to her shortly. And I'll talk to Loupe involving Duffy. If that's all the news, you'll excuse me now."

The detective nodded and turned to leave, opening the office door for Susan who held a tray with two steaming mugs of coffee. He quirked an eyebrow at her. "I'll take a rain check on the coffee, Ma'am. And don't trouble yourself," he added as she set the tray on the desk top and hastily picked up the remains of the donut, trying to brush the powdered sprinkles of sugar into her palm with a napkin from the tray. "I can show myself out."

As Owens left the office, he did an about-face, eyeing Chad, "Oh, and Mr. Chadwick, one more thing. Where were you when you left town these past few days?"

Pretending surprise, Chad looked up from watching Susan clean the sugar from the chair Owens had sat in. "Why, Lieutenant, don't tell me I'm a suspect now. For what?

Claire's kidnapping? In Paris? But I've nothing to hide. I just wanted to be by myself. Surely you can understand. I let the mountains wash away the stress of these past few months, what with the divorce and all. It will be final in a few days, you know. And before you ask, I saw no one. So there is no way for you to verify my whereabouts. You'll just have to believe me, unless of course you can prove otherwise?"

Owens only shrugged in answer and strolled out the door leaving Chad to wonder why he'd come. Wouldn't Owens think that Susan had already informed him of Claire's kidnapping and Sean's subsequent arrest? Of course she hadn't, but the detective wouldn't know that. And what did Owens mean about Duffy being kidnapped, *and returned*? How did that happen? Who returned him and to whom was he returned? Who even *knew* that the dog was at his cabin, with the exception of his neighbors down the road, and of course, Susan and David.

Chad needed to be alone while he sorted out the scenario resulting from the detective's visit. He closed his office door before Susan could buttonhole him. Officially this meant to steer clear, especially when the blinds covering the floor-to-ceiling glass walls facing onto the reception area were also closed, which he did next, then headed for his desk. He would get to Susan later.

Sitting down heavily in his leather chair, Chad swiveled around to face his favorite view of the mountains when in the confines of his office. He flexed his arms and shoulders, stiff from napping in a rather cramped position on the sofa, and with a sigh he settled back to ruminate on the recent events. When his shirt pocket began to vibrate, he took the phone out at once, glancing at the caller's number on the screen.

"Yes?" He sat bolt upright as the person on the other end disclosed the reason for the call. Chad's thundering reply formed both a question and an accusation. "*Why in hell would you do that?*" He listened impatiently, frowning, all the while unaware his thumb and second finger rolled a tiny ball of paper torn from a message in the stack Susan had left on his desk.

Susan left the office at five o'clock on the dot. She'd tried every way she could think of to corral Chad alone since the detective's visit that morning. Nothing had worked. Either he made sure he was never alone when she was able to get to him, or he ignored her attempts on the intercom to see him privately in his inner sanctum. His door had been locked and the shades closed all day. They were still closed when she'd turned out the lights and locked the entry door as everyone else had left early for one reason or another. She'd begun to think Chad might possibly not even be in there at all. He could have left anytime through his private entry and down his private stairway, although she noticed his car still occupied its reserved space as she exited the parking area.

Out on the street, she headed directly for the grocery store to re-stock her nearly empty pantry. From there, she drove to her apartment automatically, via her customary route, her thoughts absorbing her attention. Since leaving the office she'd become convinced that Chad's covertness both today and in the three days he'd been gone meant that he intended to break off their relationship. And with Sean being held in a Paris jail, she was definitely alone and terribly afraid.

The tall streetlights, although few and far between, were making some headway in lighting the night for it had grown dark by the time she finally parked in her designated spot in Building C's lot. It wasn't until she'd turned off the motor and reached for some of her grocery bags that she became aware of a dark vehicle illuminated faintly by the streetlight at the near end of the property. She heard its engine idling, and noticed the headlights were facing her way. This in itself didn't strike her as unusual as people were always coming and going around her apartment complex. Presuming the occupant of the car was simply there waiting to pick up someone who lived in her building, she didn't give it further consideration.

320

Lost in her thoughts, she sat in the driver's seat for a moment longer. Her stomach growled, reminding her it was time to get something to eat. She sighed and began gathering up the plastic bags. Susan hated going to the store because of the problem involved in getting the groceries up to her apartment on the third floor. It meant either she waited forever for the only elevator which was generally used by the older inhabitants of the building, or carry the bags up two flights of the back stairway. Tonight she was in no mood to make more than one trip, so she looped the handles of the many plastic bags over her hands and wrists. She struggled to get the last of the bags from the back seat of her car, slamming the door closed with her foot. Moving slowly because of the load she carried, Susan started across the parking lot toward the walkway on the other side near the building entry. At the sound of an engine revving and the squeal of tires, she turned her head toward the noise. Horrified, she saw the dark vehicle, that had been idling in the shadows, barreling toward her like a canon shot.

Groceries spurted every which way when she lost her grip on the bags as she attempted to get out of the vehicle's way. But at the same time, the driver veered in line with her changed direction, picking up speed. Susan knew in that split second she couldn't get out of the way in time, just as a rock hard projectile, in the form of a body with arms like a vise grip, slammed into her. They hit the pavement hard, rolling. She felt the heat of the vehicle's headlights and smelled the burning rubber as her rescuer landed on top of her—barely a fraction out of the vehicle's murderous course. She couldn't see anything with her eyes tightly closed and the side of her face pressed into the pavement, but realized from the protracted squeal of tires that the vehicle had rounded the corner of the lot and was away. All before she fully realized how lucky she was.

Shaking from the near-miss and barely able to breathe, she attempted to get out from under the muscled body that had knocked her out of the path of what she abruptly realized was

VICTORIA MASTERSON

a deliberate attempt to kill her. Still stunned, she was surprised to recognize the gruff voice that generally caused her instant stress.

"Susan, are you all right?" Detective Grady Owens pulled himself off from her and helped her to sit up. "No," he cautioned, "don't get up yet, just take it easy for a moment and get your breath back, okay? I just need to call this in." He pulled a clean handkerchief from his pocket and offered it to her, seeing her attempt to wipe the dirt off her face and hands with one of the grocery bags. "Just give me a quick sec. I want to make sure you're not injured and in need of attention by the EMTs, or a quick run to the hospital."

A crowd began to gather, coming from the apartment building and around the parking area. He flicked his badge in the glare from the headlights of his department-issued vehicle which he'd jumped out of barely a minute ago to throw himself at Susan. In his other hand he held the phone and began detailing the incident to dispatch. Several people who obviously knew Susan squatted beside her. Others began to pick up the strewn groceries and bag them. A couple of cars that had just pulled into the lot used their headlights to help illuminate the scene.

Owens finished his phone call and knelt down beside Susan. "Okay, Ma'am, I know I'm not the lightest person to hit you like a torpedo and then fall on top of you. Shall we see what the damages are?" He began at her feet, feeling for broken bones and watching her face for signs of pain as he worked his way up her legs and arms.

"Does it hurt anywhere? Your back? Neck? Head?"

Susan used that same body part to give him a negative shake. "I'm just a little d-dazed and bruised d-detective. Otherwise, I don't think there are any serious d-damages. If you hadn't been here, I'd be dead right now. Th-thank you," she stuttered, the shock of the close-call and the sudden realization left her panting for air. "How did you come to be h-here at just the r-right time?" she finally got out, marveling at the bit of luck that had brought him here to consequently risk his own life to save hers. "Lucky for me that you were, b-but I have to ask . . . w-why me? Did you get a look at who was in . . . in whatever that monster thing he was driving?"

Owens patted the blood oozing from a cut on her forehead with the handkerchief. "I was pretty busy getting you out of the way of that monster thing, as you call it. However, technically speaking, it was a full-sized SUV, but it went by so fast I didn't catch the brand. So, no, I didn't get a look at who was driving it," Owens supplied. "Do you think you can walk, Ma'am? If so, I suggest we take you and your groceries inside where it's a bit more private." He motioned to the crowd that had gathered.

"Right. P-Please help me up, Lieutenant. Ouch," she said, wincing. She felt the bruise along her elbow. There was blood and embedded dirt from the pavement where she'd landed. "It's only a scrape that needs to be w-washed and bandaged," she said upon seeing his face when she winced.

"Ms. Farrell, I'm going to get the EMT's to clean up the worst bruises, where there's dirt embedded." Even though she insisted she didn't need their attention, he took his phone out of his pocket once again and called for the team, specifying they not use their siren. "What's the apartment number, Ma'am?" Relaying the information into the phone, he got her on her feet.

Susan swayed, her limbs still shaking. Owens put his arm around her waist and taking the major part of her weight, he essentially carried her into the building. A few of her acquaintances went ahead, leading him up to her apartment and carrying the rescued groceries, the ones that hadn't been flattened by the hell-bent SUV. Using Susan's key, Owens opened the door. He bent down and picked her up, depositing her in the cradling depth of the sofa that one of her neighbors quickly covered with the plaid wool throw folded over the arm. He looked up to see the heads of the EMT team peering over the small crowd of hard-core adrenalin junkies that yet stood in the hallway outside the open apartment door.

"In here, boys," Owens called.

"Might have known it would be one of your cases, Grady. Doesn't look like we need the stretcher, Archie," the head of the team called back to his partner, "just bring the bag."

The detective ushered the EMT's in, politely thanked the curious apartment dwellers at the doorway for their assistance, and shut the door in their faces with finality.

"Ma'am," said the burly lead EMT, nodding to her. Seeing that fatigue and shock had set in, he tried to keep it light. "Let's have a look at that cut on your forehead and the worst of those scrapes. Looks like you've been in a real dogfight," he said in his Texan drawl. "Did ya get the scumbag that caused this, Grady?"

"Not yet, Jimbo, though it was a damn close call. Attempted murder. Hit and run. He flew the scene in nothing flat after I dove in front of his wheels to get Ms. Farrell, here, out of the path of destruction."

"Hot damn! Way to go, Grady. Warms the cockles of my heart to hear that. Yessiree. They ought to issue special medals for the likes of you," he said, satisfied that Susan's pupils showed no signs of a concussion. "Archie, look alive, man. Hand me that bottle and some swabs to clean these cuts. This split on your forehead, Ma'am, I'm going to put what's called a *butterfly* bandage on it. To hold it together. Don't think you need stitches, but its best to let your doctor take a look-see."

Susan sat stiffly. Keeping her head down, she winced as the paramedic finished cleaning and dressing her deeply scraped elbow. In her après-trauma state she stared at the fire-engine-red cowboy boots peeking out from his scrubs. It was such an incongruous touch that it caused her to shake in an effort to keep from laughing outright.

The EMT, too busy tweezering out the embedded dirt to look up, mistook her quivers thinking it was a sign she was in pain. "Sorry, Ma'am, I know that it hurts. But I do take my hat off to you. Yessiree," he said with respect, whistling through his teeth while gently cleaning other abrasions on her arms. "I've found that most survivors who walk away from hit-and-runs, like you, are hard-put not to quake in their boots after such a close-call."

Susan stuck out her lower lip. The alcohol stung where the big Texan had cleaned out the worst of her many scrapes.

"Jimbo, is she okay? No emergency room?" Owens wanted to make sure.

"Weeell . . . that's up to the lady, Grady. Nothin' broken that I can see . . . no concussion. But if she was mah wife, or sister . . . sorry, Ma'am, ain't no implication, ya know . . . guess I'd want a white coat to check her out. X-rays, that sort of stuff."

Susan began to bristle.

"Okay, okay. If Jimbo says it's up to you, then we'll do it your way, Ms. Farrell. No emergency room."

Owens turned to the lead EMT. "Thanks, friend, for the quick service. I know how busy you guys are."

"No problem, Grady," said Jimbo, closing his bag with a snap. "Archie, get out there and radio in that we're done here. See if they need us somewhere else." He turned to Susan and doffed the baseball cap he wore. "Ms. Farrell, as I said before, you might want your own doctor to have a lookie-see. Just to make sure, ya know. And in case you need some medication if it starts to pain ya and keeps ya awake. But I'm positive Grady here will keep a check on you. Been a pleasure to meet ya, Ma'am, a real pleasure," he said saluting her. "God bless now. Bye, Grady. Stay outta trouble, ya hear?"

Owens watched the burly Texan's rolling gait disappear into the dark hallway outside the door. "Good man, Jimbo. A little unpolished, but I'd want him on the crew if I needed help." He turned back to Susan who'd leaned back into the sofa's cushions, cradling her elbow against her stomach. She looked exhausted, trying hard to keep her eyes from closing.

"Ms. Farrell, I think what you need now is to rest. Let me help you into the bedroom, where you'll be more comfortable."

"But, Lieutenant, I won't be able to sleep knowing someone out there is trying to kill me. And what if that person makes another attempt, breaks into my place? I'm on the third floor, but there's a back stairway outside the kitchen door, every apartment on this floor has one. The back door has a lock in the handle and a deadbolt, which isn't keyed, and the top part is glass. I've got a shade covering the inside glass that I keep closed, but what's to stop someone from breaking the glass and then turning the handle and the deadbolt to get in?"

Owens recognized the fear as genuine. "Not to worry, Ma'am. I'm going to put an unmarked car out front to keep watch for the black SUV. Then as soon as you're up to it, you and I are going to have a *tell-the-truth* session that I hope will disclose the identity of the person that tried to run you down tonight, and likewise who was responsible for the attack in March on Claire Martelli. I have a feeling in my bones that these two events are definitely related. And to date, the bones are batting one hundred percent."

On hearing this last statement, Susan suddenly realized the real reason for the detective being in her parking lot at just the right moment—he still thought she was protecting Sean regarding the attack on Claire last March. But now, Susan had a good idea who had tried to get rid of her tonight. And it wasn't Sean. "Thank you, Lieutenant. I appreciate your attempt to protect me. But what if the person is already in the building? Hiding out until you leave." Her last words brought on an uncontrollable shudder.

"Would you feel better if I stationed someone outside your door tonight instead? I just thought it might upset your neighbors to see a guy skulking around there all night."

"I'd rather they might be upset than worry that someone could be in the building, waiting for you to leave. Please, Lieutenant?"

The pleading look she gave him unexpectedly touched off a compassionate chord that he generally kept well hidden behind his badge. He'd often thought that his years as a cop had left nothing but a hard and unfeeling empty shell in that department.

"Okay, Ma'am. I'll post Sweeney outside your door for the rest of the night. He's a good cop. And I'll stop by in the morning, when his shift is over. How's that sound? And so you can sleep through, I won't have him call to check in on you. Another thing, if you have the last two speed dial keys on your cell phone undesignated, I'll put his number in on the eight key and mine on the nine. That way, if you need help, you can just push eight for Sweeney, or nine for me."

He told himself that adding his number was only an act of human kindness, but it could work in his favor, because just maybe she'd drop her guard and give him the last bits of information he needed to close the case on the Martelli attack.

VICTORIA MASTERSON

12

Day Ten

Paris—Residence Saint-Germain

Madame Fontaine came out of her office on overhearing Claire and Mandy talking to Etienne at the front desk. "*Bon jour,* Mademoiselles. Such a fine morning to go shopping. Etienne will be happy to get you a taxi. Nephew? And I am also happy to see you are none the worse for your recent adventure," she said turning to Claire. "Please accept my apologies once more for my daughter's part in this whole matter. I appreciate that you did not insist on informing the clinic how Marie-Claude fell into being hoodwinked by this Shamrock person. It was very wrong of her to tell the family's secrets to a complete stranger. She has asked me to tell you how sorry she is to have caused you pain and suffering."

Once again Claire pasted a smile on her face, something she'd been doing all morning to assure Mandy and her mother that she was all right after seeing Malcolm take Cerian to his rooms last night.

"Madame, I don't blame Marie-Claude. Please assure her of that for me. I'm sure Sean would have found another way to get into the hotel. After all, he did break in to get the medallion right after we first arrived, before he knew about the passages. I'm just glad the police have him in custody at last."

"You are very gracious, Mademoiselle," Etienne broke in, "as it was Marie-Claude also who told him about the medallion Dom found in front of your suite. And where *Tante* Emilie kept it for safe-keeping."

"I suspected as much after we found out it who it was that gave Sean the information on how to get into the Saint-Germain through the passageways. But it's all over now. And I've enjoyed your hospitality and especially your lovely garden. I'm going back to the States with Abbie and Ben tomorrow, so I wanted to say my goodbyes in case I don't see you or Etienne before we leave."

"I will happily assist you with your luggage tomorrow, Mademoiselle Claire, as well as Madame Martelli's," Etienne said, beaming. "So please, let's not bid the farewells until then. Eh?" He took Claire's hand and kissed it. "It was how we French say . . . a *joie de vivre* . . . to meet you, Madame Abbie, and the Mademoiselle Man-dee here. And I can promise to take good care of her while she is staying here at the Saint-Germain. Again, as the English and you Americans would say, it would give me very great pleasure."

Madame Fontaine came around the counter and gave Claire a hug. "I will miss my charming guests from Colorado. And as a gesture of my esteem, I would like to offer complimentary accommodations to you and your family anytime you wish to return to Paris. And not to worry. I have hired trusted workmen to seal up the entrances into the mansion and the wine cellar as well as the entrances into the rooms from inside the passages. We will not live in fear of anyone else finding out about them. Their usefulness is long past."

"Thank you, Madame, but your generosity is not deserved. After all, if I hadn't come to stay at the Saint-Germain, none of this would have happened. While I am honored by your offer and wouldn't dream of staying anywhere in Paris but here at the Saint-Germain with you and your family, I couldn't accept the accommodations on a complimentary basis.

Madame Fontaine patted Claire on the shoulder. "Mademoiselle, we will be happy to see you and the members of your family at any time. This of course includes the Mademoiselle Mandy here, who I am happy to have stay in your present suite while she is working in Paris. Please allow me to do this very small service. It would be a hurt to my honor if you refuse."

So saying, the proprietress wished them a successful shopping expedition and gave a few suggestions for shops that were not widely known to tourists but whose clientele included many well-to-do French women who were both style and money conscious.

Just as the sisters turned to follow Etienne out the front door, Claire spotted Malcolm escorting Cerian down the last flight of stairs and heading for the lobby. The dark-haired beauty whose tinkling laughter had caused Claire so much pain last night was unusually disheveled at the moment, wearing one of Malcolm's shirts over the red silk cocktail dress she'd worn the night before.

Topaz eyes met sapphire. With mixed emotions, Claire broke her gaze from Malcolm and quickly hurried her sister to the sidewalk in front of the hotel, where they joined Etienne at curbside next to the open door of the taxi he'd flagged down.

"Claire, wait up a minute," Malcolm called through the open front door. He left Cerian pouting in the middle of the lobby as he rushed out to the curb just in time to see the taxi driver honking his way into the morning traffic.

"The Mademoiselles have gone shopping, *Docteur*," said Etienne, eyeing the woman standing just inside the Saint-Germain's lobby, watching Malcolm through the window. He in turn watched as Claire's taxi was carried off by a moving wave of black vehicles.

"Yes, and I'd like to think she didn't hear me. But, unfortunately I know better. Flag down another taxi, please,

Etienne. I have a guest leaving for the Ritz, "he said, adding in an undertone, "and hopefully out of my life."

He turned and retraced his steps into the lobby, muttering to himself, "How in hell am I ever going to convince Claire that it is so."

The flight back to the States and then on to Denver was both long and tedious for Claire whose nerves were strung tighter than the strings on a steel guitar. Pluck any one of them and the result would be a reverberation of discordant screeches. Across the aisle, Abbie slept with her head on Ben's shoulder. Claire was all for their seemingly wonderful new relationship. Yet it stung more than a little bit that what she had come to think of as a chance for lasting happiness with a man who she originally thought she could both trust and respect, now appeared to have faded into oblivion.

She idly wondered what the statistics were for the number of males, proportionate to the whole masculine population, who are totally bereft of the quality of fidelity.

Or is it just the ones I seem to attract? Go figure.

Determinedly, she put all thoughts of male inconsistency aside, revisiting instead her intense relief at having the sinister episodes end with Sean's arrest, and inspiring her with an uplifted sense of freedom. That proved it was Sean all along, she reasoned.

I'm safe again. As long as he's locked up in that Parisian jail. Too bad it had to be Susan's stepbrother. Not that I feel pity for her, however I can totally understand the hell she must be going through.

She leaned back and turned on her MP3 player for the final leg of the flight to Denver.

PART III
Denver

VICTORIA MASTERSON

13

Day Ten

Claire's Journal—30 May

Why is it that I can't fit back into the same life here in Denver as the Claire I was <u>before</u> I left for Paris? It was only a little over a month ago, yet <u>nothing</u> is the same as before. Try as I might, I can't seem to adjust to being back in my old world as Chad's partner . . . business partner <u>only</u>, that is. And then there's the real shocker that both amazes and blows me away. I love what I do . . . interior design . . . yet something is missing for me since I've been back. Prior to the Paris trip, the ID department was the focus of my life. And now, quite simply put, it doesn't do it for me, as before. There's that word again. Before.

Maybe, it wasn't really me before. It was really someone else living my life . . . before filing for divorce . . . before the attack in March . . . before the Shamrock incidents involving Sean in Paris. Thank God those have stopped. And definitely, before Malcolm.

Oops . . . darn! Wasn't it just this morning, after lying awake the better part of the night that I promised myself from now on I will deliberately put him out of my mind and my life? But it's so hard. He's always with me. Just a thought away. Not that it would ever work anyway, Lady Anna and Cerian would see to that. I can't imagine a worse nightmare . . . even

335

worse than the one that's haunted me for months now . . . if we attempted to pursue our relationship further.

However, something's become apparent to me since our break-up. I will call it the great dichotomy. Even though I'm hurting over a relationship too-soon ended, I'm also aware of a brand new sensation. After too many years of an emotional shut down, at least the hurt is an indication of an emotion I'm actually feeling in that department.

What a sad sham of a marriage when I actually discovered the truth of Chad's philandering and finally noticed certain deficiencies in his character that he'd been able to keep hidden until recently. I know now that I actually didn't want to accept the fact that he was unfaithful until it finally hit home. Right in front of my face. He and Susan. And now, he must be on to someone new because Susan is moping around the office, jumpy as a jackrabbit, and scared of her own shadow for some reason.

And though it's strictly a business relationship now, Chad certainly has kept me at arm's length. Now that I'm back, I swear there are times when I catch him watching me with such an intense look on his face that it's downright unnerving.

I know now that I can't make the effort it would entail to deal with a Chad that I don't like or respect anymore. It's just not worth my time given the present scenario. I've decided to put out feelers to see if anyone is interested in my portion of the business. It will be interesting to see what my half is worth if I decide to sell and leave the operation. Of course, I would give Chad first opportunity to buy me out.

I think the divorce and settlement papers should be in the mail by now. I'll call my attorney tomorrow to see if it's officially final yet, though he generally keeps me attuned to the last minute changes Chad's attorneys have attempted to throw in as to the proportion of the assets Chad and I would each receive.

But the big question is . . . then what?

That same morning, Claire headed into the office early hoping to catch Chad before he became involved with appointments and whatever other matters needed his attention. Arriving before anyone else, she walked through the reception area and headed down the hall to her office without turning on any lights. She noted that Chad's office was still dark but the shades were up. As she hadn't seen his Mercedes in the parking lot, she naturally concluded that he wasn't in yet.

But it's a very good sign that the shades are up, she thought. Since she'd been back, she'd noted that both his office shades were down most of the time and his office door locked in accordance with his peculiar 'Do Not Disturb' mode. They'd only met twice since her return. Once, to show him the photos, the result of her purchases, and to go over the expenses from the Paris buying trip. The second meeting was to go over the schedule for the completion of the New Orleans resort hotel and restaurant. After the last meeting concluded, he'd invited her to have lunch with him at the small restaurant on the ground floor of the office building.

Claire still puzzled over the track Chad's conversation had taken while they were eating. As she anticipated, he'd asked questions about the Paris incidents. He'd listened without saying much as Claire gave only brief answers that covered only the highlights of each occurrence, keeping further details and suspicions to herself.

And then he'd asked, "Was there the slightest possibility that some of the happenings may not have involved Sean?" He'd also questioned, "Had she thought about the probability there could have been more than one person involved, that Sean may not have acted on his own?" Sighing softly, he'd posed one last question: "Had she met anyone while in Paris that she'd become especially interested in and did she intend to pursue that relationship now that she was back in Denver?"

Claire only answered the last question: "I met a number of people," then couldn't help but add, "plus one dog, which I'm happy to have made friends with." She then changed the subject back to the antiques she'd purchased for the resort project and how she saw those being used in the restaurant and hotel spaces.

Turning off the bothersome thoughts from yesterday's lunch, Claire entered her east-facing office, switching on only the task light atop her desk. She opened the window shades on the floor-to-ceiling fixed glass panels bordering one wall of her work area. Outside, the morning sun sparkled the raindrops left on the trees from an early morning shower. Further to the east she watched a line of fluffy white clouds intent upon adorning the blue Colorado sky with a shimmering string of opalescent pearls. Claire smiled at the scene presenting itself outside her windows, appreciating another glorious morning in the Mile High city.

Sitting down to peruse her agenda, she noticed that Loupe had left her a small stack of messages that must have come in after she'd left work for a late afternoon appointment on the previous day.

She flipped through the messages, relieved to see that Lieutenant Owens had called to suggest a meeting at her place after work tonight. Since she'd gotten back from Paris, Claire hadn't been able to find a time to meet that worked for both their schedules. He'd been out of the office, or out of town, or off-duty when she was available.

She'd begun to think he was giving her the proverbial run-around. However, in all fairness, she thought, my days have been just as crazy since I returned. She left a voice message that she would be home by five and would put the kettle on, having previously discovered they both enjoyed tea time in the late afternoon. Hastily she'd added he needn't bring donuts, she would stop and pick up something easier on the waistline as she'd gained a couple pounds on the wonderful French bakery fare—the fabulous breakfast rolls, and especially, the whipped-cream-layered Napoleons.

Claire eagerly anticipated the meeting with the detective. She needed to find out what was happening in Paris with Sean and the status of the still-open case from the March attack. In the meantime, and with an ear out for Chad's arrival, she continued the work of placing the French antiques into the resort project layout so her team could finalize the plans for the restaurant and public areas of the hotel.

Deep into her work, her concentration ended abruptly with a commotion in the corridor outside her office. A woman's voice, hysteric and sobbing, was enough to send Claire to the door to discover the cause of the disruption that was so out of character in their normally professional office. The hoopla dialed down a notch as she found Loupe with her arm around a distraught Susan, attempting to lead the emotional woman further down the hall, away from Claire's door.

"Loupe . . . Susan? Whatever is the matter?"

At that, Susan began to cry harder.

"Here, Loupe, bring her into my office. And please see if you can come up with a cold wet towel from the kitchen for her eyes. Do you know why she's acting this way?" Claire asked, as she led the agitated woman to one of the comfortable chairs in front of her desk.

"I only know that she came flying out of Chad's office in this condition while I was out at reception to check on the arrival of an overnight package," Loupe said over her shoulder, heading for the office's kitchen.

"Right. I'll see if I can get her to talk about it. Thanks, Loupe." Claire pulled the chair next to Susan's around to face her. She offered the teary-eyed woman the box of tissues from the side table.

"Susan, please calm yourself. I'm guessing here, but I think I already know what it's about. Chad, right?" Susan nodded and broke into another round of sobbing.

"It's . . . or rather, *he's* not worth your tears. Did Chad say something to upset you? I don't have to tell you how downright rude he can be at times. And as you already know," Claire began, thinking inwardly how odd it felt to be consoling one of the *other women*, in fact the very one that became the last straw in her sham of a marriage, "I'm the star witness to the fact that remaining faithful is not one of Chad's strong points." It's funny, she thought, a month ago I certainly didn't feel as ambivalent toward this woman as I do right now. In fact, it was quite the opposite. Now I only feel sorry for her.

Loupe arrived with the wet towel which Claire placed over Susan's swollen eyes, waiting while the woman got hold of herself. "Take a couple of deep breaths. There, that's good. Are you feeling a little better now? If you would like to tell me what just happened, I'll see if I can help. Though, right now I don't think I'm one of his favorite people either." She leaned forward to give Susan a comforting hug but the woman pulled back.

Between protracted sobs Susan appeared to want to speak, opening her mouth several times to do so. Though only an unintelligible whispery sound came out. To her credit the loud wailing had stopped, turning into small hiccups on each intake of air. Claire leaned forward to hear better.

"Chad . . . he . . . he . . ." she started.

Claire put her hand over Susan's, encouraging her. "Go on, Susan. What did he do?"

"He . . . he . . . *fired* . . . me," she wailed, grabbing the wet towel from her eyes and throwing it onto the floor with a passion Claire had never before seen in her. Tears streamed down her face once more.

Claire was incredulous. "Chad terminated you? For what reason? Did he tell you why? Here," she said, handing Susan the tissue box again. "Okay, please compose yourself and start at the beginning."

Denver—Claire's carriage house

Claire turned into the tree-lined entrance to the driveway that took her behind the old mansion which her carriage house had once adjoined. She drove onto the new road that lead off to the far side of the original eighteen-acre wooded site. Rounding the curve that led into the cul-de-sac where her residence was situated, she looked forward to her first glimpse of the handsome façade of her charming new home. It was a view she never tired of seeing since she'd moved into the converted carriage house in February.

As it was still a little before five, she hoped Lieutenant Owens hadn't arrived yet. She needed time to reorientate from her day at the office. She was emotionally drained from the scenes with both Susan and then Chad. His attitude, when she finally cornered him on Susan's behalf, hadn't surprised her. He told her to stay out of his personal life and that the company's Receptionist-Girl Friday position fell under his domain.

Claire slowed to make the turn into the drive, surprised to see the detective's car already there and that he wasn't alone. In fact, a total of three cars were parked in different areas of the ample circle driveway. She slowed down and glanced over to the terrace adjoining the structure where the lieutenant and two others looked to be comfortably occupying the cushioned outdoor chairs situated among the pots of colorful flowers adorning the patio. Puzzled, Claire parked the little Mercedes in front of the garage, recognizing her mother as one of the other two. Her mind raced—had she forgotten an engagement with Abbie?

"Oh, no". Claire's lips formed the words in a whisper. She'd identified the third figure even from this distance. Stunned, she slowly got out of the car as the detective and her uninvited guests came to greet her.

Malcolm reached her first, urgency apparent in his stride. He stretched his hand out for hers but she pulled back.

"Claire, please don't be upset. I simply had to see you, to talk to you when you didn't return any of my calls. I ran into your sister at the Saint-Germain a few days ago and took her to dinner in order to get her read on the situation. Mandy's advice was to call your mother and explain everything exactly the way I'd told her. However, when I talked to Abbie, she insisted that Lieutenant Owens become involved also. So now, here we all are," he said, a tight little smile pulling his already strained facial expression a little tighter. "Please do me the favor of listening, at least, before you tell me to go away.

Then, if you still want me to leave, I will. But know this, I'm going to do everything in my power to change your mind."

By the time Malcolm finished speaking, her mother and the detective had come up to where they stood.

Get a grip, Martelli. You just need to paste one of those smiles on your face that you're so good at doing. And be pleasant. At least until he finishes what he came all this way to say. Later, you can go upstairs and cry your eyes out. But whatever you do, don't let him see what you're feeling inside.

Claire automatically greeted her mother with a hug, but the accusatory look she gave her said volumes. She turned to the detective who was politely standing a little away from the others. "Lieutenant, I'm guessing you two don't need introductions?" she asked, indicating the man at her side—the one man she most fervently wished she could wrap her arms around and the two of them escape to some desert island where there was no Cerian or Lady Anna, Chad or the business. She added under her breath, *"And to hell with everything and everyone else."*

Owens eyebrows rose dramatically hearing the frustration in her voice. "You're right, Ma'am, we met in person earlier today but we've spent some time on the phone before he left Paris last night. Your friend Malcolm has given me an extraordinary insight, actually more like legally acceptable proof concerning someone I've suspected for a while now in regard to the March attack and possibly some of the incidents that happened while you were in Paris."

"I want to hear everything you've come up with, Lieutenant, but first let's go into the house and I'll put on the tea kettle. I picked up some goodies to go with," she said, holding up both deli and pastry bags. "I hear Duffy barking through the door. Since I've been back he's afraid to let me out of his sight. Follows me everywhere."

"Nothing wrong with that. He's just happy to have you home again, Ma'am," Owens said. "Though I'm afraid I don't have a treat to give him today."

"You may not have the goods, Lieutenant, but I do." Malcolm casually took a wrapped rawhide bone out of his coat pocket. "I asked Abbie if it would be appropriate. She said Claire would be okay with it and undoubtedly Duffy. So I stopped and got one as a gift from Penny who, by the way, Claire, looks forward to making Duffy's acquaintance." He added for Owens' benefit, "My Irish wolfhound, Penelope, was the original cause of my introduction to Claire and is one of this lady's biggest fans."

Claire's only reaction to Malcolm's comment was another pasted-on smile. She took her mother's arm and led the way to the house.

"Wait up a second, Malcolm." Owens quietly said as Malcolm turned to follow the women. "There's something I need to talk to you about before you discuss what your graphology report indicates with regard to the notes you analyzed."

Claire unlocked the front door, glancing over her shoulder to see the two men engaged in private conversation. She took the opportunity to do the same with her mother. "Honestly, Mom, I would think you'd know that I've got enough problems with Chad regarding the divorce and the business. What I don't need right now is to have to deal with Malcolm too."

"Honey, I'm only concerned for your safety. Please keep an open mind and listen to what he came all this way to tell you. The detective believes Malcolm's knowledge is vital when it comes to identifying the motive behind the attack last March. This isn't about Malcolm and you personally, Claire. Though after listening to his side of the story regarding the night you saw him carrying that Cerian woman into his suite, I can only hope you'll give him a chance to explain."

Claire ignored the last part of Abbie's vindication of Malcolm's character, with a "Yeah, right. If only you knew, Mom." What she didn't reveal was that she couldn't keep her pulse from doing a spontaneous knee-jerk whenever his name was mentioned.

"Know what? Are you talking about Malcolm, dear?"

"Never mind," Claire said, impatient to hear what her mother and the detective knew that she didn't. "It's not important right now. But what possible information can Malcolm have that would be so significant to Owens in pinning down the motive behind the attack, Mom?"

"I'm afraid Malcolm made me promise to let him explain so it wouldn't be taken out of context or watered down in any way. And I agree with him. He's the expert."

"Since you described him as an expert, I would have to think his info is psychological in nature. I hope he's able to clarify all the technical jargon that only another professional in that field is likely to understand."

"Well, I don't know about other professionals, but I understood it."

Before Claire could remark, the front door opened as she'd disengaged the deadbolt on her way in. Malcolm and Owens walked through the great room into the open kitchen.

"Come on in," Claire called. "Have a seat, please. The water is about to boil and we should have our tea in a few minutes."

With that, the kettle atop the professional gas range located on the large island began to whistle. Claire poured the hot water over the loose leaves in the tea pot's open strainer and then turned to help Abbie arrange the bakery and deli goodies she'd purchased on her way home. Both men were impressed by the kitchen and complimented Claire on that room and what they'd seen of the great room when walking in a few minutes ago.

Without consulting Claire, Abbie offered to take the men on a quick tour of the refurbished carriage house which showcased her daughter's talents. Seeing the look on Claire's face, Abbie promised to make it a brief showing and Owens assured her they would get down to the business at hand as soon as the impromptu tour was finished. Claire suspected that the detective and her mother had somehow planned this beforehand but didn't take time to speculate as to why.

Claire busied herself in the kitchen while waiting for their return. She heard the men and Abbie on the stairway, coming down from the master suite, then the voices of the detective and Abbie in the garage, but not Malcolm's. She turned around to check on his whereabouts just as he came into the kitchen and took a seat at the island counter. She'd known she'd have to be alone with him after Abbie and the detective left but had wanted to forestall it as long as possible.

"Your home is very impressive, Claire," Malcolm said, in an attempt to put her at ease and dissipate the stilted mood in the room. The strain between them was palpable.

"Can I help?" He offered, nodding toward the ongoing tea preparations.

But Claire only shook her head and gave him a tight little smile while continuing to lay out the dishes and makings for the afternoon tea.

Faced with the chill of her present mood, Malcolm decided to leave things unsaid for now, hoping he would have a chance to talk with her later when the others had gone. With nothing to do for the moment, he proceeded to look around the open first level of the two-and-a-half-story domicile, studying in more depth the arresting architecture and eclectic style of furnishings Claire had chosen to use. He was quick to notice a number of unusual and refurbished architectural antiques that were placed around the great room in the manner of focal points among the cushy upholstered pieces. The warm, neutral color scheme was accented with various tints of pastel colors. The refurbished wood floor was refinished in a white wash revealing multi-shades of that color, over the warm and neutral tones of age-worn walnut laid in a large-scale diamond pattern. A fat-yarned deep-piled shag rug in a pale mushroom hue contained the conversation area invitingly.

"I love what you've done with the place, Claire," said Malcolm, coming back to the island and pulling up one of the tufted leather bar stools. "I'm getting an overall impression that is very sharp on the uptake, charming, yet sophisticated. I could take off my shoes and sink into that sectional in a second," Malcolm said, referring to the large slipcovered L-shaped sectional consisting of a pair of upholstered settees fit on either side of a wedge-shaped corner that begged to be curled up in. The sectional dominated the room in front of a two-and-a-half story fieldstone fireplace. The free-form mantel piece was comprised of a polished slab of burled elm wood, its natural bark still integral along the front edge.

Malcolm thought the room quite handsome, and on impulse he turned to her asking, "Could I hire you to help me redo my flat in London when I'm through teaching at *universite* this summer?" On seeing the look on her face that quickly changed to a polite smile, he added, "You don't have to answer now. Just think about it. Okay?"

"Well, Malcolm, I appreciate the vote of confidence, but in this case, I don't have to think for long. It just wouldn't be right or proper. It would be more appropriate to turn your decorating needs over to Cerian."

"Why in heaven's name would I do that? She's no expert in design."

"Why *wouldn't* you do that? After all, she is your fiancée, soon to be your wife."

"My what? Wherever did you get that idea?" He asked, surprise evident on his face.

"Well, you should know. After all, it was the largest announcement on the engagement and wedding page."

"Claire, slow down. I don't have any idea what you're talking about. What announcement?"

"Don't play the innocent with me, Malcolm. I would have thought that our time together although short, I grant you, deserves more than that." She stalked over to the space she used as a morning room at one end of the open kitchen and released the angled top of an ebony contemporary secretary, dropping it down to reveal a row of simply-designed wooden pigeon holes. He watched as she snatched a folded newspaper page from one of the slots and returned with it, throwing it on the counter in front of him.

"So here we have a page from the London Times that someone sent me anonymously and you're trying to tell me you don't know a thing about it." She stormed out of the room towards the garage, calling over her shoulder, "Please excuse me. I'll see what's holding up Abbie and the detective."

Malcolm unfolded the newspaper to see a headline in large type-face running across the top of the Weddings and Engagements page: "Lady Anna Worthington, Countess of Rosemore, is pleased to announce the engagement of her grandson, Dr. Malcolm Sutherland, to Lady Cerian Bradford, daughter of Sir Henry and Lady Margaret Bradford." He glanced at the copy below the headline. It went on to say the wedding would take place on October tenth of this same year at Rosemore Grange in Lincolnshire.

Malcolm shook his head. He couldn't believe he was actually seeing the printed words announcing his engagement. Knowing Cerian to be somewhat brazen by nature, one of the traits that finally made him see the light, he still doubted she had the courage to do this on her own. No, it had to be his grandmother or with her permission, he amended. He'd get on the phone as soon as he left Claire and tell Lady Anna in no uncertain terms that she must notify the paper to print an immediate retraction.

He was never keen on being the next earl and living at Rosemore anyway. That life was totally in the past. He thought he'd made that clear to his grandmother, the one person he'd always been able to trust all his life. He prayed she'd be so embarrassed when he told her to retract the announcement that she'd give up on him and choose his brother as the next earl. Jack would jump at the chance to become head of the family, especially after the well-publicized debacle a few years back when he'd coerced Cerian into running away with him. He folded the newspaper and put it back in the ebony secretary just as the other three came back into the house from the garage and gathered at the large kitchen island.

They enjoyed the tea and other treats, breaking the growing silence with small talk as they waited for Malcolm to organize the papers he took from his briefcase—his analyses of the handwritten notes he'd copied back in Paris that had dropped from Claire's overnight envelop at the Saint-Germain.

Malcolm tried to organize his thoughts as well. Could he effectively convince Claire just what had been so important to bring him flying posthaste to Denver? Why in hell hadn't he taken the time to do the analyses back then when he had Claire's confidence? Because, he admitted to himself, he hadn't wanted her to question his motives back then. He hadn't wanted to rock the boat in view of their burgeoning romance.

He knew now he should have told her there were signs in the handwriting that led him to have the notes copied in the first place. Would she have believed him back then? And now?

He shook his head to clear his ill-timed self-censure. He needed to be mentally sharp and discerning in communicating the facts that indicated she was in serious danger.

Then when the others left, hopefully Claire would listen to his explanation about the night she'd seen him carrying an inebriated Cerian down the hall to his rooms. Now, of course, he would also have to resolve the engagement announcement issue, certain to be his grandmother's doing. Malcolm knew Lady Anna would never deliberately do anything that would harm or cause him unhappiness. She had to have been sincere in placing the engagement announcement for what she thought would be for his own good. But it was high time she quit meddling in his personal affairs. He promised himself that he could, and would, make her understand just that.

Malcolm placed the written analyses of the two handwritings on the table in front of him. He decided that rather than jump right in, he would first give a quick run-down on what graphology could and could not detect in a person's handwriting. He went on to explain how, why, and by whom this science is utilized in everyday practice, as well as the fact that its legality in the courtroom is now accepted as a means of presenting informational evidence into a person's character.

The detective nodded his agreement during Malcolm's short prologue. Abbie looked surprised at the information and asked a couple of questions. Only Claire remained mute and expressionless.

Upon concluding the session with his concise findings on both individuals, Malcolm realized the disheartening reality that he'd failed to convince Claire of the very real danger posed by both of the subjects.

Covering a yawn behind her hand, Claire stood up, facing him with a polite but impassive expression. "I thank you for your concern and for what you believe you perceive in these two handwritten notes from Chad and Susan," she said. "But it's been a long day, and I'm very tired," she continued, hinting not so delicately that it was time for him to leave. "I hope you have a good trip back, Malcolm. And I do appreciate the time you've taken to travel here from Paris to inform me of your findings. I need to give it some thought."

She threw a kiss in the direction of her mother. "Mom, would you mind locking up before you leave? I'll talk to you tomorrow." She headed to the stairway before anyone could speak, leaving her guests with various expressions of surprise, disappointment and concern.

"I'm so sorry," Abbie said, watching her daughter disappear up the stairs with Duffy bounding along beside her. She turned in time to see the glum-faced expression on Malcolm's face. Impulsively, she gave him a quick hug. "She's usually not so impolite, you know. Cheer up, there's still hope. Sometimes Claire has to be alone to figure things out on her own. You've planted the seeds for her to think about. Just give her some time. Don't you agree, Lieutenant?" Abbie asked, while helping Malcolm put his papers in order.

But Owens only gave her a stoic smile. "I don't think I'm in a position to respond to that, Ma'am. I'll be off now," he said shaking hands with Malcolm. He started toward the front door and then turned back. "When are you leaving, my friend? I think we should get together one last time before you jet back to Paris. Call me," he said, once again heading for the door.

"Let me see you out, Lieutenant," Abbie said. "And thanks for including me in on the session. I do worry so about Claire," she added, following him to the entryway.

She shut the door behind the detective and turned back to find Malcolm on her heels. "Do you need a place to stay, Malcolm? I'm sure Ben will put you up at his house."

"No, I appreciate your concern, Mrs. M., but I've already booked a hotel room. And please say hello to Ben for me. He's a good man."

Reluctant to let him leave, Abbie continued. "If you're planning to stay a few days in Denver before you go back, maybe Claire will realize her error in judgment concerning Chad before you leave. I don't know Susan very well, but quite frankly, everyone in the office, except maybe Claire, knew she and Chad were carrying on. And I've never liked or trusted either of them.

"In my opinion, Claire made a rather hasty decision to marry him the night of his housewarming celebration. He proposed to her in front of a roomful of guests, you see. I think she was flattered by his proposal, as well as the size of the 'rock' he gave her, which she never wears anymore . . . but mostly, that he would think so much of her as to want to marry her.

"Professionally, they've always gotten on, although Chad was smart in his decision to make her a partner *and* marry her. He recognized Claire's talent straight away, and the fact that she's worked hard and long to make their firm a successful entity in the hospitality field. Seems to me that marriage to him was just another way to keep her harnessed to the business. He was known as a playboy before they married, and he's continued to run around with other women since. But, I don't need to tell you, do I? You know him all too well."

Abbie stopped talking on seeing the look on Malcolm's face that spoke far more than words ever could. "I'm sorry, Malcolm. I shouldn't have started in about Chad. I know Claire's reaction to your analysis is a real disappointment to say the least. But, please, just stay a few more days. For her sake." She didn't wait for him to reply, but hurried back into the kitchen, calling over her shoulder. "Just let me turn off the lights and I'll let you walk me to my car."

Dejected by the day's events, Malcolm watched Abbie's tail lights fade in and out of the trees as she drove away. He was still stunned by Claire's refusal to believe his assessment of both Chad and Susan's innate sociopathic characteristics. Worse yet, his apparent inability to convince her was a blow to both his pride and the appellations after his name that indicated his expertise by way of the doctorate he'd studied so many years to attain.

Though not in so many words, Abbie had been right in saying that Claire's present attitude and behavior were glaringly uncharacteristic of the real Claire—the one he'd fallen in love with in Paris. He remembered her last words. She'd wished him a good trip back to Paris, knowing it was her way of saying they were to go their separate ways. He kicked at a rock on the pavement, walking without cognitive observation toward the rental car he'd parked at the far end of the circle drive. It was now dark and that area was heavily shadowed by tall trees in the wooded area just beyond the drive.

He'd arrived early that afternoon for the meeting that Owens had called, hoping to talk with Claire alone before it began. But it was not to be. Abbie arrived before him. On seeing him drive up, she waved from the patio and called for him to join her, as, hose in hand, she watered the plants and flowers potted there. She explained that she usually came over a couple times a week to water the garden and plantings so Claire didn't have to try to fit it into her busy schedule.

"Just the way my luck's been going," he grumbled, still thinking back to earlier that day. His attention was diverted back into the present as something caught his eye in the shadows ahead. He'd arrived at his rental car, but stopped in the act of turning the key in the door lock on seeing a glimmer in the stand of pines a short distance ahead. A light breeze had sprung up causing the pine boughs to sway in the moonlight. His curiosity aroused, he cautiously pushed forward to discover the source of the fluctuating light. Through the lightly shifting branches, the moonlight glinted onto shiny metal that appeared to be outlining the grill panel and headlights of a parked vehicle. It was too dark to identify the brand.

Moving ahead to get a closer look, he left the paved drive and stumbled onto gravel. His feet crunched on the small rocks of a road that appeared to dissect that end of the circle drive. He stopped to listen. In the ensuing silence, his ears picked up only the ordinary sounds of the woods at night. He moved closer to the vehicle, thinking the shape and dark color looked familiar. Black? Malcolm tried to remember if he'd seen it before, and if so, where. He couldn't be sure, but he didn't think it had been there when he first arrived today.

Should've looked around more carefully, he chided himself, especially in view of the handwriting analysis that became the impetus to leave everything behind in Paris and fly to Denver to warn Claire.

When he'd pulled into the cul-de-sac earlier, he'd been so focused on the impressive carriage house he hadn't even noticed the gravel road, let alone a vehicle partially hidden in the trees. The fact that he'd been so excited to see Claire hadn't helped either. He decided there wasn't a mystery after all. This was most likely another of her vehicles, the one she probably drove in the winter while keeping her little restored Mercedes safe and dry in the garage. But what he couldn't figure out was why it was parked out here rather than inside the garage. A thought suddenly came to mind. He distinctly remembered that the garage of the carriage house was large enough to accommodate two cars when he'd toured with Abbie today. And now he was able to place a dark SUV, similar to this vehicle, parked in the other stall on the far side of the Mercedes. But how did it get out here?

Malcolm's skin prickled. A noise on the gravel. A sudden feeling he wasn't alone.

A hopeful thought skyrocketed through his head. Could Claire have changed her mind?

He was in the act of swinging around when a heavy blunt object hit him in the back of his head. He never felt his limp body dragged across the gravel, or tied hand and foot, gagged and blindfolded, then lifted into a traveling cage in the back of the SUV.

A smug voice whispered in the darkness. "Claire's just not right for you, Dr. Sutherland. Why won't you see that?"

Claire paced the floor of her bedroom. She couldn't believe she'd treated Malcolm in such a cavalier manner. After all, he'd dropped everything and come thousands of miles to warn her. The very least she could've done was afford him the common courtesy of seriously mulling over the information gained from his expertise. At the very minimum, she could have expressed her appreciation for that expert knowledge.

But the problem was accepting that Chad, and now Susan, were both capable of such shocking and abysmal deeds. There'd been red flags along the way. Had she delved further, she might have come to similar conclusions from personal experience. She was finally able to admit that she'd ignored certain signs in her marriage because she'd simply not wanted to believe the worst regarding Chad.

She stood at the top of the stairs, knowing she should go down and apologize to Malcolm for her behavior. Should she do it now or wait till tomorrow after she had a chance to think about everything. Electing the latter course, she promised her conscience she'd call Malcolm first thing in the morning.

The front door closed softly and the voices of Malcolm and her mother cut off in the midst of conversation. She concluded that the two of them had just left together. Unable to sleep and totally disquieted by the events of the day, she opted to go down to the kitchen for a glass of wine. She waited a few minutes until it was safe to assume they'd both gotten into their cars and driven away.

On her way to the cooler, she decided wine really didn't sound good after all. She began to pace through the lower level of the house, her thoughts on Malcolm's presentation, hoping for closure to the Chad-Susan problem one way or the other.

Duffy barked a couple times while gazing intently out the window beside the door, startling her out of her reverie. "Okay, pup, thanks for reminding me. Time to take you out for the night." She leashed the dog, knowing he sometimes made a dash for the woods if she didn't, usually when he heard a deer or other small animal in the underbrush. Though he always came back after a short lookout trip, tonight she didn't want to wait for him to reconnoiter. She decided to take him out to the grassy area off the patio rather than out the front door.

A feeling of exhaustion crept slowly through her body, causing her to look longingly toward the stairway. Her only desire was to get Duffy out quickly, then back inside and up to her bedroom where she could relax and think.

She opened the door leading onto the patio. At first perplexed when Duffy took off into the woods, she at once realized that the leash connection to his collar had finally failed, loosened to the breaking point. She'd intended to get a new leash, after returning from Paris to discover the loose link connection, but hadn't found the time with all the work-related problems.

"Oh, that's just great. Fine time for it to give out," she muttered out loud. "Duffy, here boy. Duffy? Come back, you little scamp." She heard him barking in the woods and knew she'd have to wait. He'd evidently flushed out some little critter, a rabbit hopefully, as her pet could never catch the speedy little cottontails and he'd give up and come back much sooner.

Plopping down in one of the chairs to wait him out, she put her feet up on the ottoman and leaned back against the cushion. The starry constellations in the night sky fought for her attention. She'd always been entranced by the tiny twinkling lights far overhead. But soon the tensions of the day preempted the grandeur above and her eyes closed on the heavens.

Claire sensed something warm and moist licking her hand. She would keep her eyes shut and maybe Duffy would let her get another ten minutes in the comfort of her bed if he thought she was still asleep. She felt for the feather comforter as an air current wafted over her bare arms and feet delivering a chilly message. Shivering, she stretched her arm out further to find the feather comforter without opening her eyes. Again, nothing. Only then did reality seep into her sensibilities. She wasn't in her bedroom at all. Startled, she awoke to find she'd been sleeping in the chair on the patio, the French doors open as she'd left them. She glanced at her watch in the light of the wall-mounted lanterns. She'd been asleep a good fifteen minutes.

"Okay, time for bed, my little hunter," she said, giving Duffy the signal to come with her into the house. He trotted on ahead, while Claire locked the doors and turned off the lights.

Upstairs in her bedroom, she found she was sleepy enough to drop right into bed. In the middle of a wide yawn, she promised herself she'd take the day off tomorrow to filter through the information received from Malcolm, some of which she just couldn't wrap her mind around yet. Or maybe she still didn't want to believe it.

Claire climbed into bed, asleep before the second hand on her alarm clock rotated twice.

From what seemed a short distance away, a dog barked, waking Malcolm. His eyes opened to pitch blackness making him wonder if he was awake or dreaming. He was lying on his back in a cramped position, atop hands that were tied at the wrist behind him and jammed against some sort of an enclosing metal framework. Unable to see in the darkness, he forced his fingers to explore along what he considered to be interlaced metal wires, thin but substantial. A cage of sort came to mind. The extreme pain in his head intensified as he attempted to sit up, instead slamming into another cage-like panel three or four inches above him. He tried moving his hands and legs, but realized it was futile. They were tightly bound. He began to panic, at once challenged by the fact someone had actually hit him over the head and then bound him hand and foot. The fear of closed spaces, especially as experienced in absolute blackness, was the final trial to his analytic abilities. And over and over came the questions. Who did this? And, as importantly, why?

With extreme effort, he forced himself to still his shaking body and lay quietly while he put his mind to figuring a way out. He refused to give credence to the nagging thought that this really could be the end. Would they eventually find his remains—a bloody hogtied corpse? Or, would his assailant bury him somewhere in the woods, never to be seen or heard from again.

He knew this kind of thinking got him nowhere. Way too dramatic for a supposedly bright PhD who solved other people's problems. As Claire once said on the occasion of the Simon Boulle-Claire-as-bait-incident in Paris . . ."Get over it." Okay, no more undue thinking on the phreaking macabre possibilities. He had to work on finding a way out.

The first thing that came to mind was to yell for help, though the very real possibility chilled him that his demented attacker might still be around. Foremost in his mind, his best professional conclusion said it had to have been someone with a probable motive. Like Chad, Claire's almost-ex-husband, whose handwriting exhibited definite sociopathic tendencies—plus the capacity for violence.

In the midst of these reflections, the claustrophobia he'd held at bay broke through his resolve and the thought he might be rescued if he hollered caused him to reject reason in favor of a desperate hope. When only a mumbling sound came out of his mouth instead of a loud shout, he nearly gave in to the blackness that threatened to cave in on him again. With great effort, he managed to push the claustrophobia further back in his mind.

Carefully, he felt around with his tongue but found nothing inserted in his mouth. The first lucky break he'd gotten. Must be some kind of tape on the outside, he thought, though it didn't feel like masking tape—something that gave a little when he worked his jaw muscles. Could it simply be the kind of packaging tape used for closing boxes? He set about to test his theory, tightening and working his jaw muscles from side to side.

The numbness growing in his hands and arms soon ended this pursuit. Again, he attempted to ignore the increasing discomfort, tentatively moving his position a fraction at a time, so that his body turned midway between his back and his side. He kept going until he could lie on his side. There was no room to turn any further. Now that he was no longer lying on top of his bound wrists, he began flexing his hands as far as he was able, to restore the circulation. He stopped when one hand nudged a cloth object. Further experimentation led him to believe that the object felt comparable in form and texture to a canvas carry-all.

Desperate to find out what was in the bag, he began twisting his hands around, though still suffering the effects of pins and needles in those members. A number of painful attempts later, he was able to drag the heavy bag closer to his body and found the place where it opened. The shock of discovering the opening was both zippered and buckled nearly caused him to give up.

In the hellish plight he'd awakened to, Malcolm only just held it together. His claustrophobia fought to take over as the shreds of his self-imposed restraint entirely deserted him. His lower body began to chill and shake, while sweat broke out on his forehead, mingling with the blood from his head wound and running into his eyes and down his face.

Why bother? Why not just accept the inevitable? But some deep inner voice held him back from acquiescing to the suggestions of his exhausted mind. With a focused effort, he started to work on the leather belts that buckled the bag top to bottom.

Success came upon working feverishly to open the first buckle. He found the desire to live was driving him on. And with it, his thoughts automatically went to Claire. He promised himself if he ever got out of this mess, he'd keep trying to change her mind. Forever, if that's what it took. At this point, he was completely void of all inner feeling which left him little doubt that his life could ever be complete without her.

He had the second buckle in hand, working weary fingers to open the leather strap, when he heard someone moving around his general vicinity.

Chad . . . or someone else? Whoever it was seemed to be searching for something, judging by the sounds made by cabinet doors opening and closing. He froze. The rummaging continued. It sounded like it came from just a short distance away. Then he heard the soft clunk of a metal container being set down on a hard surface. He heard another door open and close. Then silence. Once again questions surged into his head.

With concentrated effort, his thoughts went back to the dark SUV parked on the gravel road in the woods before he was knocked unconscious. He began to put the possibilities of the incident together. Slowly the idea came to him that someone had transported him into that vehicle and then into a building. Most likely, a garage.

That's it. He was inside the SUV that was parked inside a garage. But where? Whose garage was it? He couldn't be sure if he was alone now or if someone was still in there with him, only pretending to leave. In order to find out, he understood he must free himself.

Cautiously now, he succeeded in opening the second buckle. He gave a silent cheer. He was halfway there. As he moved the bag so that his fingers could manipulate the last obstacle—the zipper—a slight clank caused by metal hitting together came from the bag. He held his breath, listening. No sound came from outside the vehicle. He began again, much encouraged by the metallic noise, but more carefully this time.

Malcolm willed himself to unzip the bag a slight bit at a time. It was torment. A portion of his body shook from the cold, while the bloody sweat droplets continued to trickle down his face. He made himself rest each time he opened the zipper a few inches. After what seemed like hours, though actually was only a number of precious minutes, he had enough of the top unzipped to maneuver one hand inside. He felt along the first object his fingers touched. Has to be a screwdriver, he decided, a Phillips-head. No help there, but he remained hopeful that there were more tools inside that he could use to free himself. Still searching, he tentatively felt under a couple of small paper sacks, the kind screws and bolts came in. The next items he came across felt like sheets of sandpaper. Forcing himself to slow down lest he miss something more useful, he heard that soft clank again.

Upon further foraging, his fingers hit against a hard object with a flat metal handle. Overjoyed, he identified the payoff he'd been hoping for. He found the release button on the side of the object. His fingers moved across the angled edge of what could only be a box cutter. Upon feeling an acute sting and what had to be fresh blood on the flat surface of the blade, he ignored the subsequent pain and desperately hung onto the implement. He slowly pulled it out. Once clear of the bag, Malcolm grabbed the cutter in both hands, turning the blade to hold it at best advantage to saw at the rope binding his wrists. He drove himself onward, not daring to stop again until he felt the rope give way. Flexing his hands so he could finish the task, he hurriedly sawed at the bindings on his ankles. Next, he ripped off the tape covering his mouth and finally the blindfold.

Malcolm knew even before he removed the makeshift blindfold covering his eyes that he would yet encounter darkness, but he was also sure he knew the remedy. Because now he was certain he'd been transported into Claire's garage in the back of the black SUV—the whys and wherefores he'd yet to figure out. He only knew that the perpetrator, his assailant, was beginning to move without caution and now Claire was in even more danger than before.

He remembered seeing the switch for the overhead lights next to the door leading into the house when Abbie had taken them on the tour earlier. What he needed to do was to get out of the vehicle as quietly as possible and somehow get to Claire to warn her.

He was so close now. Using as much determination as he could muster, he struggled out of the wire cage through its unlocked door. By feeling the inside of the back gate for the latch, he was able to open it and then drop out of the SUV onto the cement. He huddled there, shaking, while endeavoring his stiff muscles to propel his body into an upright position. But first he needed to ascertain if he was alone.

Somewhere below, a door closed softly. Claire had fallen into a deep sleep and was now an unwilling captive of one of her frightening nightmares which hadn't bothered her since Malcolm hypnotized her in Paris. She didn't hear Duffy's soft warning bark as he raced down the stairs, paws hitting the treads on all cylinders. The dog sprinted back up to the bedroom excited to let Claire know who was there, stub tail arcing enthusiastically. He tried but couldn't wake her so he stood in the doorway peering down the dark staircase and waited.

In Claire's dream, she was hiding in a thick stand of evergreen trees. Terror gripped her as menacing footsteps approached. She crumpled to the ground, her breath catching in her chest, wanting with all her heart to be invisible from the oncoming presence she knew was about to reveal itself.

A swirling red maelstrom illuminated the darkness at the center of the stand, disclosing the same hooded creature as in her former dreams. It was extremely tall, with arms the length of an eagle's wingspan. It came toward her and then stopped out of her reach. Pure evil emanated from bony fingers that began to rise in slow motion toward her neck. Its foul breathe flowed out from under the cowled hood, freezing her in place. Frightened beyond all sensibility, she forced herself to be calm so she could do what she knew she had to do. The only thing left for her to do.

With supreme effort she forced herself to stand up. Putting one reluctant foot ahead of the other, she moved by inches closer to the cloaked figure. As she did so, the bony fingers dropped back to its sides. Her body shook violently as she reached for the demon's hood. In desperation she pulled it aside, unmasking her persecutor. Recognition struck terror and disbelief into her heart. Yet from somewhere deep inside, there came a sense of finality knowing she had just identified her innermost fears.

The face before her was the same one she'd seen in the glass of the sliding patio door the night of the attack. It hadn't been a reflection in the glass after all. The face of someone she intimately knew stared back.

Chad.

She could hardly believe it even though she now knew beyond a doubt that it was true.

Chad actually was there that night. Watching.

She realized she'd not wanted to face up to it. She tried hard to come to terms with the fact he'd witnessed her battle against the masked attacker who she now understood could only be Sean. The fact that Chad had stood and watched and had not come to her aid sent waves of shivers through her body. She'd lived with the man through seven long years of marriage.

There was something else which she could never forgive him for. He allowed Duffy to be poisoned the night of the attack. And more than likely, he was responsible for her pet's kidnapping while she was in Paris.

Blood pounded loudly in Claire's head.

Face up, Martelli, it's been Chad all along. And you actually know why.

Something bumped against her bed. She fought her way out of her dream state, opening her eyes to the same face she'd just exposed as the demon figure in her dreams. She screamed.

Chad sat on the end of her bed, casually observing her, a gun in his hand.

Chad. One of the handful of people Duffy would allow around her without barking.

"You scared the living daylights out of me. How did you get in? And just what are you doing here? Get out, Chad. Now."

"My dear little wife, shut up. I'll do the talking."

Claire estimated the distance to the interconnected security alarm installed in the wall next to her bed. Her heart pounded loudly in her head. Would he shoot if she reached for the panic button? She thought about ways of getting the gun away using her karate training. He appeared to be in a confused state. She wondered if that would help or hinder her objective.

"And, Claire, don't even think about trying any of your martial arts tricks, or to get to your security alarm. I've already disconnected the alarm wires, likewise the house phone. And the second you move from that position, I promise you I'll shoot. Not that I want to hurt you, my sweet." Chad got up from the end of the bed and moved a little farther away, the gun still trained on her.

"I'm going to give you a choice, Claire. As I haven't received the paperwork that says the divorce is final, we are still legally married. If you choose to drop the divorce proceedings and remain my wife, at least in appearances, I'll look the other way if you and your boyfriend want to meet up every now and then. Anywhere but Denver that is. Of course, it would also work the other way around.

"And, if you'll stay on as my partner in the business, I'll rewrite the pre-nup, upping the yearly figure to five hundred thousand dollars, payable annually on the first of January."

Claire shook her head. "Sorry, no dice. Look, Chad. It's time we called it a day. I'm asking you nicely to leave. Now," she said, pulling herself upright onto the pillows behind her. "If not, I won't be responsible for what happens. That's far more choice than you gave me the night of the attack. I can't believe you are so evil that you actually watched through the patio door to see if I could fight off Sean, your attack dog. And if you think I'm bluffing, try me.

"You're really a monster, Chad. And after Lieutenant Owens arrests you, it'll be jail time for you. I'm beginning to piece the whole thing together now. Denver and Paris. Time to own up. You evidently sanctioned Sean to get rid of me in Paris, didn't you? Only you made the mistake of insisting it look like an accident. I'm sure Sean might have gotten the job done if you'd let him use a gun or knife."

"Claire, I don't know what you're talking about . . . watching you through the patio door, or that I was behind your accidents in Paris. You're paranoid if you think I could do that.

"Listen to me, my pet," he coldly demanded, considering her with a tight-lipped smile. "I'm through persuading you to amend the error of your ways. You just couldn't leave well enough alone, could you? When you left our home and filed for a divorce, did you ever stop to consider how embarrassing that was for me? And talk about money, you evidently decided that half my net worth, including the business, was due you."

"Chad, be careful with that thing," Claire said, indicating the revolver he was waving around, punctuating his words. "Let's cut the pretense and tell it like it is. As your partner, I'm already legally entitled to half of the business' worth. As for your personal wealth, the investments you made in the Cherry Creek properties were all funded because of the growth of our business over the seven-year period we've been married, especially so after making me your partner. I'm sure the accountants can make that case in court if necessary."

As she talked, all her left-over fears and apprehensions vanished both in reality as well as the dream state she'd just awoken from. Claire warmed to her subject. All the information from Malcolm's session earlier that evening now came flooding back, though at the time she didn't want to believe Chad's character embodied such a negative mix of traits. Malcolm's analysis actually went so far as to name Chad as a dangerous personality—a sociopath. Through the years, she'd seen for herself the self-centered, greedy, and at times, even erratic tendencies. But the fact that he was totally bereft of human feelings and emotions was difficult to comprehend. Malcolm had also mentioned that there was an inability to take responsibility for his own actions, holding other people to blame. Never him.

She wanted him to understand that she knew exactly what was due her in the divorce. She became the voice of an avenging angel, putting it in simple terms how she would no longer put up with his philandering and lack of respect for her as his wife, plus his deceit and dishonesty in their partnership.

She watched his face turn white with rage, yet continued on, needing to get all seven years out of her system. "Then there's the little matter of the pre-nup you were just talking about. The original pre-nup agreement that *you* insisted upon by the way, gave me a sum of two hundred fifty thousand dollars a year as long as our business partnership lasted, and another two hundred fifty thousand as long as our marriage lasted. If you do the numbers, that's in the neighborhood of two million dollars at this point. Yet I haven't seen a penny of that to date. So, to reiterate, you've fallen far lower than simply being a miserable husband to being a greedy and conniving human being. It's all about you, right? Well, hear this, I no longer want to partner with you, Chad. Either buy me out at a price I'll have the accountants figure what's due me for what I've brought into the business, since that's also covered in the pre-nup, or I'll put feelers out for anyone who would like the unmitigated honor of being your partner in a going business.

"As a point of information, my lawyer called me at work today. The divorce papers *are* final. The court sent them to each of our attorneys. The legal decree will be delivered to me at the office tomorrow. Probably yours too. Looks like I end up with the business and half your wealth anyway," she said, grinning at his apparent discomfort.

Chad swept her words away with the wave of his gun. "You don't understand, Claire, read my lips: You. Must. Pay. I won't allow you to take me for half of my life's worth, especially, as your boyfriend has come between us, spoiling our reconciliation."

"What are you going to do, Chad, shoot me? And what reconciliation? If you're talking about Malcolm as my boyfriend, I didn't even meet him until after I went to Paris. And as you recall, I filed for divorce months before that."

"Well I have a surprise for you, Claire. I've got your Malcolm. He's messed up a little but still alive. And if you ever want to see him again, you'll do what I say. We'll go to my attorney's office first thing in the morning, and you'll sign a paper saying you agree to relinquish everything you received in the divorce settlement."

Trying not to be obvious, Claire fumbled to find her phone among the bedding. She'd taken it to bed. Just in case.

She finally found what she'd been searching for. The phone was caught between the sheet and feather comforter. Before she could untangle it and push the pre-programmed nine-one-one number, Chad noticed her stealthy movements and put it together.

"What are you doing, Claire? Both hands where I can see them. Now. Unless you want Duffy here to suffer needlessly from a bullet."

Claire pulled her hands out from under the covers, laying the phone on top for him to see.

He reached out, grabbed the phone and threw it on the floor, smashing it with his foot. "You won't need this anymore tonight."

A siren sounded in the distance. Claire guessed it came from out on the main road somewhere. Even though she knew it wasn't coming to her place, it was still a fortunate coincidence. She decided it just might scare Chad off if she could convince him that she'd actually called the emergency number.

"You're insane, Chad. How dare you threaten me, and Duffy, a perfectly innocent creature. We've all suffered enough because of you. And that includes Malcolm. What did

I just do? You'll find out soon enough when the police arrive to take you away."

Chad tilted his head, listening to the siren's proximity. "You didn't really call the police, did you?"

"Why don't you wait around to find out," she taunted.

With that, Claire leaped out of bed, throwing the comforter at him so he'd have to dodge it. She propelled herself forward in a crouch until within range of his gun hand. A perfectly aimed kick sent the pistol winging through the air from the force of impact. Like a hornet honing in on its next victim that had the bad manners to swat at its nest, she flew at Chad with fire in her eyes.

He didn't pause, but made for the stairs, slamming the door shut behind him and calling back to her. "You'll be sorry for this, Claire. Mark my words. And you can be sure you've seen the last of your precious Malcolm."

Claire ended up on the floor, smug in the knowledge she chased him off, though she paid for her victory with a twisted ankle in an unsuccessful attempt to stop herself from running full tilt into the closed door. She limped down the stairs in time to see Chad backing the SUV from the garage, tires squealing as he took off in the direction of the gravel road that wove through the woods to a little-used side street. She watched the vehicle disappear into the night, all the while worrying whether he really meant to kill Malcolm or was that just a bluff to get back at her.

Malcolm picked his head up from the front seat of the rental car he'd parked at the end of the circle drive. He looked at his watch, but couldn't see the time, so muddled was his eyesight. It had to be well past midnight, he thought. There was good reason to suspect that the blow to his still-throbbing head had caused a concussion. He tried to focus as objects around him swam in and out of his vision. He did a double-take when a dark vehicle roared past him, gravel flying as it hit the unpaved road into the woods.

"What the . . .?" With his blurred vision, he couldn't be certain whether it was the black SUV, but his gut told him it was someone intent on making a fast get-a-way. Thankfully he'd still been down and out of view when the other vehicle flew by, if it was the same person who'd flattened him earlier.

"Have to concentrate. Got to get back to the house to find Claire," he mumbled, closing his eyes and trying to replay what had happened just before he passed out.

His memory finally brought back the main points, like finding out he was alone in the garage with a large container of gasoline after subsequently crawling out of the SUV. He'd staggered out of the garage through a side door that stood open after several unsuccessful attempts to unlock the door into the house without knowing the code on the keypad. And after that, he tried desperately to get Claire's attention by scratching at the front door on his knees. He hadn't the strength to stand let alone pound or shout for her attention.

What an ass, he thought, finally able to recall that he'd left his phone in the car yesterday before the meeting with Claire to advise her of his graphological findings.

In his present state of confusion, he was left with the impression that it had seemed like forever to once again stagger down the drive to his rental car. He only remembered bits and pieces, like when he did reach the car, how he'd crawled into the front seat and promptly collapsed—too late to get the phone to warn Claire and call for help. He passed out before he could find the phone.

The phone . . .

He willed himself to stay alert while he searched the seat and the floor, finally locating it wedged into the console area between the driver's and passenger's sides. Hands trembling, he attempted to call Claire, pushing the pre-assigned number to her cell.

"Come on, Claire . . . answer." She didn't pick up. A pre-recorded message told him she wasn't available. Frustration caused his heart to skip a couple beats knowing all he could do was leave her a message to get out of the house at once.

Failing to alert Claire, he tried the number Owens had given him earlier. Once again, voice mail picked up. The message he left warned the detective regarding what he perceived as the immediate danger to Claire.

Malcolm opened the car door. The only plan his tired mind could come up with was to get back to the house and try to wake her. Somehow. If worst came to worst, he thought about trying to get up to her bedroom via the escape route Abbie had shown him during the house tour. Before he could put the plan into action, he slumped forward as darkness took him under again.

Too wound up to sit, Claire paced through the open plan of the ground floor in an endless circle, turning on every light as she went. Peering through the glass into the darkness, she switched on the patio and outdoor lights in the hope of seeing headlights and flashing emergency lights heading down the road and into the cul-de-sac of her circle drive. But she knew that was a futile wish. She'd tried the emergency buttons on the alarm system, as well as the house phone. Neither responded—only dead silence. Chad said he'd disconnected both systems before coming to her bedroom. And for once, he'd told the truth. But worse, he'd destroyed her cell phone.

It was not so much her own safety that worried her, knowing she could get her car keys and drive for help even though that would take more time than she was willing to spend right now. It was her concern for Malcolm that had her in this current state of unrest. She really didn't think Chad would've had time to stash him somewhere else, if indeed he did have him at all.

No, she theorized, Malcolm had to be close by. She was tempted to get Duffy and her gun and start looking for him on her own, thinking he may be lying wounded in one of the wooded areas around the property. She only held back because it wasn't light yet and she wasn't certain she could find him in the dark with only a flashlight.

She paced impatiently, trying to decide the best course of action. Malcolm was foremost in her thoughts as she pictured him in the worst situation—severely injured and unable to help himself. She opened the French doors to the patio and walked outside, peering into the dark wooded pines that edged the landscaped area. She saw nothing out of the ordinary, however she noticed that her garage door was still open. She'd forgotten to shut it down after witnessing Chad's hasty exit in her SUV.

She made a mental note to replace the present house alarm code with a new one, as well as have all the keypad codes on the entry doors changed, and to re-key the locking ones. She shook her head in dismay. Never again would she be susceptible to someone getting keys made from the extra set she kept in her office desk drawer. At first thought she couldn't figure out how Chad had gotten the codes to the key pads. But knowing Chad, she didn't question anymore. He was very ingenious at making up stories that sounded perfectly believable. He'd evidently scored another success with the company that both installed and set the codes for her home.

After closing the overhead door, she locked the access door to the garage once again. She turned to see Duffy waiting at the foot of the stairs. As soon as he got her attention, he began barking and whining.

"Sorry, pal. I can't play your game right now." Claire said, limping toward the kitchen to make tea.

However Duffy was persistent. Barking and running up a few steps then back down again, he caused Claire to stop short as she suddenly remembered she and Mandy had planned to do their weekly Skype get-together sometime this morning. So much had happened since yesterday morning that she'd forgotten Mandy's email reminder.

As well as being sisters, she and Mandy were also close friends. After discussing how they would remain in touch when either of them was away, they'd chosen to communicate via Skype on the computer. It was especially nice to be able to see each other while they talked, not just disembodied voices or strings of abbreviated text words. Claire's personal laptop occupied the desk in her bedroom so she could hear the computer signaling a call from her sister which usually took place during the night to early morning portion of the day, due to their work schedules and the time difference between Denver and Paris. More often than not it was Duffy who heard the computer's signal and woke her if she was asleep.

"Duff, I bet you're trying to tell me you heard the computer send the signal that Mandy is ready on the call. Right, fella?"

She finished making the pot of tea and poured a cup to take up to the bedroom. She would talk to Mandy and get her take on what Chad said he'd already done to Malcolm and what he threatened to do.

"Claire, that does it. I'm coming back there and I'm warning you in advance, I'm going to be your shadow. Get used to the idea right now." After being shocked by Claire's recitation of the latest turn of events, Mandy's face on the computer screen showed a determined scowl. "It's hard to believe that as creepy as Chad's always been, Malcolm's analysis of him as a sociopath is very telling regarding the fact that he was able to cover it up these past seven years. What do you think triggered his present erratic actions?"

"I would have to say the catalyst is greed. He just couldn't let me have what he thinks of as *his* money and *his* assets. You do realize he never loved me. I was just a means of making more money for him. Malcolm said in his analysis that he actually has no morals and doesn't feel emotions. But it's all over now that the divorce is final. And, no, Sis. You aren't coming back to Denver. At least not yet. You took on that project and you're going to stay there and finish it. I know you have a deadline for the upcoming issue of the travel magazine." Claire was just as determined.

"But you're in so much danger as long as Chad's on the loose. And now Malcolm, likewise. You've been taking far too many chances, Claire. You're part of the human race, you know. Not some super heroine. Who do you think you are . . . Wonder Woman?"

"Mandy, hold on a minute. Duffy just ran downstairs barking his head off. Hopefully, it's Lieutenant Owens. I'm going down to check. Be right back. Don't hang up. Okay?"

"Claire, wait a minute. It could be Chad again. Please don't go down there alone . . ."

But Claire was gone before she finished the sentence.

Mandy fumed, saying a quick prayer as she drummed her fingers. An extrasensory flash caused a shudder to run through her. She grabbed her phone from the desk in the sitting room of the suite she'd shared with Abbie and Claire just a few weeks ago. She stared blankly at the empty screen where Claire's head had been a few seconds ago, which now displayed a perfect view of the French doors leading to the deck that Claire had added onto her top floor bedroom. To Mandy's horror, the doors slowly opened. A shadow silently maneuvered into the room. The angle of the computer's camera was set too low to see the face. All she saw was a dark-clad figure moving about and then out of sight. She pressed the pre-designated number for Abbie on her phone when suddenly a gloved hand moved across her monitor and out of her line of vision. The screen went dark, shutting down her communication with Claire.

"Mom? Yes, I know it's late. Please listen. Claire is in danger. An intruder is in her bedroom and she doesn't know. You've got to call nine-one-one right now. Then call me back and I'll explain. Mom, do it now."

Abbie did one better. Besides calling nine-one-one, urging them to hurry, she also tried Lieutenant Owens. He didn't answer so she left a voice mail, flagging it important. The same with Claire. Finally she called Ben, overjoyed to hear his voice when he answered. All it took for her to say was, "Claire's in trouble."

Ben was used to emergencies by reason of his medical practice. "I'll be there within fifteen minutes," he said, adding in a calm voice, "promise me you'll wait for me. And Abbie, in no way think about going there on your own."

With nothing to do but wait, Abbie called Mandy back. She'd put it off as long as possible, terrified of what she would hear. And, she'd been right. The longer she listened to Mandy's account of Claire's disclosures on their Skype call, the more fearful she became.

In Denver's quiet early morning hours, traffic was light in the residential areas, enabling Ben to pull into Abbie's drive and give a quick honk not more than ten minutes from the time she'd called. Abbie dashed downstairs and out to his car, still on her mobile with Mandy in Paris. She handed Ben the phone so Mandy could explain what Claire had related involving the scene with Chad, and especially the part about what he'd threatened to do to Malcolm. When she repeated the frightening Skype episode, Ben, who'd been driving ten miles over the speed limit already, put his foot down on the gas. The all-terrain vehicle shot ahead, energized by the powerful engine. He only hoped they would be in time to help Claire.

Duffy galloped from the front door back up to the bedroom to find his mistress. Claire had just left her desk with the computer running after telling her sister to hold on while she discovered who was ringing the doorbell. Mission accomplished, he wheeled around and barreled down the stairs with Claire as close behind as possible, but hampered by her turned ankle. She switched on the outside lights, wanting desperately to see the detective's face through the peep hole on the other side of the door. But no one was there. All was quiet, including the doorbell. That's when she heard scratching and tapping noises coming from the other side of the door. Once again she put her eye to the peep hole, and once again she saw no one. Thoughts of opening the door to find that Chad had sneaked back were foremost in her mind. She scotched any idea of opening it. She'd hoped it would be Lieutenant Owens, or at least the police. But Claire knew she would see flashing lights through the plantation shutters on the front windows if that were the case. She decided to go back upstairs and ask Mandy to call Abbie and have her call the detective.

Limping toward the stairs, she smelled smoke. She looked in the kitchen and gasped as that room was engulfed in flames just in the short time she'd been at the door. She grabbed for the first thing at hand. An old coat hung on the wall pegs next to the back door. Beating at the blaze with the coat didn't help. The fire only leapt higher.

Claire forced herself to stay calm. She stumbled back up the stairs to get the car keys she'd left in her purse. She needed to get out of the house to call nine-one-one as it was impossible to call for help from inside. Chad had seen to that.

A crawling sensation began at the back of her neck and spread rapidly. By the time she reached the top floor, anxiety had a good hold. She forced herself to analyze why, thinking she'd get the upper hand and control her unease.

Okay, get hold of yourself, Martelli. Just because there's someone skulking outside the front door . . . and, the flames are spreading rapidly through the kitchen . . . and, I can't use either of my phones, or the alarm system, to call for help . . . and, I'm terribly afraid for Malcolm . . .

The flames . . .

Who started the fire? She was certain she'd turned off the burner after making her tea. Hadn't she? Or, could Chad have started it?

When she reached her bedroom she went directly to the desk intending to make Mandy aware of the fire and that she needed help. But the screen was black. Mandy must've given up and dropped the connection, she thought. Even as that consideration flashed through her mind, Claire didn't actually believe her sister would do that. She shrugged off the thought, figuring it was most likely some kind of computer glitch.

She quickly looked around when Duffy began barking furiously in the hallway leading to the walk-in closet. She grabbed her car keys and called for Duffy to come. He ignored her, barking even louder.

"Come on, Duffy, this is no time to be stubborn," she muttered to the upset animal.

But Duffy wouldn't budge from his post. Claire grabbed his collar and tried to pull him to the stairs. It became a tug of war. No leash, and not enough leverage. As there was no way she would leave without him, she went down on her knees to pick him up.

Her skin prickled. Knowing Duffy only barked for what he considered a good reason, she realized someone could very well be hiding in the closet. And she knew also, it most probably didn't have a cute little cotton-tail.

She prayed fervently it wasn't Chad again.

But if not him, who else?

The closet door began to open, but Claire didn't see. She was faced the other way.

Claire let go of Duffy when he wriggled strenuously to get out of her grasp. He rushed toward the closet in attack mode, yelped once and fell to the floor in a heap.

Déjà vu Claire thought, hastily turning toward the closet.

Again she saw nothing as a heavy cloth bag was forced over her head. She fell down to her knees, fighting back, in a focused effort to get the bag off. Her assailant put a knee in her back, shoving her face into the floor, capturing both hands.

She struggled, but it was no contest. With a body straddling her hips, pinning her down, her wrists were forcefully jerked together behind her and secured with what felt like a tightly knotted fabric of some kind. Claire felt the force of an arm moving across the front of her neck, in an attempt to cut off her air supply. Luckily, whoever was trying to choke her didn't know the correct place to apply the arm bar hold. Again, her first thought was Chad.

And then she realized it couldn't be Chad. Before being plunged into darkness, a whiff of a fragrance caught her attention. It was familiar. One she'd smelled many times before at the office. It was an unusual scent. One that Susan always wore. BVLGARI.

Susan . . . but why?

Claire lay still, hoping to convince her attacker that she'd passed out. Instantly the arm dropped away from her neck and the bag was ripped from her head. With her eyes still closed, she feigned unconsciousness.

A hard slap to the face ended her ruse. Her eyes flew open and she saw a darkly-clad figure leaning over her. A rubber Ronald Reagan mask covered the face, obscuring all but the tell-tale red hair that peeped out from under the baseball hat.

"That's right, Claire, open those eyes. I thought you might be faking it. And I want you awake to feel the pain when this place goes up in flames. And you'll love the grand finale. *The explosion.* It'll be seen for miles around with the help of the incinerate I splashed throughout the garage. When the inside fire reaches through that door . . . ka-boom!"

"Susan! Why are you doing this?"

Susan didn't answer. She dropped a rope with a crude noose roughly around Claire's neck and pulled her to her feet, making sure her hands were still tightly bound. Half dragging her captive by the rope, Susan got her to the task chair at the desk. There she pushed her down onto the seat and attempted to secure Claire's body to the framework using duct tape.

Claire kicked out and caught her captor off-balance, tumbling her to the floor. But Susan was up before Claire could do more damage, aiming the tranquilizer dart gun she'd used on Duffy at Claire. She slid the mask that covered her features down to her neck while pushing the bright red strands of hair back under her cap.

"Okay, Claire. We can do this the hard way if you prefer, but you need to face the very real fact that you will not be leaving this house ever again. But if you're a very good girl, I'll make sure Duffy doesn't suffer needlessly. The drug I used on the dart is something like what the vets utilize when they administer euthanasia. Only a little less powerful. So I'll give him another shot of it which should take him down and out.

Permanently." She held up a small vial with a fluid inside. "What'll it be? It's your call."

Claire didn't want her pet to die from the over-dose, but didn't want him to suffer in the fire either. She stalled by pretending to cough because of the tight rope and tried to think fast. There just might be a chance, slim as it was.

"Okay, Susan. You win. Just make sure that Duffy won't suffer before you leave. But not yet. And humor me, I'd really like to know why you're doing this. Wasn't it only yesterday afternoon you were in my office, in tears, desolate over the fact Chad fired you from both the business *and* his bed? And didn't I go to bat for you with him?"

Susan laughed softly. "But of course, Claire. I do owe you an explanation. And I promise you'll still be thinking about it when the fireworks start. But first I need to see how the fire is progressing." She ran down the stairs to check it out.

Duffy began to stir. Claire glanced over, but saw it was still going to be a minute or two before he could make it to his feet. She heard Susan on her way up the stairs. In a matter of seconds she would be back. Claire quickly swiveled her task chair so she could reach into the desk drawer, feeling for the scissors she kept there. Wheeling back around, she faced the door as Susan walked into the room. Claire could hardly keep from smiling. She wouldn't need the scissors. When she'd stretched her hands to find the scissors in the drawer she found that the fabric fastening her wrists together had loosened just a fraction. She needed to keep Susan talking while she worked at the bindings.

"Susan, you're not a murderer. Why are you doing this? Stop, now. Before you get in too deep. If you kill me, you'll get the death sentence for premeditated homicide. Better a few years than death row. They do try women and men equally now for murder, especially if it's excessively brutal.

"Huh, that's as much as you know, Claire," Susan said, her smile reflecting pure malice. "Who do you think orchestrated the attack at Chad's house in March . . . Chad? 'Fraid not. But more interestingly, he did find out about it before hand. And

I'm sure you'll be happy to hear that he gave the green light. Of course, he said to keep the damage inside the house to a minimum, but nothing about the damage to you.

"You never even guessed I was the lookout that night, did you, Claire? I waited in the alley to give Sean the signal when you drove in.

"And I'll never forgive you for taking him down like that. I was the one who rescued him before the cops got there. Had to get him up and practically carry him down the alley to where I parked my car. Sean lost all confidence in himself after that. That's probably why none of the so-called accidents in Paris worked. My brother would never admit to it now, but he mentioned once that you had to be some kind of witch because you just wouldn't die. But I'll take care of that for him in a few minutes.

"Now he's in a Paris jail awaiting trial. Who knows how many years they'll give him. And the alternative. If Owens issues an arrest warrant to extradite him back to the States, he'll face charges of attempted murder. Kind of a *lose–lose* situation, don't you think?

"And you have the nerve to ask why I'm doing this. You've caused me to lose my brother, the only family I've ever had. You see Sean only agreed to do this so I could marry Chad when you were out of the picture."

The disbelief on Claire's face drove Susan to laugh harshly. She gave the rope noose a couple of tugs, causing Claire to choke for real this time.

"You're not very good with the theatrics, Claire," Susan said loosening her grip on the rope a little. "Don't be so stupid. You should've realized. *It's the money, stupid.* Why you never picked up on this is beyond me. It's always been about the money. I was raised poor, and I got tired of being poor real fast. That and having to endure the attention of the insufferable male ego just for my looks. And sex of course. I was good enough to take to bed, but never good enough to marry.

"Then my luck changed. Chad hired me to be the poster girl for the firm. I got the job at the front desk . . . and in

377

Chad's bed. The affair went on so long that I began to think I was indispensable. I saw a way to get you out of the picture so I could marry Chad.

"However I also had a plan to get *all* the money after walking Chad and his checkbook down the aisle. With him dead, I'd end up with *everything*. So, you see, in addition to ruining Sean's life, I can't forgive you for causing Chad to get cold feet about wanting you to be the *late* Mrs. Chadwick before the divorce was final.

"Yesterday, when he gave me the boot, he told me he was ending both our personal relationship as well as my job at the office. He said receptionists were a dime a dozen. And it would be more advantageous to the business if he stayed married to you. He told me he planned it so you would cancel the divorce proceedings, one way or another."

Claire listened, both frightened and stunned. She could barely comprehend the degree of hate revealed by Susan's motives.

A murky cloud began to billow up the stairway. Both women coughed, tears running down their faces from the heavy smoke. Claire could feel the heat as the flames brightened the room.

"The police will hunt you down, Susan. You won't get away with this. It's never going to look like an accident when they find my corpse with a noose around my neck," Claire said.

Susan tightened the noose and then tied it securely to the arms of the task chair so that when Claire struggled to get free, she would in effect be choking herself.

"Well, guess what, Claire, when this place goes up like a phreaking Fourth of July fireworks display, they won't find your body at all. Unless they collect bits and pieces in a basket. But, more than likely, all that will be left is ashes. And they'll just figure you went to bed and left one of the burners on in the kitchen. Everyone at work has commented how different you've seemed since you came back from Paris."

An enormous crash rocked the whole house as one of the original timbers burned through and fell to the main floor from the open framework that formed the ceiling in the kitchen below.

"Guess this is it, Claire. You have a good last few minutes now. Bye-bye." Susan turned to go downstairs but the blaze was now out of control and roared upward, stair by stair. Turning back into the bedroom, the terror mirrored on Susan's face was painfully apparent. She dropped the dart gun and ran out onto the deck through the French doors.

Claire jerked her wrists back and forth, trying her best to loosen the bindings so she could get her hands free, but the noose cut into her neck causing her to choke and desist in her efforts. And when she tried to stand up, hoping to drag the desk chair with her out onto the deck to gain more time, the same thing happened. Between that and the billowing smoke that choked off the small amount of breath she had left, she could only think that this time her life was truly over. As Mandy had cautioned, she'd evidently used up all nine lives.

Fully awake now, Duffy ran back and forth between her chair and out onto the deck, barking his head off.

She cried out as loud as she could, hoping to lure Susan back into the room.

"Susan, please don't do this. Cut me loose. There's another way down from up here. If it's not already too late," she added in a hoarse whisper, not hearing any sounds coming from the deck.

The noxious smoke surged through the open door, completely filling the room. Her eyes teared. It was impossible to see or to breathe. She made another frantic effort to loosen the bindings on her wrists while the noose pulled ever more tightly around her throat.

She heard Duffy at her side, barking for her to get up. Her last effort was to command the dog to leave the room. "Go, Duffy! Balcony . . . outside . . ." she whispered. "Go . . ."

VICTORIA MASTERSON

14

Flames shot into the pre-dawn sky. From the main road, Owens feared the worst. Try as he might, he seemed to be moving in slow motion toward Claire's property, though his car squealed around the curves in the road as sirens wailed from the ambulance and fire trucks following him. The whole convoy of emergency vehicles slammed on their breaks as the burning carriage house suddenly burst like a bomb into a myriad of fragments, all too lately part of a beautiful home. The explosion rocked the ground, lighting up the wooded area as bits of wood and other indefinable objects rained down through the darkness that precedes daybreak.

Owens ignored the burning fallout and sped into the circle drive, waving the fire trucks and ambulance forward. The emergency team could only get to within a hundred yards of the decimated house. He turned at the sound of an insistent car's horn as the trucks made way for the Jeep Cherokee to get into the circle.

Abbie was out of the car before Ben could come to a complete stop. She ran towards Owens, picking a path through the still-burning debris in her way. "Oh my God! Where's Claire? Lieutenant, where's my daughter?"

Following right behind, Ben caught her as she made toward the burning structure.

"Abbie, you can't go in there. Even the fire company can't get inside right now. No one can be alive in there. I'm afraid it's too late, honey. We can only pray to God that she got out before the explosion." He put his arm around her and drew her head to his shoulder so she could no longer watch the blazing inferno.

Owens turned to the distraught mother. "Mrs. Martelli, please . . ." With Ben's help, he led her away from the immediate area of the house while the men from the two fire trucks attempted to get the fire under control, aiming their hoses at the densest areas of the burning structure and the surrounding pines.

Abbie swayed and would have collapsed in shock if Ben and the detective hadn't been on either side of her, steering her toward the doctor's off-road vehicle. The fire lit up the night-shadowed area at the end of the circle and Owens stopped in surprise to see another car parked there. He recognized it as the same rental car Malcolm had driven the day before. The door to the car stood open. Upon inspection, Owens found blood on the driver's seat, the steering wheel, and on the pavement outside.

"Looks like we have two people missing, Doc. This is the car Malcolm was driving yesterday. I'm afraid it doesn't look good," he said to Ben, who stood with his arm around Abbie's shoulders, attempting to comfort her. The doctor nodded his understanding.

"Abbie honey, let's get you into inside the Jeep where you can sit and rest for a little while. I'm certain the detective has everything under control," he soothed.

"But Ben, we've got to find Claire. And don't tell me she's . . . d-dead. I just won't accept that she's g-gone." With that, Abbie broke into another round of sobs.

More sirens split the air as three official cars carrying men specialized in search-and-rescue ops rushed onto the chaotic scene. Owens waved the emergency team over to him. "Men, we have two people missing. We don't know the condition of either, except to say the male is injured and looks like he's lost quite a lot of blood. The woman, we think, may have been in the house when it became engulfed in flames. We just don't know. We'll assume they're both alive at this point. Fan out through the woods and let me know the minute you find either one, or anything that could lead to their whereabouts. If they're alive, they will most likely be in shock. We have a doctor and an EMT team standing by. So, radio in and we'll have the medical team to the scene on the double." The men scrambled to get flashlights from their cars and fanned out into the woods.

For the next hour, Owens watched as the fire fighters systematically fought the blaze from outside the ruined house. One of them was getting into a special suit that would allow him to go into the house, though he would have to wait a little while longer. It was still too dangerous for the search mission the man had volunteered for. The detective tried to figure what had happened to start the blaze that ended in the explosion, causing the whole garage side of the structure to be completely destroyed. Now that the blaze was nearly tamed, the rest of the house still technically stood, but he knew it was a complete loss. It looked like an exposed framework of charred timbers, too damaged to leave standing. And Owens didn't think anyone could live through such an extensive fire.

In a way, he felt he was to blame if it came to be that Claire died in the fire. He knew he could've arrested Chad previously, on suspicion of attempted murder in the March attack. But he'd wanted to be sure. He'd wanted it to be an open and shut case so that Chad couldn't worm his way out. He'd tried to crack Susan to get proof of Chad's guilt. His gut told him she had to be involved some way, especially when the dark SUV tried to run her down in her parking lot. He figured it had to have been Chad trying to make sure she wouldn't talk. That's when he'd hit upon the idea to gain her confidence. Susan had softened, a little, but was still very much hard-core loyal to her stepbrother, and Chad—or both.

He'd actually put everything together pertaining to the motive after eliminating other possibilities, but had waited to get the goods on Chad, which Malcolm had done for him by simply analyzing his handwriting. Graphology, when done by an expert, was legally admissible in court. And Malcolm was both a psychiatrist and a recognized expert with qualifications that sanctioned him to lecture the subject at Paris *Universite*.

Owens's radio crackled alive.

"Lieutenant, we've found the burned body of a woman near the back of the house. We're bringing her in now. Ten-four."

Owens acknowledged the call with a heavy heart. He knew he couldn't face Abbie Martelli with the news at this moment. He looked over to where Abbie sat in Ben's car, encircled by his arm, head on his shoulder. She was still weeping, but quietly. Thank God for Doc Ben, he thought.

He headed toward what was left of the house, deciding it best to wait until he had a positive identification, then chided himself for stalling for time. There had been a very slim chance of finding Claire alive. He hadn't said that to her mother, not knowing how she would take it. Owens' only hope was that Claire might have escaped before the explosion by way of the emergency system she'd installed in the storage closet on the balcony—the ladder system that led from the deck down to the ground. But that hope dimmed considerably with the radioed message concerning the woman's burnt body they found in the woods near the house. If it wasn't Claire's body, he needed to satisfy his professional acumen as to the identity of the dead woman prior to saying anything to Mrs. Martelli.

Malcolm opened his eyes, wondering if it'd all been a dream. It was still quite dark, but what was left of the fire illuminated his present surroundings to a small degree. He lay on the ground, assessing whether his limbs were workable. It was difficult to tell because he hurt everywhere. He definitely wanted to learn the truth of the situation, but then again he didn't want to know if Claire hadn't survived. He gingerly reached out with his right arm as far as possible, patting for something besides dirt and pine needles. The fear factor closed in on him again.

"No . . . no. It couldn't be just a dream," he muttered into the night. He attempted to think back, his memory still under the influence of the concussion that left him unable to maintain concentration for long.

"She was there. I know she was there," he insisted to the heavens.

He almost lost his nerve, but forced himself to find out what was real and what was a figment of his imagination. To pick up his head and know instantly would be too much to bear if it was all a dream. He tried God. "Okay, Lord, I need your help. She's become my life. Please help me find her." Reaching out with his left arm, he began patting the ground for what his heart desired the most.

"Something solid, ah . . . just a stone," he said aloud, his voice gravelly. He knew he was talking to himself but couldn't help it. Continuing the search, his hand came up against something soft—furry and soft. At first, his weary mind didn't register. A few seconds later, he opened his eyes and sat bolt upright, realizing what he'd found. To hell with the pain that started in his head, went downward to his toes, and then made the circuit back up the other side.

Duffy!

Overjoyed, Malcolm looked expectantly on the other side of the furry body. His face fell as depression claimed him. No Claire. He had failed to save Claire after all. But the dream was so real.

Duffy was either dead or unconscious. After checking to see that the dog was breathing, Malcolm fell back to the ground. He knew he couldn't simply lay there no matter how desperately he needed to rest until he found out for sure if Claire had perished in the fiery explosion. He got to his knees and began crawling around her pet who was beginning to stir. Malcolm stopped and patted the dog, encouraging him to get on his feet. Duffy looked around for a few seconds, and with a whimper, attempted to stand. Before Malcolm could check him for injuries, the dog limped off into the woods.

Malcolm crawled to a pine tree and pulled himself up in an effort to get both his balance and his bearings. He could hear the sound of the fire fighters' voices remotely in the distance and could tell they were getting the fire under control as he only saw a handful of places from his vantage point where the flames still burned. He was tempted, but decided against heading toward the house lest he was kept from continuing his search because of his injuries. Though still a little distance away from the ruined carriage house, he heard the sound of something moving toward him through the woody undergrowth. At first, thinking it had to be Claire, he started to call out. But when he discerned men's voices, he ducked down into the underbrush and kept silent.

As two members of the search party passed close to him, he heard one say to the other, "Yeah, I guess the woman's body was in bad shape. Burned beyond recognition. Heard they'll have to do a positive ID through dental records. And she was supposed to have been a real looker. What a waste."

Shocked beyond belief, Malcolm slumped to the ground, dry heaves racking his body.

"Here . . . over here," he managed to call out between uncontrollable spasms that coursed like liquid fire through his whole system, plunging him first into pain, then into the depths of darkness as he fell into a numbing oblivion. Though deep down, he remained aware that he would live with the heartache of losing Claire for the rest of his life.

Lieutenant Owens stood next to the open door of Ben's off-road four-wheeler, twisting the handkerchief he used to wipe the grime from his hands. "Yes, it's true, Mrs. Martelli, we have recovered a woman's body from the woods behind the house. I didn't know that Doc Ben has the police channel on his CB in this vehicle until my men told me that the doc, here, volunteers for search-and-rescue missions." He nodded toward the man in the drivers' seat. "We need to make a positive ID, Ma'am. Most likely they're in the process of searching dental records now. And, no, I' don't think it wise for you to view the body. It looks like the woman was caught in the fire from the explosion, and the body is badly burned."

"Detective, please . . . I must be allowed to see her. I have to know," sobbed Abbie. "I'm sure I can tell if it's Claire. And, besides, who else would it be?" She broke into fresh tears, clutching Ben's hand.

The doctor gently patted her hand. He turned to get out of the vehicle. "Abbie, I'll be right outside," he soothed. "Just be a minute." Out of earshot, he said to the detective, "Lieutenant, if it will help, I will take a look and see if I can identify whether it's Claire or not. I would like to save Abbie the pain of viewing the body. If it is Claire, I'd rather she not be subjected to remembering her daughter that way."

"I understand, Doc. Let's wait and see if the dental records tell us anything. You've got your hands full comforting Mrs. Martelli which I appreciate immensely. We all understand and empathize with her pain. It's a very dark hour for her. If only I'd gotten here sooner, I may have been able to change the outcome of this," he said, gesturing toward the remnants of the house.

"None of us thought Claire would be in so much danger, Detective. This was an evil deed, pure and simple, done by a mentally sick person. Don't beat yourself up because of a flaw in someone else's character."

Owens shook his head. "But, you see, Doc, I knew where the character flaws were, thanks to Malcolm." Owens hunched his shoulders and walked slowly back toward the scene of devastation.

The radio fastened to his belt crackled. He stopped to pick up.

"Victor one to Base. Lieutenant Owens, Sir, we've found the missing male person in the woods. He's alive, but looks to have suffered a serious head injury and we don't know the degree. Victor two is coming out to lead the med team in.

Repeat. Need emergency medical for male victim. Ten-four. Out."

Owens hurried back to the four-wheeler. "Ben, I think they may have found Malcolm. The search team says it's a male with head injuries. Could you possibly take a look? I know you probably don't have your bag, but the EMTs have enough paraphernalia and equipment with them for all of you . . ."

Before the detective could finish speaking, Ben was out of the car and digging in the back for his medical bag. "Always carry a loaded one with me, lieutenant. You know, the search-and-rescue thing? Let's go. Abbie, honey, stay in the car. I'll be back as soon as I can."

"You're not leaving me here alone. All I'll do is worry and fret. And cry. I'm coming with you. Maybe Malcolm knows if . . . if Claire made it out of the house. Besides, I've grown very fond of Malcolm. He and Claire . . . so right for each other." With that Abbie scrambled out of the passenger side of the vehicle. "Wait up, Ben," she called after the two men running toward the small knot of men waiting at the edge of the woods.

Neither man heard her, so intent were they on getting to the injured man. In her haste to catch up, Abbie tripped over one of the fire hoses, turning her knee badly, then slamming it into the pavement as she fell. The group had already disappeared into the woods when she looked in that direction.

"Drat it! But, I know, Malcolm needs them worse." Abbie sat up to determine the damage to her knee where blood was already spreading through the torn hole of her jeans. She wasn't certain if she was able to get herself upright that she could put weight on that leg. Turning to look for something to use as support she felt a tongue licking the hand that she'd scraped in the process of trying to catch herself in the fall.

"Duffy? You're alive! Thank the Lord." Abbie reached for the animal, pulled him close and cuddled him. But Duffy only put up with the attention for a few seconds. Licking her hand once again, he barked and limped toward the woods, turning back to see if she was coming.

"You want me to follow you, don't you, fella? Is it Claire? Please Lord, let it be Claire. Okay, Duffy, you bet I'm coming. Just need to get myself up and I'm right behind you." Aided by a sturdy branch from a pine tree damaged in the explosion, Abbie got to her feet and hobbled after the dog. Duffy went ahead, but waited whenever she fell behind, tail wagging, for her to catch up before moving forward again.

After several minutes of fighting her way through the underbrush, Abbie stopped to catch her breath in a small clearing. She could tell Duffy was anxious for her to keep moving as he circled the tree she leaned against, tail wagging constantly. She called the dog to her knowing he was injured also. But Duffy would have none of it, barking and limping in the same direction they'd been heading. She was just about to follow him again when she heard men's voices heading her way. She hung back, thinking it had to be Ben and the others bringing Malcolm in.

When the rescuers reached the clearing where Abbie waited, Duffy barked again and again in his excitement. He limped forward in his uneven gait, heading in his original direction. Once again, he turned and waited for someone to accompany him.

"Abbie, what are you doing here? And you can hardly walk . . . what happened?" Ben ran forward and caught her in his arms. "Where did you find Duffy?" He asked, looking at the excited dog.

"He found *me* when I was trying to catch up with you and the lieutenant. He acted like he's doing now. Wanted me to follow him. I'm sure he's trying to lead us to Claire. Ben, please, we've got to follow him. Why else would he be acting this way?"

Owens caught up with the group in the clearing. He'd helped to transport the stretcher carrying Malcolm, who was deathly pale and seemingly unconscious. On hearing Abbie's story, he called one of the EMTs accompanying the stretcher.

"Frank, take a couple of guys to get our patient here to the helicopter, and go with him to the ER. The doc and the rest of us will follow the dog. I agree with you, Ma'am," Owens said, crossing the clearing to where Abbie stood. "It definitely seems that he wants us to follow him. Stand by with an ambulance, men. We don't really know who or what condition our next patient will be in. I hope and pray we find her in time if it's Claire. Be prepared for almost anything. The helicopter should be landing in the circle drive about now, at least that's the ETA they gave me when I called for one."

"Wait, Ma'am," Owens said, taking Abbie's arm. "I know how much you want it to be Claire, and for her to be alive. But we just don't know what we'll find. If it is Claire, I'd rather you didn't see her in whatever condition she's in. I mean, there's the very real possibility she might be burned. Or worse. Please do me the very great favor of waiting here with Augie, one of the med techs, while we scout out what Duffy has for us. And you're injured also. It looks like we need to do something about your knee before it gets even more serious. I'm sure it didn't help the situation to be crashing through the woods on it.

"Augie, Mrs. Martelli needs to rest and her knee needs attention. We'll pick you two up on our way back. And, Ma'am, I promise to send someone back with information as soon as we have anything to report. I can appreciate how anxious you must be."

Abbie nodded her assent, her mind working quickly on a plan to follow the men without the EMT preventing her from doing so. The detective and the rest of the team left the clearing, hard put to keep Duffy in sight.

Abbie watched them go, then turned to her babysitter. "Augie, I can't walk on this leg at all. Look how swollen my knee is now," she said, exhibiting the distended limb. "If I'm not going to be a burden to you when the group returns to pick us up, I'm going to need some way of walking on my own. Could you possibly go back to Doc Ben's off-road vehicle and get a pair of crutches? He's told me that he always carries a pair with him for his search-and-rescue missions. They should be somewhere in the back where he keeps his supplies. I'll just sit on this rock and wait for you. That way I won't hold the team up as much when they come back this way."

"I'll get the crutches, Mrs. Martelli. Just be a few minutes. We're not that far from the drive where all the vehicles are parked. But you do promise to sit here until I get back, right? And I'll bring an ace bandage back with me to wrap your knee. That will give it some support until the Doc can look at more thoroughly."

"Oh, I'm sure that will help indeed. And, I'll stay right here until you get back." She made an effort to smile sincerely at the young man while keeping her fingers crossed behind her back.

As soon as Augie was out of sight, Abbie pulled herself up with her tree staff. Ignoring the pain in her knee, she doggedly set out along the same path the rescue team had taken a few minutes earlier.

Despite his injured front leg, Duffy limped at a quick pace ahead of the search party. But, instead of his usual manner of stopping until they caught up, they could hear him barking up ahead. Eagerly, the team pushed forward. Doc Ben was in the lead with Owens and the rest of their party at his heels. After a few minutes, the barking sounded like it was coming from just ahead. They passed beyond a small opening in a dense stand of trees, crashing through a deep pile of last year's fallen aspen leaves. There, anchored by several downed trees in a hollow of the downward-trending trail, they found Duffy waiting for them.

Ben pulled up short. The others did their best to keep from running into him. At Ben's feet lay a woman's body clad in dirty and ragged night clothes. Her head was wrapped in a towel, quasi turban style. She was face down in the leaves. From what they could see, she appeared still and silent, even as Duffy excitedly pawed the ground around her, barking incessantly.

Ben and Owens both knew in a second.

391

It was Claire.

The doctor bent down and felt for a pulse in her neck. He straightened up, reacting quickly to his discovery. "She's alive. Hurry, men, turn her over. Gently now. Let's get a stretcher in here. I don't like the sounds in her lungs," he said, listening with his stethoscope. "Detective, can you call for another emergency helicopter? We need to get her to the ER as quickly as possible to treat her for smoke inhalation and to check for other injuries. Her breathing is very ragged," Ben said, his frustration evident in his voice.

"You found her. Thank the Lord. And she's alive. Right, Ben? Tell me she's alive."

The whole team looked up for a quick second from their emergency attentions. Abbie stood on the other side of the fallen tree, attempting to get across it without asking for help. In a last-ditch effort, she sat down on the trunk and swung the injured leg across, proceeded by the good one. Then she limped the short distance to where the men were hooking up an IV to her daughter's arm and an oxygen mask onto her sooty face. Another checked her pulse while Ben examined her legs and arms for broken bones.

After a quick field examination, he breathed a sigh of relief. He saw no signs of internal bleeding, thinking she might have jumped from the third-story deck outside her bedroom to escape the fire. And she may have, he thought further, but if so, something had broken her fall. Or somebody, he guessed, remembering Malcolm's injuries and his ranting about it not being a dream.

"But how in the world? Okay, okay," he said under his breath. "Not going to do me any good to keep guessing." The doctor curtailed his curiosity, knowing he would have to wait until one or the other of his patients was able to tell what actually happened. He saw that Claire was beginning to come around, aided by the extra oxygen that was helping her lungs begin to process the smoke she'd breathed. Time to get her onto the stretcher and to the helicopter.

He watched Abbie's attempt to kneel beside the stretcher. The doctor was definitely not happy to see the woman he'd never stopped loving in forty-some years, unable to walk due to the injury that had been made worse by her refusal to stay off the leg and out of further impairment when concerned with one of her daughters.

He sighed. "Abbie, is this sort of behavior going to be a constant occurrence the rest of our lives?" But Abbie only smiled, and continued massaging her daughter's clammy hands.

Ben looked toward the detective, who had just radioed for the helicopter for Claire.

Owens gave him a perceptive look and then got back on the radio to ask whether the chopper was big enough to carry two patients. They both knew Abbie wouldn't leave her daughter's side.

Ben was tired. It'd been a long night's work, or early morning to be exact. But he was happy. All three of his patients would recover. No, make that four, he said to himself, as Duffy hobbled toward him, tail wagging. "Being in love helps," he murmured to Duffy, who patiently held up his paw to Ben. "It will be interesting to see how you and Malcolm's Penelope get along, fella, because I think that's where we're heading.

"And may Heaven help us."

VICTORIA MASTERSON

15

"Claire . . . Claire . . ."

The insistent voice floated through the subliminal layers of her subconscious.

But Claire didn't open her eyes. She didn't want to leave the peaceful place where the sun was shining, birds were trilling, and she was walking through a field of gently waving wild flowers as tall as her waist. She was searching for Malcolm, hoping he was near.

But that voice. Definitely sounds like Mandy. But it can't be. Mandy is in Paris.

"Come on, Sis. Open those eyes. I came all the way from Paris to be with you. And here you are sleeping the day away."

"Easy, Mandy. Let's not make her feel guilty," Ben broke in. He'd been splitting his hospital time plus his personal off-time for the past day between Malcolm and Claire, their private rooms being adjacent at his request, in the same hospital he used when one of his juvenile patients required admittance.

They'd both been treated for various injuries and smoke inhalation, each still wearing an oxygen nosepiece for that purpose.

Abbie entered the room on crutches with a hopeful look on her face. She had on a backpack from which she withdrew a paper bag with three steaming insulated cups of tea marked with their names. "She's not come around yet?" she asked, distributing the tea.

"No, not yet, Abbie. But as I told you on the phone this morning, the fact that her bodily functions have returned to the normal range is a very good sign. It's just that her mind isn't ready to face up to what she's gone through. She'll wake up when she's ready." Ben offered a silent prayer that it would be so while continuing to check the monitor for Claire's oxygen level, pulse and heartbeat.

"How is Malcolm fairing, Ben?" Mandy asked. She sat back in her chair, but kept hold of one of Claire's limp hands, concentrating on sending energy to her sister through the connection. It was something that they'd done in their younger days when one or the other needed an energy uplift from the occasional jammed finger or sprained ankle to the broken hearts of their teenage years. It had worked then, and Mandy was hoping it would bring her sister out of her deep sleep now.

"I just looked in on Malcolm before I came to see Claire. It's the darndest thing, but then the mind is the most wonderful and yet strangest feature of being human. He responds to my voice, even opens his eyes. But then looks around as if he's searching for something or someone, and when he doesn't find what he's seeking, he closes his eyes and withdraws to some private place. I'm betting it's Claire he's looking for. It's like he doesn't want to live without her." Ben rubbed his forehead, and was about to get up from his place at Claire's side, when Abbie stopped him. She sat down behind him on the bed, and began rubbing his neck and shoulders.

"Of course, regarding the physical damage, Malcolm's injuries are worse than Claire's. So his body is necessarily going to take longer than Claire's to heal," Ben added. "Seems as though somehow she blessedly escaped with only a couple of broken ribs, a sprained wrist, a turned ankle, plus some insignificant scrapes and cuts, and with only minor burns that should heal without leaving visible scarring. The only thing that could possibly scar is where the noose cut into her neck. It was still around her neck when we found her. Of course, if it leaves a scar, it could be corrected with plastic surgery. She's really a very lucky lady."

"Oh no, a noose? Mom, you didn't tell me about that. Who put the noose around her neck? Chad?" Mandy asked, frowning. "I'd like to put a noose around his neck, but then I'd probably keep tightening it until he went blue in the face and quit breathing. And then, instead of being thanked for a community-minded service, I'd be arrested and charged . . ."

". . . With murder in the first degree, and you'd go to jail for life," came a new, but familiar, voice from the door. "And we wouldn't want to see that happen. Would we?"

They all turned to see Lieutenant Owens standing in the open doorway. "Besides, it wasn't Chad, regarding the noose, that is. But he does have to answer for his part in all this. And he will. I promise," said Owens, his eyebrow cocked significantly.

"I stopped by to give you the good news. I've just been notified that Chad's been arrested while attempting to leave the country by way of the Dallas-Fort Worth International airport. They found forged passports and other identification in his pocket in several fictitious names, and, a ticket to Rio de Janeiro. I'm sending a man to Texas first thing in the morning to bring him back to Denver.

"But, may I come in? I can only stay a few minutes. Just thought I'd check in personally to see how the invalids are doing, besides giving Claire the news about Chad, of course. But I see I'm a little premature," he said, gesturing toward the bed where Claire lay.

"Please do come in, Lieutenant," said Abbie, getting up from the side of the bed. "This is all so fascinating. If only Claire would come back to us."

"Mom, I'm going to get a wheelchair for you unless you sit down and rest that knee. Tell her, Ben. She listens to you more than the rest of us."

"Never mind, Ben. Look, Mandy, I'm sitting. Thank you, Lieutenant," she said from the chair Owens pulled in from the outer corridor for her use and placed beside Claire's bed.

"We're very interested in the motives involved in Claire's case."

Owens leaned against the wall by the door, preferring to stand. "When I came in, you were wondering who put the noose around Claire's neck. That had to have been Susan's doing. You already know that before we found Claire, the charred body we discovered behind the house was actually Susan's. And after hearing Malcolm's analysis of her character, I reckon her motive was both greed and revenge. From what I've been able to piece together, it looks like she held Claire responsible for all the rotten things that happened to her, especially those having to do with her stepbrother, and then Chad. In reality, it was due to her own choices that caused all the problems in her life.

"Regarding the attack last March, it appears Chad became aware of Susan's intentions to get rid of Claire, and become the next Mrs. Chadwick. Chad was clever. He didn't want to get his hands soiled by doing the actual deed himself, so he was content to mastermind the whole scenario by manipulating Susan as his weapon of choice. Susan, in turn, persuaded Sean to do the actual dirty work, promising that she would share the money with him And, once again, as we know from Malcolm's handwriting analysis, Chad, like Susan, had many character flaws that lead him to blame everyone, except himself, where the rightful blame belonged. That, along with the fact that it would personally cost him more than he was willing to pay to Claire when they became legally divorced.

"The two of them, Chad and Susan, were both unable to accept responsibility for their own actions, and both were greedy. Susan thought she was tough enough to get rid of Claire, prior to the divorce becoming final, so she could marry Chad and not have to share the money with his ex-wife. She just didn't figure on Sean's incompetence when it came to doing the actual deed."

"Whoa . . . hold up a second, Lieutenant. What you're not saying in so many words is that it was Susan, not Chad, who set Claire's place on fire, tied her up, and rigged it so she'd be killed in the explosion?" Ben asked the question before either Mandy or Abbie could get the gist of what Owens was saying.

"Then, continuing in that vein, I suppose it was poetic justice that she was the one caught in her own trap. But then I wouldn't wish the manner in which she died on my worst enemy . . ." Ben's voice trailed off at the shocked look on the Martelli women's faces.

"Well, I'm going to call it instant karma," Mandy said, squeezing Claire's fingers tightly. "I'm sorry Susan died in that manner, but they do say that bad karma will get you in the long run."

Mandy noticed that her mother's eyes were wet and a trail of tears rolled down her cheeks. "Mom, don't cry. If she hadn't been trying to kill Claire, she wouldn't have gotten caught in the fire. There wouldn't have been a fire."

"I know, dear. It's just that I remember how I felt when they found the body, Susan's body, as it turns out. But at the time, not knowing whose body it was, I was devastated. To save myself the all-consuming agony, one that I wouldn't wish on *my* worst enemy, I simply refused to believe Claire could die that way. So I clung to hope, and then Duffy showed up. You know the rest. What a tragedy, for anyone to die in that manner." Abbie quickly crossed herself, adding, "Lord, have mercy."

"She was her own worst enemy, Ma'am. That's a fact," Owens agreed.

Mandy nodded her agreement. "Lieutenant, regarding Chad. Didn't he have a part in the fire scenario also? Because, if it was Susan who started the fire, could it have been Chad who had a change of heart and actually saved her? I'm sure all of us want to know how Claire escaped."

All eyes were on the detective, waiting for his answer, when a small voice came from the bed. "Malcolm . . . it was Malcolm. He . . . saved me . . . then went back for Duffy."

"Claire. Oh, my dear girl, you're awake." Abbie forgot to use her crutches and almost fell in her haste to get to Claire's side. Fortunately, Ben was near enough to catch her.

"Okay, Abbie," he said in a mock stern voice. "You are to please sit down in this chair while I see to Claire. At this moment, you are ambulatory, and I much prefer you stay that way. I'd rather not have another patient confined to bed."

Used to Ben's normally laid-back manner, a surprised Abbie sat down where he indicated, though she inched her chair nearer to the bed so she could be closer to her daughter.

Claire pulled off the oxygen tube affixed to her nostrils. "There, that's better," she said, keeping her eyes closed. She squinted them open. "Too light," she said, indicating the light shining in her eyes that was located on the wall behind her bed.

"Better?" Ben said, adjusting the light away from her face.

"Much." she answered, opening her eyes all the way. "Mandy. It *was* your voice I heard. You shouldn't have come all that way for me." She looked around greeting first her mother and then the detective in turn. "Where's Malcolm? Why isn't he here? Something's wrong, isn't it? And Duffy? Please, I've got to know. Did . . . did they make it?"

Before anyone could answer, her eyes fastened on Ben, who was at her side. It was *déjà vu* all over again as she remembered waking up in Paris after drinking the glass of wine containing the knock-out drug. And, prior to that, when Sean had pushed her down the one-way stairs at Notre Dame. Ben had taken care of her then too. She made an effort to sit up, but her ribs told her in no uncertain terms to lay still or suffer the consequences.

"Ben, I realize this is getting to be a habit. If this kind of happening keeps up, I'll be the only adult in your pediatrics waiting room," she commented dryly. Claire felt the need to change position and tried using the guard rails to pull herself up into a sitting position.

"Ouch and double ouch," she groaned, giving her sister a wry look.

"Easy now," Ben said, placing another pillow behind her head. "To answer your question, Claire, both Malcolm and Duffy will be fine. No need to worry. A few injuries here and there is all. Nothing too serious. And, speaking of injuries, you've cracked a couple of ribs," he explained, before she could question him further regarding Malcolm and Duffy. "And ribs do heal. But I'm afraid this will force you to lay low for a little while," he said, taking the pain pump from the bedside stand and handing it to her.

"For right now, you'll be able to control the pain by just giving this a push and the pain medication will go into this tube and on into the IV apparatus you're wearing. The drug will make you sleep a lot, but that's the best thing for healing. Glad you're back with us, Claire. Though, right now, I've got to go check on another patient. But not to worry, I'll return soon. Right now, I'm leaving you to your mom and sis. And, Claire, save the story of how Malcolm rescued you till I get back. I want to hear it too." Ben smiled and headed for the door giving Abbie a quick admonition to stay off her injured leg and a hasty pat on the shoulder in passing.

Mandy, who had moved out of Ben's way, came back to the bedside. "It's so good to see you awake, Sis. Speaking of ouchies, I think you'd be allowed the ultimate *triple* ouch in this case. You know, I don't remember either of us having any hurt beyond the double ouch level when we were growing up."

Mandy picked up the remote control that made adjustments to various parts of the bed. "Here, I think this will do the trick. I'll raise the head of the bed slowly and you tell me to stop if it hurts too badly. We can do it in stages, ready?" She asked, pushing the control toward the Head Up position.

Claire held her breath for fear of moving her ribs while Mandy slowly raised the head of the bed. When she got to a more comfortable position, Claire took as deep a breath as she dared and allowed her body to relax. "Thanks, Sis. That's good for now." She looked from her mother to Mandy. "Before I can rest, I've got to know the worst. My house . . . How bad is it?" Claire asked. Seeing the look on both their faces, she didn't question any further. She simply sighed and closed her eyes.

Lieutenant Owens quietly left Claire's room after hearing her statement that it was Malcolm who'd rescued her, as well as Duffy. He admonished himself to wait until she got a little rest and some nourishment before he asked her to describe how Malcolm had actually achieved that miracle as he hadn't seen either of them on the scene right after the explosion.

After getting a cup of coffee from the patient-visitor's snack area where he unhappily discovered that donuts were not an approved item on the list of provided refreshments, he headed for the room adjacent to Claire's to see if there was any change in Malcolm's condition. If not, he planned to go back to the precinct and come back later.

He needed to wrap up the final details of the investigation. Of the three identified perpetrators in the case, two would stand trial and one was dead. Owens shook his head. Such an unnecessary waste of a life. He still needed to officially notify the Paris police of the warrant he'd just put out for Sean, alias the Shamrock, so he could be extradited to the States to stand trial for attempted murder. And then he needed to make the final arrangements for the return of Mr. E. Forde Chadwick back to Denver. Owens knew Chad would have the best lawyers that money could buy. But the only way they'd get him off would be to plead insanity. And what a fitting end that would be—the prison's mental asylum. Owens smiled to himself. He liked the idea. Talk about karma.

Claire Martelli is one lucky woman, he thought. True, she'd been both physically and mentally harassed by all three of the identified perpetrators in the case, and subsequently suffered severe psychological distress in the form of those horrendous nightmares she'd told him about. But she's certainly lucky to have the love of a wonderful family. Soon, he predicted, to be expanded to include Ben and Malcolm, both exceptional men in his opinion.

In the middle of these thoughts, he literally walked into Ben who was coming out of Malcolm's room. "Oh, sorry,

Doc. I was just thinking about Malcolm. Any good news in that quarter?"

"Yes, there is as a matter of fact, but I need your help, detective," Ben said. "Malcolm is awake, but looking around once again as if he's searching for someone. My best guess is that he's still looking for Claire. I know this is rather unorthodox, but can you help me wheel Claire's bed into his room? We've got to be quick about it before he goes back into a state of unconsciousness. For some reason he seems to think she didn't make it because he keeps murmuring her name even when he's insensible."

The two of them hastened into Claire's room, where Ben abruptly announced, "I don't have time to explain, but Claire needs to come with us. Now." Ben took the head of the bed, Owens the foot, and they pushed and pulled it toward the open doorway.

"Mandy, grab the IV stand and follow us," Ben directed. "Abbie, get your crutches and come along. And *please* be careful. Let's get a move on, everyone."

The little procession headed from Claire's room down the hallway to the next room. Visitors and hospital personnel alike moved aside, staring as they hustled by. Claire clung to the side rails, a little dizzy from the ride but in no pain thanks to a small pump of pain killer. A nurse blocked their way into the next patient room.

"Doctor, for heaven's sake. Whatever are you doing? This is highly irregular."

"Out of my way, nurse. This is an emergency. Move aside, and open the door while you're at it," Ben commanded.

"Er, yes, Doctor. Right away." The nurse only agreed after seeing the determined expression on Ben's face.

In the lead, Owens pulled Claire's bed past the wide-eyed nurse, while Ben pushed from the bed's head. Once in the room, they moved the beds side-by-side.

"Claire . . . look. It's Malcolm," called Mandy, who entered the room with the IV stand and realized her sister was still dazed from the brief but wild ride. Abbie eagerly piled in

403

behind her moving as fast as she dared on the unfamiliar crutches.

Claire stared at the man in the bed next to hers. His head was covered by a bonnet of gauze bandages, completely wrapping his skull from the forehead up. A hard white cast concealed his left leg to the knee. Cuts and red burn marks were sporadically strewn over his face and neck, but the sapphire blue eyes were as deeply eloquent as ever.

"Oh . . . it *is* Malcolm. It really is," she cried, attempting to take hold of his hand without disturbing the loosely wound dressings of gauze.

At the sound of her voice, Malcolm focused his gaze in her direction. "Claire? Oh darling, you're alive. I really did get you out before the house exploded. I'm not dreaming, am I? You're truly here?"

Delighted, Claire chuckled at the expression of amazement on his face. "Yes, I'm really here, Malcolm. It's wonderful to see you, too. Just minutes ago, I woke up with the thought playing through my head that maybe you didn't make it. I can never thank you enough. You are a true hero. In spite of your injuries and the danger posed by the smoke and fire, you came through a blazing inferno to rescue me. I owe you my life. And Duffy's too." She looked around in askance at the people gathered around her bed. "You did say Duffy was okay?"

"Claire, rest assured. Duffy is definitely okay," said Lieutenant Owens, from his chosen position next to the door as he'd not wanted to intrude on the family's privacy and the intimacy of the reunion between Claire and Malcolm. "Just a little stress fracture on one of his front legs that the Doc here took care of already. But you know Duffy. In fact, he was the one that limped into the woods searching for you, then came back to lead first your mom and then the rescue team, in to find you. Believe me, he's not letting a little thing like a walking cast slow him down now," he ended, chuckling.

Ben, who'd been checking Malcolm's vital signs, nodded his agreement. "He's doing fine, Claire. I took him home with me and fixed him up. Then when Mandy got here, I took him to Abbie's so that the two of them could look after him. He's loving the attention. You know what they say about not keeping a good . . . ahem, man down."

Ben looked into Malcolm's eyes to see if his pupils were still dilated. "I'm happy to say that it looks like the concussion won't leave any permanent damage, Malcolm. But please understand, both you and Claire have been basically out for a day or so. And you both need to rebuild your strength which takes a little time.

"Besides, there's gossip going around the hospital that I'm changing over to an adult practice and it's beginning to worry some of my colleagues. So here's the way it's going to be. My orders for both of you are to rest, eat, and get well both physically and mentally. I need to get back to my pediatric practice. You both need to get strong enough so I can send you home." Ben stopped, then looked at Malcolm and continued. "Except I'm not ready to release you to leave Denver yet. And, Claire, sorry, I forgot for a second about your home," he paused and looked away uncomfortably as Abbie took up the conversation.

"They're both coming home with me, Ben. I'll get them up and around in no time. It'll be nice to have house guests again. And, Mandy, you can afford to stay another few days while your sister recuperates. I'm sure Claire will have plenty of options to consider regarding work and a place to live while her ribs are mending. And, Malcolm, you've become like a son to me. So that makes you family, too."

Abbie bent down from her place beside his bed and kissed him on the cheek. "I'll never be able to thank you enough for saving my daughter," she whispered in his ear, "so don't even think about jumping ship now. After all, families stick together."

"I can see that Ben is about to kick us out of here and send sis back to her room," Mandy said, eyeing the doctor for confirmation. "So, please, I have one small request before that happens. If it's at all possible for either Claire or Malcolm to give us at least the bare bones on how he was able to get up to

VICTORIA MASTERSON

her bedroom and get her down to ground level after Susan left her for dead, I'd appreciate it. I don't think I'll be able to sleep tonight without knowing how that miracle happened."

Malcolm smiled. He grasped Claire's hand as if he'd never let go. "You want to tell the story, Claire?" He asked, his voice hoarse from disuse and the smoke inhalation.

"No, you are the superhero, Malcolm," Claire stated positively. "You did the rescuing. I was merely the sack of dead weight you came up two and a half stories for and then brought down in one piece while all along you were badly injured yourself. You're the reason I'm alive today. You tell it. And don't forget the part about saving Duffy, too."

They all settled closely around Malcolm, the better to hear. Ben shushed the nurse who kept repeating that the situation was highly irregular. In a kind but firm manner, he asked her to come back later and to please close the door on her way out. After she left, still complaining under her breath, he pulled up a chair next to his patient. Mandy and Abbie sat on the foot of Claire's bed, while the detective leaned against the wall close by, eager to hear the rest of the story so he could figuratively put the case to bed.

Though physically weak, Malcolm's sense of humor was definitely intact, as he began. "Once upon a time, there was a princess in need of rescuing . . ."

Four people groaned in unison.

"Okay, okay," Malcolm said in a cracked and whispery voice. "I'll tell it straight. It was really a relatively simple task. And I'm no superhero. I was simply lucky that Abbie had taken me on a tour of Claire's place earlier. When we were up on the top floor, the master bedroom suite, I asked to see how Claire handled the balcony outside the bedroom because I had the idea I wanted to add that feature to my list of must-haves if I ever built a home," he said, pausing to cough.

"You know, Malcolm, as your doctor, I'm going to suggest that we do let you rest for now," Ben suggested. He held the pitcher of ice water so his patient could sip through the straw. "We can hear the story later, when you're stronger. You've been unconscious for a couple of days. Takes a toll on the physical body, you know."

"I don't want to be the cause of Mandy not sleeping tonight," Malcolm joked, his voice slightly stronger after drinking the water. "So, just roll me up a little. Feels as though I breathed at least a ton of smoke, if that's possible. I think I'll feel better with my head higher. Thanks," he said as Ben rolled the head of the bed to a more elevated position.

"Anyway, to continue. When I was out on the balcony with Mrs. M., I noticed an area that looked like some kind of storage closets, with locking doors that blended into the siding. I liked the way they created an alcove for the French doors, rather than it being just a flat wall. I asked Abbie what was stored inside the closet areas. She told both the detective and me that Claire had thought long and hard about a way down from the top floor in case of an emergency and she couldn't use the stairway down for some reason . . ." he said, his voice trailing off. Then remarked dryly, "Fire being one of those emergencies . . ." His voice broke on the last word. Once again Doc Ben held the ice water for him to sip.

Claire quickly piped up so that he had the opportunity to rest his voice before continuing his account. "And to think I was upset with mom for taking the men on a tour of the house. Turns out mama really does know best. Mom, you must have had a hunch that it would be good if Malcolm and the detective knew about the secret stairway," Claire said, smiling at Abbie, who had a pleased look on her face.

Owens interjected at this point. "Unfortunately, I knew about it, yes, but as I had to use the facilities just then. It was extremely lucky that Malcolm took the opportunity to give the escape system a quick look. Without that, your guess is as good as mine how our hero here would have been able to reach Claire's bedroom and save her. But I'm certain he would have found some way," the detective said, smiling at Malcolm's discomfort at being called a hero.

"So the ladder system was hidden in the storage area?" Ben asked, getting back to the subject. He knew his patient should rest, yet he was eager to hear the whole story.

Gamely, Malcolm gave a thumbs up sign. "I thought you'd never ask. Well, one side *was* simply a storage area to over-winter the outdoor furniture. But inside the other, the one adjacent to the backside of the house, was where she'd located the so-called emergency escape system. Custom-built, I'm assuming. Right, Claire?" He didn't wait for an answer upon seeing her nod in agreement. He took another sip of water from the pitcher Ben held out to him.

"It appeared to be made up of a series of light-weight aluminum ladders fastened together on special hinges that raised and lowered the whole system," he continued. "I didn't have a chance to actually study the workings as I was in such a hurry to get up to Claire's floor when I saw heavy smoke rolling out onto the balcony. Also, I should say at this point that she designed the system so cleverly that the ladders weren't visible from the ground level. If the fire hadn't exposed the bottom part of the chase area, I wouldn't have known that the escape system was located right there, and I'd never have been able to get her out," he explained, giving Claire's hand a squeeze. He couldn't help but think how different the outcome could have been. "And if that had been the case, I would just have soon died in the fire with her," he said, giving her an intense look. She gently squeezed his hand in reply.

"But, to finish the story, I guessed the escape apparatus operated by means of an electronically controlled switch. Most likely there was one installed somewhere at the top as well as the bottom of the chase. However, I noticed the system also had a manual hand crank, to be used as a fail-safe operation, in the case of an emergency situation like a power failure. And thank God, you thought of that, Claire, because without that hand crank I couldn't have operated the ladder system. The fire was so out of control, it had to have knocked out the electricity."

"So there you have it. I manually operated the crank that let the ladders down. Then I climbed up to the deck. Duffy greeted me . . . barking his head off, running inside and then back out again for me to help his mistress. I found Claire in the bedroom tied to a chair with the noose around her neck. She was pretty much out of it, half strangled and groggy from inhaling the smoke that was everywhere. I cut the end of the noose that was fastened to her wrists and tied to the arms of the chair. The fire and smoke were so bad that I ran into the bathroom and wet some towels to protect our heads from the flames that were beginning to engulf the room. I knew we'd be able to breathe a little easier close to the floor where it was a less smoky. I kept low and dragged her out onto the deck, then carried her down the ladders over my shoulder, fireman fashion. End of story."

"Oh, no. Not quite. Malcolm you're making it sound like a walk in the park," Claire objected. "You see he did all that with a number of very serious injuries, no thanks to Chad," she told their audience who hung on every word. "Blood dripped down his neck and face from a head wound. And his hands were burned and blistered from the hot metal of the ladders. Then to top it off, after he got me down and either dragged or carried me far enough away that I wouldn't be in danger, he actually went back for Duffy, because he couldn't lug both of us down at the same time," Claire said, ignoring Malcolm's obvious embarrassment.

"Claire, I only did what *anyone* would have done given that situation. Believe me, I'm no hero." He picked up the tale again, intent on downplaying his actions in the last part of the story. "It wouldn't have been so bad if Duffy hadn't leaped from the deck into my arms when he saw me come back for him. I'd already started up the first ladder when he jumped. I tried to catch him, but his front leg hit the ground as I fell backwards with him in my arms. At least I broke *his* fall. That's how both of our legs got injured," he said ruefully looking down at the cast covering the lower part of his left leg. "But it could have been worse. And I'm not sorry. He's one spunky pup. Anyway, somehow I grabbed hold of his collar and we crawled away from the fire, and both collapsed. And that's why I thought it was all a dream because when I woke up, Claire wasn't with us. It was just Duffy and me. I guess I forgot exactly where I left her in all the commotion. Then Duffy limped off into the woods and I must have passed out again."

"Okay, you all know the rest better than we do. *Now* end of story," said Claire.

"Actually, Claire, I must disagree." Malcolm said, looking at her with clear promise in his sapphire gaze. "It truly isn't the end. It's only the beginning."

Claire caught her breath. A sunny warmth sparkled in the golden eyes as she silently nodded her assent to that promise, realizing that together nothing was impossible, including the formidable Lady Anna. She responded to the incomparable smile that always lit up her world, smiling back and answering, "Malcolm, I've heard the English countryside is beautiful this time of year . . ."

In the midst of the hearty congratulations that followed, a grinning detective stole out of the room on the mumbled pretext of going to find some donuts, certain that no one would notice.

EPILOGUE

Denver—Offices of the Martelli Design Group

Not that it mattered to anyone but Lieutenant Grady Owens, but he had to set the record straight, even if it did bring back memories he knew Claire would rather forget. It was a hot August day when the elevator opened onto the second floor to see Claire and her staff admiring the company's new name on the freshly lettered door of the architectural design firm. He noted the healthy color in her cheeks and happy smile when she greeted him.

"Lieutenant, welcome. To what do I owe the honor of your visit? Please join us. We're having an informal grand opening of our newly reorganized company. Then I'm off to England in a couple days. Malcolm said if I wasn't on that overnight flight he would come get me."

"And how is Malcolm, Claire? Is he completely recovered from his injuries?"

Claire smiled at the use of her first name, knowing it was the detective's way of saying she was no longer just a case to him. "Pretty much. He's still walking with a cane, but that's about the worst of it. Thankfully, his mind seems to be unscathed by Chad's attack. I just couldn't get him to stay at mom's any longer. He said he had to get back before Lady Anna took flight herself, and showed up on Abbie's doorstep."

Owens laughed. He'd heard about the grandmother-countess. "I see you're wearing a new trinket." He nodded toward her left hand where a large oval-cut center diamond sparkled in a frame of smaller round diamonds, the gold band girdled with emerald-cut sapphire stones.

"It's beautiful, isn't it? It belonged to Malcolm's mother. Said he'd brought it along when he flew over here, hoping he could persuade me to say the magic word. And I did. But only after so much needless suffering resulted because I wouldn't

411

allow myself to believe what his analyses of Susan and Chad's handwriting revealed."

"Claire, speaking of Chad, could I talk to you in private?"

She looked surprised, but only nodded and led him into the architect's old office that now reflected a warm harmony of furnishings in a strong play of whites and neutrals.

"What a change. Your new domain?"

"No, it's Loupe's office. I've promoted her to Associate Director as I will be back and forth a lot. What did you want to talk to me about, Lieutenant?"

"Claire, I feel you should know that the D.A. made a deal with Chad. In return for giving us the complete story, the D.A. would ask for a lesser sentence—*with the possibility of parole*—if he admitted to masterminding the attempts to kill you."

Stunned, Claire sat down on the arm of the white sofa.

"And there's one more thing. It was Chad, not Sean, who drugged your wine and kidnapped you from your bedroom at the Saint-Germain. He told us he thought about making it look like you found where the panel in the wardrobe opened into the secret passageway, and that you most likely fell several floors to your death as the old wooden passage boards had given way. He'd actually put a 'bug' in Susan's phone and listened in on Sean's calls. That's when he decided to leave Duffy at the cabin and fly to Paris, where he hid in the Saint-Germain's shed, watching while Sean opened the stone panel into the passageway. Why did he change his mind not to kill you? He actually wanted you to believe Malcolm was involved in the attempts on your life. So, he found where the panel opened into Malcolm's suite and left you in his bed . . . and you know the rest." Owens stopped, waiting for a response to his disclosures, hoping the news wouldn't create havoc with her peace of mind—or worse, her new life with Malcolm.

"Thanks for filling me in, Lieutenant," was all she said in a strained whisper. It was the look on her face that told all.